DON'T FORGET TO WRITE

a novel

SARA GOODMAN
CONFINO

T0036166

LAKE UNION
PUBLISHING

Published by Lake Union Publishing, Seattle

www.apub.com

Amazon, the Amazon logo, and Lake Union Publishing are trademarks of Amazon.com, Inc., or its affiliates.

ISBN-13: 9781662512223 (paperback)
ISBN-13: 9781662512230 (digital)

Cover design and illustration by Philip Pascuzzo
Cover image: ©tigerstrawberry / Getty

Printed in the United States of America

DON'T FORGET TO WRITE

ALSO BY
SARA GOODMAN CONFINO

She's Up to No Good

For the Love of Friends

*For my parents, who never banished me to New Jersey
(even when Bruce was playing and
I wished they would).*

CHAPTER ONE

"Stop it," my father hissed at me as I jiggled my leg.

I did try not to roll my eyes, but Rabbi Schwartz's sermons were as boring as the news about the presidential campaign. Although that Kennedy fellow *was* pretty dreamy. I didn't mind hearing about him.

But this sermon about duty and honor?

My father was lucky my leg was all I was shaking.

Still, I thought as I looked around the sanctuary, Daniel, the rabbi's son, provided a distraction at least. I hadn't looked twice at him when we were in school. (Not that we went to the same school. Daddy would lose his mind if I was in a coed program, even for college.) But now that the mouthful of braces was gone, and his hair wasn't in that ridiculous Caesar cut that looked like his mother did it over the kitchen sink—well, now he was worth looking at.

Normally, I would stay far away from anyone related to the old man droning away about some goat in the wilderness. But he had winked at me last Saturday as my father spoke to his after the service. And I did like a challenge.

We didn't have the place of honor in the front row that his family did, of course, but we were close: just two rows back and a few seats over. I studied his profile and began counting. If he turned around before I got to twenty, he was fair game. If not, I would take it as a sign to be good.

On seventeen, his head started to move, and by eighteen, his blue eyes were locked on mine.

I grinned slowly and he smiled back. I inclined my head toward the door, then turned away and whispered into my father's ear that I needed to use the ladies' room.

I could feel Daniel's eyes on me as I walked out, demure as could be, in my sheath dress with a Peter Pan collar. I was far too old for such fashion, but for shul, it was better not to argue. I was on thin ice with my parents as it was. I hadn't been home a week before the dean called my father, claiming I needed to focus more on my schoolwork and less on boys when I returned in the fall.

Which was entirely ridiculous because the whole reason my father sent me to college was to meet a good husband.

The reason I agreed to go was because he wouldn't be there, and I could do as I pleased.

I leaned against the lobby wall just outside the sanctuary doors, counting again. Daniel wouldn't keep me waiting if he knew what was good for him.

This time I only got to eleven.

He shut the door softly, looking for me, and I tapped his shoulder.

"Hi," he said quietly.

"How long before your parents realize you're missing?" I asked, flashing a flirtatious smile.

Daniel shrugged. "My father won't notice. He never looks up during his sermons." I let out a giggle and he shushed me.

"He must be fun at the dinner table," I whispered. "You spend more time here than I do. Where can we go and actually talk?"

"Aren't we better off out here? Where it's public?"

I shook my head and watched the battle between good and bad play out across his face. It didn't take long. "No one will be in my father's office," he said slowly.

I slipped a hand through his arm. "Lead the way."

Rabbi Schwartz's office was messy, and I wondered if I was the first woman to ever set foot in this holiest of holies. Beth Shalom was part of the conservative synagogue movement—which was still relatively new and a little shocking to the more traditional members of the community in that it modernized some of the customary religious practices. The genders sat together, and services weren't nearly as long as at the neighboring orthodox synagogues. Still too long for my liking, but when I was home from college, those Saturday mornings were nonnegotiable no matter what I had been up doing Friday night.

Papers and books covered nearly every available surface, including the chairs opposite the gigantic cherrywood desk. Even the books weren't immune to the mess, I noted, as there were papers crammed between the pages. Not how I pictured that extremely stern man working. But I didn't want to think about him. Daniel had taken my hand from his arm and was tracing the outline of it with a finger, sending a tingle of electricity up and down my spine.

The only clear surface was a small table in front of a stained glass panel that looked just like the one at the back of the ark, where the Torahs were kept. I sat on the table, crossing my legs in a way that meant he got an eyeful of garter. "Have you got a girlfriend?" I asked.

"No." He swallowed, his Adam's apple moving up and down as he did. "Do you have a boyfriend?"

A slow smile spread across my lips. "Would I be alone in here with you if I did?"

He had moved closer. "You tell me."

I threw my head back and laughed. "Good gracious, Daniel! I'm practically an angel. Can't you just see me floating around in heaven with wings and a harp?"

He was closer still. "Jews don't believe in heaven."

"Good," I said. "I probably wasn't getting in anyway."

"Doesn't seem like much fun," he agreed. I tilted my head up to catch his lips, and he kissed me gently. "Is this okay?"

I nodded and reached up, grabbing his tie and pulling him back in to kiss me again, which he did less gently, pushing my back up against the stained glass as his hands roved my sides and up into my hair and then—

Something cracked loudly and suddenly we were falling backward.

The next thing I knew, both of us had tumbled through the open ark, shards of colorful glass all around us, and the whole congregation staring in horror at the remains of what had been the rear of the vessel that contained the holy Torah scrolls. Apparently the stained glass in the rabbi's office was the backside of the one that was visible when the sacred texts were removed. I glanced at Daniel, whose face was smeared crimson with my lipstick, then back out into the sanctuary. Everyone was on their feet, as was customary while the Torahs were paraded through the congregation for people to touch with their books or prayer shawls.

"It could be worse," I whispered to Daniel. If the Torahs had been in the ark and we had knocked them to the ground, everyone present would have to fast for a month.

"Marilyn Susan Kleinman." My father's voice boomed as my mother sank into her seat, her friend Mrs. Singer fanning her with a prayerbook.

"It's worse," he whispered back as his father came storming up the aisle, the poor cantor following behind him as fast as he could while carrying the Torah, which jiggled precariously in his grip.

I glanced down and saw blood on my dress. I examined myself, looking for the source. I would hate to die from a stained-glass injury obtained while making out in the rabbi's office on Shabbat. But, a quick glance at my father's now-purple face told me there were worse ways to go.

Finding no injuries, I looked to Daniel, who had turned whiter than the robe his father wore, blood pouring from his left hand. I grabbed the first thing I could find, which was the altar cover, snatched it free, and wrapped it around Daniel's hand while everyone except our two fathers watched with eerily identical expressions of horror.

Daddy reached me first, yanking me off the raised platform of the bimah at the front of the sanctuary and ordering me outside. Everyone was still staring at me, so I pulled my right arm free from his grip and waved to the assembled crowd. "Thank you, Temple Beth Shalom," I said loudly. "I'll see you next week!"

My father grabbed my other arm and dragged me out of there, his neck resembling an eggplant.

CHAPTER TWO

I picked at my bedspread in annoyance at being sent to my room like I was a child. I was twenty, for goodness' sake!

And come to think of it, it was time to redecorate this room. The pink wallpaper and bedding had been cute when I was nine, but now I felt like I was trapped inside a piece of Coney Island cotton candy.

But I could still hear my father ranting downstairs, and there were no sounds of the midday meal being prepared over that. I crossed the room to the window seat, complete with pink cushions, and gazed out the window onto the city street below our brownstone.

When I was little, I used to daydream that I was a princess trapped in a tower, waiting for a prince to come rescue me. Like every little girl did, I supposed.

But now? Princes were overrated. Look at that eleven-year-old kid with the Dumbo ears who was eventually going to become the king of England. And if you married a prince, sure, you got nice jewelry, but you never got to have your own life again. No thanks. I'd much rather rescue myself.

Which was easier said than done in 1960.

Sighing, I went to my closet and changed into a pair of cigarette pants and a short-sleeved sweater.

Eventually, my father's yelling died down, and I heard the telltale sounds of lunch being prepared. I wondered if I would be summoned or left up here to starve. I could always start a fire, Mrs. Rochester–style, if they didn't feed me. Probably said a lot that I preferred her to Jane Eyre.

But it wouldn't come to that. I had been in trouble enough times to know I would soon hear the soft footsteps of my mother placing a plate outside my door. Jewish mothers didn't let you go hungry, no matter what you had done.

To be fair, this was one of my bigger offenses. But a few moments later, those familiar sounds appeared in the hall. I waited until she was gone to retrieve the sandwich—brisket from last night, sliced thin on thick slabs of challah bread. Shabbat lunch was always leftovers from the previous dinner.

My stomach full, I lay down and fell asleep quickly, unbothered by any of the twinges of conscience that should have accompanied my misdeed.

~

I awoke to the sound of the doorbell and muffled voices downstairs. The alarm clock on my nightstand told me it was nearly five—I had slept over three hours.

Then my father bellowed my name.

What now?

I thought about not going. But that would only make things worse. The best way to handle Daddy was to pretend I was sorry, then go back to doing whatever I wanted to when he wasn't looking.

I opened the door a crack. "Coming, Daddy," I called. Then I went to the bathroom down the hall to relieve myself and put on a little lipstick. Whoever was down there would be easier to tame if I had my armor on.

I dashed down the stairs and skidded to a stop at the doorway to the living room. Rabbi Schwartz was seated on the white sofa. The one that I still wasn't allowed to sit on at twenty unless my parents were telling me someone had died. Daniel was next to him, a bandage wrapped tightly around his hand, and Mrs. Schwartz was on the other side.

I weighed my options. I could run away and become a nomad. But tents really weren't my style. And joining the circus would come with the same tent issue, plus I couldn't walk a tightrope or grow a beard to save my life.

"Sit," my father commanded in a tone that implied the death I was about to learn of on that sofa was my own. I did as he said, on the love seat opposite the Schwartzes.

"Look, he kissed me—" I began. "I might have said it was okay, but it takes two to tango and all that jazz." My father's eyebrows came dangerously close to meeting in the middle. Apparently accusing the rabbi's son of misdeeds didn't make the situation better. I closed my mouth and folded my hands demurely in my lap.

"This is obviously a scandal for both of our families," Rabbi Schwartz said gravely. "As well as the whole congregation."

Great. I ruined the entire synagogue now. I debated going for broke and telling him that if his sermon hadn't been as exciting as watching paint dry then we wouldn't be in this situation. But then I wasn't sure a crowbar would be strong enough to separate my father's eyebrows. So I said nothing.

"Luckily, we have a solution that Daniel has agreed to." Rabbi Schwartz prodded his son, who looked first to his mother, then his father. When neither budged, he slid off the sofa and knelt in front of me.

"So, uh," he said and swallowed, looking decidedly less attractive than when he was nervous in his father's office. "They think—I mean—I think"—he cleared his throat—"maybe we should get married?"

I stared at him for a long moment. "You're joking." He looked at the floor. "Tell me you're joking."

"I—uh—it'd fix the situation." He finally looked up at me. "And you're a nice girl. I like you."

"You *like* me? You don't know me! Haven't you ever made out with anyone before?"

8

"Marilyn!" My mother sounded horrified.

"Mama, honestly, it wasn't even *that* good of a kiss—"

"MARILYN!"

"Look, I appreciate that you all want to save face, but it's 1960, not 1860. I'm not marrying you just because we got caught kissing."

"You absolutely will marry him," my father thundered.

I stood up, hands on my hips. "I will *not*. I barely know him. And I want love, not like, if I ever do get married. Besides, it's not like we did anything that would get me pregnant—"

There was a soft thud behind me. I turned around to see my mother unconscious on the ground. Apparently that was a step too far in front of the rabbi.

Grace, our maid, came running in and began fanning my mother, confirming my suspicion that she listened outside doors. She tapped her wrist urgently. "Mrs. Kleinman! Mrs. Kleinman!"

I turned to Daniel, who was now standing awkwardly, unsure what to do about his unconscious intended mother-in-law. "I'm sure you mean well and all, but ask a girl on a date if you like her."

CHAPTER THREE

I paced my bedroom for a solid hour after I was sent back upstairs. The Schwartzes left in an insulted huff, my now-conscious mother moaning that we could never show our faces at the synagogue again. And apparently my suggestion that Daddy just donate a new ark—preferably one with a sturdier back—went over as poorly as Daniel's proposal.

They couldn't *make* me marry him. But they could disown me. The only family I knew who had sat shiva for a daughter had done so when she eloped with a Protestant boy. But they were orthodox, and even my father said that was too steep a consequence. Granted, he said that with a warning that I'd better not get any ideas. He didn't seem to understand that I had no ideas about getting married anytime soon. Not that either of my parents could grasp that the world was different now. When they got married, it was still the Great Depression, and they were worried about war breaking out. Now we worried about the Soviets, but that was no reason to rush to the altar. I didn't want to be married by twenty-one and a mother by twenty-two.

I shuddered at the thought. I wanted to live my life first.

Supper was a plate left in the hall outside my bedroom. But around eight, my mother knocked on my door.

I opened it, plate in hand, assuming she was cleaning up and remembered she was missing one. She looked at it blankly for a moment. "Your father wants to speak with you," she said.

"Mama, you have to calm him down. It was just some kissing—even you had to have kissed someone before Daddy—"

She held up a hand. "Downstairs."

My mother had always been on my side. I was a daddy's girl when I was younger—what little girl wasn't? But he didn't have a lot of tolerance for my rebellious streak. And she always smoothed him down when I broke the rules.

Steeling myself for the lecture, I sighed and followed her down the stairs.

But this wasn't a living-room-white-sofas conversation. Instead, he was in his office, seated behind the mahogany desk that he swore once belonged to one of the lesser Rockefellers. He inclined his head toward the chair opposite him, and I took it, my mother going behind the desk and perching on the arm of his chair. He hated when she did that, but he didn't comment on it or shoo her away.

"You've gone too far this time," he said. "And now I'm forced to issue an ultimatum. If he'll still have you, you'll marry the Schwartz boy."

If he'd still have me. Hah! But no. That wasn't happening.

"Or?"

The brows closed in again. "Pack your things," he said darkly. "You leave in the morning."

"Leave? Daddy, I just got home. School doesn't start for more than three months."

He waggled a finger at me. "You're not going back to that school. I'm not paying another penny for you to learn to be promiscuous. I told your mother it was pointless to send girls to college, but *she* thought you'd meet a better husband there. You won't find someone better than a rabbi's son."

"You're a doctor," I shot back. "Are you saying Mama could have done better than you?"

The purple hue began creeping up his neck again, but Mama put a calming hand on his arm as he began to sputter. "You're going to your great-aunt Ada in Philadelphia."

"My—who?"

"My aunt," my mother said.

"I've never heard of her."

"You have. And you met her at . . ." She thought. "Walter, was she at Harold's bar mitzvah?"

"I was eight at Harold's bar mitzvah." My brother was five years older than me and could do no wrong, despite having followed in my father's footsteps as a doctor instead of joining the clergy, which was apparently now the preferred profession—at least when it came to my prospects.

"Either way, you're going."

"You can't send me to Philadelphia to go spend the whole summer with someone I don't even know. Mama, please."

"You won't be in Philadelphia all summer. She goes to the shore for most of it."

"The Hamptons?" Okay, this wouldn't be so bad after all. Yes, I would have to dodge an elderly chaperone, but I could do that in my sleep.

"No, New Jersey."

"Mama!" I looked to her pleadingly. "You can't banish me to *New Jersey* of all places! I won't go!"

"You will go," my father said. "Or you will not return to this house."

I eyed him cautiously, looking for any sign of weakness. But there was none. "What am I supposed to *do* there all summer?"

"Straighten out," my mother said. "Ada is tough. She won't tolerate poor behavior."

"Mama—I'll behave. I shouldn't have done that today. You can't send me away like this."

"It's already decided," my father said. "And Ada agreed to take you in. Her assistant has to be away for the summer."

"Assistant?"

My mother nodded. "She's a matchmaker. The assistant, Lillian— she's more of a companion, really. Ada isn't as young as she used to be and needs help sometimes. Lillian's mother is sick."

"A *matchmaker*?"

My father's eyes gleamed with the first hint of amusement I had seen all day. "We told her she'll have her hands full finding someone for you, but she's up for the challenge."

~

My mother was pulling clothes from my drawers and placing them into my trunk while I paced my room again. "Mama, I mean it, I'll never do anything like that again. Cross my heart." I made the gesture across my chest.

"Don't let your father see you doing that," she said distractedly. "It'll be much cooler at the shore. Philadelphia is even hotter than the city in summer though."

"I won't get on the train."

She turned to me. "You will. And I'll spend the summer working on your father to get you back to college. But that means you need to be on your best behavior. Ada is . . . strict. If you don't mind her, she's going to send you right back. And if that happens, you can kiss college goodbye."

Great. A *mean* old woman. Who was going to try to marry me off to someone named Herbert with a bald spot and a lisp.

"I'm not letting her play matchmaker with me."

My mother smiled grimly. "Ada doesn't play." Then she shook her head. "Besides, she might find you someone good. She's the premier matchmaker in all of Philadelphia."

"That's like being the safest taxi driver in New York."

"Perhaps. But it's better than being the worst taxi driver. And you'll like the shore. I spent a summer there as a girl."

"If you liked it that much, you'd have gone back," I grumbled.

But the reality was, however strict my mother thought this Ada was, I would be able to get around her. And at least it would get me out of the house and away from a forced marriage to Daniel Schwartz.

I cursed that flimsy stained-glass panel as I grudgingly pulled a pile of undergarments out of my drawer.

CHAPTER FOUR

My first impression of Philadelphia was that it was hot. My second was that I had just stepped back in time. This wasn't a city; it was a time capsule. Trolleys, which had stopped running in New York City three years earlier, outnumbered the cars. Few of the buildings required craning my neck up toward the sky, unlike at home. Except for the clothes and handful of modern cars, it was much more how I would have pictured New York decades earlier.

I tapped my foot impatiently as I waited for a porter to bring my trunk, counting silently in my head to see when this mysterious Ada would arrive, hoping desperately that we weren't about to try to wrangle my belongings into a trolley car.

A young man walked up to me and removed his hat, his brown face shining in the warm sun. "Miss Kleinman?"

I eyed him suspiciously, as any New Yorker does when a stranger knows their name. "Maybe."

He smiled. "You look just like your aunt Ada." He held out a hand. "Thomas."

I shook his hand—and my head—at the same time. "I should hope not. Isn't she ancient?"

"Best not let her hear you saying that," he said as the porter brought my trunk and hatbox. He thanked the porter and took control of the dolly, taking my valise from my hand and placing it carefully on top of the other luggage. "Glad I brought rope. Otherwise we'd have to send these along later."

I imagined him securing my trunk with rope to the back of a horse and buggy. What had I gotten myself into?

"The car's just this way," he said, gesturing toward a row across the street. He started walking but turned around when he realized I wasn't following. "Miss?"

"How do I know you're actually here to collect me?"

"Excuse me?"

"I don't know you from Adam. And my mother said Ada would be picking me up."

"Miss Ada is in the car," he said slowly, as if explaining to a child. "You can't expect her to carry your trunk up all the stairs."

"So you're her driver?"

He shook his head, chuckling. "No, ma'am. Miss Ada doesn't allow anyone else to drive that car. And I'm in medical school at UPenn. I just help out when she needs it."

Served me right for making assumptions. "I'm terribly sorry."

He smiled broadly. "Words you'll never hear from that aunt of yours. Come on. Let's get a move on before she comes after us."

This time I followed. Even if he did kidnap me, it might be a better fate. Besides, he was handsome. Although I knew better. If Daddy threw a fit at the rabbi's son, I could only imagine what would happen if I got caught flirting with Thomas—even if he *was* going to be a doctor.

He stopped at a Daphne Blue Cadillac convertible, the top down, the sun glinting off the absolutely blinding chrome. A woman sat behind the wheel, platinum blonde hair peeking out from under a baby blue Hermès scarf. She wore matching driving gloves, one hand holding the wheel, tapping impatiently with a forefinger, while the other held a lit cigarette that she brought to her mouth periodically. From behind, she could have been Marilyn Monroe.

In the rearview mirror, she lowered her cat eye sunglasses, a web of fine lines around her rich brown eyes dispelling the youthful image.

"Good grief, how much did you pack?" she asked without turning around. "Thomas, we might have to send that trunk along later."

"I came prepared," Thomas said, opening the car's trunk and pulling out a length of rope. "If she's related to you, she wasn't packing light."

"Cheeky," she said, but there was a smile in her voice. "You're the only one I let talk to me like that."

"Don't I know it," he said, lifting my luggage with a small grunt. "We have rocks here in Philadelphia, you know. You didn't need to pack your fancy New York City rocks."

"We don't have rocks in the city, we have skyscrapers and taxis."

"And attitude problems," Ada said, finally turning her head and removing her glasses to fix a stern stare on me. She looked me up and down. "The dress will do," she said, looking over my black-and-white checked dress, belted at the waist, then flared out over a crinoline. "But that lipstick makes you look like a tart." She held out a gloved hand. "Let me see it."

"Excuse me?"

"The lipstick," she repeated, waggling her fingers to indicate she expected it. I fought the urge to clutch my handbag to my chest to protect it and instead opened the clasp, found the offending lipstick, and handed it to her. "Much better. See, Thomas? She's not as bad as her mother said." She dropped the lipstick into her own handbag.

"No, Thomas," I said. "I'm much, much worse." Ada's mouth turned down at a corner.

I finally held out my hand to my great-aunt. "We haven't been properly introduced yet. I'm Marilyn."

"Why, whoever else would you be?" she asked, ignoring my hand completely. "Thomas, it's not going to fit." I lowered my hand.

"With all due respect, Miss Ada," he said as he finished tying off a knot. "You can drive like the devil himself is after you, and that thing's not going anywhere."

"More's the pity," she said. "Climb in, girl, we haven't got all day."

I opened the door and went to sit in the passenger seat, but Ada stopped me. "The back. Thomas rides in front."

Thomas objected, "The back is just fine—" Ada stopped him with a look. Without a word, I climbed through into the backseat.

Thomas had barely closed his door when Ada peeled out of the parking spot, down the lot, and out onto the street, seemingly without looking. I leaned forward to be heard over the wind of the convertible. "What should I call you?"

She turned to look at me. "What kind of a question is that?"

"Well, Great-Aunt Ada is a little bulky."

"Don't you dare put that 'great' part in front of my name. I don't need 'aunt' either. *Ada* will do just fine."

I stared at her a moment longer, then shrugged, wishing that I had a head scarf as well. My hair was going to be a knotted mess from riding in the backseat, especially the way she drove.

We stopped at a traffic light, and Ada pulled my tube of Guerlain Rouge Diabolique lipstick from her bag, pursed her lips in the rearview mirror, applied it, and then returned it to her bag. I leaned forward again. "What happened to that looking tarty?"

"On you. I can pull off anything."

This was going to be a very long summer.

CHAPTER FIVE

Ada wound the car through the city, whipping around turns and narrowly avoiding both oncoming trolley cars and pedestrians. We only saw maybe two dozen other cars and no taxis. Thomas seemed unfazed, but I saw his right hand gripping the car door tighter than the rest of his posture would imply was strictly necessary. And I did wonder how much of this was theater for my benefit. Was she actually the kind of woman who would make her niece sit in the backseat so a man of a different race could ride in the front? Or was she putting me in my place? I tended to believe it was the latter, based on the inherent xenophobia I had seen from the older people back home. But none of the septuagenarians I knew looked or acted anything like Ada. So maybe it was real.

Eventually, she pulled to an abrupt stop in front of a large duplex in a neighborhood full of cookie-cutter houses.

"I told you the rope would hold."

"I stand corrected," Ada said, smiling up at Thomas. And for a moment, I could have sworn she was flirting. "You don't mind bringing it upstairs to the guest room, do you, darling?"

Darling. Interesting.

"No, ma'am, not at all."

She thanked him, then turned to me. "We're going to have to establish some rules before you get too settled."

Here it was. My mother warned me she was going to be strict.

"Number one: you'll do as you're told. I don't have time to be disciplining errant children."

"I'm not a chi—"

She held up a finger, shushing me. "As I said, I don't have time to be disciplining you. So you'll behave, or you'll be right back on that train. And from what I hear, you don't want that any more than your parents do."

I crossed my arms sulkily but let her continue.

"Number two: no men. My reputation in this community is my livelihood, and I don't intend to let something like your stained-glass incident affect that. Am I clear?"

I nodded, seething inwardly, but there was no way I was letting this witch see it.

"Number three: no one enters my house without my permission. I don't care who your little friends are. I don't trust them around my things. Number four: you touch nothing without my permission. No 'borrowing' without permission. And I won't be granting permission."

"So it's okay to steal my lipstick, but if I take anything of yours, I'm out?"

She smiled. "Now you're understanding."

Mama, what did you do to me?

"And number five: no lies. I don't care how ugly the truth is. And I see that bottom lip, missy. I know you're thinking you can get around me. You can't. I see through you, little girl. Don't you ever forget that." Thomas returned after having brought the trunk inside and this time took my valise and hatbox. "He's off limits," she said, following my gaze.

"Why? You want to date him?" I asked tartly.

"Don't be rude," she said.

"Any other rules?" I asked.

"Yes," she said. "But we'll start there for today." Thomas returned to the car. "Hop in, I'll take you home."

"Thank you, but I don't mind catching a trolley. I need to stop off at my father's shop."

"I can take you there."

He nodded toward me. "I think you've got your hands full already."

"Don't I ever?" Ada said. "Why my family thinks I'm running a home for all these wayward girls, I couldn't tell you." She removed her driving gloves and held out a hand to Thomas, who shook it fondly. "You tell your folks hi for me."

"I will, ma'am."

"And for the millionth time, stop with that *ma'am* business. It's Ada. Just Ada."

He smiled, showing off perfect white teeth. "Yes, ma'am," he said to her, then turned to me and nodded. "Miss Kleinman."

Ada shook her head as he walked away, then turned off the car and climbed out. "Come on," she said. "No one ever got ahead by being slow."

I climbed out the passenger side, prepared to argue that I was hardly a "wayward girl," when something dawned on me. "Ada—who else has the family sent you?"

"Sent me what?"

"You said you're not a home for all these wayward girls. Who else got sent to you?"

She turned at the bottom of the stairs up to the door on the right side of the duplex, a sly smile spreading across her face. "You think you're the only bad one? Your mother spent a summer with me too, young lady. And look how she turned out."

My eyes widened, but she was already halfway up the stairs. Mama—here? She'd said she had spent a summer at the shore and that Ada was strict, but she'd never even hinted at a past. I wasn't naive enough to believe she had sprung out of the ground prim and proper and had done nothing until she married my stodgy father. But it also never occurred to me that the reason she took my side so often was that she had gotten herself into trouble as well. And I was determined to pry that story out of Ada if it took me the whole summer to do so. What had Mama done?

Ada opened the heavy oak door, and a small gray ball of fur launched itself at her, yapping shrilly. "My baby," Ada crooned, picking up the terrier. "I missed you too, darling. Mumma is home now." She looked at me. "Shut the door. You wouldn't want Sally to escape."

"Sally?"

She held the dog out toward me, and the little creature bared its teeth, growling. "She's an excellent judge of character," Ada said, pulling her close to her chest. "You know a problem when you see one, don't you, sweetheart?"

"Lovely creature," I murmured. I held out a hand toward the dog's face, hoping it wasn't about to get bitten off. "I'm friendly," I told Sally. "I promise." Sally snapped her teeth as if she didn't weigh all of fifteen pounds soaking wet.

"Champion bloodlines." She set Sally down, and the dog scampered off to a bed in the living room below a window, where she lay, eyeing me suspiciously. Ada removed her scarf, hung it on the coat rack beside the door, and fluffed her hair in the mirror next to it, pursing her lips slightly to admire my lipstick.

I looked around my new home. It was furnished tastefully in modern decor with an emphasis on Scandinavian minimalism, despite the clearly prewar hardwood floors and ornate woodworking on the banisters. Not at all what I pictured for a matchmaking spinster. I expected the look and smell of a grandmother's purse, not these clean lines accentuated with bright pops of color. But Ada obviously had money, and, if her car and scarf were any indication, she cared about fashion and appearances. "Matchmaking must be profitable," I said.

"It's rude to discuss one's finances," Ada said. "I'll show you to your room. Dinner is at six sharp. At seven, we take our evening walk."

"And in bed by eight, I assume."

"Don't be foolish. Ed Sullivan is on at eight."

"Of course. Silly me."

She looked at me sharply as I followed her up the stairs. "Impertinence will not be tolerated either."

"Duly noted." I continued in silence as we went down a long, narrow hallway. There was a small staircase at the end, which I assumed led to servants' quarters. Knowing my luck, that was where I would end up.

Instead, she stopped at the last door on the right and turned the knob. The room was austere, with a brass bed covered in a white eyelet coverlet, a dressing table, a nightstand, and a freestanding armoire instead of a closet. It smelled vaguely of mothballs and disuse. "Home, sweet home," I said with as much fake cheerfulness as I could muster.

"The bathroom is next door. My room is down the hall. Lillian's room is next to mine. You're not to open closed doors."

"Lillian?"

"My companion."

"Ah. Mama said she had to go home—sick mother or something?"

"'Sick mother or something,'" she mimicked. "Her mother is dying. A little compassion goes a long way."

"I'm sorry for her—impending—loss."

Ada nodded curtly. "You'll be taking on some of her duties until she returns."

"Which will entail . . . ?" If she intended for me to do the cooking, she was about to be sorely disappointed. I could barely make toast.

"Doing as you're told."

"Right, of course."

She nodded. "I'll let you unpack. I have work to do."

And she was gone, closing the door to my new jail cell behind her. I sat on the bed, which creaked. No radio. No books. And while I was sure she had both downstairs, I wasn't allowed to touch anything.

"Daniel Schwartz was *not* worth this," I said to myself. Then I stood up and pulled the key from my purse and opened my trunk.

As I went to put away my underthings, a piece of paper in the back of a drawer caught my eye. After glancing over my shoulder to make sure this wasn't a test and that Ada wasn't watching me from some portrait on the wall with eyeholes cut in it, I removed the page. But it wasn't paper—it was a photograph. Two women stood on a boardwalk,

Atlantic City's Steel Pier behind them. The younger had her arm around the elder and was planting a kiss on her cheek. The elder was clearly Ada, younger, her hair darker, but vibrant and smiling, an arm raised in the air in a celebratory pose. And the younger—I squinted. It was hard to tell from the profile, but I was pretty sure the younger was my mother. I flipped the photograph over and sure enough, in my mother's script were the words "Rose and Ada, August 1932."

I looked to the door again. Did she put this here on purpose? Or was my mother the last person to stay in this room? Turning back to the image, I studied it more closely, spinning a story in my head about the circumstances that could have led to her arriving in this room. And how on earth did she look so happy with Ada? Had the fun been sucked out of my great-aunt in the preceding twenty-eight years by age or some tragedy?

No, Mama said Ada was strict. So none of it made sense. And my mother would have been nineteen when the photograph was taken. A year before she married my father. Three years before Harold was born. Did Ada arrange their marriage?

I left the clothes on top of the dresser and dug through my trunk for pen and paper. There was a small chair at the dressing table, and I sat down, already composing the letter.

> *Mama,*
> *Why didn't you tell me why you spent a summer here?*
> *What did you do? Was it scandalous?*

I stared at the page. She would never answer that question, especially not in writing. But that didn't mean I wouldn't ask it.

> *Ada is strict, as you said. And she's said I'm not to bor-*
> *row any of her things—can you send my radio and some*
> *books? I'm afraid I'll die of boredom otherwise. And while*

Daddy might be okay with that, I know you'll take pity on your only daughter.

    Love,

    Marilyn

    PS: She stole my lipstick! Would you please run into Saks and get me another? I'm not sure they actually have real stores here . . .

I folded the monogrammed paper and slipped it into the matching envelope, licked and sealed it, scribbled the address, and placed a stamp in the corner. But then I realized I didn't know the address here. So, being flippant, I wrote my name in the return address corner, and under it, "Ada's house of horrors."

    Then I returned to unpacking.

CHAPTER SIX

Dinner was less the quiet affair than I imagined, Ada peppering me with so many questions that I was hardly able to take a bite before I needed to answer the next one. Though the food was excellent because she employed a cook. But she wanted to know absolutely everything from my dress size to my favorite books to what happened with Daniel.

And much to my surprise, when I told her what I'd said as my father dragged me out of the sanctuary, she laughed. "No, I don't suppose Walter would have handled that well at all. Though how your mother managed to keep a straight face, I will never know."

"Why did my mother come stay here?"

She waved a hand at me. "That's her story to tell, not mine. I don't meddle."

"You're a matchmaker. Isn't that professional meddling?"

That elicited a small smile. "I didn't matchmake her. She found that fuddy-duddy all on her own." She leveled a gaze at me. "But apparently you can't breed out exuberance."

I tried to imagine the word *exuberance* being used to describe my mother. Sure, she was more fun than my father, but exuberant? Then again, she certainly looked so in the picture in my room.

But Ada wasn't done. "And you refused to marry the boy?"

"It's not the Dark Ages. And it wasn't like I was going to—" I stopped myself. If my mother had fainted at me saying I wasn't pregnant, I didn't want to kill Ada.

"Find yourself in a fix," she finished. "No, I agree."

"You do?" She nodded. "Mama fainted when I said that in front of the rabbi."

Ada threw her head back in a deep belly laugh. "Oh my goodness. Yes, we have our hands full, don't we?" She pushed her plate away and blotted at her mouth delicately with her napkin. "Go get ready for our walk. I think you'll be good at this part of the business."

"Business?"

She winked at me.

~

I didn't think I needed to get ready specifically, but Ada rejected my first three outfits. "Aren't we just going for a walk?"

"A working walk."

"I don't know what that means."

She pulled a dress from the armoire and held it out at me, closing one eye. "This one."

"Can I have my lipstick back?"

"No." And with that, she left the room so I could change.

Once I was dressed suitably enough for a walk down Fifth Avenue back home, Ada adjusted my hair and neckline.

"You're not trying to fix me up with someone, are you?" I asked warily.

"You?" She laughed. "Goodness no. You'd be the end of my business."

"Then what—?"

"Come on. Let's see how good you are."

"Good at *what* exactly?" She smiled, and I put my hands on my hips. "I'm not leaving this house until you tell me where we're going."

"To the park, darling. Honestly, do you think your parents would send you down here to do something sinister?"

I didn't tell her that I had tried the doors upstairs. They were all locked other than mine and the bathroom. And mine didn't lock.

We started down the block, Ada's heels clacking loudly along the sidewalk, her pace betraying her New York roots as she zigzagged around slower walkers and narrowly avoided the careening trolley cars.

"Do you get used to the trolleys?" I asked.

"I never got un-used to them."

After four blocks, we came to a park—large by New York standards if you didn't count Central Park. Tiny compared to that. There were several paths, and Ada chose one to the right. Rounding a grove of trees, we came upon a tennis court, where a group of young men played, a half dozen others watching.

"This is where I leave you," Ada said, handing me a small pad of paper and a pen.

"What am I supposed to do with this?"

"Get names, phone numbers, and ages. Get their heights too. Some girls are picky about that."

"Of who?"

She gestured toward the court. "As many of them as you can."

"Ada, I'm confused."

She turned to me, hands on hips. "Good grief, girl. You go, you bat your eyelashes a little, and you get their information so I have young men to set girls up with. It's not complicated."

"But how do you know they'll make good matches?"

"That's where we see how good you are. Rate them. One through ten. Ten means marriage material." She looked me over again. "One means someone you'd sneak out of synagogue with."

"And you won't do this yourself because . . . ?"

"Because I already have. But when they see you, they'll see the kind of girl I'm offering." She gave me a little push. "Now go. I want at least six men."

Well, if I wanted to go home, a single letter to my father detailing this part of my stay would do it. He would have me packed and back in my childhood bedroom in no time flat. But this definitely sounded better than going home. So I sauntered toward the court, swaying my hips and waiting for them to notice me.

Which would have been a lot smoother if I hadn't tripped over an errant rock in the path and tumbled into a bush with a yelp.

As I tried to disentangle my hair from the branch it had gotten stuck in, a pair of hands reached in and helped. "Allow me," a male voice said. I became distinctly aware that my dress had ridden up significantly.

"Heck of a way to meet someone," I said, letting him pull me to my feet. He smiled, and I dusted off my dress, then held out my hand. "Marilyn."

"Freddy."

"Freddy, I'm afraid I have a favor to ask you."

His eyes twinkled merrily. "Ask away."

"I need you to introduce me to your friends over there."

"I was hoping it was more along the lines of dinner."

Under normal circumstances, I would have said yes. He *had* rescued me from that bush after all. And it didn't hurt that he stood six feet tall, with a jawline that would have made Gregory Peck jealous. But Ada said no men, and I didn't plan on staying here long enough to form an attachment, even if it was just for a little fun.

"Maybe another time."

He offered his arm and I took it. Apparently that path was treacherous. We reached the court, and he called out to the other men. "Hey!" The players stopped and turned to him. "This is Marilyn. She wanted to meet you all." He turned to me. "Anything else?"

Now what? I thought as they all stared at me. "Right. Not how I wanted to do this, but here goes. My name is Marilyn, and I'm here to help you find the girl of your dreams."

"Looking at her," one of them called out, then let out a wolf whistle.

"Cute. I'm not available though. I mean, I am, but not like that. But I've got . . . friends."

"You don't sound so sure about those friends," the one with the tennis ball said. He bounced it impatiently. "You working for that Ada woman?"

"Working implies getting paid. No."

"Then what?"

"Listen, I'm not the kind of girl you want to marry. I can't cook, I'm a mess, and I got sent down here because I got caught making out with the rabbi's son during services." A couple of them laughed. "I wish that were a joke, but it's not. We crashed through a stained-glass window and everything. Then he asked me to marry him—I don't think he'd ever kissed a girl before. But Ada's got nice girls who will actually take care of you. That's what you really want in the end, isn't it? Someone to come home to?"

"I don't know," Freddy said. "You sound like more fun."

"I tell you what, you give me your info and agree to go on three dates. And if Ada doesn't find you the perfect girl by then, I'll let you take me out instead."

"What if none of us find girls we like?"

"Then I will have quite a reputation, won't I?" Three of them chuckled. "Come on, fellas, help a girl out here. She said I need six names and that I'd better get them in time for her to get back and watch Ed Sullivan."

They all checked their watches.

"Have you got paper and a pen?" Freddy asked. I pulled both out of my dress pocket and passed it to him. "I'm game."

"Freddy, you're an angel," I said and told him to put his height down as well. "Who's next?"

With eight sheets of information in hand, I walked back to where Ada sat just around the corner on a bench, throwing a quick backward glance at the boys, who were all watching me walk away.

"Done!" I proclaimed, holding the papers out toward her. "And with twenty minutes until Ed Sullivan."

"Eighteen," she said. "You're cutting it close. Good recovery from that fall though."

I was hoping she hadn't seen that. "Men like a damsel in distress. Even if they're just saving her from a bush."

"I know. That's why I threw the rock."

"You—what?"

She grinned. "Don't ever think that I don't know what I'm doing."

CHAPTER SEVEN

Back in my sterile room after a "really big shew," I pulled a notebook from my trunk and sat at the dressing table. Daddy always said my writing was a waste of time—he wanted me to learn to cook and keep a house and become a good little wife. But Mama encouraged it. She was the one who pushed for me to go to college too. Every spare moment, she could be found with a book in hand, often even while standing at the kitchen counter stirring a pot. Daddy bought three different ovens over the last decade, never realizing that the burned meals came from her being engrossed in a good story, not the malfunctioning stove that she blamed it on.

Ada was—I didn't know how to describe her. But she was an excellent character study. Who was she? How did she get such a large house? Did matchmaking pay that well? Yes, it was a duplex, but so were all the houses in this neighborhood. Why was she so secretive about the upstairs rooms? And why hadn't she ever married?

While I was curious to learn the real answers, I was also just as quick to make up my own backstory. When I finally stopped to flex my hand, my watch showed that an hour had passed.

I closed the notebook and yawned. I had woken up in New York but would be going to sleep in an entirely different world. And if Ada's rock-throwing skills were any indication of what was to come, the following day would be another unexpected adventure.

Stifling another yawn, I pulled my toiletries bag from the dresser and went to wash my face and brush my teeth.

~

At home, I always awoke to the smells of coffee and breakfast being made, the sun peeking through my curtains. The never-ending sounds of the city outside my window.

In Philadelphia, I awoke to a fully dressed and girdled Ada throwing my bedroom door open and telling me I couldn't sleep all day.

"Clients start arriving at nine sharp," she said. "Get dressed. Breakfast is on the table."

"What time is it now?" I asked. The bed was too soft, but that didn't mean I was ready to leave it.

"Seven thirty."

"I don't need breakfast," I murmured, rolling over to clasp the pillow.

But she pulled the covers off me. "I don't tolerate tardiness. Get up. Now."

Glaring at her, I sat up and swung my feet off the bed onto the floor. "I'm going."

She tapped her foot impatiently until I stood.

~

An hour and a half later, I was seated in a hard-backed chair in the corner of Ada's "office," which was really another sitting room, minus the television of her actual sitting room, while Ada sat across from a mother and daughter, who perched on the edge of their seats with such ramrod-straight posture that I worried they would break in two if they tried to sit farther back.

A notepad was on my lap—Ada had told me my job would be to take notes on the girl's qualities and concerns. Apparently it was also my job to fetch coffee and the platter of pastries that Ada's cook had prepared. All of which sat untouched on the coffee table, despite her chastising me in front of the guests for not knowing to bring them.

"So, Stella," Ada began. "Tell me about yourself."

Stella opened her mouth to speak, but her mother cut her off. "She's a good girl. She just needs a husband already."

"And we will take care of that," Ada said smoothly. "But I want to hear from Stella herself. What are your hobbies?"

"Hobbies?" Stella squeaked.

"Yes, darling, what do you do for fun?"

"We don't encourage frivolous pursuits for the girls," the mother said. "She cooks, she cleans, she sews, and she can play bridge."

Ada pulled out a gold cigarette case and offered one to the mother, who shook her head. Ada selected one for herself and lit it from a matching lighter, taking a long pull before responding. It was my only sign that she was annoyed, and had I not been so carefully observing her, I wouldn't have noticed.

"What sort of books do you read? Magazines? Television shows?"

Stella again opened her mouth, but her mother began talking. Ada stopped her. "Mrs. Edelman, with all due respect, I'm not looking for a husband for you. Let the girl speak."

Mrs. Edelman's mouth snapped shut. But she strangely didn't look offended.

"We don't have a television," Stella said quietly. "I liked the movie *Pillow Talk*."

Ada grinned. "Rock Hudson. Now we're getting somewhere." Stella smiled back shyly.

After they left, Ada turned to me. "Let's see those notes." I handed her my notepad. "You don't know shorthand, I see."

"Why would I?"

She ignored me as she read through what I had written. "You're right that Mrs. Edelman will be a nightmare of a mother-in-law. We're better off finding either someone with an equally awful mother or someone without a mother at all." She continued reading. "Now that's not fair.

Stella will make a lovely wife for the right partner. Did you see that smile when she talked about movies? She just needs to get out from under her mother. No domineering men for her. Someone quiet who will let her blossom is who she needs."

"You got that from talking about Doris Day and Rock Hudson?"

She turned her head to look at me from the corner of her eye. "Yes. You, for example, need someone who will stand up to you. You'll never respect anyone who caves too easily. And you'll bulldoze over anyone who gets in your way."

"Explains why you never got married, then," I said, unable to stop myself.

Ada smiled. "We know our own kind. The next client will be here in five minutes. Don't make me ask for the coffee this time."

~

Four more mother-daughter pairings came in and two mothers dragging sons, with a break for lunch before the final two customers. The heavy female-to-male ratio explained why she had me soliciting young men.

Then, after the final set, Ada turned to me. "You can take the afternoon off."

I wanted to ask, "To do what?" But the reality was that I didn't care what as long as I wasn't sitting in that chair listening to people who couldn't wait to get married. I was, however, curious how her method worked.

"What do you do now?"

"Find them matches."

"But how do you do that?"

She wagged a finger at me. "I don't share my techniques, and I don't need competition. Go. You're dismissed."

After climbing the stairs to freshen up before going out to explore my new city, I paused at the end of the hall. She had said the other bedrooms were off limits, but she never said I couldn't look around the rest of the house. With a backward glance over my shoulder to make sure I wasn't being observed, I ascended the second set of stairs.

I was right about the third floor having been intended as servants' quarters, but the rooms seemed to be primarily storage. I peeked in a box and found an extremely old collodion photograph of a man and a woman in wedding regalia. I knew that one. It was my mother's grandparents—she kept a framed copy on her dresser. But a peek below that one showed a whole stack of family photos from the late 1800s.

There was a noise below me, and I quickly replaced the lid. But I would be back up here. I knew that much. There were more boxes labeled "photographs," along with discarded furniture, luggage, and several armoires. I peeked inside the armoire closest to the stairs, hoping for flapper dresses. But if Ada was seventy-five, that would mean she was born in 1885 and in her thirties when Zelda Fitzgerald was hopping into fountains. Too old for the costume wear I wanted.

Then again, with that bleached hair . . . But no. That particular armoire held an impressive collection of fur coats, capes, and stoles.

I wondered again how much she charged for her services. She hadn't made that clear in the meetings—the mothers handed her a check of a predetermined amount.

I had never seen a woman manage her own business before. Sure, there were domestic workers, and I knew plenty of girls who went into the business world as typists and secretaries—but mostly to meet husbands. No one ran a company or managed their own money. And her age—along with the fact that she had been in this profession for nearly fifty years—made that even more impressive.

And despite myself, I was envious. Yes, I wanted love and passion and excitement. But the idea of being my own person—of doing what I wanted when I wanted and bossing everyone else around—was intoxicating. More than that though, when Ada spoke, everyone listened.

And I vowed, throwing my notebook into my handbag, to learn from that while I had to be here. It was the exact opposite experience that my father would have wanted. But my mother—I began to wonder if she secretly wanted me to learn this very lesson all along.

CHAPTER EIGHT

The door to Ada's study—her real office—was closed, so I didn't disturb her as I left the house to explore. I walked down the street. Much like many New York neighborhoods, once you left Ada's street, it became a mixture of residential and commercial properties seemingly without zoning. The difference was no buildings blocked out the sky this far uptown, and trolleys replaced the unending traffic I was used to.

I found a mailbox easily and dropped my mother's letter inside. I hadn't wanted to risk my defiant return address with the cook. The shops were all locally owned, and, from the names, we were in a heavily Jewish neighborhood, delicatessens dotting corners like street signs. Which also answered another question I hadn't wanted to ask—How did Ada know the tennis men were Jewish and therefore acceptable matches? On this side of town, apparently everyone was.

Yet crossing a single street brought me out of Eastern Europe and into Italy, immigrants hawking their wares and working in their fully mustachioed glory, surrounded by churches instead of the two synagogues of my aunt's neighborhood. The smells from the restaurants here began to feel more like home, and I inhaled deeply, wondering if there were any areas where cultures mixed as in the city of my birth.

I wandered for close to two hours, observing my new surroundings. My parents had taken me to Washington, DC, and to Florida as a child, but this was my first time as a solo tourist anywhere. After returning to

Ada's neighborhood, I stopped a young woman about my age and asked how close I was to the Liberty Bell—my sole Philadelphia landmark—but she laughed. Apparently it would be a two-trolley ride to get there and therefore not plausible today.

"Doesn't anyone take taxis?"

"Why? The trolley cars are cheaper." She looked me up and down. "You're not from around here clearly."

"What gave me away?"

"Everything," she said, laughing again. "Wait. Are you Ada Heller's niece?"

"Great-niece. How do you know that?"

"This isn't New York. We all know everyone's business."

"I'll keep that in mind."

She held out her hand. "I'm Shirley."

"Marilyn."

"We leave for the shore next week, but my parents' house isn't far from Ada's if you want to get together."

I remembered Ada's comment about my friends and wondered if Shirley would be an acceptable playmate in her eyes. But it didn't really matter. A friend would be nice while I was in exile.

"Ada hasn't mentioned the shore, but if we go, I'll look you up."

"Oh, she'll go. She goes every year. The city empties out, and she follows her business." She dug into her handbag and pulled out a piece of paper that she wrote a phone number on. "I've got to go—but give me a call." She walked away, her skirt swishing behind her.

Encounters like that wouldn't happen in New York. We assumed everyone was a murderer. And, quite honestly, she was too cheerful. She might have been one. But I dropped her information into my purse and popped into a delicatessen for a cup of coffee and a sandwich, grabbing a local newspaper at the door to flip through while I waited.

～

On the block before Ada's house, I wandered into a drugstore and bought myself a new lipstick. It was a knockoff of mine, but it was better than nothing. And, being a drugstore brand, probably beneath Ada's dignity to confiscate.

When I arrived back at the house, I heard Sally barking before I even made it up the stairs. She had sat peacefully through every single client who entered the house that morning, but apparently I was an invader and not to be trusted. She growled and backed away from me as I walked through the door.

"Marilyn?" Ada called from down the hall.

"It's me," I said back.

"Don't yell from room to room," she yelled, oblivious to the irony. "Come to my study."

I walked in, and she gestured for me to sit. I did, and she proceeded to rip up two sheets of paper. "Two of the men you got information from last night are already engaged. Didn't you ask any questions?"

"You mean after you almost killed me with a rock? No, I only asked what you told me to."

"If you die falling into a bush, you deserve what you get. What did you tell them anyway? You were a little too far out of range to hear."

I hid a smile. She didn't know everything after all. "That I'd hop into bed with anyone who gave me their number."

"Bed? I thought defiling holy places was more your preference." She cocked a finger at me. "Just don't make promises you don't intend to keep." She waved a hand dismissively and bent her head over the large ledger in front of her. "You can go now."

I turned to leave, but she called my name again. "The lipstick."

My shoulders sank as she held out a hand. "This one cost fifty cents," I said. "From a drugstore on the corner. It'd be below you to wear it."

She wiggled her fingers again, and with a sigh, I handed it over. She examined the tube, then dropped it into the trash can next to her desk.

"If you *must* wear lipstick, the Guerlain is preferable. But you should be wearing something lighter. You don't have enough life experience to wear the red, and you look like you broke into your mother's makeup while she was out."

"Can you even *get* Guerlain in this little hamlet you call a city?"

"Careful," she warned, holding up a finger again. "This 'little hamlet' was the nation's capital for ten years." She wrote something down on a piece of paper, then handed it to me. "Tomorrow, when we're finished for the day, you can take the trolley into Center City and go to a department store. I'll even let you put a lipstick—that's *one* lipstick only—on my tab. As long as it's a more demure color."

I took the paper, examining the multiple trolleys she had written down, wondering if it was worth it for lipstick. It wasn't like I was going to see anyone interesting here. But an adventure was an adventure. And I wasn't going to turn down a chance to see something that resembled an actual urban center.

She was looking at me, an eyebrow raised. "Thank you," I said finally.

She nodded, then returned to her ledger, and I slipped out into the hall. When I reached my room, an alarm clock was now resting on the nightstand, a piece of paper sticking out from under it. I pulled out the paper, and, written in the same spidery hand as the directions to the store, were the words "Don't oversleep."

I sank onto the bed. "Please don't leave me here all summer," I said quietly, willing my mother to hear me. Then, realizing no help was coming if I didn't make it happen, I pulled out my stationery and began a letter to my father.

> *Dearest Daddy,*
> *I'm writing today to let you know that I have seen the*
> *error of my wicked ways. I understand why you sent me*
> *away—you were right to do so. But, Daddy, please let me*

come home. I promise to behave and never pull a stunt like that again.

But then I stopped writing. What if, in coming home, I would be expected to marry Daniel? A summer of torture was better than a lifetime of mediocre marriage.

I balled up the letter. No. I could do this.

CHAPTER NINE

I awoke to the clanging of the alarm clock. I swatted at it, putting the down pillow over my head, but then I remembered Ada's note and wrenched myself out of bed. It was still too soft, but there was something comforting in being in it. Like a cocoon had enveloped me. I stretched out my arms, but they weren't wings. And if my work in rounding up young men was any indication of what I was doing here, I wasn't improving from caterpillar to butterfly. No, I was definitely going from rebellious daughter to procuress.

I thought about the balled-up letter in my bedroom's wastebasket. Daddy would certainly bring me back home in a hurry if he knew that Ada was employing me to flirt with potential clients. But he might ship me off to a convent then. Better Catholic than soliciting young men.

Me? I'd take the soliciting. It was fun when Ada wasn't throwing things at me. Although she did offer to help me trip again.

So I pulled the scarf from my head and began unwinding the rollers I had slept in. I knew better than to be late to breakfast now.

Immaculately dressed and made up, sans lipstick, I descended to find Ada drinking coffee and reading the newspaper, a piece of dry toast untouched beside her.

"Thank you for the alarm clock," I said.

She looked up, taking in my appearance. "Who are you, and what have you done with Marilyn?"

"If I'm going to be here all summer, I want to make the best of it."

She closed the newspaper. "You won't be here all summer."

"I won't?"

"No. We leave for the shore next week."

"Shirley mentioned that."

"Shirley? Shirley Goldman or Shirley Cohen?"

Everyone did know everyone's business here. "Um—the one whose shore house is near yours?"

Ada rolled her eyes. "Goldman."

"What's wrong with Shirley Goldman?"

"Nothing really. The family are social climbers though. Wealthy, but vulgar. No class."

"Does that really still matter in this day and age?"

"It does in my line of work. There's absolutely nothing wrong with roots in trade, only with the people who try to hide who they are for appearances. They only want to meet established families, and if I bring them to any of the established families, I'll never work in this town again."

Frannie, the cook, brought a plate of eggs, fruit, and toast and set it in front of me. "Coffee?"

"I will never turn down coffee," I said gratefully. Especially when I had to be up by seven. She got the pot from the sideboard and poured me a cup, bringing it with a small pitcher of cream and a bowl of sugar. "Thank you, Frannie."

"You should take it black," Ada said, watching me dump half the pitcher of cream in, along with a heaping spoonful of sugar. "Better for you."

I looked at her black coffee and shrugged. "I'll walk it off later," I said, taking a sip of the delicious sweetness. In reality, I would sweat it out. The day was already sweltering. I understood why the elite left the city for the shore like in New York. "How many clients are coming today?"

"Seven."

"Is that every day?"

"There are only three certainties in this world, Marilyn. Death, taxes, and Jewish mothers wanting to marry their children off."

"Why didn't you ever get married?"

She reopened the newspaper and held it up in front of her face. "Because there were no matchmakers as good as me when I was young." She lowered the paper just enough to see me over it. "Any other impertinent questions? Or may I continue reading about the election? I certainly hope people are willing to overlook the fact that Kennedy is Catholic. It would be nice to have someone who doesn't look like a constipated Howdy Doody running the country. And that wife of his is pure class."

~

A little over an hour later, I found myself in the straight-backed chair again, notepad on my lap. Opposite Ada was one of the most unfortunate-looking young women I had ever seen. Gawky and tall, she towered over her normal-sized mother, with a large nose and buck teeth that would make a beaver envious. Her mother sat there wringing her hands, bemoaning her daughter's appearance to Ada.

"I understand if you can't do anything with her, I do," she said. "But she's twenty-six now, and time is running out."

The poor girl's eyes were trained on the floor the whole time, her shoulders hunched as she tried to hide her size.

Ada looked from mother to daughter and back to the mother. Then she turned to me. "Marilyn, darling, perhaps you could take Mrs. Stein with you to fetch a fresh pot of coffee?"

I eyed her with confusion. Sending me for the coffee was one thing, but taking Mrs. Stein to the kitchen? I didn't understand what she was getting at, but I rose and asked Mrs. Stein to come with me. She followed without a word.

When we reached the kitchen, I dumped out the pitcher of still-hot coffee and began to brew a new pot. It was the extent of my kitchen skills. Mrs. Stein sank to the kitchen table while the coffee brewed, and I added fresh cream to the pitcher.

"If only I had a daughter like you," she said miserably. "You must have men lining up to marry you."

"Just one," I said. "And that's why I'm here. I said no, and my parents sent me to Ada."

"You're so lucky. With that figure and that complexion."

"Looks aren't everything," I said delicately. What I wanted to say was that she was an awful mother. She had sat there telling my great-aunt what a wonderful cook her daughter was, how she could sew and mend anything, how obedient she was. Heck, I would marry her if I were a man. Looks fade for everyone—except maybe Ada—but someone who can cook, darn socks, and listen to every inane word you say was forever. "I wish I had half her domestic skills."

"You don't need them. You'll marry well."

There it was again. That assumption that I would stop existing except to pop out babies and pick up some husband's dirty socks.

It took every ounce of self-control I had not to let her have it. Instead, I bit my (thankfully un-made-up) lip and kept quiet. When the coffee was done brewing, I let it sit a moment longer, hoping I had given Ada all the time she needed, before leading Mrs. Stein back to the sitting room.

Where I almost dropped the entire coffee tray.

We had been gone six minutes. Maybe seven. But the girl in front of us wasn't the same girl who had slunk through the door after her abusive mother.

Yes, she was nearly six feet tall, looming over the rest of us, but her shoulders were back now. Ada had belted her dress neatly at her almost nonexistent waist, brushed the hair out of her gorgeous chocolatey brown eyes, and applied rouge and lipstick, which, upon closer inspection, was mine.

She would never be beautiful. But with her mouth shut over her teeth and her posture corrected, her cheekbones stood out, giving her a handsome appearance despite the large nose.

Mrs. Stein's mouth was open, her eyes bulging. Ada instructed Hannah to twirl around, which she did.

"How did you—?"

"She's got wonderful bone structure," Ada said. "You're going to take her to Gimbels, down on Market Street. Ask for Charlotte. I'll call ahead. She's going to take care of you. And I'll call you later this week with some matches."

"You're a true *bal-shem*," Mrs. Stein breathed.

When they left, I asked Ada what *bal-shem* meant.

"Miracle worker. Yiddish." She shook her head angrily. "The real miracle was me not slapping that awful woman. Who treats another human that way, let alone their own child?" She went to the desk in the corner and made a note. "But she'll worship the ground any future husband walks on for taking this problem off her hands. Meanwhile most of the men in this city should be so lucky." She looked back up at me. "When you go buy a lipstick, get me another one in that same shade. I gave yours to Hannah."

I smiled at this glimpse into her true colors but turned away so she wouldn't see it.

CHAPTER TEN

When Ada dismissed me for the afternoon, I took the paper from my pocket and began my adventure on the Philadelphia trolley system. We were in Oxford Circle, far from Center City, as the talkative woman next to me on the first trolley explained. I wasn't used to strangers being so polite and tried to ignore her at first, but she made that impossible. But my aunt had chosen to live in the community she worked in.

I wanted to ask how far Market Street was from the Liberty Bell, but after realizing I sounded like a tourist for asking Shirley how to get to it from Ada's house, I decided to keep the question to myself.

It was nearly an hour, much longer than when Ada drove at breakneck speed back from the train station, before I stepped out under the gold awning of Gimbels. The store took up a full city block. I had been to the New York one, of course, but with its Philadelphia roots and reputation for skimping on frills, it wasn't the New York icon that Macy's, Saks, or Bergdorf Goodman was. But it would do.

Two lipsticks later, I was back on Market Street, looking at the people going about their daily lives and wondering where they were going and where they had come from. There was a little boy on the corner selling newspapers, and an electronics store with a window full of televisions, a sign above them reading "Watch the future as it happens."

I stepped off a curb and narrowly missed being hit by a trolley; I was used to the traffic in New York City that could smoothly move around pedestrians with a honk and outburst of profanity from the driver if the pedestrian was in the wrong, an extended finger and outburst of profanity from the pedestrian if the driver was. This would take some getting used to.

But there, across the street, was a sign with the shape of a bell on it. I smiled in my new lipstick.

That smile faded, however, as I reached Independence Hall, after walking along the tree-lined street outside the building where the Constitution was signed. There was no line, and a sign on the door read "Closed for Renovations."

"Who renovates the Liberty Bell this close to the Fourth of July?" I asked out loud in frustration. I tried the door, but it was locked, the windows papered over to hide the view of what was happening inside.

I stomped my foot, cursing this town, and then turned and made my way back toward the trolley stop for the long ride back to Ada's house.

~

When I arrived back, tired, hot, and dirty from nearly two hours of travel time just to get a lipstick, Ada was in the living room, laughing into the phone.

I held out her lipstick wordlessly, and she gestured for me to put it on the table. "Darling, Marilyn is here. I'll call you back from the bedroom." She replaced the receiver and rose.

"Who was that?" If it was my mother, I would have liked to have said hello.

"No one you know," Ada said. "And that's another impertinent question."

"Do you have a boyfriend?"

She turned to look at me. "Two impertinent questions. My, we're feeling brave today, aren't we?"

"Well, you called them darling."

"Darling, I call everyone darling. Now if you'll excuse me."

46

She swept up the stairs grandly, and I heard the door to her bedroom closing.

I looked at the telephone on the table. If I picked it up very quietly, I could listen in.

I waited long enough for her to have dialed and then carefully removed the receiver—but the sound of a dial tone greeted me. I waited and tried again two more times before Sally started barking, at which point I gave up because I couldn't listen in without that evil little monster giving me away.

With a sigh, I went upstairs to rest until dinnertime. But as I passed Ada's room, curiosity got the better of me, and I crept back to the door and leaned my ear against it.

I couldn't make out the words, but I heard the low murmur of her talking, as well as another laugh. I had been outsmarted. There was another phone line in her room.

There was no way to prove it, but I felt my guess had been correct. That wasn't the laugh of someone talking to a friend. It had a flirtatious lilt to it.

Then again, Ada had seemed to be flirting with Thomas, who was more than fifty years her junior, so what did I know? On my tiptoes, I made my way to my room, shutting the door quietly behind me.

CHAPTER ELEVEN

Two days later, instead of dismissing me after the morning's matchmaking work, Ada looked me over again. "Have you got a bathing suit?"

"Of course."

"With you? Or in New York?"

"Here. Mama said I would need it for the shore."

"Show me," she said, rising and leading the way up the stairs.

Uncertainly, I followed her to my bedroom, where she sat at the dressing table chair. I went to the drawer where I had put it and pulled the stretchy fabric out.

Ada pursed her lips. "No. That won't do at all."

"Whyever not?"

She rose and gestured for me to follow her. "We're going to Gimbels."

I sighed. The absolute last thing I wanted was to be stuffed into some bathing contraption from the Victorian era that covered me from shoulders to knees. The tan lines would be atrocious. "Ada, I like my suit."

"I don't recall asking."

"Or listening," I grumbled.

"What was that, darling? I wasn't listening."

"Nothing," I said through clenched teeth.

She turned and patted my cheek. "Keep it that way."

But at least with Thomas not around, I was allowed into the front seat of the Cadillac. Though it was a more terrifying ride with the full, unobstructed view of what we were narrowly missing. I wondered if there were so few cars on the road to avoid the terror that was Ada.

She parked on the street near the store, leaving the top down.

"Aren't you worried someone will steal the car?"

She looked at me as if I had just asked if she was worried aliens would land and shave her head. "You're not in New York anymore."

That much was for sure.

Entering the store with Ada was an entirely new experience. I had been ignored until reaching the makeup counter on my solo journey. But a doorman held the door for her, greeting her by name, and a young woman came rushing over to her. "Miss Heller! I'm so sorry; we didn't know you were coming."

"I do like to keep you on your toes."

She smiled politely, clearly flustered. "I'll go fetch Charlotte. One moment, please."

"We'll meet her upstairs."

"Of course," she said, rushing away.

I followed Ada toward an elevator, where a uniformed man stood, ready to push the buttons. I hadn't seen an elevator operator in years.

"Hello, Miss Heller," he said, tipping his hat.

"George," Ada said with a nod. And that was all he needed. He knew where she was going.

We arrived at the top floor, where a young woman was waiting. "Ada," she said, leaning forward to kiss my great-aunt on the cheek.

Ada embraced her, then held her away to see me. "Charlotte, darling, this is my niece, Marilyn. And she's going to need a shore wardrobe."

"Of course. Right this way." She looked me over carefully. "A perfect size ten."

I nodded, and she led us to a private viewing area, with a three-way mirror, changing room, and settee. "Would you prefer coffee or champagne this afternoon?" she asked Ada.

"Coffee." Ada waggled a finger at her. "You always talk me into things when I choose the champagne."

"Never," Charlotte said, feigning outrage but giving a conspiratorial wink. "You two sit right here, and I'll bring a selection right up for you." She started to leave but turned back to Ada. "And I have a few new things for you to look at as well."

"Nonsense. We're here for Marilyn today."

"Why don't I just bring them, and we'll see how you feel?"

Ada smiled. "Maybe it's not the champagne."

We sat, and another young woman brought a tray with a silver coffee pot, two cups, and cream and sugar. Ada indicated that I was to pour. I handed hers to her black, looked longingly at the cream and sugar, but took a sip of the plain brew instead. She said nothing but watched approvingly.

When Charlotte returned, we began with dresses, pedal pushers, and several lightweight blouses. Nothing as exciting as I would have gotten had I done my normal seasonal shopping with Mama, but Ada explained that I wouldn't need much formal wear at the shore. And the pile of clothes to buy grew larger with each round.

Finally, Charlotte presented the bathing suits. Ada walked up to the rack of them and flipped through while I waited. Her style had been impeccable for the clothes, but if she disapproved of my admittedly modest suit, I was in trouble.

"This one," she said, handing something to Charlotte, who put it into the changing room and gestured for me to join her.

Hanging on the room's hook was a baby blue bikini. I had asked for one the year before, citing the images of movie stars in magazines, but my mother refused. Daddy would have thrown a fit, and she didn't want that fight on her hands.

I poked my head back out. "Really?" I asked Ada.

She shooed me back in. "Try it on."

Stripping off the sheath dress I had tried on last, I stepped out of my underthings and pulled on the midriff-baring suit. I had never been this publicly unclad before, but I had to admit, it flattered my shape, and the color would look lovely with a tan.

I stepped out, climbing onto the pedestal at the three-way mirror.

Ada smiled, lifting her eyebrows twice. "And you thought you weren't going to have any fun this summer." She turned back to Charlotte. "We'll take it." She thought for a moment. "Add a second one in green while we're at it."

~

Back on the street, we waited as the concierge brought the bags to the car. "Not as barbaric as you assumed when you arrived, is it?"

"Philadelphia?" I asked. She nodded. "It's not New York—"

"Nothing is New York," Ada said. "Just like how nothing is Paris."

I had never been. "But I suppose it has its charm." I gestured down the street. "I tried to see the Liberty Bell the other day, but it was closed for renovations."

"I didn't take you for the history type."

I shrugged. "When in Rome . . . or in this case, Philadelphia."

She eyed me carefully. "I also didn't take you as the type to give up so easily." She gave a dollar to the concierge, then slipped a hand through my arm. "Come on. Let's go see your cracked bell."

"But, Ada, it's closed. The door was locked and the windows were covered."

"Pishposh. Nothing is *that* closed." She walked, taking me along with her. "Keep up, please."

We walked the three blocks arm in arm, then down the tree-lined avenue to the entrance. "See?" I said, showing her the sign. "Closed for renovations."

"Oh, ye of little faith." She shook her head. "Come along." And she half pulled me to the corner, rounding the building to the rear entrance, where workers were cutting wood on a sawhorse. "Hello, boys," Ada called merrily.

One of the workers tipped his hat, but another looked less pleased. "You can't be back here, ma'am. It's restricted."

"Could I speak to your supervisor, please?" she asked sweetly. "I won't be but a moment."

I was sure he would say he was the supervisor. Or that he wasn't going to get whoever was. But when Ada flashed a smile, seventy-five or not, he softened.

An older, heftier man, who clearly did none of the manual labor himself, came outside a moment later. He looked up at the sun and wiped his brow with a stained handkerchief before directing himself to us.

"How can I help you today, ma'am?"

"Ada Heller," she said, sticking her hand out. He studied it for a moment before shaking it. I wasn't sure I would have offered mine. He didn't look overly clean and was sweating profusely. "My niece here is from New York and hasn't seen a single thing that makes her think this city of ours is worth even a penny." The supervisor shot a dirty look at me. *Thanks, Ada.* "I took her to Betsy Ross's house." *Lie.* "And the Christ Church Burial Ground to see Mr. Franklin." *Another lie.* "We even went to Declaration House." I didn't even know what that was. All I had seen so far was the train station, Gimbels, and Oxford Circle. "And she's simply impossible to impress." She leaned in conspiratorially. "But the one thing that can't fail to impress is the Liberty Bell. You know it as well as I do. If we're going to sell her on Philadelphia, that's what she just has to see." She took his hand again. "I do know that you're not open to the public, but do you think you could make just the tiniest of exceptions to let her see this piece of history while she's here? If she doesn't, she may never visit her aunt again, and what a shame that would be."

52

The supervisor considered this for a moment, and Ada flashed another one of those smiles. He looked left and right to make sure no one else was watching, other than the workers, who hadn't done a lick of work since we arrived.

"You can't tell anyone," he said quietly. "And you have to walk exactly where I tell you. And don't touch anything."

Ada mimed crossing her heart. "You're an absolute gem," she told him. "We'll be as good as church mice."

"Come on, then," he said, gesturing for us to follow him into the building.

"Isn't it as *poor* as church mice?" I whispered to Ada.

"How should I know?" Ada whispered back. "I don't spend time in churches. Or places with mice, for that matter."

Scaffolding lined much of the walls, but the supervisor brought us into a darkened room, then flicked the switch on the wall. The construction so far seemed to be confined to the outer rooms, as this one appeared untouched. The bell sat on a large wooden pedestal, a staircase with white-painted wooden balustrades next to it, separated by a crisp American flag, with all fifty stars for the newly added Alaska and Hawaii. The iconic crack spread from just below the name of Pass to the bottom.

"What do you think?" Ada asked.

"It's bigger than I expected."

"May you say that on your wedding night," she said quietly.

"What?"

Ada laughed.

"Can I touch it?" I asked the supervisor.

"Absolutely not."

Ada touched his arm. "What if you just turned around for a moment? I promise she won't harm it."

He looked down at the hand on his arm, then back up to her face, lingering a little too long on her bosom on the way there. "I suppose I need to check that scaffolding over there," he said gruffly.

Ada nodded to me, and I walked up, laying a hand on the split in the metal. This piece of Americana had been here much longer than my family had been in this country.

"Let's go before our sweaty friend gets into trouble," Ada said, taking my arm again. "Sir?" she called. "We've taken up enough of your precious time. And I think we've hooked the young lady."

"Impressed yet?" he asked me.

I nodded my head. "Consider me converted."

He nodded. "I'll walk you out. And I'd best not hear about this or find out you're reporters."

"Of course not, darling. But you've given this girl a precious memory, and we both thank you for that."

He tipped his hard hat to us at the door, then retreated to the cooler air of some unseen office when we walked out.

"How did you do that?" I asked once we were safely back around the front of the building.

She smiled. "You catch more flies with honey than with vinegar. And don't ever let anyone tell you we're the weaker sex."

CHAPTER TWELVE

There was a letter bearing my mother's flowing script waiting for me when we returned to the house. I grabbed it and made a beeline for my room, where I flopped onto the bed and tore open the envelope, inhaling the scent of her perfume that rose from the page.

> *Dearest Marilyn,*
>
> *I hope you are enjoying Philadelphia more than when you first wrote. I know it's a change, but you will adapt beautifully. Your father is still angry, of course, and vowing he can never return to Beth Shalom. Personally, I think he just likes being able to sleep in on Saturdays and read the newspaper. But I'm working on him.*
>
> *I have sent several books that I believe you will enjoy along to the shore house, as well as your radio. It didn't make sense to send them to the Philadelphia house just for you to pack and move them in a few days' time.*
>
> *Try to enjoy yourself. I know this wasn't how you wanted to spend the summer, but I think you'll find this is actually a welcome respite once you settle in.*
>
> *Love always,*
> *Mama*

*PS: If Ada took your lipstick, far be it from me to
replace it.*

I made a face at the postscript. I had held out hope of wearing
my signature color when I wasn't around Ada. But at least I would
have entertainment when confined to my room at night, unlike now,
when I got an hour of television—whatever Ada watched—after
our nightly prowls for available men, then was sent off to bed like
a child.

I went to refold the letter when I realized there was a second postscript on the back.

*PPS: Do not let Ada see you write a return address
like that. If she sends you home now, I don't know what
your father will do.*

Grimacing, I shoved the letter back into its envelope and grabbed
my stationery to send a reply thanking her for the books and radio.
Excited, if for nothing else, that in a few days I would have a distraction.

~

When the day came to leave for the shore, it looked like a mass exodus
as families were running up and down stairs with suitcases and other
bags all along the street, which was now lined with the first taxis I had
seen since arriving, as well as private cars.

"Does everyone leave on the same day?" I asked as I loaded our
suitcases into the car. We had sent trunks along ahead with most of
our things so that we wouldn't need help unloading when we arrived.

"The women and children do. The men tend to come down for
the weekends."

"How will we work if there are no men most of the week?"

Ada lowered her sunglasses and winked. "Much more efficiently."

Suitably prepared for her driving this time with sunglasses and scarves, the two of us matched as Ada peeled out of the parking spot in front of her duplex and careened skillfully around the other cars and down the street, Sally sitting between us on the bench seat.

The traffic lessened considerably once we left Ada's neighborhood. "How long is the drive?"

"About two hours. The train is faster, of course, but I want my car. And the train only goes to Atlantic City now."

"Isn't that where we're going?"

"No." She glanced over at me. "You'd probably enjoy that better—more nightlife. But no."

"Then where?"

"Avalon." When I looked at her funny, she said, "You'll love it. You complain too much."

"I didn't say a word," I said coolly. "Will King Arthur be there?"

She took her eyes off the road for far too long for my liking. "I don't follow."

"You didn't read *The Once and Future King*?" I realized I hadn't seen a single book in her house. "Sorry. It's a book that came out a couple of years ago. About King Arthur and the knights of the Round Table and Guinevere and—"

She held up a hand. "I'm familiar with the story. Arthur and his knights do predate me believe it or not. But I don't tend to read children's books."

I shook my head at her dismissal. "Avalon is where Arthur goes at the end to be reborn as the future king."

"I believe your parents hope the one in New Jersey is where their prodigal daughter will go to be reborn as a good little girl who listens to them and marries the rabbi's son."

"I'd as soon kiss a pig."

"We can arrange that. There's a lot of farmland to pass through."

I laughed, the feeling of the wind and the open road proving a balm to my soul. "Imagine Daddy's reaction to that. Kissing *and* pork. Poor man would have a stroke."

"We wouldn't want that. Although your mother could do better."

"You don't like my father? You called him a fuddy-duddy before."

She lowered her glasses again. "What would you call him?"

I didn't have an answer. "I don't know. He's my father."

Ada sighed. "And I knew your mother before him. She was so full of life." She glanced at me, and I felt the weight of what she was implying. "I understand why she wanted the stability of marrying him. Don't get me wrong. It's what most of the women who bring their daughters to me want. But for Rose, I wanted more."

"More?"

"Love. Passion. All of it."

"She loves Daddy," I said defensively. Didn't she? The opposite was obviously true. He was smitten with her, going along with buying those ovens rather than believing it could be her fault when the brisket was too dry again. And she was the only one who could smooth him over when he was upset. I certainly couldn't. Granted, I was usually the reason he was upset. But I never saw them show affection. I had always chalked it up to the era they grew up in. But the pitying look Ada was giving me made me wonder.

We rode in silence for the next half hour as Philadelphia changed to Camden, then to marshes and farms.

I had so many questions I wanted to ask, but Ada had made it clear she wasn't answering any about my mother.

"Do you like ice cream?" Ada asked suddenly, breaking my reverie.

I checked my watch. It was only ten o'clock in the morning. "Yes."

"Good. The two best ice cream parlors you'll ever see are on the island."

"I thought cream was bad for you."

Ada laughed. "This is worth it."

"Avalon is an island?"

"All of the shore towns are. But Avalon is special. It's a mile further out than the others, so the temperature is always cooler." She fell silent for a moment. "It's changed a lot since your mother was here. The storm in 1944 wiped out a good chunk of the pier. They rebuilt, of course, but it isn't the same."

"How far is it from Atlantic City?"

"Now? A little over half an hour. The Garden State Parkway, which opened a few years ago, makes it a breeze. Cape May is just under half an hour in the other direction too." She glanced over at me again. "Don't you worry. We'll have plenty of fun."

I wasn't sure her idea of fun was the same as mine, but at least with men off the island for five days of the week, I should get a break in the evenings to . . . Well, I didn't know what I would do without men around. Her assurance still sounded awfully dreary as we drove past mile after mile of farms and swamps. I leaned my arm on the windowsill and rested my head on it, letting the air whip around my face, blissfully unaware of what the future might hold.

CHAPTER THIRTEEN

Once we exited the Garden State Parkway, a left turn onto Avalon Boulevard took us through marshland with thick channels cutting through the seagrass, a lone house sitting out in the marshes accessible only by a raised dirt road that would be treacherous to traverse at night. Unlike the valley of ashes that one went through to get to Gatsby's version of the Hamptons, this barren wasteland made me wonder if we would be the first people to ever access this island. And if not, perhaps King Arthur would, in fact, be sitting there waiting for us.

But as we crested a new-looking bridge, the town came into focus. Houses dotted the horizon, a few larger buildings straight ahead, growing smaller as they radiated out from the center of the town, a pier jutting out into the ocean.

No, this wasn't where the mythical king was healing himself. And it looked like I was going to need those books to provide entertainment after all.

Ada inhaled deeply, urging me to do the same. "This is the best part of my year," she said. "I'm so sorry Lillian is missing it."

"Are you two close?"

"Would I keep her around if we weren't?" She stared ahead contemplatively as we reached the town, turning left onto a road labeled Dune. "I'll go to the funeral, when it happens, of course. It doesn't sound like her mother can hold on much longer."

I thought of Mama, some hundred and fifty miles away, and shuddered slightly. Mothers should live forever.

Which reminded me—I studied Ada's profile, looking for a resemblance between her and my grandmother, who had passed some ten years ago.

"It's rude to stare," Ada said, not turning around. "What's the matter with you?"

I pursed my lips in annoyance. "I was just thinking how you look much younger than Bubbie did when she died."

Ada fluffed the ends of her scarf-covered hair and ticked a finger at me. "That's because she had children. And grandchildren. Nothing ages you like children."

"So it's my fault she looked old?"

"And your mother's. Why do you think I wouldn't keep either of you around for more than a summer? I value my youthful appearance."

She pulled into a driveway on 18th Street. "Here we are."

The house was grander than most around it, on a large lot with stones instead of grass, edged in seashells. It stood two stories high, with a wraparound porch in the Victorian style and wooden shake siding. It was almost more window than wall.

"No more duplexes?" I asked.

"I own enough of those."

"More than just yours?"

She got out of the car. "It's rude to ask about others' finances. But yes. Be a dear and bring the bags inside." And, without a backward glance, she climbed the steps to the summer home, leaving me to struggle with our suitcases, hatboxes, and other assorted bags that Ada didn't trust to send ahead.

The first thing I noticed when I climbed the steps was how bright the house was. The multitude of windows, which Ada was currently going through the house opening, provided natural light everywhere—even in the bathrooms. It would hardly be necessary to turn on a lamp until dark, which was late this time of year. The walls and furnishings were all pastels, creating a feeling of clean air throughout the entire house. I pictured myself lounging on the overstuffed sofa, a novel in hand, eating fresh fruit from a farm stand. A far cry from New York, but delicious nonetheless.

"Don't just stand there," Ada said. "We have work to do."

"What work? I'm here to relax."

"Relaxing takes work. Come on. Those bags go upstairs."

"Can't we get lunch first? I'm famished."

Ada put a hand on her hip. "I lived through the Great Depression. You'll live another half hour."

"You were alive in the 1800s too. That doesn't make me less hungry."

"Watch it," she said. "I was younger than you when they sank the *Maine*."

"I don't know what that is."

Ada held a hand to her chest in mock outrage. "You know about King Arthur but not the USS *Maine*? What *are* they teaching you in that fancy college?" She smiled. "You know what? It doesn't matter. Unless you mend your wicked ways, you're not going back there anyway. Now get those bags upstairs. I'm hungry too."

~

Lunch was a couple of blocks away at a hotel called the Whitebrier, with a dining room overlooking the water. The owner greeted Ada with a kiss on the cheek and asked if I was her new companion.

"Only for the summer. Lillian's mother is quite ill. This is my niece, Marilyn."

"She could be your sister," the man said with a wink. "Your usual spot outside?"

"Please."

"I don't like him," I whispered to Ada as he led us toward the deck.

"Really? I adore him."

Diners stopped eating to greet Ada as she entered, a reigning queen, waving gently to her subjects as we were settled along a rail, closest to the water, seagulls sitting on the dune nearby waiting for an opportunity to strike.

The owner held Ada's chair for her, then placed menus in front of us. "No need," Ada said. "We'll both have the usual."

"Very good, of course," he said, pulling the menu from my place and retreating.

"What if I don't like 'the usual'?"

"Then you have no taste, darling. Try it first. I doubt even you will be able to complain."

I scowled at her, but there was nothing I could say to that that wouldn't be branded a complaint.

"And don't make that face. It'll cause wrinkles," she said.

"More so than children?"

She winked.

Not more than a moment later, champagne flutes of orange juice arrived. "To Avalon," Ada said, raising her glass to me. "The jewel of the Jersey shore."

"I'm not sure that's saying much."

"Hush," Ada said, taking a sip. I followed suit, realizing as soon as the vibrant liquid hit my tongue that it was a mimosa. Ada was watching my reaction, so I kept my face blank. "I lived through Prohibition too," she said. "Cheers."

The usual proved to be a summer salad topped with crab meat, a combination I would never have tried on my own. My family didn't keep kosher, though we avoided shellfish and pork. But Ada was right. Perhaps it was the sea air or the view or just the food itself, but it was delicious.

"Is the town Jewish?" I asked as the waiter cleared our plates.

"No. Two churches, no synagogues. We'll be heathens for the summer."

I ignored the "heathen" comment. There had been no mention at all of going to a shul the one weekend I spent in Philadelphia, and I wasn't going to be the one to suggest it. Especially not when I knew what sort of comments she would make about why I might want to attend—not that I did. "Then who will your clients be?"

"Here? Everyone with an unmarried daughter over twenty-five in Cape May County. Atlantic too. They don't mind driving." She drank the last sip of her mimosa. "Which is where you come in. When the young men come to visit their families, we swoop in."

"You're not going to push me off that pier, are you?" I asked, gesturing to the pier in the distance.

"Now there's an idea. Weeds out the ones who can't swim."

"Did Lillian round up men for you?"

"Lillian? Goodness no. We always hired a girl to help."

"Does that mean you're going to pay me?"

"If so, I'll also be charging you rent."

"I have a feeling I'll come out of that arrangement owing you money," I said.

"Best not look a gift horse in the mouth. Come on. I'll pay you with an ice cream cone. Springer's is better, of course, but we would have to drive to Stone Harbor for that, so another day. Avalon Freeze is absolutely worth the walk."

"Do we walk everywhere in this town?"

"Mostly. I have bikes in the shed as well if you fancy a ride."

"I haven't ridden a bike since I was a kid."

Ada pushed back her chair and stood. "All of five minutes ago, then." And she strode away, leaving me to chase after her.

CHAPTER FOURTEEN

Frannie appeared mysteriously at seven the following morning to prepare breakfast. "Does she stay here with us?" I asked when Frannie returned to the kitchen.

"Of course not."

I was apparently supposed to know her living arrangements without asking. "Does she take the train down from Philadelphia at five every morning?"

Ada lowered her newspaper. "Is it really your business where Frannie lives?"

I supposed it wasn't. But I was still curious. Especially if Ada actually paid her a living wage. She had been beyond generous with Hannah, the homely girl looking for a match, and ridiculously so when it came to buying me a summer wardrobe (though I suspected that was more about me being a reflection of her than anything else), but I was still curious, especially given the fact that her paid companion lived with her year-round with time off for an ailing mother. But I said nothing—until Frannie came back in with my coffee, that is.

"Frannie," I asked, ignoring a warning look from Ada. "Where do you stay when you're in Avalon?"

Frannie looked in confusion to Ada, who shrugged. "Why—Miss Ada gives us a house for the summer. On Ninth Street."

"Who's 'us'?"

"My family—my husband, the children, and my sister comes to stay with us."

"How lovely," I said as Ada returned to her newspaper.

"It really is. We could never afford a place here."

"That'll be enough, Frannie," Ada said from behind her newspaper. "And you can have the night off tonight. We'll be having dinner with the Katzes."

"Of course, Miss Ada. Thank you."

Ada nodded, and she retreated to the kitchen.

"Just how many houses do you own?" I asked.

"Real estate is never a bad investment." She lowered the newspaper again. "What exactly is it that you want to do anyway?"

"Do?"

"Well, you don't seem to have any interest in getting married. And while there *is* money to be made in the type of exploits that got you sent here, I don't imagine that's a career 'Daddy' would approve of." I sat in silence for a moment, catching a satisfied smile on Ada's face. "Oh my. Did I actually stump you? I thought you had a comeback for everything."

"That's you," I said.

"And I told you not to make that face if you don't want wrinkles. I think you're destined for children. You'll look older than me within five years."

I felt my face scowling and tried to smooth it out. "I'm not *against* marriage," I said finally. "I just don't want to be forced into it. If I do, it'll be for love."

"Love fades," Ada said, putting her newspaper back up and flipping the page. "You're better off marrying for compatibility at that point."

"Have you been in love?"

She kept her face behind the newspaper. "We're discussing you. And you're dodging the question."

"I don't know exactly. I suppose I'll need a job if I don't marry."

"Did that just occur to you?"

I threw my hands up. "Maybe it's *you* who causes wrinkles."

She lowered the paper enough to catch my eye. "Just call me Dorian Gray."

We were both silent as she returned to reading. "I enjoy writing," I said quietly. She didn't respond. "But there's no real money in that if you're not a literary genius. And I'm no F. Scott Fitzgerald."

"A better thing than you realize. Scott was a mess."

"You're not about to tell me you knew Scott Fitzgerald!"

"I wouldn't say *knew*. But I met him." I stared at her in wonder. "Close your mouth. You'll catch flies." I mulled this over, trying to picture any circumstances where Ada could have crossed his path. "I imagine your father thinks writing is a waste of time."

"Completely," I said. "Mama doesn't though."

"Your mother always had her nose in a book. I suppose it's an escape from the tedium now."

"Her life isn't tedious."

Ada folded her newspaper and set it down, rising from the table. "Then why don't you want a similar one?" And without another word, she left the room.

~

The client meetings began promptly at nine the following morning. I wondered when she arranged them, but then I realized that was probably what she did when she dismissed me in the afternoons. Or it had been Lillian's job.

I was a fast learner and had gotten much better at taking notes, to the point where I earned a nod from Ada when she reviewed them. She raised an eyebrow when I suggested that our second client would be a good fit for a young man we had met the previous week. "And why is that?"

"Well, they both enjoy music and art. She's shorter than him. They're about the same level of attractiveness. And neither of their mothers seemed awful. I think they'd get along."

"Excellent appraisal. We'll try it and see how you did."

I was suddenly apprehensive. "What if they hate each other? You'll blame me."

"It's a risk you must be willing to take if you're going to make suggestions."

"So I should keep my mouth shut?"

"Are you capable of that? Besides, if you're right, you're guaranteeing two lifetimes of happiness."

"Happiness or tedium?"

Ada shrugged. "Once they reach the altar, that part is up to them. We can only teach them to fish. We can't also teach them to cook, chew, and swallow."

CHAPTER FIFTEEN

We broke for lunch, and then Ada informed me we were done for the afternoon. I raised my eyebrows, wondering if this was a result of fewer families being in town or if it was because she actually treated her time in town as somewhat of a vacation. But following her dictum of gift horses and mouths, I didn't question my good fortune.

Instead, I raced up the stairs and changed into my new blue bikini, admiring myself in the bathroom mirror before throwing on a caftan and packing a bag with a towel and one of the books my mother had sent. Then I called to Ada that I was going to the beach.

"Don't burn," she said. "No one wants to give their number to a lobster."

"I've got my Coppertone."

"There's also something to be said for umbrellas."

I rolled my eyes. "I'll take that into consideration."

Ada's house wasn't directly on the beach, but it was just two lots from the dunes. She claimed it was safer from storms and she had no intention of losing her house to the ocean. But it had an unobstructed view from the second floor, where my bedroom was. And the walk to the dunes only took a couple of minutes. The dunes themselves were harder to traverse, but soon the ocean spread out before me and I breathed deeply, as Ada had when we entered town. My parents may have preferred the Catskills, but I would always choose the ocean. Even if it *was* New Jersey.

It was a weekday, and only a handful of women with small children dotted the coast. I selected a spot far from their sandy feet and sticky fingers and spread my towel in the sand.

After applying the tanning lotion, I sat watching the ocean. Daddy certainly wouldn't approve of this punishment—I looked down at my pale stomach, exposed to sunlight for the first time—or of what I was wearing. But despite Mama's conservative dress, I somehow thought she would. Whatever part of her that spent the summer with Ada all those years ago, that part would approve of me here now. Even if she *had* fainted when I said I wasn't going to get pregnant in front of the rabbi.

I opened the book—it was an advance copy. One of Daddy's friends was in publishing and often gave my mother books before they were in stores. Daddy never knew how many burned dinners Mr. Stein had caused. This was called *To Kill a Mockingbird*. Mama wrote inside the cover, as she always did when she passed me books, that it was due out the following week. Before I knew it, I had read a hundred pages and realized I had better flip onto my back if I didn't want to look like a pancake Mama made while reading. She always served them burnt-side down, but they didn't fool us anymore.

I lay on my back and pushed my sunglasses up onto my forehead, closing my eyes against the brilliant sunlight, and slowly I began to drift off into a doze.

"Well, if it isn't the siren of the shore," a male voice said, waking me. I squinted against the sun, but I could only see the silhouette of a man in a pair of Avalon Beach Patrol trunks. Sitting up and holding my hand above my eyes, I could just make out the young man who had pulled me from the bush my first night in Philadelphia.

"Freddy, isn't it? I hardly recognize you when I'm not sprawled in shrubbery."

He grinned. "I'd know you anywhere." Looking around, he asked, "Are you on the clock? I don't see that aunt of yours lurking around corners."

"She's back at the house. Apparently we get to relax in the summer." I lowered my sunglasses so I wouldn't be squinting, and he sat on my towel next to me. I was very aware of the heat of his leg almost touching mine—and even more aware of how unclothed I was. "Wait—I didn't tell you she was my aunt."

"Maybe I asked around about you."

"Who would you ask? I just arrived!"

"There are no secrets in Oxford Circle. Or Avalon, for that matter."

I gestured to his trunks. "Are you here for the summer, then?"

"I am. My last summer of freedom before I graduate and have to decide between law school and the family business."

"Which is?"

He looked sideways at me. "Sizing me up as a match or asking for yourself?"

"If there are no secrets in Oxford Circle, Ada already knows all your business."

Freddy swept some sand off the towel, brushing against my leg in the process. "She does. You know, she called me after you got my number, and I asked about you. She said you weren't available."

"Did she now?"

He nodded. "Is it the rabbi's son? Or was that whole story a red herring?"

I scrunched up my nose, making a face that would surely upset Ada and her concern for future wrinkles. "True, unfortunately. But I did refuse him."

"Then you're not available because—?"

"Because Ada says I'm not."

He smiled, then rose off the towel. "We wouldn't want to go against Ada Heller, now would we?"

I felt a slight sense of disappointment as he prepared to leave. Ada had said no men, but what Ada didn't know . . .

"I have the afternoons free," I said. "Maybe I'll see you around."

"Maybe. How strong a swimmer are you?"

"Decently so."

"Shame," Freddy said, his lips spreading into a flirtatious grin. "I'm certified in mouth-to-mouth."

"Good to know," I said. "I'll make sure you're around before I start drowning."

Suddenly he was kneeling back on the towel. "We could practice now."

I pushed his chest away playfully and he tumbled over into the sand, clutching his heart. I couldn't help but laugh. "Get up, you fool."

"I can't. I'm mortally wounded. Only true love's kiss will break the spell."

There was another lifeguard sitting in a chair a little ways down the beach, and I pointed toward him. "Should I go get him to help you? I bet he's certified in mouth-to-mouth too."

"Another dagger to the heart. Maybe I should give up and try one of Ada's matches after all."

That sobered my mood quickly. He should, actually. I was off limits, especially if she was working with him. Ada made that much clear.

"Hey," he said softly, sitting up. "What just happened? You stopped smiling, and it's like the sun went away."

Against my better judgment, I leaned over and kissed his cheek. "That'll have to do."

"For now," he said, standing up again. "I'll see you soon, Marilyn."

And he took off jogging down the beach toward the lifeguard stand.

I reached up and touched my own cheek. I was smiling. Not smart at all. But a little flirtation couldn't hurt anyone. As long as Ada didn't find out.

CHAPTER SIXTEEN

Ada sent me to the small grocery store in town two days later.

"Isn't that Frannie's job?" I asked. It wasn't like I did any of the cooking.

"Frannie deserves days off just like everyone else," Ada snapped. "It won't kill you to pick up some produce."

Yes, Frannie deserved a day off, I grumbled to myself as I walked the half mile to the store. But so did I. Okay, I had the afternoons, and Freddy had come to find me on the beach both days. Of course, even on the days we didn't have clients, Ada had errands or other jobs for me to do. I would have liked a morning to sleep in and do what I wanted instead of catering to her.

But that was my penance, I supposed. Had I any idea that Daniel would have been so much trouble—well, who was I kidding? I probably would have done exactly what I did regardless. But maybe I would have stayed away from that stained glass. I had no regrets about anything except getting caught.

I soon found myself in the produce aisle, utterly confounded by the melons. Ada said to make sure they were ripe, but short of cutting one open, I had no idea how one would go about doing that. And I feared they would frown upon me cutting them all open and sampling them.

"Marilyn?"

I turned around to see Shirley. "My goodness, you're here to save me, aren't you?" I threw my arms around her neck.

Shirley laughed. "What do you need saving from?"

"These blasted melons. Ada said to make sure I got a ripe one, and there's no way to tell with the rind on. You create a distraction, and I'm going to try to crack one open like a coconut."

She looked at me like I had grown a second head. "Or I could show you the trick. Might be easier than smashing them."

"I suppose that'd do."

"Here," she said, pressing a thumb to the indentation on the top. "You press the belly button and then smell it. If it smells like you want to eat it, it's a good one." She held it out to me to smell, and the aroma was heavenly.

"Thank you. There's no greater joy than thwarting that woman, and she clearly expected me to fail. What do you know about peaches?"

Shirley shook her head. "Haven't you ever bought fruit before?"

I remembered Ada's disparaging comment about Shirley's family. Grace did most of our shopping even though Mama insisted on cooking. I had accompanied my mother a few times as a child when she went, but after I destroyed an entire tower of canned goods by plucking some from the bottom, she began leaving me home—a tradition that continued to this day.

It was amazing they hadn't sent me away sooner.

"Far too much of a troublemaker for that, I'm afraid."

Shirley linked her arm through mine. "Come on. We'll have Ada thinking there's nothing you can't do in no time."

After we had fulfilled both of our shopping lists, Shirley asked if I wanted to grab a cup of coffee at the diner across the street. I did, but Ada expected me back.

"Dinner, then? My family would be happy to have you—Ada too, of course."

I didn't think Ada would say yes, but I told her I would ask. Shirley rattled off her phone number, telling me to just let her know. We walked back together as far as 21st Street, when Shirley turned to go to her family's shore house.

Ada sighed when I asked her. She took a bite of a peach. "You picked well," she said.

"Shirley helped me."

She waved a hand at me. "You go. Send my regards but say I already had plans."

"Do you? Have plans?"

She leveled a gaze at me. "Believe me, when my plans become your business, you'll be the first to know."

I wondered again about the mysterious caller. The two phones in this house seemed to be on the same line, but when she had gone to her bedroom to take a call the night we arrived, I hadn't been able to eavesdrop without being caught. Her tone again sounded more like she was talking to a lover than a friend. Was he here, whoever he was? Did she have a date?

But that, too, would be considered not my business.

So I shrugged and called Shirley to tell her it would just be me for dinner.

~

Wearing a new eyelet sundress that we had purchased at Gimbels, I twirled to show Ada before I left. "It suits you," she said. "But you really should be sitting under an umbrella. All that sun you're getting . . ."

"Yes, yes, will cause wrinkles. So will everything else I do."

She threw up her hands. "Far be it from me to stop you if you want to look like a raisin when you're thirty."

"What a lovely image," I said, refusing to let her get my goat tonight. Instead, I leaned down and kissed her on the cheek, surprising her. "Enjoy your plans—whatever they may be."

"And you yours," she said with a knowing smirk. "Just remember the rules, please."

I didn't know what that meant because I wasn't bringing Shirley here. But I shrugged and headed out the door to walk the three blocks to Shirley's house.

Traversing those blocks in heels, however, was slightly more complicated than I expected. The houses all had the same white stones for a lawn that Ada's did, but not everyone had a gardener as fastidious, so there were many opportunities to turn an ankle on errant stones. I chuckled, mentally thanking Ada for all the practice she had given me at dodging rocks in my path, and arrived at the house unscathed.

The house rose before me, and I saw what Ada meant about the family trying too hard. Ada's house was designed to look like a classic beach cottage, if a large one. Shirley's family's summer home was a stone behemoth, designed to show off wealth. It lacked the airy windows that provided such welcome breezes and constant sunlight and was built for effect more than comfort. It would have looked at home across from the White House, not here among the clapboard and shake-sided cottages, with its columns and porticos.

I hoped they had fans. I didn't want to sweat my makeup off before dinner was served.

I climbed the steps and rapped smartly on the oversized oak door, expecting Shirley to throw it open (or a butler, if they were really trying to impress).

But when the door opened, Freddy stood there, dressed in a dinner jacket. "Well, hello there."

I leaned back to look at the house number. "I must have the wrong house, but hello to you as well."

"Right house," Shirley said breathlessly, elbowing Freddy out of the way. "Don't mind him. He'd flirt with a corpse if it had lipstick on."

"My sister exaggerates," Freddy said, leaning against the doorpost.

"Your sister? This just got more interesting."

Shirley looked from me to him. "Oh no." She turned to Freddy, hands on her hips. "Can't I have one friend whose heart you don't break?"

"First of all you have Julia—"

"Only because you said Julia looked like a potato with hair!"

Freddy turned to me. "She does. Very unfortunate girl—I don't think even your aunt could save her." He looked back at his sister. "And second, the only heart being broken here is mine. She's refused to go out with me multiple times now."

Shirley threw an arm around my shoulders. "I knew I liked you. Come on, Mama and Papa want to meet you. We have cocktails in the living room before dinner."

Mr. and Mrs. Goldman rose to greet me warmly as we entered the living room. I needn't have worried about fans—instead I worried my hair would look worse than after a ride along the coast with Ada driving and no scarf.

"Shirley has told us so much about you." Mrs. Goldman spoke loudly to be heard over the noise of the fans. I shot a glance at Freddy, wondering both if he had mentioned me and if he had made the connection that I was his sister's new friend before I arrived.

"All lies," I said. She looked confused. "I'm kidding."

"Of course," she said and laughed loudly to punctuate it. And I immediately understood that Ada would never set foot in this house. They didn't know my family in New York—they were trying to impress me because Ada was Oxford Circle royalty. And Mrs. Goldman's desperate laugh to prove she got a joke that went over her head was entirely so I would form a good impression. Freddy and Shirley or no, this was going to be a long evening.

Mr. Goldman insisted I sit in his chair, the place of honor in the living room, which was mildly uncomfortable as the whole family sat on two sofas, staring at me.

"Tell us everything about yourself, dear," Mrs. Goldman said. "I want to know everything there is to know."

"Goodness, that would be terribly boring."

"Not at all," Freddy said with a laugh. His mother shot him a death stare, and he hid his smile behind his glass.

"You're from New York, of course. What does your father do?"

"He's a doctor."

"And your mother is a Heller."

If you went back to my great-grandparents that was true, but it didn't make sense to correct her on the branches of my family tree, especially when she was telling me, not asking. So I nodded, taking a sip of an extremely weak sloe gin fizz.

"Do you have any siblings?"

"A brother, Harold."

"A brother," she said, looking at Shirley. "How wonderful. You'll have to invite him down to meet our Shirley. We could have a double wed—"

"Mama!" Shirley interjected.

"You're right, of course," Mrs. Goldman said, smoothing her dress. "He could be twelve. How old is he?"

"Twenty-five and married—sorry, Shirl." It was my turn to hide behind a drink. There was a good chance I was going to start laughing if I didn't.

Shirley shook her head. "Mama, really. Enough."

"Marriages don't always last—do they seem happy?"

"Mama!"

"What? I'm just trying to look out for you, dear." She leaned in toward me conspiratorially, as if I weren't there at her daughter's request. "You're not offended, are you?"

"Ah—um—no, of course not."

Mrs. Goldman leaned back in her seat, flashing Shirley a closed-mouth smile of victory before turning back to me. "And you? Are you engaged?"

"Quite the opposite."

Mrs. Goldman nodded sagely. "Which is why you're here, of course." Then she looked to Freddy, who was glaring at her, and her husband, who was making a *stop* gesture across his throat. "I don't mean *here*," she said, gesturing wildly around the room. "I meant with your aunt. To find you a match." She wrung her hands fretfully until her husband reached over and put a calming hand on her leg.

"Let the poor girl breathe, Arlene," he said. "She didn't come here to be interrogated."

To be honest, I was wondering what I was doing there at all now. Neither Shirley nor Freddy reeked of the desperation of their parents, so it was no wonder I had accepted the invitation, but it would take a lot more gin and a lot less fizz to get me back here again.

"It's fine," I reassured Mrs. Goldman. "But no. I'm not here to find a husband. I have two more years of college left and then—well, we'll just see what happens. I don't go in for all that matchmaking business."

Freddy hid another smile. "No?"

"Not for me." He winked, and I raised my drink again. At this rate it was probably a good thing that whoever made the drinks had barely waved a bottle of gin over my glass.

A maid in a crisp uniform entered and announced that dinner was served. She stood in stark contrast to Frannie, who wore what she chose. Ada, stickler that she was for so many traditions, seemed to be the champion of workers' rights.

The meal itself was a preposterous affair of a multitude of courses, all of which were far too heavy for a hot evening, leaving me worried that I would doze off before we even reached the turkey that was finally brought out. I wanted to ask if they ate like this every night or if they had gone all out for little old me. But I knew the answer already. And I wished there was a polite way to tell them to stop trying so hard. It was the primary difference between their family and my own. We had nothing to prove. The Goldmans tried so hard to impress everyone that they failed to impress anyone.

But finally the meal ended with a seven-layer cake, and Mr. and Mrs. Goldman retired to the den to allow me and Shirley to spend some time on the porch swing. The sun was setting over the bay, and the air had finally turned cooler on the porch, which faced the ocean, away from the street, though the view was heavily obstructed by the dunes.

"Sorry about them," Shirley said quietly while we rocked gently in the breeze.

"All our parents are ridiculous," I reassured her.

"You'd be hard pressed to find a more ridiculous pair than Howard and Arlene," Freddy said from behind us, startling me. He struck a match on one of the porch columns and lit the cigarette held between his lips.

"Have another one of those?" I asked.

"Do well-bred young ladies smoke?" he asked, grinning as he passed me the one he had lit and pulled the pack from his pocket.

"I wouldn't know."

"What say you, sis? Want to try a puff?"

Shirley shook her head. "You know they'd kill me. And you for offering."

"Me? Their golden child? Never. You—well, they'd be dredging the bay for your body."

She looked to me. "I wish he were wrong. But they want me to be absolutely perfect."

I gave her a sympathetic smile. "My parents did, too, but they gave up on me a long time ago. I'm a bad egg."

"Make some room," Freddy said, nudging his sister away from me and coming to sit between us over her protests. "You don't seem like such a bad egg," he said softly.

"Frederick Joseph Goldman, don't you even think about it," Shirley said, jumping up. "Marilyn isn't interested. Go smoke your cigarette somewhere else."

"Why not let Marilyn decide if she's interested?"

"You said she already did multiple times. You leave the poor girl be."

I tried not to laugh. I did. But being referred to as a poor girl was too much and I couldn't hold it in. And once I started, so did Freddy. Shirley's face fell. "Oh, Shirley. No. Freddy knows I'm not allowed to date while I'm here. They'd be pulling my body out of the bay along with yours. Or worse, shipping me back to my parents, and you'd never find my body in the Hudson along with so many others."

Relieved, Shirley went to the edge of the porch and craned her neck. "Do you think they're above us listening?"

Freddy leaned down and planted a quick kiss on my neck, in the hollow where it met my shoulder, before she turned back around, and I looked at him in amused surprise. "No," he said, like nothing had just happened. "We'd have heard them. Howard stomps about like a hippopotamus." He waited a beat. "Definitely not. We'd hear them grumbling about that comment." He looked over at me. "Do you want another drink?"

"Depends. Will it actually have alcohol in it?"

Freddy laughed loudly. "You're quite the firecracker. Or glass breaker. Which is it?"

"I like to think I'm a polymath when it comes to destruction."

He grinned. "Shirl—go fetch us some more drinks."

"You fetch them. I'm not a puppy."

"Tsk, tsk, tsk. Wait until Mother hears you're not taking care of your guest's needs."

She glared at her brother, and for a moment I thought she would stomp her foot, but her shoulders dropped, and she opened the door into the house.

Freddy's arms were suddenly around me. And as much as I knew I should throw them off, I didn't want to. "I've been dying to get you alone since I first found you in that bush," he said, his face just inches from mine.

"And just what do you intend to do with me?"

His face moved closer to mine. "I've got a few ideas."

"Which are?"

And then he kissed me. This wasn't a tentative first kiss like Daniel's. This was a man who knew what he wanted and intended to make sure I was aware that what he wanted was me. I knew I should pull back. Shirley or the Goldmans could walk out and catch us at any moment, but that danger only added to the deliciousness of the moment, and I kissed him back as if my life depended on his lips and tongue meeting mine.

He pulled back, placing a finger to his lips at footsteps that I hadn't noticed, so wrapped up in the feel of his mouth on my own. My heart was beating so quickly I thought for sure Shirley would see it through my skin. No one had ever kissed me like that before.

"You can get your own," Shirley said to her brother, handing me a glass and keeping one for herself. "I'm not serving you."

"I don't need one," he said, putting an arm around my shoulders on the swing. "Marilyn here is intoxicating enough for me."

He looked at me to see what I'd do. And I decided to play offended, for Shirley's sake. "Take mine, then," I said, removing his arm and thrusting the glass she had given me into his hand. "I should head home anyway. But please thank your parents for me." I rose to leave.

"I'll walk you there."

"It's only three blocks. I can find my way home."

"You could twist an ankle in those shoes. Fall into another bush."

"I think I'll manage."

"What about the Jersey Devil?"

I had gone down the first step, but I turned back at his words. "The what now?"

He nodded wisely. "It haunts the pine barrens a couple of miles inland. And preys specifically on unprotected young women."

"None of that is true," Shirley said, rolling her eyes.

"Why do you think Mother and Father don't want you out alone at night?"

"Not because of some monster, I'll tell you that much."

He angled his head knowingly. "Or they just don't want you to be too afraid at night." He rose from the swing and took my hand, placing it through his arm. "If the Jersey Devil wants to get to you, he'll have to get through me first."

"So gallant," I murmured. "Shirley, thank you, darling—let's go to the beach together this week. I'm free most afternoons."

She was pouting but agreed as Freddy led me down the steps and around to the front of the house. But instead of turning left to go up toward the main road, he turned right. "The house is this way," I said, gesturing in the other direction.

"But the beach is this way and it's so much more romantic than a street."

I stopped walking. "Now, Freddy, that was fun and all, but I told you, I can't get involved."

"That's too bad," he said, turning to face me. "Because I'm already absolutely smitten." He grinned impishly. "Besides, you said if we didn't like Ada's matches, you'd go on a date with any of us."

"You haven't met any of Ada's matches."

"I already know I don't like them. They're not you." He tugged my arm to get me walking toward the path over the dunes.

"I definitely can't walk on the sand in these," I said as we reached the sand pathway, my heels already sinking in.

"Then take them off," he said, kneeling to remove first my right and then my left shoe, holding them both in one hand by the heels as he rose to take my hand with his other. "Or I can carry you, if you'd rather."

"I can walk just fine," I said. But as we crested the dune, the ocean sparkling below us in the reflected moonlight, I pictured us re-creating Burt Lancaster and Deborah Kerr's scene in *From Here to Eternity* in the surf. I was in dangerous territory, and I knew it. "We probably should have taken the road," I said quietly.

"I was just kidding about the Jersey Devil, you know. Besides, he hates water." I laughed, despite myself. "You're perfectly safe with me."

"Are you safe with me though?"

He stopped walking, pulling my arm until I was facing him, and wrapped one arm around my waist, his other hand tangling itself in my hair. "You tell me," he said quietly as he leaned down to kiss me again.

When we finally broke apart, both panting for air, Freddy said he should get me home. As much as I knew he was right, I felt a tingle of disappointment radiating through my body. "I want to win that aunt of yours over. And that means returning you without making it obvious what we've been up to."

His mention of Ada sobered me quickly. Even if he were from a different family, Ada made it quite clear that she would not approve of any romantic liaisons that summer. And the fact that she had his number as a potential match made the situation that much worse. "I'm not sure you'll be able to do that."

"Just watch," he said. "I've been told I'm too charming for my own good."

"You're not that charming."

"Oh no?" he asked, pulling me in for another kiss. "Your lips beg to differ."

I told myself it was the setting, but I couldn't help it. I kissed him back. And again when we reached Ada's street. "Not too close to the house," I whispered. "She sees everything."

"Then we'll say goodbye here," he whispered back. "When can I see you again?"

"Like this? I don't know that you can."

"What a terrible answer. Shall I ask Ada for her permission? Like she's your father?"

"My father would grant it easier than she would."

He looked down at me in the darkness. "You strike me as the type who knows how to sneak out of a house if the mood suits you."

I laughed quietly. He had me pegged. "Maybe."

"Will you be on the beach tomorrow?" I nodded. "We'll make a plan then." He kissed me one more time, then turned to walk away, and I went up the path to the house, climbing the steps to the front door that Ada told me didn't need to be locked.

I didn't call out. I had no idea what time it was or if she would be awake, but she was in the den, on the phone. "Marilyn?" she asked.

"It's me, Ada."

"Come in here, please." I did as she asked, arranging my face placidly as if I had just come from a family dinner with no siblings in the house. Her mouth turned down in a frown as she looked me over. "I believe you had lipstick on when you left this evening."

My mind was racing, but I kept my face bland. "Came off on my napkin," I said, thinking fast. "And I left the tube in the bathroom here so I couldn't reapply."

She pursed her lips, and for a moment I was sure I was sunk. Then she waved a hand at me to go and returned to her phone call. "Yes, I know. It's hard for me too."

I started up the stairs, wondering again who she was always talking to. And what was hard? But I didn't really care. I wanted to wash my face, change into my nightgown, and dream of Freddy on the beach.

CHAPTER SEVENTEEN

"I think I'll join you on the beach today," Ada said the next morning. Frannie was back, and I was beginning to question why she brought her in to make breakfast. She didn't eat much of it. Not that I minded. I was famished.

I froze, mid-bite, wondering if I was somehow caught. But there was no way she could know Freddy said he would see me there today, was there? No, she would have had to have been outside with us and she was clearly on the phone. She lowered her newspaper because I hadn't responded, and I composed my face. "Of course," I said, smiling innocently. Her eyes narrowed, and she made a small *hmmph* sound.

When she raised the newspaper back to reading level, I felt my shoulders drop, and I pushed my plate away, appetite gone. I had to tell Freddy we couldn't see each other. For real. I would never be able to get away with anything. Ada was too wily, and she somehow could read my every move before I made it. I didn't understand how, but she did.

I just hoped he was smart enough to stay away when he saw me with her.

Getting Ada to the beach was much more of an ordeal than tossing a towel and a bottle of Coppertone into my bag. While she dressed, Frannie prepared a light lunch of sandwiches, bottles of soda, and fruit to take with us, which she packed into an ice-filled Styrofoam cooler.

Then, Frannie helped me lug a wagon out of the shed. In it we packed the cooler, my beach bag, a chair for Ada, and a beach umbrella. "Do you know how to put this up?" Frannie asked me.

I did not. But how hard could it be? I could open a regular umbrella. And you just stuck it in the sand. Frannie eyed me warily. "I'll be just fine," I assured her.

Frannie wrung her hands. "I can send my husband to help. Let me just call him."

I put a hand on her arm. "Frannie. I can handle a walk to the beach and setting up Ada's things. It's fine."

"I wish Lillian were here," she said.

"Well, she's not. I am. And I'm not an imbecile. Truly. I'm in college. I can figure out an umbrella and a chair."

She looked unconvinced, especially as I began trying to drag the wagon over the white rocks of the yard. That part took her pushing while I pulled. But once we reached the sidewalk, it was smooth sailing. "See? Right as rain."

"You just come back to the house if you need me to call my husband," she said.

"Shoo," I said, waving her away. "And don't you sit at the house waiting for us. Go enjoy the day. I've got everything under control until dinner."

Ada descended the stairs in a caftan covering everything except her head, hands, and feet, and a sun hat so gigantic that I wasn't sure how she fit through the front door. It took a lot of effort not to laugh.

"What are we waiting for?" she asked. "It's a beautiful day!"

"Miss Ada, let me send my husband to bring your things. I can call him in a moment."

"Traitor," I said quietly. "I can handle it."

"Take the afternoon off, Frannie," Ada said gently. "I'm sure Marilyn is quite capable of getting me situated."

"But—"

"No buts. I want to hear all about the lovely time you had with your family later. Go." She turned to me. "Don't prove me wrong."

"It's an umbrella, Ada."

Ten minutes later, I was heavily regretting my words as it fell over for the third time. I stabbed again at the sand. "Why—won't—it—go—*in*?"

Ada stood, arms crossed in irritation, as I had also been unable to unfold her chair. And dragging the wagon up the path over the dunes had almost been the death of me.

"There!" I exclaimed finally as the pole seemed stable. I bent to open the top and—the whole thing toppled into the sand and blew away, leaving me to run after it, expelling a stream of profanities that made a mother near us cover her child's ears and glare at me.

But someone else reached the umbrella before I could. "Need a hand?" Freddy asked.

I glanced over my shoulder. Ada had her sunglasses on, but she appeared to be looking in our direction. "Ada's here. Pretend we don't know each other."

"She knows you got my phone number *and* knows Shirley is my sister. Probably not the best plan."

"Fine. Pretend you didn't kiss me last night."

"Should I pretend you didn't kiss me too?"

"Freddy!"

He smiled and picked up the errant umbrella, jogging it over to where Ada stood. "Miss Heller," he said, nodding his head. "As a member of the Avalon Beach Patrol, it would be an honor to help you set up today."

She lowered her glasses. "Freddy Goldman?"

"Yes, ma'am."

She looked to me. "Suspicious timing."

"Ma'am?"

"You two having dinner last night and then you showing up here?"

He feigned an excellent look of confusion. "I'm afraid I don't know what you mea—wait." He looked at me. "Are you the same Marilyn my sister is friends with?"

I wasn't sure what game he was playing, but I nodded.

"That explains it. I ate at the pizzeria on the boardwalk last night with a friend from school. And I work the Eighteenth Street lifeguard chair."

I didn't think Ada bought it, but she allowed him to set up first her chair and then the umbrella. I watched as he dug out a small hole, then borrowed a bucket from the child whose mother I had offended with my blue vocabulary and poured water after planting the umbrella, patting the sand to make it firmer. He looked up and noticed me watching him. "Aim it against the wind," he said. "That way a gust won't pull it out and hurt someone."

"I knew that part," I said tartly.

He suppressed a smile.

"Thank you, Freddy," Ada said. "You can go back to your actual job now."

"Yes, ma'am. And don't forget me if you find anyone as pretty as your niece here." He winked at her and jogged back to the lifeguard stand.

As soon as he was out of earshot, Ada turned to me. "No."

"No what?"

She wagged a finger at me. "You know what. Once you gave me his information, he became off limits. And I said no men from the get-go."

"Ada—"

"Not up for discussion."

I threw my hands up. "Can I say anything at all?"

"Not if it's about Freddy Goldman."

"And if it's not?"

Ada settled into her chair in the shade of the expertly assembled umbrella. "Then I'm all ears. What would you like to say?" But I had nothing to say anymore and just stood there sputtering. "That's what I thought. Close your mouth, please. You look like a fish when you keep standing there doing that."

Angrily, I shook out my towel, taking small pleasure in some sand flying onto Ada, and spread it in the sun several feet from her. I pulled out my book.

"Are you reading a hunting manual?" Ada asked.

I rolled my eyes, then realized she couldn't see them through my sunglasses. "No."

"Then what on earth is that?"

"A new book that Mama sent me."

"You remind me of her. Nose in a book at every opportunity. Except when there's a boy around."

I raised my sunglasses to the top of my head to make sure she saw my eye roll this time. "The only time I've been around boys, except for Freddy helping with the umbrella, was when *you* made me go talk to them. That's not a fair assessment."

"And what brought you here again?"

I lowered my sunglasses and returned to my book. At least it didn't insult my virtue.

So wrapped up in the trials and tribulations of Maycomb was I that I didn't even notice Ada had removed her own novel and was reading—quite a large one at that. I squinted to see the title. *Hawaii*, by James Michener.

"I didn't know you read," I said.

"How impertinent," Ada said without looking up. "Of course I read."

"I meant for fun. You don't keep books around."

"I do," she said, turning the page. "But they're not on public display."

What does that mean? "Uh, okay."

"Don't say *uh*. It makes you sound uncertain. Speak with assurance and people will treat you as intelligent."

I willed her umbrella to blow away and land on her head. "Where are your books, then?"

"I have a shelf of them in my room. The rest are boxed in the attic. I donate most of them to the library on the island at the end of each summer."

"There's a library here?" I yelped, sitting up. "Where?"

Ada looked at me curiously. "In the basement of the elementary school." I smiled at the thought that I wouldn't have to depend entirely on the generosity of my mother for entertainment this summer. Even if it was located in a school's basement and largely Ada's hand-me-downs. She sighed. "I suppose you can browse my collection as well."

Freddy forgotten, I returned happily to reading, the sun shining on my back, the surf crashing in the background, and Ada grumbling periodically about wrinkles.

CHAPTER EIGHTEEN

Eventually, Ada rose from her chair, stretched her arms over her head, and removed her hat and voluminous caftan. "I believe I'll go for a swim," she said.

I looked at her curiously as she pulled on a bathing cap. Her swimsuit was a green one-piece, which clung to her wiry frame.

"It's rude to stare," she said.

She was facing the ocean, so how did she know I was looking? She turned and grinned at me. "I told you, it's children that age you." Then she pointed at the sky. "And that sun you're sitting under. When you're my age, you'll regret not sitting under that umbrella."

She sauntered to the shore, waded in a couple of feet, and then dove through a wave, surfacing in a strong and sure freestyle stroke.

I turned to the lifeguard stand. Freddy had seen her go in and was climbing off the chair, with a quick word to the other lifeguard. He laughed at something the guard said, then walked over toward me, shaking his head.

"We've got a little while," he said. "She does long swims."

"How do you know that?"

"She's down here most mornings, early. You're not supposed to swim before the guards are out, but, well, we were told to leave her be if we see her out there unless she's in distress."

"Still," I said, looking out to where her white swim cap cut through the water. "You shouldn't be over here. She sees everything."

"She can't possibly." He leaned in. "No kiss today?"

I shoved him away playfully. "There are children and a very nosy aunt present."

"They might enjoy the show."

"I think I see why your sister warned me about you."

"You can't listen to anything Shirley says. She probably thinks kissing is how babies are made."

I shook my head. "If that were true, she'd have a passel of nieces and nephews running around."

He held a hand to his heart. "I'll have you know I'm a perfectly virtuous young man. It's not my fault you've stolen my heart."

"No one virtuous kisses like that. That takes practice." I couldn't help but smile at him though. And after the previous night, the way his bronzed torso shone in the sunlight was not lost on me.

"I can't remember a single girl before you. Were there some? Maybe. You're the one who matters."

I knew better. I did. I knew anyone who talked this smoothly was trouble—and I knew it because it was how I had hooked Daniel with no intention of following through on anything. But there was something in the way Freddy never took his eyes off me. The way he watched my mouth as I spoke, as if he wanted to devour my very words. The way he made me feel like the most irresistible girl in the world—the only girl in the world. I couldn't hold out against that.

"She's in bed by ten," I said quietly. "I could slip out after that."

His lips spread into a smile that I longed to kiss. "I'll be outside waiting for you."

"Now shoo, before Ada catches us and ships me back to New York."

He kissed my cheek quickly and jogged back through the sand.

~

It was Sunday, and Ada insisted on watching Ed Sullivan, as always. I felt like my insides were vibrating, but I forced myself to sit still and act like I cared about Rosemary Clooney and Dave Barry. I laughed when she laughed, but I was really watching the clock on the mantel behind the television. Would this show never end?

But eventually it did, and Ada turned it off and went up to get ready for bed, which I pretended to do as well.

She turned to me at the top of the stairs, and I held my breath. She knew. Somehow, she knew.

But all she said was, "Tomorrow is the Fourth of July. I've given Frannie the day off, so you can sleep in as late as you like. We'll watch the fireworks on the beach in the evening."

"That," I squeaked, then cleared my throat. "That sounds lovely."

"Are you coming down with something?" She put the back of her hand to my forehead. "Or just too much sun?"

I felt my cheeks flushing. "Maybe. I'm sure a good night's sleep will fix whatever it is."

"Don't stay up too late," she said, turning to her door.

"Excuse me?"

She looked back at me with those shrewd eyes that missed nothing. "Reading."

"Of course. No, I'll go right to sleep tonight."

"Good," Ada said. She went into her room and shut the door. But I couldn't shake the suspicion that she knew anyway.

I didn't want to chance the front door. It was heavy and it stuck, and while she didn't lock it, there was a high likelihood that either opening or closing it would give me away. Not to mention I would have to walk past her room to get down the stairs. But my bedroom windows opened, and the roof of the front porch was right outside. And even better, it was on the other side of the house from Ada's window. I waited until ten minutes after the light under her bedroom door went out, and then I slid my window open and unlatched the screen.

I did hope Freddy couldn't see me, as my shuffle down the roof to the edge was far from graceful, but it was an easy climb to the porch railing and then down from there. Freddy was practically invisible aside from the light of his cigarette glowing in the darkness.

"I knew you were the type who could sneak out," he said, his teeth shining in the moonlight as he smiled, holding out his arm to me. "Let's go. I left my car around the corner so it wouldn't wake the old bat."

"Don't call her that," I said, taking his arm. "She's strict about certain things, but she's not what she seems."

"If you say so."

Then I thought about what he had said. "Car? Where are we going?"

I saw the flash of his teeth again. "To have some fun."

"I'm good for some kisses, but I'm not *that* kind of girl, buster."

He threw his cigarette into the rock lawn of a nearby house and grabbed my waist, pulling me to him and kissing me deeply. "Who says I'm that kind of boy?" he breathed into my ear when he broke the kiss. "Come on." He pulled me along again. "I promise. All clean fun tonight."

His car was a red-and-white Bel Air convertible, a few years old, but immaculately kept. "Let's go," he said, opening the door for me. He climbed into the driver's seat and held out a scarf. "Stole this from Shirley. She won't ride with me unless her hair is tied up."

"How thoughtful." He looked over as I secured the scarf around my hair. "What?"

"You look beautiful," he said. "Like you belong in this car."

I shook my head as he lifted my hand to his lips and kissed it. Then he started the car and drove off toward 30th Street, the road out of town, the moonlight shining over the bay and the channels as we passed through the marshlands, which held a beauty in the darkness that I had failed to see on the drive in. He turned right onto the Garden State Parkway, and the wind whipped around us, making conversation impossible. But Freddy reached over and took my hand around the exit for Ocean City, and I felt a shiver up and down my spine as he traced a thumb along my palm.

The road was empty and dark, surrounded by pine trees on the left and the shore towns in the distance on the right, the moon and stars our only companions. It felt terribly romantic. Like we were running away together. I wanted to slide over and let him put an arm around me, but I felt it was best to keep my wits about me. The last thing I needed was for us to not make it to our destination, but wind up in the backseat on the side of the road.

Eventually Freddy exited the highway, and the sign read "Atlantic City." "Really?" I shouted over the wind.

"Have you been?" I shook my head. "I'll take you during the day sometime. A proper visit."

Ada would never allow it. But I didn't want to spoil the fun.

Instead, I watched the horizon as the lights of the most famous boardwalk came into focus.

Avalon was quiet by ten o'clock. Atlantic City was just getting started. We parked and walked up a set of stairs to the boardwalk, and I immediately felt overstimulated by the sights, sounds, and smells that accosted me. And this coming from a New York City girl!

Everyone wore their finest. Suits and ties on the men, dresses with starched crinolines on the women. Ignoring the heat, many women wore faux mink stoles around their shoulders and were dripping with rhinestones. The few children who could be seen were asleep in strollers or their parents' arms.

I felt almost underdressed in my sundress and espadrilles, but if I had learned anything from Ada, it was that confidence was everything. So I didn't smooth my skirt or fluff my hair. I walked along on Freddy's arm as if I were the one whom everyone else had come to see. And the two of us did turn heads.

"You look like a movie star," Freddy said, taking my hand and twirling me around. He pulled me toward a photography booth. "Come on. Let's get a picture."

But I resisted. "I don't want a trail of evidence for Ada."

"Why doesn't she like me?"

Well, there was certainly no way to explain about his family, which was a sobering thought in and of itself. Even if marriage had been an option, the idea of being tied to his parents was quite disconcerting. "She said I'm not allowed to date while I'm here."

"Does she have someone in mind for you?"

"Oh no! Nothing like that!" But I did remember her comment about needing a man who would stand up to me. *That could be Freddy,* I thought, looking up at him. He refused to take no for an answer, and while he didn't overpower me, he got me to cave with charm. I could see where that would be appealing in the long term. "No, she's got strict rules about her business. Once you gave me your number, you became off limits."

"But I gave *you* my number. Because you said you would go out with me if I didn't like Ada's matches."

"I, technically, wasn't authorized to say that."

"Well, you did. And I don't like any of her matches."

"You still haven't met any of them!"

He grinned down at me. "Doesn't matter. I still know I like you better."

I turned away so he wouldn't see my smile.

Freddy paid the admission for us to go onto the Steel Pier. The smells of fried foods and popcorn assailed us as a man directed us toward the diving horses. "One last dive tonight, folks. Just one last dive tonight."

"Is that real?" I asked.

"Of course." He pulled my hand. "You have to experience it." I let myself be tugged along, and Freddy secured us a spot in the stands. The announcer told us we were about to experience one of the greatest wonders of the world.

"Is this safe?" I asked.

"Perfectly so."

But I remembered my mother telling me about Sonora Carver, who lost her sight in a diving accident. So when the bathing suit–clad girl climbed to the top of the tower, I felt a flutter of anxiety in my stomach. And when the horse began barreling his way up the ramp to the tower, I clutched Freddy's arm in sheer terror, holding my breath as the girl jumped onto the horse and the two of them flew together through the air, seeming to hang there for an impossible moment, before plunging into the tank of water below, emerging to the sound of such thunderous applause, shouts, and stomping of feet that I wondered if the pier would tumble into the ocean.

"You all right there?" Freddy asked me.

"Perfectly so. Why?"

"If you hold my arm much tighter, I'm afraid you'll wrench it off."

I laughed a little and released him. "I've never seen anything quite like that."

He put an arm around me, pulling me to him comfortingly with a squeeze. Then he took my hand and led me out to get an ice cream cone to soothe my nerves.

We ended the evening dancing in the Marine Ballroom as a band played. Had it been the afternoon, I wouldn't have dared, as Ed Hurst broadcast his "Summertime on the Pier" dance show live there every Saturday and Sunday. But this late at night, we were safe from cameras, other than the roving boardwalk photographers. Not that I thought Ada would watch anything so frivolous, nor did she turn on the television before dark, but I was enjoying whatever this was with Freddy and didn't want to see it come crashing down.

By the time we returned to the car, it was after one. "Sure you want to go back?" Freddy asked.

"Wherever else would we go?"

"Why, anywhere we want. We could just drive south and live in Florida. Or west to California. We could stop at the Grand Canyon on the way. I've always wanted to see that."

"We can't just run away."

"We can do anything if we're together."

Suddenly he was kissing me, my back pressed up against the car. And for a moment, I believed him, that anything was possible. What if we *did* just keep driving? Start fresh someplace where parents and aunts didn't dictate our futures?

As we drove back through the moonlight, I leaned against Freddy, my shoes off and legs up, feet hanging out the open window. My posture was drowsy, but I was awake with the possibilities of what life could be like if we just escaped.

But we eventually reached Avalon, and Freddy parked his car on the main road again to avoid detection. "I'll help you get back upstairs," he said quietly.

"I can do it."

"What kind of a gentleman would I be if I weren't there to catch you if you fell?"

I shot him a flirtatious look. "Or try to catch a glimpse of what's under my dress, you mean?"

"If so, I'd have brought a flashlight," he said, winking. He held a finger to his lips. "Let's get you to bed safe and sound."

He kissed me one more time on the path up to Ada's house. "I had a wonderful time tonight," I said.

"We'll have to do it again."

The reality was that it would be close to impossible to fool Ada a second time. But I nodded, thinking as I climbed up the railing and onto the roof that I probably could have flown up to my window instead.

CHAPTER NINETEEN

Ada's version of "sleep as late as you want" apparently extended until nine, at which point she entered the room, opened the curtains, and pulled the covers off me.

"Ten more minutes," I moaned, burying my face in my pillow.

"How long can one person sleep? You're missing a gorgeous day!"

"Every day is a gorgeous day here."

"And when you're my age, you'll learn not to take that for granted."

The reason I was so tired returned to the forefront of my mind and I smiled, happy my face was buried in my pillow so Ada couldn't see it. Instead, I feigned grumpiness and rolled over, stretching my arms above my head with a yawn.

"There. Are you feeling better this morning?"

"Better?" I asked, then I remembered she thought I was getting sick the night before. "Yes, much."

She peered at me sharply. "You don't look well rested."

My eyes flicked to the nightstand, looking for an excuse, where I found one. She had given me her copy of *Hawaii* when she finished it. "I stayed up too late reading."

Ada shook her head. "Youth is wasted on the young. Get dressed."

I was going to have to read that book fast and it was a behemoth. *It better be good,* I thought, hoping desperately that she wouldn't quiz me on it over breakfast.

She was in the living room, note cards spread out on the coffee table in front of her, when I came downstairs for breakfast. "What are those?"

"Never you mind," she said, gesturing for me to leave her alone.

Never one to be deterred by a hand wave, I walked around behind the sofa to get a look. "This is your matchmaking system? You pair them up on cards?" She glared at me. I shrugged innocently back. "You shouldn't make that face. It'll cause wrinkles."

Ada glared for another moment, then threw her head back in laughter. When she stopped, she patted the seat next to her. "Come on. That earned you a peek into how I do this."

I was mildly curious. I *really* wanted a cup of coffee, but I wasn't going to turn down the first real offer of trust she had given me.

"I grade everyone I meet on their values and interests. One through ten. How large a family they want. How religious they are. How close they seem to their own families. Social class—that one can sometimes be negotiable, but often not in this business. Physical attractiveness. Do they read for fun? Do they enjoy the outdoors? How educated are they? How traditional or modern are they? Sense of humor. These are the main attributes that contribute to a happy marriage."

I looked over the cards, wondering how she got some of that information from the interviews we had conducted together. "But you don't ask all those questions."

"When you've done this long enough, you don't have to. Remember Stella? The one with the horrible mother and who liked Doris Day and Rock Hudson?" I nodded. "If she were a reader, she would have mentioned a book, not a movie, when she said she didn't have a television. And her choice of a movie tells me she likes to laugh and is more modern than her mother."

"How long have you been doing this?"

"Formally? Forty years. Informally? Much longer than that."

Forty years ago she would have been thirty-five. "What did you do before that?"

"I was a nurse. Then the Great War broke out, and I went to Europe. My father died while I was overseas. He only had daughters and the rest were married, so I inherited the bulk of his estate. I used some of it to start my business and invested the rest."

"Didn't the stock market crash wipe you out?"

She shook her head. "I told you. Land is always a good investment."

I looked at her in awe. I had never known a businesswoman before. I had known secretaries and nurses and teachers. But not someone who fully managed her own finances for a lifetime without the help of a man. Without a father or husband, credit would be largely out of her reach. But she had built an empire that survived the worst economic crisis of our country through her own shrewdness—something that most of the men had lacked. "Was it hard?"

Ada sighed. "It still is. But the only things in life that are worth it are hard. It was worth it to maintain my independence. And now I can help others."

She drove me nuts. But I also admired her more than anyone I had ever met.

When I retreated to the kitchen to make myself coffee and some toast, I mulled over her system, thinking about how I would grade Freddy. He certainly didn't seem to be particularly attached to his family. I hated the idea of not living in New York or near Mama, but he could probably be convinced. Neither of us showed much interest in religion. I didn't know if he enjoyed reading—I wanted someone who did; Daddy had no interest in the books Mama wanted to talk about. Attractiveness was no issue. Neither was sense of humor. The social class thing—well, Ada had said that could be negotiable. And I certainly didn't care. Besides, he was going to go into either business or law school. This was America. Anyone could be anything.

Then I realized how foolish I was being. We had gone on one secret date. I shook my head. A little fun was one thing, but I wasn't planning to fall in love.

"Are you done in there yet?" Ada called. "We should go to the beach. They do a boat parade."

"Let me just eat my toast and throw on my bathing suit," I yelled back.

"Don't yell from room to room! It's rude!"

I laughed, shaking my head.

CHAPTER TWENTY

The fireworks show over the ocean was no match for that over the Hudson, but it was on par with the ones I had seen in the Catskills as a child, so it wasn't hard to feign interest for Ada. Though I did keep peeking around the dark beach as children darted around waving sparklers, drunk on ice cream and the late hour. Freddy would likely be with his family, three blocks away. And I didn't dare interact with him while I was with Ada. But it didn't stop me from looking.

Tuesday morning was back to business as usual, Ada reminding me before bed to set that alarm clock, which went off promptly at seven. Ada was already at the table, as always, her newspaper in front of her face, her coffee half-drunk, her toast untouched.

"Ada," I said. "When you went for a swim the other day, Freddy said you swim every morning?"

She didn't lower the paper. "You seem awfully chummy with that Goldman boy."

I could have kicked myself. "I told him to leave me alone and go do his job, which was watching you swim."

"I don't need to be watched. I'm an excellent swimmer. And if a shark gets me, I've lived my life."

"Yes, that's about what he said. I'm just curious. Do you actually swim every day?"

The newspaper didn't budge. "Weather permitting."

Frannie placed a plate of food in front of me, and I thanked her. She had made muffins with fresh Jersey blueberries, which looked and smelled heavenly. I took a bite, savoring the explosion of flavor as a berry opened.

Apparently the talkativeness of the previous morning had not extended to today. I didn't see Ada's face until she rose to prepare for the day's clients. A single errant curl at the nape of her neck was the only clue that perhaps she had been near water that morning.

The curl had been subdued by the time the first girl and her mother arrived. I observed both Ada and the girl, this one plump and cheerful, confident Ada would have no trouble finding her someone, through new eyes having gotten a glimpse at Ada's methods.

"Do you enjoy dinner parties?" Ada asked.

"I adore them," she said. "Especially hosting. I love cooking and seeing others enjoy what I've made."

Needs someone social, I wrote.

"Do you have a favorite book?"

A quick, panicked look entered her eyes. Ada's face didn't change, but I knew she saw it too. "Let me think," she said. "Honestly, it was probably something from school."

"That's fine," Ada said smoothly. "Movies? Television shows?"

"Oh my goodness, that's much easier. Let me see . . ." She began rattling off a list of generic comedies.

No education beyond high school, I wrote. *Doesn't read. Wants a sense of humor, but nothing dry or sarcastic.*

When we finished for the morning, Ada flipped through my notes as she always did, but this time she nodded approvingly. "You're a fast study."

"I do try."

"I'll have to watch my back. You'll be my competition before long."

I had no interest whatsoever in matchmaking. Nor did I believe for a moment that I could do what she did. If a girl came in with a domineering mother, I'd probably tell the girl to run away and start her own life. And I could never knowingly send someone into a meeting with someone I found repugnant.

But Ada's praise was seldom given and never undeservedly. And there was no higher compliment than seeing me as potential competition. If I ducked my head in modesty, the corner of her mouth would turn down—which was just fine, as modesty wasn't exactly my forte. Instead, I laughed. "Apples and oranges. No one can do what you do."

She turned me loose after lunch, citing my becoming too good at her line of work to be allowed to be involved, but she said it with a wink. "Take an umbrella to the beach," she warned.

"I will," I lied merrily.

Ada shook her head. "It'll be 2015 when you're my age. And I'll be long dead. But you'll look in the mirror one day and think, *I should have listened to Ada.*"

"Oh, Ada," I said. "You're far too cantankerous to die. You'll make it to a hundred and thirty for sure, and then you can tell me yourself."

She swatted at me and told me to get out, but she was laughing. "You should be so lucky."

I was smiling as I walked to the beach sans umbrella. I *was* lucky my parents had banished me here. And not just because Freddy came jogging over soon after I set up my towel in the sand and picked me up, swirling me around in a kiss.

"Why, Mr. Goldman," I said, feigning shock. "In broad daylight? What will the neighbors think?"

"That Freddy Goldman has finally settled down," he said, flopping onto my towel. "I have an hour break. Thanks for setting up such a great nap spot."

I pouted, kicking sand over his foot. He opened his right eye to look at me. "You could always sleep with me. All puns intended."

"Freddy Goldman!"

He leaned up on his elbows. "Was worth a shot. Come on. Let's walk down to the jetty. Sometimes you can find crabs at low tide." He stood up and took my hand, and we strolled leisurely down the beach together.

~

When I arrived back at the house, I yelled a hello to Ada, who yelled back that I wasn't to yell room to room, and went upstairs to shower. But when I entered my bedroom to grab my bathrobe, I stopped short.

On the dressing table was a baby blue portable Underwood typewriter, an unopened ream of paper next to it. As if in a trance, I approached it, running my fingers over the feel of the new keys.

"Do you like it?" Ada asked from the doorway. "I suppose we'll need to get you a proper desk, too, though I chose this model so you could write anywhere."

I swallowed. "I—I don't know what to say. This is for me?"

"Who else would it be for? I'm not planning to write my life story anytime soon. You said you wanted to write."

"This is—" I stopped, afraid the lump in my throat would betray me. "Thank you."

"Well, don't get all mushy on me about it," Ada said gruffly. But she didn't fool me. I threw my arms around her neck, suddenly understanding the picture of her and my mother. She wasn't warm and she suffered no fools. But no one had a better heart than this indomitable battle-ax before me.

She squeezed me back once, then peeled my arms from her neck. "Go shower. You smell like you've been working on the docks." Then she was gone. But I sat at the dressing table chair before I went to shower, opened the ream of paper, and slid a crisp, white sheet onto the roller, feeling like a proper writer, envisioning a day when I would be walking along the beach and seeing people reading my novel. Even if I had no idea where to begin.

CHAPTER
TWENTY-ONE

That blank paper was still sitting there two days later when Ada walked by my room. She sighed. "You do know it works, right? I didn't get you a typewriter-shaped paperweight."

I looked up from where I was sprawled on the bed, my nose in *Hawaii*. It was engrossing. Ada's good taste extended beyond clothes, decor, and my lipstick.

"I'll write the Great American Novel tomorrow," I said flippantly and turned a page, hoping I had one-eighth of Ada's sass in page flipping.

"I had you pegged as serious," she said coolly. "But I can take it away." She moved toward the typewriter, and I sat up suddenly.

"No, please, don't!"

She stopped and turned. "Your parents didn't send you here to lounge on the beach all summer."

"No. They sent me here so either my mother could smooth my father down or you could marry me off and make me someone else's problem."

One hand went to her hip. The other pointed a finger at the typewriter. "And *that* is your way out of both problems. You said you wanted to write. The only one who is going to make that happen is you. If you lie on a beach flirting with boys all day, the best you can hope for is marriage."

I was ready to throw that stupid typewriter at her head. Or the copy of *Hawaii*. At almost a thousand pages, it probably weighed about as much as the typewriter.

"I'm not you," I said bitterly. "Maybe I just want to fall in love before I get married."

"That's well and good," she said. "But love doesn't always work out."

"What would you know about that?"

She let out a short, barking laugh. "More than you do, I know that much. But fine. You want me to be the villain? I don't mind. As long as you write something."

She left and I flopped back onto the bed.

Then, after a few minutes, I went and sat at the typewriter. But all I had was the idea of being locked in a tower again. And that was such a baby story. I wanted to write something sweeping like *Hawaii* or universal about the human condition like my favorite, *The Great Gatsby*. And all I knew was my own spoiled existence.

The phone rang, and I heard Ada's bedroom door shut. So I stomped down the hallway, not bothering to be quiet, and went downstairs, then slipped on my shoes and left the house. I avoided the beach—I didn't want to see Freddy in this mood—and headed toward town instead. I walked up the two blocks to Dune Drive and then turned, almost colliding with Shirley.

"Hello, Marilyn," she said coolly.

"Hi," I said, surprised by her lack of effusiveness compared to when I had seen her previously. Shirley moved to keep walking. "Wait," I said, grabbing her arm. "Are you mad at me?"

She glared. "I thought you wanted to be my friend. Not use me to get to Freddy."

"Excuse me?"

"That's the only reason you came to dinner."

"It is not. I had no idea he was your brother." She made a disbelieving face, and I mimed crossing my heart. "Swear. I had no idea. And I wasn't even a little interested."

"Past tense," Shirley said. "I don't understand why he goes after all my friends. Can't he find his own girls?"

A slight alarm went off in my head, but I needed to know. "All your friends?"

"Most of them."

"Not the one who looks like a potato though?"

She tried not to laugh, but couldn't quite contain it. "Honestly, Marilyn, he's such bad news. I don't know why you'd want to go out with him."

I linked an arm through hers. "Darling, I'm having a rough day today. Can we put this behind us? I'll buy you an ice cream cone."

She hesitated a moment, then let me lead her into town. "Why is your day so rough?"

I sighed. "Where to begin? Ada got me a typewriter—I told her I wanted to be a writer. You're only the second person I've said that out loud to. And she's mad I haven't written something to rival Shakespeare yet."

"What *have* you written?"

"Don't you start now too, Shirl."

"Well, they say people write what they know. You've got this big, glamorous New York life. Write about that."

"It's not so glamorous."

"You know about rakes like my brother."

I chuckled. "So the glamour girl and the rake? Sounds like one of the paperbacks I have to sneak out of my mother's closet because they're off limits."

Shirley grinned. "My mother has a box of those too."

"We should trade notes."

She laughed. "What about Ada?"

"If she has a box of racy novels, I wouldn't know. Her bedroom is strictly off limits. She probably has suits of human skin hanging in the closet."

"That's horrifying. But no. She's interesting. Write about her."

I studied Shirley's profile, an idea forming. Her family actually made the much better story. Imagine marrying blindly into that mess. What if a Freddy-like character met a Marilyn-like character, but away from his family? They have a whirlwind romance and elope, only to meet his parents and—no, that read like a horror novel. I was no Shirley Jackson.

"I'll think about it," I said eventually. "And you don't need to worry about me and Freddy. It's just a little bit of fun."

"He likes you."

I smiled, but I played it off, framing my chin with my hands. "Who doesn't?"

~

The idea that had formed with Shirley continued to intrigue me though. What if it was more of a comedy of manners? The two sets of in-laws clashing while the young couple tries to begin a life together? Ada's bedroom door was still closed when I got back to the house, a murmur through the wall telling me she was on the phone, so I went to my room, closed the door, and sat at the typewriter, where I began to write.

CHAPTER
TWENTY-TWO

"I wish we didn't have to sneak around," Freddy said as we walked to his car Sunday night. I had written three chapters, but I hadn't yet told him that I was working on a novel. Then again, he never asked what I wanted to do with my life other than the assumed marriage and children either.

"I know," I said.

"Why can't we just talk to your aunt?"

I didn't respond as Freddy opened the car door for me. When he had shut my door, climbed in his side, and started the engine, I finally said, "It's complicated with her."

"What about your parents? Surely they'd approve. I'm going to be a lawyer after all."

I looked over at him. "Have you decided, then?"

"I believe I have." He took my hand and brought it to his lips. "New York has a lot of law schools. Some of the best in fact."

"You wouldn't stay in Philadelphia?"

He looked at me. "Would you want me to?" My heart was racing. "You sure you want to go to the boardwalk tonight? We could take the Garden State all the way up to the city."

I looked at the clock on the dash. "And scare my parents half to death. It'd be two in the morning by the time we got there. Not the impression you'd want to make."

"No," he said. "But I'm serious. Tell me which dragon to slay and I will."

I rested my head on his shoulder. "No dragons. Let's just keep getting to know each other and the rest . . . Well, it'll work itself out when it needs to."

He wrapped his arm around me, and the night enveloped us as we crossed the marshes, going south this time on the Parkway to the much closer and more casual Wildwood boardwalk. This wasn't a place to see and be seen like Atlantic City. Kids ran amok, chased by tired parents, who looked as if they regretted all their choices under the amusement park that loomed over the boards.

"Good clean fun," Freddy said as we walked past a motel. "Unless you wanted to rent a room."

"Freddy," I said warningly.

He threw up his hands. "I'm kidding. I mean, I wouldn't say no if you wanted to. But no. Our first time should be more special than that." He pulled me in and kissed the top of my head. "And I would never pressure you."

I looked up at him warily. "Shirley says you've been with practically all her friends."

"Shirley's mouth is too big."

"Is that all this is though?"

Freddy stopped walking. "I'm insulted that you would ask that."

"That's not an answer."

"Marilyn."

I didn't reply.

He took a deep breath. I hadn't seen him mad yet, but I could sense he was getting there. "No. That isn't what this is. If it were, yes, I'd be pressuring you. Is that what you want to hear?"

No. It wasn't.

"We all have a past," he continued. "You do too. The first thing you told me about yourself was about that rabbi's son. I'm not grilling you about whether you're with me because you're bored." He took my hand. "I'm here with you because I like you. You're not like the Philadelphia girls. I wasn't kidding when I called you a siren. I don't understand it. I don't want to get married. I don't want to settle down yet. And I definitely don't want an Ada match. But I look at you and . . ." He trailed off.

"And?"

He looked at me imploringly. "Haven't I subjugated myself enough tonight? I'm yours. Can we just go ride the stupid roller coaster and hold hands and kiss on the Ferris wheel and pretend we don't have to hide how we feel from your aunt?"

I rose up on my tiptoes and kissed his cheek. "You left out the ice cream."

"I'll give you the moon if you ask for it."

"Rocky road will suffice."

"Marilyn, I—"

I shook my head, pressing a finger to his lips. "Let's go ride the stupid roller coaster and hold hands. We'll figure out the rest later."

He looked like he wanted to say something else, but then the cloud over his face passed. "Okay. Let's see if it's better than Coney Island."

"Nothing is better than Coney Island."

"Will you show me someday?"

I nodded, and he pulled me along with him toward the amusement park, where we kissed on the Ferris wheel and spun around and around on the Tilt-A-Whirl until we couldn't have worried about the future if we'd tried.

CHAPTER
TWENTY-THREE

The phone rang unexpectedly during the next morning's session with prospective clients. Ada jumped. I didn't know how people knew that they were supposed to call her between two and four in the afternoon to set up a meeting, but it was an unspoken rule that all adhered to.

"Excuse me," Ada said, rising.

"I can get the phone."

"Sit," Ada directed me. I did as I was told, and Ada left the room and went and picked up the receiver in the den.

I desperately wanted to know what was going on, but Mrs. Geller and her daughter, Janice, both turned their heads in the direction Ada had gone and also seemed interested in whatever the phone call was about. And Ada wouldn't like that.

"Janice," I said, coming to sit in Ada's spot. "Tell me about your favorite books." She looked to her mother uncertainly. "I'm training as Ada's apprentice," I lied smoothly. "That's why I'm taking notes. But I can go down her list of questions easily."

Her mother nodded, and Janice named a couple of romance novels, which her mother did not know the contents of, based on her bland expression. I wondered if Mrs. Geller didn't have a box of off-limits books so Janice had resorted to swiping them from a friend's house.

"And movies?"

Ada returned quickly and shooed me back to my seat. But she seemed distracted as she finished the interview. When the Gellers left, she went to the desk in the corner and wrote down four names and phone numbers from her planner. She brought the paper to me. "I need you to call the rest of the day's clients and reschedule for next week." She hesitated. "The rest of the week's clients. I'll write out that list next, but take care of today's first."

"What's going on? What was that phone call?"

She looked tired, as if someone had simply pulled the plug on all her energy and sass and it just ran out onto the floor, leaving an empty Ada bottle. "Lillian," she said, closing her eyes and pinching the bridge of her nose. "Her mother died. I need to go to her."

"When is the funeral?"

"They don't know yet. I'll probably have to help. Her sister is . . . not going to be useful."

"What can I do?"

Ada looked at me as if she had forgotten I was there. "Oh. I didn't think about arrangements for you. Yes, I suppose you'll have to come with me."

"Ada—"

"I can't leave you here unsupervised."

"Ada, I'm twenty. And I've followed every rule you've given me this summer."

"Have you?" she asked. I just looked at her. "Your parents would be furious."

"I'm quite good at keeping secrets from them."

"Except when stained glass is involved."

I held my arms out wide. "Luckily, you don't have any of that here. Seriously. I can manage for a few days just fine. I promise. I'll sleep late,

I'll read, I'll go to the beach, I'll read some more, I'll go to bed. And I'll watch Sally."

I could see her wavering. She didn't want to babysit me while helping her friend. And she hadn't figured out a plan for the dog. "That's all you're allowed to do."

"Can I get ice cream with Shirley?"

She pointed a finger at me. "Don't push it." Then she went back to her desk. "I'll make that list for you. And I need to get a train. And pack—Frannie, can you come help me, please?"

Frannie came in, wiping her hands on her apron. "Of course, Miss Ada."

"I'll go make those calls now," I said, retreating to the den to start calling families.

But I was worried she would be able to hear how fast my heart was beating from the other room.

~

Ada left the following morning, amid a frenzy of packing and last-minute instructions. "Frannie will look in on you every day," Ada warned. "And she's got strict instructions to call me if a single hair looks out of place."

"Just go," I told her. "I'll be fine. Take care of your friend."

She opened her mouth to say something, then closed it and nodded tightly. I pulled her in for a hug that she did not reciprocate before she climbed into the car and put on her sunglasses.

"Are you sure you don't want me to drop you off at the train station?"

She lowered the sunglasses to look at me. "You'd be walking back if you did." Returning the glasses to her eyes, she began backing out of the driveway. "No one drives this car but me. And remember: no guests, no dates, and no Freddy Goldman."

I felt her eyes piercing me through my sunglasses. "What about a different Beach Patrol boy?"

"You're not funny," she called from the street as she put the car into drive and pulled away.

"I thought that was funny," I muttered as I watched the bumper of her car disappear around the corner.

But for the next few glorious days, Ada would be the least of my worries. It wasn't even ten when I went upstairs and changed into my bathing suit, packing my bag with my towel and a new bottle of Coppertone that I had purchased at Hoy's, the island's 5 & 10, after finishing the last of the old bottle.

I padded to the bathroom, slipped my thumb into the bottom of my suit, and pulled it down, studying the crisp line where my skin turned pale. I looked at the little girl on the Coppertone bottle and smiled. Sally would be all too happy to bite me right there if I presented her the opportunity to re-create the image.

Which reminded me, I needed to walk Sally. And the only grass to be found anywhere was on the median strips up on Dune Drive. "Don't bite," I said gently as I slipped the leash onto her collar. She and I had been getting on better. Which Ada believed was a testament to Sally's good nature, not my character being adequate to meet her approval. But the dog allowed me to take her to do her business before I headed down to the beach.

I grabbed the copy of *Goodbye, Columbus* that my mother had mailed me and put it in my bag as well. *Somewhat scandalous. You probably shouldn't read this one. But c'est la guerre,* my mother had written on the title page. Nothing could make me want to read a book more. Though to be honest, the book was the last thing on my mind.

It took effort not to skip the entire way up the dune path, run to the lifeguard stand, and throw myself at Freddy, re-creating the scene from *From Here to Eternity* that I had thought of the night he first kissed me.

But I wanted to get the full effect of telling him that I was home alone. So I spread my towel in the sun and started the book, waiting for him to notice me. Which didn't take long. Through my sunglasses, I saw when he looked over his shoulder, then a smile spread across his face as he leaned over to say something to his chairmate before climbing down.

"Don't you ever actually work?" I asked, sitting up as he reached me.

"I'm working right now," he said, nudging my legs so he could sit on the towel. "I'm making sure you don't drown."

"On dry land?"

"You never know. Drownings can happen anywhere."

"In that case, I might need more protection. Maybe dinner tonight?"

He turned his head, looking at me sideways. "Don't tell me Ada finally came around?"

"Now, you know better than that."

"Then I'm afraid I don't understand. Do you want to come to my house?"

I shook my head. "Ada's gone for the week. Her friend's mother died."

The smile that spread across his face was worth everything. "I'll pick you up at six," he said. "There's this Italian restaurant down in Cape May . . ." He kissed his fingertips, then spread them in the air, his eyes alight with possibilities.

"Sounds lovely."

He leaned in and kissed me.

~

I shaved my legs with extra attention in the shower after the beach, then lay on the upper deck's lounge chair in a light robe to dry my hair in the sun before getting dressed. I selected my fanciest girdle, the one that cinched my waist down to practically nothing, and the seafoam-green sundress with the matching lace overlay. It was low cut, but the lace extended up two inches, giving a peek-a-boo glimpse of decolletage. Dabbing Chanel No 5 on my wrists and behind my ears, I studied my reflection in the mirror. What the outfit *really* needed was my lipstick. And not the new color Ada wanted me to get.

I had never entered her bedroom. But there was no chance of getting caught now—except by Sally, who couldn't tell on me. And I was already breaking a major rule. What was one more?

I stepped out of the bathroom, went down the hall, and put my hand on the knob, half expecting her to have locked it. But the knob turned easily under my hand.

The room was large, with a queen-size bed covered in a white comforter, a baby blue crocheted afghan residing at the foot of it. The dressers were white as well, with an oversized vanity table covered in facial creams and cosmetics. The picture window held a cushioned seat, the perfect place to take in the ocean view. And underneath it, white built-in bookshelves lined with paperbacks. I knelt, examining the titles. None of the books were the kind Shirley and I would steal from our mothers, though there was a D. H. Lawrence book I wasn't familiar with, but a wide variety of genres and authors, from modern to classical. I pulled one out and looked at the cover. It was called *The Price of Salt*. I remembered hearing something whispered about it, but couldn't recall what the controversy was.

Replacing the book, I turned to the vanity to complete my mission in here. And yes, there was my Guerlain Rouge Diabolique. The same lipstick Marilyn Monroe wore. I applied it at Ada's dressing table and pursed my lips at my reflection, smiling at the result. Then I dropped it in my clutch. I'd want to touch it up after dinner of course. And I would put it back before Ada ever knew it was missing.

Sally alerted me to Freddy's presence before he rapped on the door. "Shush," I called to her, banging my knee on Ada's vanity as I hurried to stand. But then I took a breath and smoothed my skirt.

Freddy stood outside in a suit and tie, like when we had gone to Atlantic City, but holding a single red rose, the exact color of my lipstick.

His eyes traveled up my legs to my waist, lingering at my bosom and lips before meeting my own. "Wow," he breathed. "You look . . ." He stopped himself. "Like you didn't have to climb out of a window."

I laughed. "You may need to work on your compliments."

"I think that one was quite good. Because you looked gorgeous climbing out that window. If you were a cat burglar, I'd give you everything I had."

"Do I have to be a burglar for that?"

He took me in his arms. "You do not." And he leaned in and kissed me deeply.

I would need to reapply that lipstick in the car too.

~

Dinner was just as excellent as Freddy had promised, and we split a bottle of wine. I had two glasses and was a little tipsy by the time we finished. I half expected Freddy to make a comment about how I should drink more before he took me home, but he took the last half glass from me after I dropped my fork on the ground and laughed. "Probably enough of that," he said. "Come on. Let's go walk through town. It still looks like it would have when Ada was young."

"I don't want to think about Ada tonight," I said.

"Me neither."

The sun was starting to set, and we walked on the side of the pedestrian street that was covered in the long shade of the buildings, hand in hand. A caricaturist sat in the square near a fountain. "Should we?" Freddy asked.

"You'd have to keep it for us."

"I can do that. Then someday, we'll frame it and let our children laugh at it."

"Children?"

"I said, 'Someday.'"

"What else do you have planned out for us, Mr. Goldman?"

"Plenty of things," he said, guiding me to the chairs in front of the artist and handing him a dollar. "I figure you'll take a year off school so that I can finish, then we'll both go to New York, and you can finish college while I go to law school."

"You expect me to take the year off?"

He smiled disarmingly. "It would be harder for me to take two off for you to finish first, but I can if I have to. Or transfer."

"You'd transfer to a New York school for your senior year?"

"If it was the only way to be with you? Yes."

If we lived in New York, the issue of his family disappeared except for infrequent visits . . . but no.

"I think you're the one who drank too much of that wine, buster."

He kissed my hand. "I'll show you I'm serious."

I leaned against him. "Well, I suppose I'm glad I don't look like a potato, then." Freddy threw his head back in laughter, causing a crease to form between the caricaturist's eyebrows. "I'm sorry, sir," I told him. "I'll behave. I promise."

"Don't make promises you can't keep," Freddy said.

It was my turn to laugh.

~

Cape May wasn't a boardwalk town the way Wildwood and Atlantic City were, and at around ten things began closing down. "We should head back," Freddy said.

"Do you want to go to a boardwalk?"

"Do you?"

I shook my head as Freddy opened the car door for me. He drove back to Avalon with his arm around my shoulders, my hand holding his as it rested just above my breast.

Freddy parked around the corner where he always did. I hadn't interacted with any neighbors yet, but I didn't need anyone telling Ada that Freddy's car was in the driveway. We walked hand in hand down the sidewalk, my stomach aflutter as we neared the house.

He kissed me at the top of the porch steps, his right arm tight around my waist, his left hand wrapped in my hair. Then he stopped. "Well," he said, his lips so close to mine that I could feel his breath. "This is where I leave you."

I knew I shouldn't say it. I had promised Ada. I had already broken my promise by seeing him at all, but I didn't have to break it further. But every fiber of my being strained against what I knew was right. And in the end, I couldn't stop myself.

"Or . . ."

"Or . . . ?" Freddy asked, his eyes twinkling merrily.

For a long moment, neither of us spoke, our breathing ragged with the fire of what we felt. "You could—maybe—come in—for a couple minutes . . ."

He pulled back and searched my face in the dim porchlight. "Are you sure?"

I bit my bottom lip, his eyes trained on my mouth, then nodded ever so slightly.

Freddy smiled, but it was sad this time. "Be more sure than that first," he said, kissing me lightly. "I called off work tomorrow. We can spend all day together." Then he turned to leave.

But before he got to the first step, I grabbed his arm and pulled him back to me. "Come in," I said, much stronger this time.

"You're sure?"

"Stop asking me that or you're not invited anymore."

Freddy laughed and made a bowing gesture. "After you."

I opened the door and—

Sally came barreling in from the living room, yapping her head off at the intruder. "Sally, hush," I said. But she hid behind me, baring her teeth and growling at Freddy.

"Sally?" Freddy asked. "Are you sure it's not a nickname for Satan?"

"Ada says she's a wonderful judge of character, but she normally hates me."

"Apparently she prefers you to me," he said as he leaned in to kiss the side of my neck. "I can't say that I blame her."

"She can sense a rake a mile away."

He was still kissing my neck, pausing only to answer me, his breath hot at my collarbone. "Reformed rake. You're making an honest man of me."

"You're not going to show up with a ring tomorrow, are you?"

Freddy took my left hand, kissing the fourth finger where a ring would go. "I will if you want me to." Then he wrapped his arms around me, Sally still growling by my feet. "I meant what I said, Marilyn. I'm yours. I'm not leaving unless you tell me to."

"And if I tell you to?"

"You'll break my heart." He leaned down, kissing along my neck, from my earlobe to the hollow where it met my shoulder, then down to my breastbone, just above where the lace of my dress started.

"Then stay," I whispered, taking his hand and leading him toward the stairs.

CHAPTER TWENTY-FOUR

"What time is it?" Freddy asked drowsily. We had dozed in and out, our bodies entwined in the bed, fitted together like pieces of a puzzle.

"I don't care," I said, nestling in deeper to the crook of his arm.

He chuckled and shifted slightly, reaching over my head for the alarm clock on the nightstand, its radium dial glowing green in the darkness. "Do you want to go watch the sun rise over the ocean?"

I sat up. I did. I wanted to watch the day dawn over the new world I was living in. "Let's go!"

Freddy laughed as I jumped out of bed, then I winced slightly at the soreness in my thighs. "You might want some clothes," he said. "Although I'll never object to none."

I leaned over the bed, kissing him lazily, as if we had all the time in the world instead of just a few days. He started to pull me back to him, but I resisted. "Shouldn't have mentioned the sunrise if you didn't want to go," I murmured. "Come on."

Freddy heaved himself out of the bed, and pulled on his pants and then his undershirt as I stepped into a pair of underwear and put my beach caftan on over them.

He looked at me, silhouetted in the light from the hall. "What are you waiting for?"

"Just memorizing how you look right now."

"You mean a mess?" I pushed my curls back.

"Perfectly you," he said, coming and kissing my forehead. "Let's go."

I grabbed the beach towel that had been hanging on the porch railing to dry, and we ran down the steps together, then climbed the path over the dune in the gray darkness.

The beach was empty and the air chilly. I should have been self-conscious in just the sheer fabric of my coverup, but after the previous night, I couldn't imagine ever feeling shy around Freddy again.

He spread the towel just above the line where the wet sand indicated that the tide was going out, then sat and held a hand out to me to sit next to him.

Freddy wrapped his arm around me, and we watched the horizon for a pinprick of light. But his lips soon found my neck, and my breathing hitched as they slipped lower, his fingers reaching up to unbutton the caftan. Before I knew it, he had shifted us and was laying me down on the towel, while I reached for the button on his trousers.

I turned my head as our bodies found their rhythm, catching sight of the first beam of sun peeking over the water, and I called Freddy's name. "Look," I said.

"I'm looking at something much more beautiful."

But after, as Freddy buttoned his pants and reached down to fasten my caftan, he shook his head. "We shouldn't have done that."

I looked at him suspiciously. Here it was. "No?"

"No, no, no, don't look at me like that. I meant without . . ." He trailed off.

I could feel my face flushing, and I bit my lip as his meaning became clear. "Oh."

"It was just the one time," he said. "I'm sure it will be fine. And if it's not, well, we'll just move our timeline up."

I made a wry face. "You do know that you haven't asked me, and I haven't said yes."

"And I don't intend to—yet. I'm just saying you don't have to worry about me."

Leaning into him as the sun separated from the ocean, I turned my face toward his. "I'm not."

He kissed my hair, and we sat together contentedly for a long time.

~

Eventually, Freddy went home for a shower, fresh clothes, and a nap. He would return in the afternoon, after Frannie had finished checking on me, promising another fun outing. "I don't care what we do," I protested. "I'm happy to just lie on the beach with you."

He grinned lasciviously.

"I don't mean like that!"

"I'm crushed. But I still want to take you out."

I walked Sally, then went upstairs, intending to shower. But I wasn't quite ready to wash off the feel of Freddy's skin on mine, and I was too invigorated to sleep. Instead, I sat at my typewriter and pulled a fresh sheet of paper from the ream.

I understood so much more about my characters now. About how the circumstances of their families and births would pale in comparison to their feelings.

By the time I heard the front door open and Frannie greet Sally, I had filled six pages.

I called down a hello and went to take a shower, thinking about how it might be smart to have dinner with Freddy's family again. I could use more material. Though I was now certain there would be plenty of opportunities for that later.

CHAPTER
TWENTY-FIVE

Ada called later that morning to check in, concerned far more with Sally than with me. "Is she eating? She's never been without me before."

I leaned way back, trying to see if her bowl was empty. I probably would have noticed if there was still food in it when I fed her that morning. "She's perfectly fine. I promise. She's even warming up to me." I smiled at the memory of her growling at Freddy, as if she were a wolf instead of a tiny little creature who would have difficulty battling a large squirrel.

"Are you sure she feels all right?"

"Ada! She's fine. How's Lillian holding up?"

Ada sighed. "Not so well. It's good that I came."

"When will you be back?"

"What's today? Wednesday?" I confirmed. "Sunday, then. The funeral is set for Friday."

I did the math in my head. Four more glorious days of freedom before my now-colorful world went back to black and white.

But Ada was still talking. "Make sure you water my hydrangeas."

"What are hydrangeas?"

"What *are* they sending you to that college for?"

"Not agriculture."

"Agriculture is food crops, you ignoramus. You mean botany. And the hydrangeas are the purple and blue flowering shrubs in the front. They're in peak season and they need water. Unless it rains, then you'll flood them."

"Got it. Water purple and blue flowers."

"Some are violet—water them all."

"I will think of nothing else but the health of your hydrangeas," I said.

"I'm not in the mood for your sass," Ada said. "Put Frannie on the phone, please."

I called for Frannie and scooped Sally up with only minor protests on her end. "Your mommy is a nut," I crooned to her, hoping it was loud enough for Ada to hear. Then, quieter in her ear, "But I'm very glad you can't talk."

~

"Don't your parents wonder where you are?" I asked on our third night as we lounged in bed. "Or haven't they noticed that you're gone?"

Freddy shrugged. "They don't keep such close tabs on me. I'm a good boy after all."

"That's *not* what your sister says."

He leaned up on an elbow to look at me. "It's fun to tease her. But they practically keep her under lock and key. It's different for boys. As long as I don't bring home someone they wouldn't approve of, they don't really mind if I go out."

"And they approve of me?"

"You, my dear, are the gold standard."

I flinched, knowing what that meant. "And does all that matter to you? Is that why you're here?"

"If it did, I wouldn't be here. I'd be doing the proper courtship that they think I am. I don't care who your family is—actually, that's not true. I wish you weren't part of your family because then Ada wouldn't disapprove, and we could be together in the open." I looked away, but he put a hand under my chin and turned my face back to his. "I didn't fall for you because of some status symbol. I fell for *you*. And the rest just gets in the way."

He lay back down on the bed, pillowing his head on his crossed arms. "What about you? Does my position as the son of a man who owns a clothing factory put you off? Are you secretly happy we're sneaking around?"

A tiny trickle of guilt ran down the inside of my chest, like a drop of rain along a window. It wasn't that I wanted to sneak around, and I couldn't have cared less what Freddy's family did for a living. But I knew Ada now. If I pushed her hard enough, she would tell me to date Freddy and learn for myself. But if I did that, I would also lose the respect that I had fought and clawed to earn from her. And I didn't know why that was more important than a true courtship, but it was.

There was no way to explain that to Freddy. And if someone tried to say the same thing to me, I would have shown them the door. Quite possibly by kicking them through it. But I reassured him, the fingers on my left hand crossed under my leg, where he couldn't see them, that no, I didn't care about his family at all.

"We'll still live nearer to yours," Freddy said quickly.

I laughed, and he rolled on top of me, kissing me, while he laughed as well.

CHAPTER TWENTY-SIX

Ada arrived home on Sunday wearing a black dress, her hair wrapped in a leopard scarf to protect it from the wind on her drive from the station. I had made sure to slip her lipstick back into its place Saturday night.

She immediately swooped Sally up, cradling her to her chest. "Did Marilyn even feed you? You're skin and bones. Don't worry, darling, I'm back."

Sally looked exactly the same as she always did. "Welcome home," I said drily.

Ada looked me up and down, and, for a moment, I was sure she knew. Somehow, she knew. But all she said was "Hmph" before going up the stairs. "Be a dear and bring my suitcase," she called down.

I exhaled. She didn't know anything.

I picked up her inordinately heavy suitcase, lugged it up the stairs, and deposited it outside her room. "I told people we'd pick back up with clients tomorrow."

"Excellent. I'm going to change and lie down for a bit. It was a rough week." She went to pull the suitcase into her room, but stopped and reached into her purse instead. "Wait. I brought you something."

She held out her palm, in which sat a snow globe of Chicago. "It's silly, of course. But other than the abomination that they call pizza, it was the most Chicago item I could find to bring back."

I smiled at the fact that she had thought of me at all, even if it was a child's gift. "I'll keep it next to the typewriter."

Ada nodded and retreated into her room.

I turned the globe upside down, then righted it, watching the flecks of glitter settle over the city skyline. The return to reality wasn't welcome, exactly, but I had missed her nonetheless.

~

After dinner, Ada suggested we drive to Stone Harbor, the other town on the island, for what she claimed was the best ice cream I would ever experience.

We drove the four miles to 96th Street. The town ended around 33rd Street, leaving nothing but houses and scrub brush until we reached Stone Harbor. On a Sunday night, with most of the men on their way back home before work the following morning, it was a quiet stretch of road. Ada parallel parked on the street outside an ice cream parlor on Third Avenue with a sign reading "Springer's."

"This is Lillian's favorite," Ada said. "She asked us to go get some in her honor." The line wrapped halfway around the block. I expected Ada to just skip it and waltz in, but she went to the back with the rest of the patrons.

"Does she come with you to the shore every year?"

Ada nodded. "She needs to spend a few more weeks getting her mother's estate in order. She'll be able to join us for a week or so before we go back to Philadelphia."

The line inched forward. "Have you ever thought about retiring? You clearly don't need the money anymore. And you could live here year-round. You seem to love it so."

"It's impertinent to talk about money—especially when it's not your own."

"Okay—but the rest?"

She sighed. I was clearly ruining her good time. "I love it here in the summer. There's nothing to do in winter. Most of the town is only open seasonally. And I'm not ready to retire. What would I do all day?"

It was a thought that hadn't occurred to me. She had no children or grandchildren to spend her twilight years with. All she had was Sally and a paid companion—which didn't rule out any true friendship that might exist between her and Lillian. But I envisioned her coming to stay with me someday when I was much older and married with children running around, a vaguely Freddy-shaped husband in the blurry background.

Then I had to hold in my laughter at the idea of a child rubbing its sticky fingers on Ada's handbag. No. I wasn't sure she was cut out for that type of retirement anyway.

But was that how she had always been? Or was it her age and the fact that she had spent so long doing only as she pleased?

"Were you ever in love?" I asked.

"My, how your mind jumps about from impolite question to impolite question." She peered at me carefully as we moved closer to the steps leading up to the store's entrance. "This better not be about that Goldman boy."

I couldn't let her see me flinch. "Freddy? Good grief, Ada, you see me talk to one boy, one time, and you think I'm in love? By that logic, you're having an affair with Thomas."

That got the desired laugh. "When you marry, you'll do far better than Freddy Goldman. But yes. I've been in love a couple times."

"Who—?"

She shook her head. "A lady doesn't tell stories that don't belong entirely to her." She nudged me up the stairs and into the shop. The sign on the door said it had been open "since Prohibition."

"How old *is* this place?"

"Younger than me, so watch it." Ada stepped to the counter and ordered herself a cup of strawberry ice cream. I decided to try the Dutch apple.

We went back outside, where we sat on a bench, and I touched my tongue to the oversized scoop atop my cone. My eyes widened. "Okay, I like Lillian already."

A real smile lit Ada's face at that. "She has immaculate taste. I think you'll enjoy her company."

"I hope I've been a decent substitute."

"Decent," Ada said, musing. "Although if you go into my room and take that lipstick again, you'll be finding yourself a decent seat on the train home."

I almost dropped my cone.

"I—"

"Eat your ice cream," she said mildly.

CHAPTER
TWENTY-SEVEN

Ada and I settled back into our routine quickly. She didn't ask why I took the lipstick, and I volunteered no information. I secretly suspected she knew and was just biding her time. Toying with me seemed to be one of her primary sources of joy. But she said nothing and returned to the task of meeting with the clients we had rescheduled—though she did keep me off the beach for three days, ostensibly to catch up, but I wondered if it was really her way of making sure I didn't see Freddy.

We hadn't planned for when we would see each other next. But each of those three nights, I sat with my window open, listening for cars. Tuesday, I went so far as to climb out onto the deck, peering down into the darkness, hoping to see Freddy waiting on me, missing me enough to take the chance that I would be outside.

Okay, what I really hoped for was a pebble thrown up to my window. Our whole lawn was rocks! All he had to do was show up, select one, and gently toss it at my lit window. It wasn't like I was asking him to slay a dragon or climb up my hair.

But there was no sign of him.

When I finally went to bed Wednesday night, more than a little heartsick, I vowed to find a way to get to the beach Thursday afternoon.

Ada sometimes stopped work early on Fridays and often went with me on weekends and if I missed this last opportunity, I wouldn't see him alone before Monday—and that was if Ada didn't decide I was finally ready to do some of the actual matching and start making me work afternoons every day as well.

"We have a lighter load today," Ada said as the first clients climbed the porch. "I think you'll be able to go to the beach this afternoon." I tried not to smile too widely. The corners of Ada's mouth turned down. "It's a working trip," she warned. "We're running low on men. Ask that little friend of yours for any Jewish members of the beach patrol—or other friends he may have."

"Can I borrow your lipstick to ask him?"

"No."

The morning crept by, but it didn't matter. I was going to see Freddy finally, and all would be right with the world again.

~

I crossed the dune path, a notebook and pen in my beach bag this time. If I failed, Ada would know and the jig would be up.

Instead of setting up my towel, I went straight to Freddy's chair. He was sitting, his chin in his hands, his elbows resting on his knees, staring listlessly out at the ocean.

"Hey," I said, coming around the side.

"Marilyn!" He jumped down, then picked me up and swung me around. "Where have you been? I thought you threw me off."

"No. Ada kept pushing work at me. And I couldn't exactly say I *had* to go to the beach." *Don't say it, don't say it, Marilyn, do NOT say it.* But the words slipped out anyway. "I waited for you on the deck the other night. I hoped you'd come even though we didn't have plans."

"When you didn't come to the beach, I thought—I'm sorry. I should have come."

"Pick me up tonight?" I asked.

"Of course. Where do you want to go?"

I smiled. "Anywhere. As long as we're together." I started to walk away to set up my towel, but remembered my official reason for being there. "Wait, Freddy!" He had started to climb back up. "Ada sent me today because she's running out of men. Do you have any friends who might be willing to go on a few dates?"

He shook his head. "She's something. She won't give you up, but I'm supposed to give you all my friends?"

"She's not my father—remember that. I'm only living with her for the summer."

"Yes, but I don't want her poisoning your parents against me." He sighed and turned to Louis, the other lifeguard on the chair. "Give the girl your number."

"I don't want to get married anytime soon," he said, holding up his hands.

"No one's saying you have to get married," I explained. "But Ada is *really* good at this. I've seen her system. It works. Worst case scenario, you go on a couple dates. Best case scenario: the sky's the limit!"

He hesitated for a minute, then wrote down his name and phone number in my notebook.

"I'm almost a little jealous," Freddy said.

"Don't be. Once their numbers go in this book, they're off limits forever according to Ada."

"Yes, but mine was the first one you got."

"That just makes you all the more special."

"Get a room, you two," Louis grumbled.

Freddy and I both laughed.

～

When I got back to the house, Ada wasn't downstairs. I went up, planning to shower, and saw the door to her bedroom was open. *That's new,* I thought.

"Ada? You okay?"

"Perfectly so," she said. I looked through the open door. She was seated in the window nook and for a panicked moment, I wondered if she could have seen me and Freddy from there. He had taken a break and come to sit on my towel with me and there had been some kissing. I craned my neck, but it was impossible to tell what her view was from there. "You can come in."

An alarm bell went off in my head. I had been with her five weeks now and I had never been invited into her bedroom. I stepped in cautiously. She was holding a stack of papers, a pair of reading glasses on the bridge of her nose. As I approached her, I breathed a sigh of relief. The dunes blocked everything but the water.

"These are good," she said, gesturing toward the pages.

"What are?"

"Your chapters."

My eyebrows approached my hairline. "My what?"

"Unless someone else wrote them."

I felt stripped bare, naked. I wasn't ready for anyone else to see what I had written, and the audacity of just *taking* it—

"How did you get that?"

She shrugged. "It was next to the typewriter. I was curious."

"If you wanted to read it, you should have asked."

"And if I didn't want to read it, I wouldn't have given you a typewriter."

I could feel my chest heaving with righteous anger. How *dare* she?

But Ada swung her legs around to the ground and patted the seat next to her. "Smooth your ruffled feathers. If it wasn't good, I wouldn't have wanted to keep reading. And I did—enough to bring it in here and finish."

That was enough to make me sit, invasion of privacy or no. "You really liked it?"

"I did. And I don't typically read romances."

"It's not a romance. It's going to be a comedy."

Ada tilted her head. "I suppose I can see that."

"They're going to get married quickly—without meeting his family first. And they're going to be simply awful. So they'll have to navigate that."

"Not writing from experience, I hope."

"Yes. I'm secretly married."

Ada smiled wryly. "You know what I mean."

"I do. And Freddy gave us a couple of numbers and is going to work on more."

"And how does he like my lipstick?"

She was watching me carefully to see if I had any tells. "I wouldn't know," I said. "But my secret husband loves it."

Ada swatted me playfully with the pages. "Get out of here." I took the papers, but she called my name at the door. "You know what it needs?"

"What's that?"

"A sassy aunt."

I shook my head with a small laugh, exhaling a huge sigh of relief as I reached my room.

CHAPTER

TWENTY-EIGHT

"I hate sneaking around like this," Freddy said. We were parked down by the jetty at the north end of town and were in the process of readjusting our clothes in the backseat of the car.

"We'd be sneaking around no matter what. No one is letting us do this anywhere."

"You know what I mean."

I sighed. As desperately as I wanted to spend time with Freddy, I didn't want him talking to my father. I didn't want to get married and move to Philadelphia and keep house for a year while he finished school. If he wanted to transfer to New York, and we could keep seeing each other, that was one thing, but that didn't necessitate a conversation with Daddy. I wanted to live first. And Freddy wanted a wife who was going to have dinner on the table for him.

But the only thing I could see in my future if I went that route was me sitting at a Formica-topped kitchen table trying to focus on the typewriter in front of me while a brisket dried out in the oven, a baby crying in the background.

It was the same future I didn't want with Daniel. And I didn't understand how these men could claim to be attracted to the fact that I was free, then try to cage me.

"Let's just see what happens."

"Marilyn, we're going to be a two-hour train ride apart in another month and a half if we don't make some decisions."

I looked up at him in the moonlight. "Is a two-hour train ride the end of the world?"

"I don't want a two-minute walk separating us."

The lights of another car startled us. It parked behind us, high beams on.

"What—?"

"Cop," Freddy said. My eyes widened. "Let me do the talking."

The police officer came around to the car. "Evening," he said. "What are we doing out here in the backseat like this?"

"Trying to figure out which boardwalk we want to go to tonight."

"Shouldn't you be doing that from the front seat?" I kept my face down, not wanting to be recognized. "Everything all right, miss?"

I nodded and he peered down to get a look at me. Freddy laughed. "I promise she's fine. I'm trying to convince her to let me talk to her father and she's putting me off."

The officer laughed as well. "Might as well let him make an honest woman of you."

I felt my cheeks coloring, but I said nothing. If I opened my mouth, I was going to tell that police officer exactly what he could do with his opinion of my virtue. And that didn't end well for anyone.

"Let's move along. The Wildwood boardwalk is nice and close and then I don't have to cite you for necking in the car."

"An excellent idea," Freddy said, climbing out and coming around to open the door for me. I ignored him and climbed through into the front seat. He got into the driver's seat and began to pull away. "Wildwood, then?"

"Take me home," I said, arms crossed.

Freddy looked over at me. "What's wrong?"

"Why did you tell him that? About talking to my father?"

He moved his mouth in confusion before he answered. "Because it's true?"

"You haven't asked *me* Freddy. And *I'm* not ready to say yes. You can ask my father until you're blue in the face, but even if he says yes, *I* matter. *What I want matters.*"

"And you don't want to marry me?"

"I don't want to marry *anyone* yet. That's why they sent me here."

For a moment, Freddy said nothing. "So it's not a no, it's a not yet?"

"Yes."

He put an arm around me and pulled me in close on the seat. "That's all you need to say, then. I won't keep pushing it."

I finally nestled into him. "Thank you."

"Now how about that boardwalk?"

Once I no longer felt like my future was spinning like a carnival ride, I was willing to agree to that.

CHAPTER
TWENTY-NINE

The following afternoon, Shirley and I had plans to meet up and go to the library in the basement of the elementary school, followed by a trip to Hoy's and the new little boutique in town that had bikinis in the window.

Shirley was late though. Very late. Eventually, I walked down the street and got myself a milkshake from Avalon Freeze. If she wanted one, she could get one when we were done. I sat on a bench with it, waiting and people watching. The story I was writing would be set in New York, but I could still pick up mannerisms from the pedestrians here.

A woman a few years older than me walked by, holding the hand of a young girl, her husband on the other side of the daughter, an even younger daughter on the husband's shoulders.

"You have to admit it's lovely here," the man said to his wife.

"It is, darling," she said. "Of course, it's no Hereford."

The man rolled his eyes with a small laugh. "You don't think anything is as good as Hereford, Evelyn."

"That's because nothing is. But if it means we get an extra two weeks of beach time with you, I can make an exception once in a while."

The husband smiled at her.

"Who wants ice cream?" she asked the girls. "Joanie? I know you do."

The little girl on her father's shoulders squealed and clapped her hands. "It does make everything better, doesn't it?" the husband said.

"I thought that was you?"

He chuckled and leaned in to kiss her cheek.

I watched them as they walked away. They seemed so very much in love, which, with two young children, felt like an accomplishment. I tried to remember the last time I saw my parents show each other affection, and I couldn't think of anything.

Eventually, I gave up, assuming Shirley forgot about me. I debated going to the library myself, but I had a new box of books from my mother and decided to wait. We could always go another day. It was too nice out to be in a moldy basement anyway. I could sit out on the porch and read with a glass of lemonade quite contentedly. Or maybe take my typewriter out there and work at the table. I wanted to use the easy way that husband looked at his wife so adoringly somehow.

But as I reached 23rd Street, I saw Shirley practically running toward me. I looked to see who could possibly be chasing her, but there was no one. "You don't need to run—it's okay that you forgot," I called to her.

She reached me, panting heavily for breath. "Marilyn—you—won't believe—what—just happened."

"Catch your breath," I told her. She took a moment to collect herself.

"Freddy is getting married," she said, still huffing slightly.

I felt my shoulders tense. I *told* him I wasn't ready for any of that. He said he understood. And now he was telling his family that he was getting married?

"Not anytime soon," I muttered darkly. But Shirley didn't seem to notice.

"A girl he was dating in the spring showed up with her parents—she's pregnant. And Papa said if Freddy doesn't step up and marry her, he's going to cut him off!"

My blood turned to ice, and my vision narrowed to a pinprick of light. I reached out and grabbed at Shirley's arm dizzily, close to fainting for the first time in my life. Shirley was still talking, but she sounded far away, like a buzzing insect somewhere out of sight yet trapped in the house.

I kept breathing, and finally my vision cleared. "Stop," I said weakly. "I—you must have misunderstood."

Shirley shook her head, then finally seemed to notice I was in distress. "Wait—I thought you weren't keen on him." I couldn't answer. Shirley's face turned suspicious, and she crossed her arms. "You said it was just a bit of fun."

"I suppose I didn't realize he was 'having fun' with so many people."

"You're not in a fix too, are you? That'd make this a lot more interesting." She grinned gleefully at the idea.

I turned abruptly and started walking home. Shirley trailed after me. "He'll likely choose you if you are. Especially because Papa will definitely cut him off if he got two girls pregnant, and you've got plenty of money—"

"Please just let me be," I said, shaking off the hand she tried to put on my arm.

She stopped walking but shouted after me. "It's not my fault, you know. I told you what he was like. If you were stupid enough to fall for him anyway, that's on you!"

~

Ada was sitting at the desk in the living room when I walked in. Sally didn't even bark at me anymore. "Are you all right?" she asked, rising.

"Too much sun, I think," I said. "I'm just going to go lie down."

I didn't look to see if she believed me. I just went up the stairs. But the tears wouldn't come. It had to be a mistake. Or a mean joke from Shirley. There was just no way . . . Was there?

No, I knew I wasn't Freddy's first, but even if the girl showing up were true, would he—could he marry someone else when just the night before, he was planning for our future?

I went to the bathroom and retched, then returned to my room, where I lay down and stared at the ceiling for an eternity, wondering if this was my punishment for refusing to marry him after what we had done.

At some point, I dozed off. Miserable and curled on my side in the fetal position, I awoke to the sound of Sally barking wildly. *Dumb dog*, I thought, burrowing further into my pillow. If I was asleep, I didn't have to feel anything.

But Sally kept barking, and above that, I heard Ada talking to someone. Sally's barking cut off abruptly in a sound I knew—Ada was holding her mouth shut. I stood and crept to the door and opened it a crack.

"Absolutely not," Ada was saying. "And even if I were going to allow her an audience with a young man, she's unwell today."

A young man. It was Freddy. I knew there was a mistake!

I ran down the stairs, nearly tripping, and then skidded to a stop on the wood floor. They both turned toward me. Freddy looked wretched—like he had aged ten years overnight. There were dark circles under his eyes, he was pale under his tan, and his hair was disheveled. Ada looked from me to him and back to me. A muscle ticked in her jaw, which was set firmly.

She finally turned back to Freddy. "You have ten minutes. On the porch. And I keep the windows open."

I was frozen in place. The fact that he was here. That he looked as miserable as he did. Shirley had been telling the truth. And if I didn't go on that porch, I didn't have to hear it from him. I could run back upstairs and pretend it never happened. But Ada looked at me. "Unless you don't want to go. I can send him away," she offered.

I blinked heavily, and then walked forward. The air had turned to soup, too heavy to move through as I normally would, and I was afraid it would drown me.

"Ten minutes," she reminded us. "And not one second more."

Freddy held the door for me, and I went and sat in a wicker armchair. Freddy pulled another up to face me.

"Shirley—" His voice was thick, and he stopped himself, cleared his throat, and tried again. "Shirley said she told you. Marilyn, I—" He tried to take my hand, but I pulled them both away and put them under my thighs.

"It's true, then?"

He ran his hand through his hair, disheveling it further. "I didn't know. I swear. We broke up almost two months ago. It was the week before I met you. I never . . . It was before."

"And now?"

He got up and walked to the railing of the porch. "I didn't have a choice. I wasn't home when they showed up, and her father talked to mine before I even knew they were there. He's going to make me a partner in the business and buy us a row house. If I say no, I won't even be able to finish school. I won't have a penny to my name."

Then he crossed back and knelt in front of me. "But, Marilyn—there's another option. We could elope. You and I. Your parents would never cut you off. And I can finish school, and we'll be okay."

I stared at him in horror as he continued. "I was thinking about going to New York anyway—if your parents don't want to give us a house right away, we can live with them. I don't mind that. Maybe your father can even find me a position somewhere and—"

I held up a hand. "Stop. Please stop."

He took the hand I had up. "Marilyn, please, you have to see. This is the only way. I—I can't marry her. I love you. I know you don't want to get married yet, but this—this is the way we can be together."

My chest was rising and falling at a rather alarming rate. "And what about the baby?" I asked quietly. "You'd just abandon your child and the mother?"

Something so ugly crossed his face. "I don't even know that she's telling the truth. That baby could be anyone's."

I stared at him again, truly seeing him for the first time. *You're not in a fix too, are you?* Shirley asked blithely in my head. I could have so easily been this girl. Too easily. Ruination or salvation hanging in the balance of what he—selfish, carefree Freddy—wanted. "You told her you'd marry her."

"To appease my father until I could talk to you. You have to understand that."

I stood up. "Go home, Freddy. Go clean up your mess."

He grabbed my arm. "Marilyn—no! You don't understand. I—let me explain again."

"Freddy, let me assure you, I understand completely. And the fact that you would abandon this girl and your own child . . ." I shook my head. "Go home."

"But I love you."

"That isn't my problem anymore."

I pulled my arm back and went into the house, shutting the door firmly behind me.

Ada rose from where she had been sitting in a chair under the open window. She started to say something, a heavy frown on her face, but I burst into tears.

I don't know how I got to the sofa, her arms around me as I wept into her lap, but she simply held me, stroking my hair as I cried out all my sorrow.

When I finally sat up, she handed me a handkerchief.

"We have a few problems here," Ada said finally. "How careful were you?"

This was the absolute last thing I wanted to discuss with her, but I didn't have it in me to be coy or to lie. "We were careful."

"Every time? It only takes one mistake."

I colored, remembering the sunrise on the beach and Freddy's concern at being caught off guard without protection.

Ada swore, rising from the sofa and beginning to pace, then swore again more forcefully. "You and your mother—two peas in a stupid, stupid pod."

"Mama—?"

Ada waved a hand in the air, dismissing that. "I assume this was all when I was in Chicago?"

I nodded, and she began counting on her fingers. "When is your cycle due?"

I asked what day it was, doing the math in my head. "Monday."

Ada set her jaw again. "If your cycle is late, then we go to the doctor for a test."

A tingle of fear ran down my spine. "And if it's . . ." I couldn't say the word.

"Then you decide what you want to do, and we either find someone to help or you extend your stay with me," she said. "But we'll cross that bridge if and when we come to it and not a moment before."

CHAPTER THIRTY

I retreated to my room, too distraught to contemplate dinner. The news would have been enough of a blow without the added worry, and I cursed myself for counting on Freddy to know what he was doing on the beach that morning. There was no solace in knowing I wasn't the first girl he had been indiscreet with; it only made me feel worse about my own decisions. I was the one who asked him to come in—he refused unless I was sure. This was my fault. And around midnight, I vowed not to let him know, no matter the outcome. He was going to marry the other girl and that was that. I couldn't ruin someone else's life for my own any more than I could trust Freddy to do the right thing if it wasn't what he wanted.

In the morning, I slept in. Around nine, Ada entered with a tray of breakfast. She opened the curtains and set the tray on my bed. "I know heartbreak feels like the end of the world, but you need to eat and keep going."

Heartbreak. That word jarred me. Was my heart broken?

And I surprised myself by realizing the answer.

"My heart's not broken," I said, sitting up.

She raised her eyebrows. "No?"

"No. I'm angry. And I'm hurt. And embarrassed. And I'm worried about"—I made a gesture circling my nightgown-clad stomach—"that. But . . ." I shook my head. "He wanted to marry me. I said no."

Ada tilted her head but said nothing.

"I hardly knew him—and it turned out I knew him less than I thought. And he didn't know me. He didn't care what I wanted. He just assumed I'd be lucky to have him." I thought for a moment. "I told him I didn't want to marry anyone yet, which is true, but . . ."

"But?"

I shook my head again. "I don't know."

"When it's right, you will."

"No. It's never going to be 'right.' I see that now. It's me. I don't want to be someone's wife. I want to be myself."

Ada had the first pitying look in her eye that I had ever seen. "When it's right, you'll find you can be both."

I started to ask her how she knew that, having never been married. But she rose, finished with the conversation. "I'm canceling all my clients for Monday. News is going to be all over town about the Goldman boy, and I don't want anyone suspecting. Instead, you have influenza. You should be recovered by Tuesday or Wednesday."

I was too drained to argue and resigned myself to being contained in the house for the next three days like a cat in heat.

~

When she returned midafternoon, I was still in bed. "This won't do. Get up."

"Let me wallow," I moaned, my face in the pillow.

"Now, if your heart were broken, we could have a day of wallowing, but it's not. So you'll dress. It'll make you feel better."

"Nothing will make me feel better."

Ada took a moment to reply. "I'd say work on your novel, but I have a feeling that roman à clef hits a bit too close to home now."

I winced. "It's not a roman à clef."

"Please. An upper-crust New York girl and a boy from a horrendous family meet and marry?"

"Well, that certainly didn't happen."

"And aren't you glad now that it didn't? What if this girl had shown up with a child six months into your marriage? Then you'd *really* be stuck." She thought for a minute. "Actually, *that* would make quite the book."

"No."

"Well, find something to entertain yourself. The more you sit around and worry about your cycle, the longer it's going to take to arrive."

I turned my head so I could see her with one eye, the other still buried in my pillow. "Is that true?"

"In my experience it is."

In her experience—I sat up. "That's a story I want to hear."

She pointed to the typewriter. "Write one of your own, and I'll think about telling you mine. But take a shower first. Just because some writers choose to be bohemians doesn't mean I'll tolerate that kind of behavior in my house."

~

For three days, Ada kept me entertained. We watched television and played card games and swapped books. And when I could, I tried to write. But the words weren't coming.

"Don't write your own story," Ada said. "You haven't lived enough for that. But use what you've learned."

"What have I learned? Other than that I should listen to you?"

Ada smiled. "What a lovely start."

I kept expecting her to light into me about breaking the rules. About ignoring her advice and dating Freddy anyway. But she never did. In some ways, I would have preferred if she did—it would have alleviated some of the feeling of dread that I hoped was all that was wrong with my stomach. I had some cramping, but Ada warned that could go either way.

"How do you know so much about this?"

"You don't get to my age without learning a few things."

I looked at her. It was obvious she had been extremely beautiful when she was young—she was still handsome now. "Why didn't you ever get married? The real reason."

She sighed. "I was engaged once. But he died."

"How old were you?"

"Your age."

I did the math. It would have been 1905. She must have been very in love with him to never marry after losing him so young. "How did he die?"

"It was a fire. They think his father fell asleep while smoking a cigar. None of the family got out."

Whether it was hormones or the excitement of the past few days, I felt tears springing to my eyes. I couldn't imagine being so in love and then having to live the rest of my life—

"Don't look at me like that," Ada said, interrupting my thoughts. "I said I was engaged. I never said I was in love with him."

I blinked rapidly. "Excuse me?"

"We were friends, yes. And I suppose I loved him. But it wasn't passion and fireworks—it was a *shidduch*."

"A what?"

"'A what?'" Ada mimicked. "A match."

I stared at her. "Your parents hired a matchmaker for you?"

She shook her head. "No. It was informal. Our parents agreed on it and told us we were getting married. I was happy, as things went. They could have picked someone far worse for me. Plenty of my friends wound up with much older widowers who could provide for them."

She plucked at the blanket on the back of the sofa. "When Abner died—well, I told my parents I wanted more time. And that more time kept growing until suddenly I was an old maid. And according to my father, too ornery to make a good wife."

I made a sour face at the idea of her father saying that. Although it was something my father would say as well.

"Wrinkles," Ada said, tapping my forehead. "He didn't mean it like that. He was fine with my choice as long as I was happy. And he helped me train to be a nurse. I cried far more when he died than when Abner did, I'll tell you that much. Papa was—Papa was born out of time, I think. He would have been down South fighting for civil rights if he were alive now." She looked at me. "He'd have loved you."

I knew almost nothing about my great-grandparents, but there was something comforting in knowing he would have approved of me. Especially now.

"You said you'd been in love though—if not with Abner, then with who?"

"That's enough for today." She opened her book to end the conversation.

I shook my head, picking up my own book, pretending to read while actually studying her, spinning a tale about her tragic past in my head. "Are you going to read that book or not?" she asked. I never understood how she could know what I was doing without looking at me, but she always did.

Sticking my tongue out at her, I flipped the book facedown on the sofa and stood, stretching out the crick in my back from sitting for so long, then shuffled down the hall to the bathroom.

When I wiped, a streak of blood came away on the toilet paper.

I put my head in my hands, my elbows on my legs, near tears in relief.

Before I went to get a sanitary pad, I returned to the living room. Ada looked up anxiously as I approached—the first sign I had seen that she was actually worried. I shook my head, smiling widely. "We're in the clear."

Ada sank back against the couch cushions, closing her eyes. "Thank goodness for small favors," she said. Then she looked at me. "Do you feel better?"

"Much."

"Good," she said, rising. "But you're out of the business now."

"What?"

"You broke the rules. And I don't tolerate that. Don't worry. There are plenty of other ways I'll put you to work. But you're out."

She strode past me to the kitchen, humming softly, and I stared after her.

CHAPTER

THIRTY-ONE

When Ada's clients returned on Tuesday, I was banished from the living room. "I can at least show them in," I argued.

"You can stay out of sight is what you can do," Ada replied. "I don't care if that means upstairs or out of the house entirely, but I meant what I said: you're out."

I skulked upstairs and sat at my dressing table-turned-writing-desk, huffing loudly and staring out the window. There was no way to return to what I had been writing. I couldn't quite throw it away though either. Instead, I shoved the pages onto the shelf at the back of the closet and put a new sheet of paper in the typewriter.

But I could feel the old story behind me. Almost like it was calling my name.

It was too close to real life—I could see that now.

Sighing, I leaned my head in my hand, elbow on the table, thinking with disgust how readily Freddy would have thrown that poor girl off if he could live off my family's money instead of his family's. He might have been able to doom that child to the stigma of growing up father-less, but I couldn't do that. And the assumption that I would marry him because of this, with no consideration of my repeatedly saying I didn't want to get married. And that my parents would support us—he had never even met them. Did he expect my father to support his child with another woman too? Literally everything was about what he wanted. His choices. His decisions. Where was I? Did I matter at all? Or was I just a means to an end? Would he have even come to talk to me that afternoon if my family didn't have money?

And Shirley's delight in the idea of me also being pregnant by her brother was nauseating as well. I would never understand how anyone could enjoy the misfortune of others. Even if she wouldn't be a constant reminder of my mistake, that wasn't the kind of person I wanted in my life.

But who was I to write anything when I was such a poor judge of character?

I pushed back my seat, opting to go for a walk to clear my head.

I would have preferred the beach. Freddy was unlikely to still be working—he had a new life to build as a soon-to-be father and husband. But the chance of running into him was too much. And if he repeated his entreaty in any way, I just might vomit on him.

Instead, I went north toward the jetty. It was wide, jutting out between Townsends Inlet and the sea, dotted with a handful of sport fishers and crabbers.

For a long moment, I stood at the entrance, looking down at the families in the cove, who opted for the waveless beach of the inlet, then down the beach toward Stone Harbor, the pier reaching an arm into the ocean at the center of town. The fourth lifeguard chair down was Freddy's.

I made a face and, grabbing a rock, hoisted myself up onto the jetty. There were signs warning about tides and fishing seasons, but I ignored them all, picking my way along the rocks until I reached the end. I slipped off my shoes and sat, legs dangling over the water as the waves crashed and the spray reached up to tickle my legs, my hair blowing wildly in the breeze. Except for two tiny boats on the horizon, I could have been the only person in the world.

A pelican flew past me, diving for a fish it spotted, snagging it, and lifting up to soar again. I watched as it disappeared into the distance. It had never occurred to me to be jealous of a bird, but that pelican—minus the diet—had the freedom I wanted. It knew where it belonged, which I no longer did. It knew what it was supposed to do—eat, fly, and swim. And there was no one chastising it for not living the way *they* wanted it to.

Ada lived like that bird. But I wondered if she was lonely. I supposed I would meet Lillian in a few weeks' time. Was she really a substitute for a family though? And if not, why did Ada seem happier than most women I knew?

A fin popped up ten feet away, and I quickly pulled my feet up, away from the water. But I laughed at my silliness and allowed them back down when I saw several more curved fins bobbing. It was a pod of dolphins.

Behind me, a child shouted. I turned to see a little boy pointing, his mother close behind. I smiled reflexively, observing the boy from behind my sunglasses, the way his mother picked him up so he could see better, planting a kiss on his cheek while he watched.

A pang of—something—hit me. I wasn't ready to write that life off and be Ada. But I didn't want it now either. And what I really needed was someone who understood and appreciated that.

That wasn't Freddy. He never asked what I wanted to be or do because in his world, wife and mother was the be-all, end-all answer to that question for women. It never occurred to him that I might have a different answer.

Ada had said that social class was sometimes negotiable in making matches, but often not. And I finally understood she didn't mean money. She meant values. Core beliefs. The way we treated others. You could be rich as Croesus and still not have class. And while Freddy and I fell into the same category financially, the divide between how we viewed the world was as wide as the ocean in front of me. Shirley as well. Neither of them grew in a vacuum. And she couldn't care less whom

Freddy married or how many children he fathered, as long as she got a front-row seat to any resulting dramatics.

I had dodged a bullet, I realized, turning my face toward the sun. And that was something to be happy about.

But it got me no closer to knowing what to write about. And when I eventually stood, dusting off the seat of my trousers, I realized that finding the answer was going to be the best thing I could do for myself. Ada pulled no punches. If she thought my writing had merit, it did. Now I just needed to find the right story to tell. And perhaps a touch of disappointment wasn't such a bad thing to be able to write from experience.

I started to walk back along the road, then stopped. I had nothing to fear from Freddy. And I wasn't going to alter my life over him. So I turned left, going up the dune path at the end of the beach, my shoes in my hand, and walked down to the waterline, where I continued until 18th Street.

Approaching that chair, I snuck a peek from the corner of my eye. Freddy was still sitting there, looking tired. But he didn't turn in my direction, and I continued home. "Goodbye, Freddy," I whispered. I hoped he found some kind of happiness in his new life, but I doubted he would. When I pictured him in a duplex with a wife and a screaming baby, I imagined him sneaking away to spend his time at some gin joint, sitting next to a girl who looked like a poor imitation of me.

But he had made his bed. And I had my own to make, unmake, and make again without him in it.

CHAPTER THIRTY-TWO

There was a dark sedan that I didn't recognize parked in the driveway, but the person who belonged to it brought a smile to my face. Thomas was lugging a stack of cardboard boxes into the house.

"Hello there," I called to him.

"Miss Kleinman," he said, nodding.

"Please call me Marilyn. I'm younger than you are."

He smiled, wiping sweat off his forehead with the back of his hand. "That may be, Miss Kleinman. But I know my manners, and ladies are Miss."

I shook my head. "What are those?"

"Miss Ada asked me to bring them down from her attic at home."

Ada came out onto the porch. "You let Thomas be," she said, scolding me. "He doesn't have time for the likes of you."

She turned to direct him to the den, and I stuck my tongue out.

"What are all these?" I asked Ada.

"Your new job."

I groaned. "If you're not going to let me do the matchmaking, at least let me lie on the beach and ruin my skin."

"I'll do no such thing," she said, taking my face between her hands and smushing it around with her thumbs to look for wrinkles. "Though it may be too late for me to save you."

I shook her off, but I was smiling. "Fine. What's in here? Heirlooms? Jewelry? The bodies of the people you kill to steal their youth?"

"Don't be silly. I keep those in the basement of the Oxford Circle house. And I'd better be good and dead before you even think about my jewelry."

"Oh, Ada, you're too mean to ever die."

She cocked a finger at me. "And don't you forget that." She gestured for me to follow her into the house and opened the top of a box. "No. These are photographs."

I counted up the boxes. There were eight of them. And they were good sized too. "And you want me to . . . ?"

"Organize them into scrapbooks. They're mostly labeled on the back. I want you to label them in the books in chronological order."

I looked at her like she had suggested I eat the fish that I saw the pelican go for whole.

"I know you're mad, but come on. This will take me until I'm your age."

"I don't get mad. You shouldn't either. It—"

"Causes wrinkles, yes, I know."

"Actually it causes stress, which makes your hair turn gray."

I blinked heavily. "Can we please just move on? I promise I've learned my lesson."

She shook her head. "It's scrapbooks or back to New York you go."

Yes, I missed my mother. But no. Her last letter had said my father was starting to waver on college, but warned that I had better keep behaving down here. It had arrived right on time, the day after I learned about Freddy's impending marriage.

"What year do they start?"

"How should I know?" Ada asked as she walked away and offered Thomas a glass of lemonade.

"She's never once offered me a glass of lemonade," I grumbled. But I was mildly curious. And the sooner I started, the sooner I would be done. So I pulled the top box down, put it on the floor, and sat cross-legged next to it.

The box I opened must have been the one I saw in her attic in Philadelphia because the same wedding photo was on top. Below it, two little girls in matching dresses sat with my great-grandmother, my great-grandfather standing stoically behind them. Only my great-grandmother had a hint of a smile. It was a studio portrait, and I looked at the two little girls, trying to determine who was who. The younger had to be Ada. It was hard to imagine her as a child. But she held her sister's hand, and I squinted at my grandmother. I was only ten when she died, and she had been sick for a couple of years before that. But I remembered hugging her and a feeling of safety when she was with us. It was an irreplaceable feeling, one that had never been remotely imitated since. And I remembered my mother crying randomly for weeks after we lost her, Harold trying his best to comfort her, me not really understanding. She was old—I thought dying was just what old people did.

But she wasn't that old, if Ada was still here and my grandmother had been gone ten years. That thought was jarring and made me miss my own mother, who was now only twelve years younger than her mother had been when she died.

I set the photo down and reached for the next one.

When Ada returned, walking Thomas out, I had started stacks for different years, organizing the photos by actual date when they had one. She looked at my piles approvingly, but said nothing.

The next morning, I set out to Hoy's early. I bought a set of pens, some folders, index cards, rubber bands, and rubber cement. I moved the first box up to my bedroom, being respectful of Ada's wishes that I stay out of sight, where I took over the floor and then spread out into the hallway.

By the time Ada was finished for the day, I had cataloged most of the first box by date.

"At some point, I'd like those to go into albums," she said.

I looked up at her. "Do you want the job done quickly, or do you want it done right?"

She held up her hands. "Proceed."

~

I watched Ada's childhood blossom in front of me, piecing together what I could from what I saw and what I didn't. Her mother's stomach swelled, there was a baby, and then there wasn't. Her stomach swelled once more, but no baby followed.

"What happened to the baby?" I asked over breakfast.

"What baby?"

"Your mother's—there were pictures of a little boy. And then there weren't."

Ada shook her head. "The Asiatic flu pandemic of 1890. I barely remember him. He was only a couple of months old. I don't know who got it first, but we all did. The rest of us recovered." She stared into the distance. "Well, physically. My mother—she struggled."

"She got pregnant again though."

Ada looked confused. "No. I don't think she did."

I pushed back my chair and ran up the stairs to get the photo. I handed it to Ada, who studied it closely.

"I suppose you're right. I don't know what happened."

"When did she die?"

"A year after my father."

I looked at her, surreptitiously, from the corner of my eye so she wouldn't make a comment about my impertinent staring. She was still studying the photo of her mother. *So much death*, I thought. I wasn't sure I would marry either if I were in her position. She lost her fiancé, her brother, her parents. It had to feel like everyone was temporary.

"It's how things were," Ada said finally. "You can stop looking at me like that. Everyone my age has similar stories, Marilyn. You had large families because things happened."

But as I went through the photographs that morning, I realized something—her mother never smiled in a picture after the baby died. Not once.

CHAPTER
THIRTY-THREE

In the mornings, I sorted pictures and began placing them in the first scrapbook, carefully labeling each picture with the information from the back. There was something soothing about returning to these now-familiar faces, watching them grow and change.

After lunch, I took a break, walking two blocks north to the beach. It was a necessary change. The first day that I chose to return, I went to my normal spot, and Freddy came over.

"Can we talk?" he asked.

I opened a single eye. I had been enjoying a little "siesta" as Ada called her afternoon naps, typically taken on the wicker love seat on the porch.

"I'd rather not."

He sat in the sand next to me, knowing better than to try to sit on my towel now. "Marilyn, please. I'm miserable without you."

I pushed my sunglasses to the top of my head and leaned up on my elbows. "What do you want me to say to that?"

He looked perplexed, which wasn't attractive. When confident, no one was more handsome. When confused, he resembled a chimpanzee.

"That you miss me too," he said finally.

My eyebrows approached my hairline. "Darling," I said. "I do not intend to lie to you." I pulled my sunglasses down and lay back on my towel.

"Marilyn, you have to understand—"

I sat up, annoyed now. "Freddy, my dear, I don't give a damn." The chimp face again. "Look, we all make mistakes. And we have to live with the consequences. Yours was not using protection with your new fiancée. Mine was getting sent down here in the first place. Because while I appreciate the life experience, I honestly wish I had never set eyes on you. And if you ever actually cared about *me*, not just yourself, you'd do me the favor of making sure I never had to again."

He started sputtering excuses, protesting that he still wanted to be with me, until I finally picked up my towel and left the beach.

From then on, I selected the 16th Street beach, where he wouldn't think to look, to enjoy my solitary time communing with nature, reading, and processing my next steps.

I brought a notebook to the beach. There was something about lying in the sun, the sound of the waves crashing in the background, punctuated only by the laughter of seagulls, that sparked creativity.

My new story started with a broken heart—while I had told Ada the truth about the state of my own, I felt I could write about such things now with a sense of accuracy. I began borrowing from the photographs as well, though my timeline was modern. The unsmiling mother. The close-in-age sisters. The father who supported them through it all. I didn't know exactly where the story was going to wind up yet, nor whether it was a comedy, a tragedy, or a biting social commentary. But it was mine to create. Where I had felt trapped my whole life by society and the expectations of everyone around me, I was free in this world that I had begun to spin around my characters.

And I realized that, while I told Freddy I didn't want to lie to him, I had. My mistake wasn't being sent to Ada; it was not listening to her in the first place. I didn't regret being here at all. And truth be told, I didn't regret Freddy. I needed that experience to write about relationships and the all-encompassing emotions that come with desire.

When I had gotten my fill of sun and sand for the afternoon, I walked the two blocks home and rinsed off in the outdoor shower at the back of the house. It was what Ada did each morning after her swim, and the first day that I tried it, I cowered at every noise. Yes, it locked from the inside, but I was still certain the door would somehow open, and I would be exposed to the world. What world I thought would be gathered in Ada's shore house backyard, which contained only a shed and a clothesline, I could not say.

But by my third time bathing in there, modesty had been forgotten. I loved the sunlight that I could see through the roof slats as I washed my hair, the feel of the stones warmed by the sun and water beneath my bare feet. I began singing so loudly that Ada later told me I was scaring away small children and cats. I hit her with a verse of "A Bushel and a Peck," doing my best Vivian Blaine impression until she shook her head and walked away muttering that I'd scare Frank Sinatra away too with that rendition.

We ate dinner together, then when Ada retired to the den to watch television, I went upstairs to write.

"Don't stay up too late," Ada said each night, coming to my doorway before she went to bed.

I promised her I wouldn't, even though I usually lasted past midnight. It was a code between us. Ada would never show me affection, but her admonition was as good as telling me she loved me.

And the reality was, whether she kicked me out of the business or not, I had grown to love her as well.

So I smiled every night when she left my room, giving another zinger to the sassy aunt in my story in her honor.

CHAPTER THIRTY-FOUR

I presented Ada with the first scrapbook, which covered the photos before she was born up until her tenth year.

She flipped through the pages, taking her time. I knew if I made any errors, I would hear about them, in great detail. Ada was stingy with her praise and generous with criticism. But it made the actual praise so much more valuable when she gave it.

"Yes," she said finally, when she reached the end. "This is what I had in mind."

She rose, setting the book on the coffee table. "Get your purse. We're going out."

I looked down at my clam diggers and knotted blouse. "Let me just get dressed first."

"No need. We'll do that after."

"After what?"

She grinned. "Get your handbag."

~

Ada's definition of "going out" was a trip to the beauty parlor in town. I looked up at it warily, uncertain about its ability to live up to my New York hair standards. But I wasn't about to say that to Ada. And if they butchered it, well, the beauty of hair was that it grew.

We entered a world of pink and turquoise, customers and stylists alike greeting Ada as if she were the mayor. I looked at her as she waved to everyone, scolding a couple of people for not coming to see her, and wondered if maybe she WAS, in fact, the mayor. She knew everyone, their business, and what to do about it.

Ada's stylist of choice led us toward two chairs, one of which was in use, but the client was quickly relocated to another spot to accommodate us. Ada introduced me as her niece, then gave detailed instructions about her own hair. I let my attention drift to the mirror, observing the women behind me, looking for mannerisms I could use in the book.

Ada was saying, "—a bob, I think. Something like what that Jackie Kennedy is wearing."

I looked at Ada's platinum hair, which was already in a bouffant bob. Then realized she was talking about me. The stylist agreed, coming around to put her hands in my shoulder-length hair.

"Wait, what?"

Ada smiled at me in the mirror. "It's 1960, darling. Let's make you look like it."

"And the color?" the stylist asked.

"I'll leave that up to her," Ada said. "Marilyn, would you like to look more like your namesake? We can go blonde."

I held up my hands. "Let's start with the style."

Ada laughed. "Probably for the best. They say gentlemen prefer blondes, and we don't need more of them sniffing around."

I cringed, but the stylist didn't seem to notice. "Does that sound good?" she asked.

"Do I have a choice?"

She laughed. "I do what your aunt says."

"You and everyone else."

~

An hour and a half later, freshly coiffed, we left the salon. "I bet your head feels lighter," Ada said.

"It feels . . . bigger, for sure."

"You mark my words. If Jackie is wearing it, everyone else will want it. If her husband wins the White House, it'll be half because he's handsome and half because she is."

I didn't follow politics enough to argue. I knew he had my vote for the reasons she listed. And as we passed a shop window, I admired my new style. It did look appealing.

"Thank you," I told Ada. "A new look is exactly what I needed."

"Oh, we're not done," Ada said.

"We're not?"

"No. Go get dressed in the fanciest thing you brought. We're going to Atlantic City tonight."

My shoulders drooped.

"What's this?" she asked impatiently.

"I—Freddy took me there. When we first—"

"When you first started sneaking out at night?"

I stared at her.

"I told you the day you arrived—I miss nothing."

"Couldn't you have warned me?" I said.

"I did."

"No, I mean, said, 'I know what you're doing, here's why it's a bad idea.'"

"Would it have stopped you?"

I opened my mouth to say yes, but the word got stuck in my throat.

"That's why," she said. "We all have to make our own mistakes and learn some things the hard way."

I studied her profile, wondering what mistakes she had ever made. If I asked, she would either say that it was an impertinent question or that she was the exception to the rule. But she wouldn't have said it in the first place if that were the case.

"But get dressed and put some makeup on. You haven't done Atlantic City the right way yet because you haven't done it with me."

~

Half an hour later, I left my bedroom in a baby blue sundress, paired with my highest heels and the lipstick Ada actually allowed me to wear. I pursed my lips at my reflection in the bathroom mirror. Ada was right—the haircut suited me.

Her bedroom door was open. "I'm ready when you are," I called in, taking care not to cross the threshold.

"Not yet you're not," Ada replied. "Come on in."

I hesitated briefly, wondering if she was going to let me wear her lipstick, then entered.

Ada was dressed to the nines in a beaded dress cut similarly to mine. A white mink stole was draped over her arms, held up at the elbows, and a long strand of pearls hung around her neck, gigantic matching earrings dangling from her lobes.

"Hmmm," she said, circling me.

"This is the best I have," I told her. "And I won't fit in your dresses." I was curvier than Ada, and anything that fit her was likely not going over my hips or bust.

"No," she agreed. "You won't. But accessories are more forgiving."

My eyes darted toward her vanity. "Don't you even think about that lipstick," she warned. Instead, she looked me over, then went to her closet, emerging with another white stole. "This one is older," she said. "I don't know why I kept it. But it's yours now."

It was in absolutely perfect condition. Perhaps a trifle wider than the one she was wearing, but otherwise identical. "Mine?"

"Was that not clear?"

I raised my eyebrows but thanked her. Mama would be pea green with envy. She had exactly one mink coat, which Daddy claimed was enough for anyone.

But Ada wasn't done. She was riffling through a jewelry box on her dresser. "This is *not* yours," she said. "But for tonight—well, you can pretend."

She came around behind me and fastened a necklace on me. I looked in the mirror. It was a large diamond. "Is this real?"

"Do you really think I'd wear paste?"

My eyes were as round as the stone dangling from the chain on my neck as Ada studied me. "You'll need earrings too." She returned to the jewelry box and came back with a pair of teardrop diamonds that she handed me to slip into my ears. She made one more trip to the jewelry box and returned with a sapphire ring, which she held in her closed palm a minute before offering it to me. "This was my mother's engagement ring," she said.

I studied the oval sapphire surrounded by small diamonds on a gold band. "It's beautiful."

Ada nodded approvingly. "Center diamonds weren't in vogue yet. That came later."

But contrary to what Marilyn Monroe would say, this was the ring I would choose, if actually given a say, for my own. It drew the eye more than a solitaire, and the colored stone was unique—I didn't want something that some nebulous man in my future picked from a velvet tray of nearly identical rings in a jeweler's shop. I wanted something with character—like me.

"Oh, Ada—"

"Don't get all sentimental on me now," she said. "And like I said, it's all loaners."

"Except the stole?"

"Ask me that again and I'm taking it back."

I wanted to hug her, but I was worried that would result in her taking back these gorgeous jewels before I had a chance to wear them.

"Can I wear the red lipstick?"

She pointed to the door. "Get out. I'll be down in a minute."

When she came down, she was wearing the Guerlain, of course. I didn't say a word.

CHAPTER
THIRTY-FIVE

We pulled into town with the top down, our hair protected in scarves, and Ada drove to a parking lot. There were valets, but she refused. For a moment, I thought the valet would argue, but a supervisor came over and greeted her by name, telling her to go ahead.

"Thank you, Teddy," she said.

"Mrs. Miller isn't with you?" he asked, peering at me.

Ada shook her head. "Her mother died. She'll be joining us in another week or so. I'll be dining with my niece tonight."

"My condolences," Teddy said, bowing his head. "Would you like me to let Hackney's know you'll need a table?"

"Yes, darling, thank you so much."

"Anything for you, Miss Heller."

Ada pulled away, directed by the first valet to a parking spot. "Is Lillian married?" I asked.

She looked over at me as if that were a bizarre question. "Why would you ask that?"

"He called her Mrs."

"She was," Ada said. "A long time ago now."

"Do you two come here a lot?"

"Once a year," she said, removing the scarf from her head and fluffing her hair in the mirror. I did the same to mine. "I suppose it may be twice this year if she's up to it when she finally arrives. Poor dear. She's having such a hard summer. A little fun is just what she needs." Ada opened her door and stepped out. "Are you coming?"

I scrambled to follow her, but she was already halfway up the steps to the boardwalk by the time I caught her. It had been much later when Freddy and I arrived, and the boardwalk was now dominated by families, many of which had younger children in carriages or riding on their fathers' shoulders, all in their finery. Couples, young and old, strolled arm in arm. Women wore cocktail attire, and more than a handful of men wore tuxedoes despite the heat.

A little boy, about ten or eleven years old, narrowly avoided colliding into us. "Bruce!" his mother scolded. "Wait for your sister!"

He grinned up at us impishly with a pronounced underbite before he ran back to her.

"It's too hot for a stole," I complained to Ada.

"That's the trick, darling," Ada said. "To look like you're chilly enough to need it."

I looked at her from the corner of my eye. "Since when do you care what people think? Why not just be comfortable?"

She suppressed a laugh. "I don't, honestly. But everything here is an illusion. And if we don't put on a show, why would anyone else?"

I looked around at the glittering gem of the shore and wondered what she meant. "Because no one here is actually as rich as they seem? Except you of course."

Ada smirked. "It's rude to discuss one's wealth. But that's only a part of it. The city itself isn't what it was. If you leave the boardwalk, well . . . I don't recommend straying too far. And it's always been a bit of a sham. They may have finally gotten Nucky Johnson, but that didn't take away the darker elements of the town."

I didn't know who that was. But it was hard to imagine this whole place being a facade.

"Where are we going?" I asked as Ada led us directly past the Steel Pier with hardly a glance.

"To dinner, of course."

I had trouble picturing Ada eating on the boardwalk, but as we neared the northern end, the lights of a huge establishment greeted us. I looked up, reading the sign, which said "Hackney's," with a logo of a giant red lobster.

At the door, the host greeted Ada with a bow. "Miss Heller," he said. "And your new friend, of course."

"My niece." He gave me a bow as well.

"We have your usual table prepared, overlooking the water."

"Thank you so much," Ada said, and we followed him through the largest restaurant I had ever seen. It was noisy, with the sounds of china and cutlery, clinking glasses, and mealtime chatter. Waiters buzzed through the aisles, some carrying gigantic trays of food, dodging patrons and other servers with practiced skill.

Two waiters appeared as we approached what was clearly a place of honor, the table empty with a card reading "Reserved" on it. They pulled out our chairs, pushed them in after we sat, and, with a flourish, opened our napkins and laid them delicately across our laps.

A third man came seemingly out of thin air. "Miss Heller," he said warmly. "It is always a pleasure to have you here."

"Thank you, Michael."

"Can I start you with some champagne?"

"Of course."

He signaled to another waiter, who had a bottle at our table, complete with glasses and an ice bucket, in under nine seconds. I was counting.

Michael expertly popped the cork without spilling a drop and poured first for Ada, who took a sip and then nodded, before he filled my glass, then hers to the top, holding the bottle, label out for her to see.

Menus were placed in front of us, and Michael set the champagne bottle on ice, saying he would give us a moment to peruse the menu.

Ada didn't touch hers.

"You know what you're having already?"

"And what you are, if you know what's good for you."

"And what's that?"

"Mussels followed by lobster."

I glanced around at the multitudes of people, all of whom seemed to have the boiled shellfish on their plates in various stages of consumption.

"I—I've never had either." I picked up the menu, uncertainly, looking for some kind of safer fish option.

Ada put a hand on the top of my menu, pushing it down. "Because you're so religious? Or because you're afraid to try?"

I kept my face neutral, though it was trying to scowl. She knew I wasn't religious. But there were certain dictums of my childhood I wasn't quite ready to abandon. Eating a lobster seemed awfully sacrilegious.

"You already tried crab and loved it," Ada said as if she could hear my thoughts. "The rules are archaic and from a time when food poisoning was likely to kill you." She lifted her own menu, though I was sure she didn't need to even glance at it. "I'm sure the flounder will be excellent here as well. If you're not feeling brave enough to try something new."

I set my jaw.

The waiter returned as promised and asked if we were ready or if we needed more time. "I believe we're ready," Ada said, gesturing to me.

She was infuriating. "Can I start with the mussels, please," I said. "And may I have the lobster after that?"

Ada's brows came together, but she smoothed them before the waiter turned to her. "I'll have the same," she said, handing him her menu. But as soon as he was out of earshot, she turned on me. "That's not how you order."

"Excuse me?"

"Did your mother raise you in a barn?"

My hackles rose. "My mother—"

"Knows better," Ada said. "And I would know, because I brought her here before you were born."

I tried to picture Mama eating shellfish and sitting in the seat I now occupied, perhaps in this very mink stole. But in my mind's eye, it was Mama as she was now. Not the younger version I had seen in the boardwalk photo.

"What did I do wrong?" I asked.

"You don't *ask* for food. It's their job. They're not your mother. Say either, 'I would like,' or 'I will have.' Not 'May I have.' The answer is yes, you may."

"What's the difference?"

Ada closed her eyes for about three seconds. "The difference is etiquette. You can get away with a lot of things when you reach my age and stature, and you can get away with a lot when you're young, but neither means you should."

I winced and sipped my champagne. I would correct my restaurant ordering style beginning now and lasting for the rest of my life.

Waiters placed plates heaped with black-shelled mussels in front of us, giving us each a small bowl as well, then were gone. I looked to Ada. I had no idea what to do with these things.

"Why are you looking at me like that? Eat." Then her expression softened. "Watch me," she said.

I watched as she took a small fork, pried the meat out of a shell, and popped it into her mouth. She chewed, then held the shell up like a tiny castanet. "You use this to pluck them out of the rest," she said, demonstrating on another set of shells.

After I failed at three attempts with the fork, Ada handed me her shells. "Try now," she said. "Or we'll be here all night, and we do have plans after this."

"What are we doing after?"

"You'll find out soon enough." I pried the first mussel from its shell with ease and looked at it, clamped between the two black shells I had used as tweezers. "It's better as food than art."

Certain I was about to chew something with the consistency of shoe rubber, I placed it on my tongue, pleasantly surprised by the taste—it was salty and sweet, chewy but not tough.

"They're delicious," I said after swallowing.

"You sound surprised. It's not like I told you to order cod liver oil."

I opened the next. I hadn't realized how hungry I was until the first mussel hit my tongue.

When we finished, the bowls and plates were cleared, and two lobsters appeared in front of us. "I suppose you'll need help with this too," Ada said. "This takes considerably more skill than the mussels, I'm afraid. But you seem to be a fast learner."

Ada described the anatomy in far greater detail than I expected or needed, then showed me how to eat it, piece by piece.

"So?" she asked.

"I understand why it's a delicacy now."

"Always say yes to new things," Ada said. "It's the only way you'll be able to write about life—if you actually go out and live it." She laid her fork delicately across her plate. "You asked why I didn't warn you off Freddy—that was part of why. You can't expect to write about things you've never felt in a real way."

I copied Ada's fork placement, and Michael returned, offering us a dessert menu, but Ada waved him away. "No, we have a show to get to tonight."

"Of course," Michael said smoothly. "You two always arrive in town on the same nights."

"By no great coincidence, I can assure you," Ada said, smiling almost flirtatiously. She handed him a stack of bills. "Buy your wife a present."

"Thank you, Miss Heller." Ada patted his arm as busboys cleared our plates.

"Let's go," Ada said, rising. "We have a rather long walk, but it's a pleasant night."

"What show are we going to?"

"It's a surprise."

I assumed it would be some old-time band to remind Ada of her youth. But we walked back past the Steel Pier. Many of the families had retired, but some were still going, children starting to look sleepy if they hadn't just eaten their body weight in sugar—the children who had were running circles around their tired parents.

At Missouri Avenue, we exited the boardwalk, and I glanced around, looking for signs of the decay that Ada had said was occurring in the city. But we walked only two blocks before we hit a large crowd of people, a neon sign advertising "The 500 Club" in front of us. *A nightclub?* I thought. I had never been allowed to go to one, though the braver of my college friends and I had snuck into a few in New York. I wondered if this would be some sort of vaudeville act.

Ada sidestepped the line, however, bringing us right to the front. "Miss Heller," the man at the door said, unhooking the velvet rope for us. "Your table is ready, right in front."

"Thank you so much," she said. "Does he know I'm here tonight?"

"He does," the doorman said with a wink.

"Wonderful." Ada walked in through the door he held for us, people in line craning to see what celebrities we were to be allowed in ahead of them.

We walked through the main bar, fitted in the Art Deco style of the 1920s, zebra-patterned wallpaper lining the walls. There was a waterfall in this first room, lined in imitation foliage. But Ada kept walking, moving us through to the Vermillion Room. The walls were dark red velvet, and the floor was filled with tables covered in white cloths. It was mostly full, with a small table in front holding a "Reserved" sign for us. Ada led us purposefully through the room to the table by the stage, and a waiter appeared, pouring champagne without asking what we wanted. "On the house," he said. "Mr. D'Amato sends his regards."

"Tell Skinny I said thank you," Ada said. "But he's still too young for me."

The waiter chuckled. This was apparently a running gag.

I looked around the room, spotting Jayne Mansfield on the opposite side of the stage from us. My eyes widened. Scanning the rest of the tables, I saw Paul Newman with Joanne Woodward as well. A man and woman approached the movie stars, and I smiled, recognizing the couple I had seen in Avalon the other day, sans children this time. They snapped a picture with the famous couple, and Paul Newman signed a napkin for the woman—Evelyn, I believe her name was—before they returned to their seats farther back in the house.

"Ada," I said, leaning across the table. "Who are we here to see?"

She smiled as the lights went down and a spotlight rose on the stage, just inches from us. "Ladies and gentlemen," a voice boomed. "The 500 Club is proud to present to you tonight the Chairman of the Board, Old Blue Eyes himself, Mr. Frank Sinatra."

CHAPTER
THIRTY-SIX

By the time the show ended, my voice was hoarse from screaming along with every other woman—save Ada—in the house. He had come over and held my hand during "I've Got You Under My Skin," and I was certain I would never wash that hand again.

But I never expected Ada to usher us backstage, where Frank Sinatra—FRANK SINATRA!—greeted her with a hug and a kiss, then, after she introduced me, he gave me the same.

"Is this a present for me?" he asked Ada.

"Watch it, Frankie," Ada said, elbowing him playfully in the ribs. "This is my niece, Marilyn."

"You sure you don't want to make me a match? I'd be great entertainment at the holidays."

Ada laughed, and I felt myself melting into an absolute puddle at the idea that Frank Sinatra was even joking about marrying me. Ada said she would let him get back to his fans, but before we left, he grabbed a photograph of himself from a stack of them and signed one to me. I clutched it with a shaking hand as we left the club and headed back toward the boardwalk.

"Same Atlantic City Freddy Goldman showed you?" Ada asked. I shook my head, my eyes as wide as the Ferris wheel on the pier. "You're all right? I'm not catching you if you faint."

"How—how do you know Frank Sinatra?"

"Darling, I've been coming here since Prohibition. I know everyone in this town. Not the tourists, of course. But the actual heart of it." She looked pensive for a moment. "When your mother was here, she got to meet Bing Crosby."

I turned to Ada in surprise. "Is there anyone you don't know?"

"I don't know most people. But if they're regulars here, I've probably been introduced. I had much more of a social life when I was younger."

I remembered the picture of Ada and my mother on the boardwalk, my mother's exuberant kiss on Ada's cheek, something held tight in her hand. "Did Mama get his autograph?"

"She did. I assume she still has it somewhere."

We stopped for fudge and saltwater taffy on the way back to the car, but I felt like I was walking on air instead of the boards. No one was going to believe that Frank Sinatra kissed me on the cheek and asked if I was a present for him. I didn't believe it.

At the car, Ada took off her stole, draping it carelessly in the backseat. I held on to mine. It was the first fur I'd owned, and I didn't want it getting messed up in the wind from the convertible, no matter how hot it was. And it was still hot, in late July, even at night.

We tied our hair up, and Ada put the car into gear, reversed out of the parking spot, and pulled out into the street, taking the Black Horse Pike back to the Garden State.

"Thank you," I said as we cruised along in the darkness, the pine barrens looming to our right, the barrier islands and sea to the left.

She said nothing, though whether she was lost in thought or just concentrating on the unlit road, I did not know.

"Ada?" I asked as we passed Ocean City.

"Hmm?"

"Why did my mother spend the summer with you?"

"I told you. That's not my story to tell."

"Except you called us 'two peas in a stupid pod' when you thought I might be . . . in trouble. Did she—" I swallowed. "Do I have a sibling I don't know about?"

Ada was silent for a long moment, and I braced myself for the worst. "You do not," she said eventually.

"Then what—"

"Give me a minute," she said, still staring at the dark road. For a mile, she said nothing as I counted the road markers.

Then she began to talk. "It was 1932. She was eighteen years old. And she met a boy who she thought was going to marry her." Ada glanced over at me. "It was *not* your father."

"I assumed as much."

"Your grandfather didn't know. Your grandmother—my sister—called and explained the situation. I told her to send her down to me. When Rose arrived, she was terrified. The boy had vanished when she told him. And when she showed up at his house . . ." She shook her head. "He told his parents he had never met her."

I took that in. Freddy's response to the girl he got into trouble was horrendous, but compared to that . . . Then again, if I had agreed to have Freddy, he would have left her just as high and dry as my poor mother.

"I sat her down and told her she had about a month to decide what she wanted to do. The decision was hers to make. If she didn't want to go on, well, we'd find someone to help. And if she did, she would stay with me until it was time, and we would find someone to adopt the baby."

A shiver ran down my spine. *You do not,* she had said when I asked if I had another sibling. *Oh, Mama.*

"In the end, she didn't have to decide—fate or her body took care of it for her."

Neither of us spoke. I was trying to reconcile this with the mother I thought I knew. The one who spent her days lost in books, but who doted on her children beyond anything. When she held us, did she think of the baby that never was? Did my father know? I thought of her weeping at her own mother's death, the woman who protected her honor and allowed her to go on to become my mother instead of some fallen woman, which, in 1932, she would have been.

"She struggled with it for some time," Ada said finally. "She really thought she was in love and his response . . . Well, I'm not sure which was more devastating." She shook her head slightly at a memory. "She was herself again by the end of the summer. But I think that's why she married your father the following year. She wanted stability. Someone who couldn't hurt her like that."

Daddy worshiped Mama. We all knew that. He refused her nothing. And she loved him too—but not with the passion I had seen in the books I snuck from the box in her closet. Harold and I—we were her true loves. And the rest? She found her solace in books.

But Mama *had* been that deeply in love. And I vowed to myself, on that dark stretch of road, never to do what she did and settle for something bland to keep from being hurt.

Ada put a hand on top of mine. I looked down in the moonlight, seeing the veins and wrinkles on hers, weighed down with heavy rings. "I shouldn't have said that."

"Yes, you should have. I asked. I'm glad you told me."

She shook her head again. "No. The 'two peas in a pod' thing."

I tilted my head questioningly. Our situations certainly merited the comparison.

"You won't wind up like her." I lifted my chin, realizing she was right. I would have married Daniel if that were the case. "You're too much like me."

I looked at her profile, illuminated in the moonlight as she pulled off the Garden State onto Avalon Boulevard. She was wild and free, but she was alone.

And I didn't know if that was exactly what I wanted or what I was most terrified of becoming.

CHAPTER THIRTY-SEVEN

July turned into August, bringing warmer temperatures and men to the shore for more than just the weekend as they took their two-week vacations to join their wives and parents. The beach and town grew more crowded and, as I experimented one day with returning to the 18th Street beach, I discovered Freddy was noticeably absent from the lifeguard chair. I returned the next three days, looking cautiously at the stand before deciding where to set up camp, but when he didn't appear, I stopped looking for him.

Ada left her newspaper at my place at the lunch table, folded to a wedding announcement in the *Philadelphia Inquirer*. It featured a picture of the couple, Freddy smiling but looking like he wished it were a funeral announcement instead. I wondered if they would also publish a baby announcement in a few months or if they would skip that to make it less obvious to anyone who paid attention to dates.

Probably the latter.

I looked at the girl with great curiosity though. She was pretty, but there was nothing striking about her. I wondered if marrying Freddy was what she wanted or if her parents had strong-armed her into it. From the perspective of a writer, it was a fascinating study. But none of them were my problem. I mentally wished them well and then put them entirely out of my head.

Besides, I had more interesting things to discuss with Ada. There were several undated photos, and I needed her help categorizing them. I was nearly done with the second scrapbook, covering the second decade of Ada's life. I met Abner, Ada's fiancé, and had studied him, going so far as to get a magnifying glass from the kitchen drawer to look even closer at the handful of photos of them. There was an engagement portrait, along with a newspaper clipping announcing their news. But another clipping soon followed, detailing the fire and loss of life.

The photos stopped for almost a year after that.

Ada came to sit at the table, nodding to the newspaper. "I thought you'd want to see."

"I hope they're happy."

"They won't be," she said darkly.

I shrugged and let it drop. I didn't want to spend another moment of my life on Freddy. "I'm almost done with the second album, but I had a few questions." She peered at me. "Where are all the pictures from 1905 after Abner died?"

"Excuse me?"

"There's nothing for almost a year."

"Why would there be? We were a house in mourning."

"So you just—sat there?"

"Of course not. But it would have been considered bad form to go about documenting our lives."

"What did you do that year?"

"I went to nursing school."

That answered my next question; of the undated photos, most of them featured Ada in a nursing uniform.

"Are these from nursing school, then?" I asked, passing them to her. "They don't have dates or names."

She inspected them. "They are. Which would mean they're sometime in late 1905 or early 1906."

"Who are the other girls?"

Ada named a couple of them, and I wrote the information down. But she didn't remember everyone. "It was so long ago. And women came from all over to train at the New York Hospital Training School for Nurses—it's part of Cornell now. But that happened much later. I never saw most of them again."

"So you really *are* a nurse, then?"

"Not for forty years."

"But if I sliced my finger open, you could fix it up."

Ada pursed her lips. "Yes. I believe my experiences in the Great War qualify me for your finger."

I tried to imagine this woman, who was basically royalty among the Jews of Philadelphia and apparently among everyone at the shore, in a nurse's uniform tending to wounded men. But all I could picture was her telling them they had best not bleed on her if they knew what was good for them.

"In other news," Ada continued, "Lillian arrives next week."

I was curious to meet her, but I also didn't want her to join us. I liked having Ada to myself, and I didn't want someone who wasn't family coming in and upsetting the dynamic. Something had shifted between us since the Freddy situation, and I enjoyed the closeness we had found—even if we spent less time together in the mornings.

"She's wrapped everything up in Chicago?"

Ada nodded. "They found a buyer for her mother's house. Her mother didn't have much, but should Lillian ever leave me, she'll be comfortable at least."

"How does your arrangement work anyway? Will she retire someday?"

"I doubt it. I would assume we'll live out the rest of our lives together. She enjoys our arrangement as much as I do."

"But you pay her?"

"It's—"

"Impertinent to discuss money, yes, I know. I'm not asking how much. I'm just asking how it works."

"I'm afraid that is our business. Lillian is quite content with her life as it is. As am I."

I changed tacks, wondering if I would be able to get more information out of Lillian herself or if she would be as cantankerous as Ada. "You said once you weren't ready to retire. Do you think you ever will?"

"Lillian thinks I should."

"But you don't agree?"

Ada looked past me pensively. "I think I'll know when it's time. I'm not there yet. But I have a little place in Key West waiting if we get to that point."

"Why Key West?"

"Because Havana is too iffy these days. I'm too old for Europe and the like, and I never did care for Palm Springs. And in Key West, no one cares who you were before. You can just disappear and exist without the world watching."

I was surprised at Ada wanting anonymity. She thrived on the recognition she received everywhere she went. Without it, I assumed she would shrivel up like a raisin.

"But in all likelihood, I'll stay here," Ada continued. "If demand dries up or I grow tired of being Ada Heller, well then, Key West is waiting. Though I don't see marriages going out of fashion anytime soon."

"Does anyone ever question the fact that you never married, yet you're the expert on what makes a happy marriage?"

Ada grinned. "Once in a while. I just explain that I can't match myself and I wasn't going to settle for someone inferior to an Ada Heller match."

"You said you've been in love though."

"I have. Twice, in fact."

"Then why didn't you get married?"

"Because love alone won't always make a good marriage." She pushed her chair back from the table. "Enough questions for today. I have work to do."

Frannie cleared the dishes while I remained at the table, trying to figure out exactly what she meant by that—especially because the main character in my writing was just now falling in love. What secrets did I need to know to make her actually be able to find happiness?

I shook my head. I could write a seduction from experience now, but I still knew nothing about being in love. When I eventually rose from the table, I went back to the photographs, thinking that when I finally found these two loves of Ada's, I would be able to learn enough to write it convincingly.

CHAPTER
THIRTY-EIGHT

It was early afternoon when I heard the knock on the door. I was packing my bag to head to the beach, but I ran down the stairs. We had been getting deliveries at all hours in preparation for Lillian's arrival, and Ada had set me to work with Frannie airing out her room—it was the second-largest bedroom and located directly next to Ada's—and washing all the linens. But it seemed we had done most of what needed doing now, and I was anxious to dig into one of the newest books that Mama had sent.

"Lillian's trunks are here," I shouted up to Ada, skidding to a stop at the front door.

"Don't yell room to room," Ada yelled back.

I chuckled and flung the door open. "If you don't mind bringing them upst—" My eyes widened.

Daniel Schwartz stood on the porch, a bouquet of white roses in his hand.

"No," I said, slamming the door shut just as Ada was coming down the stairs.

"What's wrong with you?" she asked. "Have him bring the bags in!"

"It's not—" But it was too late. Ada had opened the door.

She stopped and looked Daniel up and down. He was dressed in slacks and a short-sleeved button-down shirt, which Ada gave an approving nod. She gestured to the flowers. "I assume you're not here to bring Mrs. Miller's bags."

"I'm afraid not," Daniel said. "I'm here to see Marilyn."

Ada looked from him to me to him again before holding out her hand. "Ada Heller. And I believe you're the infamous rabbi's son."

I groaned internally. The handshake was a sure sign of approval. I wondered if I could just run away and never come back. Key West sounded nice.

"I see my reputation precedes me. Yes. Daniel Schwartz."

"Daniel? Or Dan?"

He smiled. "Dan to my friends."

Oh no. Ada was eating this up with a spoon. "Well, Dan—if I may be so bold to presume we're going to become friends—please, do come in." She slipped a hand through his arm, leading him into the house.

"Ada!" I hissed.

"Where are your manners?" Ada asked, smirking at me. "You have a gentleman caller."

"This isn't the 1800s. No one says that anymore."

"So rude," Ada murmured. She took the flowers from Daniel and whacked me in the chest with them. "Go put these in some water while I get to know our guest."

"Good. Get to know him. Maybe you can find him a match who *isn't* me."

"Ignore her, darling," Ada crooned up at Daniel. "Come with me. We'll go sit in the living room."

I stood there for a long moment, seriously debating stealing Ada's keys, hopping in the car, and never coming back. But having grown up in New York City, I didn't know how to drive. And I wasn't quite ready to abandon the burgeoning manuscript upstairs. So I took the flowers to the kitchen, where I put them on the counter.

"Let me just get a vase," Frannie said, wiping her hands on her apron.

"No need," I said. "I don't want them."

"Such pretty flowers," she said. "I'll put them in water."

"Frannie."

"Miss Ada said to. I heard that much. And I work for her, not you."

"Do you know how to drive?" I asked.

"What?"

"Never mind."

I heard laughter from the living room, and, lacking a clear escape route, I took a deep breath and then went to join them.

Daniel was on the sofa, Ada in the chair opposite him. Sally had apparently fallen in love and was on Daniel's lap, kissing his hand. That traitor. "Sit," Ada told me, still laughing. "You didn't tell me how funny Dan was—or how handsome."

I ignored her. "What do you want, Daniel?"

"I—uh . . ." He looked from me to Ada and back, then he took a deep breath. "I'm just going to lay it all on the line. I can't stop thinking about you."

I stared at him as if he had just said he murdered people for fun.

"How sweet," Ada said. "Marilyn, darling, isn't that sweet?"

"You're enjoying this, aren't you?" I asked her.

"Immensely." She turned back to Daniel. "And you drove all this way to tell her that?"

He nodded. "I went to your house—I went a few times actually. Your mother finally told me where to find you."

I exhaled forcefully, blowing the air out over my bottom lip. "Daniel—"

"Dan," Ada corrected. "I believe once you crash through a piece of stained glass in an act of passion, you count as friends."

Driving couldn't be that hard, could it?

"Dan," I said through gritted teeth. "I'm sorry you drove this far, but my answer is the same as it was two months ago. No."

He looked vaguely confused—but unlike Freddy, it was cute on him. As much as I hated to admit that. "I—oh—no—I'm not here to propose—again. That was my father and I—I don't know why I went along with it." He ducked his head, then looked back up at me. "Actually, I do. I like you. And I thought—" He stopped for a moment to collect his thoughts. "My parents were a match. And I always liked you, even when we were kids. And I just figured it'd help our families, and we already knew each other better than most matchmade couples . . ." He turned to Ada. "No offense, ma'am."

"None taken at all."

I glared at her. Why was she suddenly being so nice?

"It was stupid. I know that. But I thought, if you were game, why not?" Dan asked.

"I wasn't."

Dan smiled ruefully and ran a hand through his hair. "I know that now." He turned so he was actually facing me, and I inched slightly away. "I came here to ask if I could take you on a date. A proper one."

"Of course you can," Ada said. "Marilyn, go get dressed."

"Ada!"

She held up her hands in a gesture of innocence. "What? I can't speak for you, certainly, but I give my wholehearted permission."

"Look, Dani—Dan. I'm not interested in dating anyone right now. I want to focus on myself. And my writing. And I don't—"

"Your writing?" he asked. "What are you writing? I'd love to read it."

I could have kicked myself.

"He'd love to read your writing, Marilyn," Ada said. "How very modern and interesting compared to so many *other* young men."

If looks could kill, even her meanness wouldn't save her. She would have been six feet under and cold already. The actual last thing I needed was her bringing Freddy up and Daniel taking that information home to my parents. I could kiss college goodbye forever if that happened.

"That's not the point," I said through gritted teeth. "I'm just not dating right now."

"Nonsense," Ada said. "Dan, if Marilyn won't go out with you, you'll stay for dinner tonight."

I made eye contact with her, trying to communicate how entirely unwelcome this was through telekinesis or some other psychic ability, but like my nonexistent driving skills, I seemed to lack the power to save myself that way.

And when Ada just smiled at me in response, I realized that if I *didn't* go have dinner with Dan, she was going to invite him to stay with us.

"If I agree to have dinner with you tonight and I'm still not interested, will you leave me be?"

For a moment, I felt sympathy for him. He drove all this way, thinking he would get a warmer welcome than I was willing to give.

But they also had these amazing things called telephones and he could have saved himself the effort if he had just picked one of those up and dialed.

"If you really don't want to, I'll leave now," Dan said. "I just thought—you seemed like the type who would appreciate a grand gesture."

"She is," Ada assured him. "And she wants to go out with you. She just doesn't know it yet."

"Ada!"

Ada smiled broadly. "Go upstairs and start getting ready, Marilyn. Dan, darling, I'll call the Princeton and get you a room—I'd offer to let you stay here, but I'm afraid that wouldn't be fitting with two unmarried women and I'd *hate*"—she winked at him—"to do anything that would force you two to get married to save your reputations—as much as you may still be able to salvage them, that is." She rose and Dan followed suit. "I'll make you a reservation for dinner as well. Did you bring a tie? If not, there's a haberdashery in town."

"I did."

"Lovely," she said, taking his arm and leading him to the door. "The Princeton is just a few blocks over. You could walk, really. I'll make the call and then you just come back here at six and pick our Marilyn up. I'll make sure she's ready."

Dan looked over his shoulder at me, sulking on the sofa. "I'll see you tonight."

"Can't wait," I said with as much sarcasm as I could muster.

Ada shut the door behind him and then came back to me. "What are you waiting for? We need to figure out what you're going to wear!"

"Why are you doing this to me?"

She pointed a finger at me. "Because I can spot a good one a mile away. He cares about your interests. He respects what you want. And he drove all this way to try. Even Sally approves, and I told you, she's an excellent judge of character. Now you're going to stop pouting and go set your hair while I call the hotel." I didn't budge. "Now. Move."

Sighing, I pulled myself off the sofa. This was going to be a very long night.

CHAPTER THIRTY-NINE

After Ada arranged accommodations for Dan and made a reservation for our dinner, she marched into my room without knocking.

"Hey! What if I was naked?"

"It'd be nothing I hadn't seen before," Ada said as she crossed to the closet and began riffling through my dresses. "No. No. No. Maybe. No." She looked at her watch. "We probably have time to go get you something new in town."

"I don't need anything new. Especially not for dinner with Daniel Schwartz."

"He was good enough for you to neck with during services, but you can't be civil enough to have dinner with him?"

"That was before he proposed."

"And what's so wrong with someone who would be willing to save your reputation?"

I threw my hands up, exasperated. "I don't *want* to be saved. I want—" I stopped. What exactly *did* I want?

Ada rolled her eyes but plucked the light green dress I had worn to Cape May with Freddy from the closet and laid it on the bed.

"Not that one," I said.

"Why not?"

I scrunched up my nose and she held up a hand. "Say no more." She returned it to the closet. "Unless you want me to burn it?"

"Might as well. Unless you know an exorcist for clothes."

She pulled the pink dress that she had designated as a "maybe" and put it on the bed, then came and sat next to it. "I know. You want romance and passion and butterflies in your stomach. But you clearly felt some of that two months ago or you would never have gotten yourself into any of this."

Had I? I tried to remember why I did what I did, other than boredom. I thought back to him turning to look at me in shul, as I counted to see if he would. Yes. There was something there in my stomach that day. But— "It was the forbidden aspect," I said. "That's all."

"That's what it was with Freddy Goldman, that's for sure. But what's actually wrong with this one?"

I didn't know how to explain that it was what he represented. The stodgy Upper West Side life that left me at the stove with a book. Okay, I probably wouldn't actually be at the stove. But he could ask what I was writing all he wanted—he would still want me to put the silly hobby away as soon as he had me. And there was so much of the world I wanted to see before I resigned myself to that life. California and Paris and London and Havana and, yes, even Key West. Maybe I could convince him to honeymoon in Havana instead of Niagara, but that wasn't enough for me. And it wouldn't have been even if I had never experienced the freedom of living with Ada. But now that I had . . .

"You said you needed more time after Abner died," I said, reaching desperately. "I need more too."

"Oh, darling," Ada said, patting my leg. "Nice try. But no. I'm not saying you have to marry him, but you're going on this date. Now, are you going to get in the shower yourself, or do I need to join you?" I made a face and she laughed. "You're so old-fashioned. Even if you married him, divorce is a thing now." I fought the urge to throw a shoe at her. "Now go get showered."

~

At five minutes to six, Ada had me dressed, made up, and sitting in the living room. She refused my request for the red lipstick, saying it made me look "fast."

"He liked it well enough in June."

"And he proposed after that. If you want a different outcome, change the way you get there."

"Do you have to have a comeback for *everything* I say?"

"Yes," Ada said without missing a beat. "It's one of the benefits of age. I can say exactly what I want. And the good lord help anyone who gets in the way of your tongue when you're my age."

I would be her age in 2015. We would have flying cars and be living on the moon by then.

She fussed over my hair, and I swatted her away. "I swear, it's a good thing you never had daughters."

"For me as well if they'd be as disagreeable as you."

We were interrupted by the sound of a car door closing. "Now you behave tonight."

"Didn't say behave like what," I muttered as she went to open the door.

"Like a lady," she hissed back, then threw the door open just as Dan was raising his hand to knock. He held another bouquet of flowers.

"For you," he said to Ada. "Thank you for arranging things."

I was in trouble. Ada was smiling up at him.

"You look beautiful," Dan said as I rose from the sofa.

"Yeah, yeah, let's get this mess over with."

"Stay out at as late as you like," Ada called after us. "I'd say don't do anything I wouldn't do, but really it's better if you do everything I would."

"Goodnight, Ada."

I clomped down the front steps as indelicately as possible, pausing when I saw his car.

"Do you have something for your hair?" he asked. "Or I can put the top up."

In front of us was a canary-yellow Impala. I started to answer, but Ada came running out of the house, waving one of her Hermès scarves at me. "I'm keeping this," I told her, plucking it from her hand.

"Small price to pay," she said. "Now go have fun."

I made a wry face at Dan. "You know she's going to show up in sunglasses and a scarf and try to hide in a plant to watch us, right?"

He laughed. "Sounds about right. I like her though."

I do too, I thought. "She's something all right."

He opened the door for me and I sat down, then tied up my hair while he closed the door and went around to his side. "It's a cute little town," Dan said. "I like the name too."

"It's a literary reference."

"I know. I loved that book." I stared at him—this was a setup, right? Ada prepped him somehow. Maybe she called the hotel while I was in the shower? "Are you ready to return to New York and claim your throne, or are you planning to stay into the fall?"

"Depends on my father, I guess."

"Is he still angry?"

I nodded. He hadn't spoken to me all summer. Granted, I also hadn't written to him, following my mother's advice to let him cool down. Her last letter said he was closer to coming around on college, but wasn't there yet. And had I never laid eyes on Dan, that wouldn't have been in jeopardy in the first place.

"I'm sorry," Dan said, genuinely. "If I'd known—actually, wait. Is he most angry about us getting caught or you turning me down?"

"Both."

"Well, I *am* sorry. I thought I was helping, agreeing to my father's plan. If I had realized I was making things worse, I would never have . . ." He trailed off. "I'm just sorry."

"Yeah, well, that and a dime will get you a Coke." His shoulders sank and I felt a little bad. I was being mean and his only crime was trying to help. "You don't need to apologize. I made my own choices. You didn't coerce me. I was the one who suggested someplace private. And I was the one who said I wasn't getting married over some kissing."

"I didn't stop you either."

"I don't want someone to stop me. I want someone who will respect that I made a choice and want to clean up my own mess."

He was quiet for a moment. "I understand that."

We rode in silence for another couple of minutes until we arrived at the restaurant Ada had selected for us. I took the scarf off my hair as Dan got out and came around to my side, but I made sure to open my own door before he could.

Once we were seated, menus in front of us, Dan asked if I knew what was good there. I shrugged. It was new to me. "If Ada picked it and didn't tell us what to order, everything is good. But knowing her, she called in an order when she made the reservation."

"She's not what I expected when your mother told me where you'd gone."

"I don't think Ada is what anyone has ever expected anywhere."

A waiter arrived, holding a bottle of wine and two glasses. "Courtesy of Miss Heller," he said, setting the glasses down and opening the bottle.

Dan smiled at me.

"Told you," I said.

He tasted the wine and nodded his approval, then the waiter poured mine. I immediately took a long swig. The corners of Dan's mouth turned down. *Good*, I thought. *He doesn't like women who drink. This will be easy.*

"We don't have to do this if you don't want to that badly," he said. I almost choked on the wine. "This was probably stupid. I know that. I just—I needed to try."

I took a smaller sip of the wine, feeling like the worst person on the planet. He was reminding me that I *did* like him. It was why I had him meet me outside the sanctuary that day. And if we hadn't gone crashing through the glass at the back of the ark—well, who knew what might have happened? But I wasn't the same girl I was before all that. And it wasn't because of Freddy. I had seen that life didn't have to look like my parents'. And that opened up a whole world before me that I never knew existed. I couldn't go back now.

"It's not you," I said eventually, softer. "I'm sorry. I'm not trying to be mean to you—okay, I am. But it's because you have to realize, I'm not like all those other girls who must be dying for you to ask them out. I—I want more than getting married and going to temple and having babies at twenty-one."

"I know that," Dan said.

"You can't possibly know that."

"I mean, you told me. But it's why I like you. You think all those other girls would make out with me in my father's office?"

I shook my head. "Okay, so you like me for being fast? That's not really who I am either."

"No." He reached over and put a hand on top of mine. I looked at it for a moment, but resisted the urge to yank mine back. "I mean, I like you because you're different. You're—with other girls, I don't know what they're actually thinking. They say and do all the right things, and I never know what they really want. And you're the exact opposite. You're like a tiger. You might destroy me. And I kind of think that might be worth it."

My head tilted. "Probably a good thing you went with a cat analogy over a dog of my sex, or we'd be having a very different conversation."

Dan laughed heartily. "This is what I mean though. I don't know what you're going to say or do. And I want to—I want to be here to hear it and see it and experience it all. I know we don't really know each other yet, but I'm saying I want to."

What excitement do you have to offer me though? I wanted to ask. I didn't. I understood what he was saying. But he wasn't going to be able to keep up. And so I made a decision to show him that.

The waiter arrived. "I'll have the lobster," I said, handing him the menu, then looking at Dan defiantly. A rabbi's son would never go for shellfish.

He chewed his bottom lip for a few seconds as he pondered this, the waiter looking at him expectantly. "Will you show me how to eat it if I order the same?"

I inclined my head again. "Whatever would Rabbi Schwartz think?"

"I couldn't care less."

I nodded and he ordered the lobster as well. I sipped my wine. This had gotten a little more interesting after all.

CHAPTER FORTY

When the lobsters arrived, Dan hesitated briefly, both of us wearing our ridiculous bibs. "You don't have to eat it," I said, cracking a claw open. "But you're missing out."

He looked up at me, then his gaze traveled down to my hands. He picked up the claw in front of him and copied my gesture, breaking it open with a satisfying snap. I lifted mine to him in an approximation of a toast, then took a bite. Dan followed, gingerly, unsure what to expect. "It's—almost sweet," he said as he finished chewing.

I nodded, taking another bite of claw meat. "Practically melts in your mouth." He took a second, heartier bite, and I grinned. "We'll go get some bacon next. Maybe on a cheeseburger."

Dan looked up at me in horror and I laughed. He swallowed his food and then shrugged. "In for a penny, in for a pound. If you say it's worth trying, I'll try it."

I felt the corners of my eyes crinkling. "Sounds like a challenge."

"If it gets you to smile, I will dive into the ocean and find one of these myself."

"You'd have a long way to swim. There are crabs here. I don't think there are lobsters."

"Whatever crustaceans there are."

He was looking at me the way he had in his father's office. And I didn't want that. He might have said he liked me because I was wild, but the reality was he still wanted to put me in a cage. And if I fell for sincere eyes and a smile, I was going to be walking into that cage myself while he locked it behind me.

"What happens if I don't go back to New York?" I asked, leaning back in my seat and crossing my arms.

"Are you thinking about that?"

I wasn't. The plan was always the summer. Ada was supposed to straighten me out or marry me off. And despite her machinations to get me on this date, she had done neither. It sounded like college was still on the table, and Ada hadn't offered to extend my visit. But it was a way to make him realize this wouldn't work.

"Maybe."

"Would you transfer to Bryn Mawr?"

I studied him carefully to see how much he had gotten out of my mother. I didn't have the grades for Bryn Mawr. Not by a long shot. But it seemed to be a genuine question. "I have no idea."

"Just staying with Ada, then?"

"Maybe."

He shrugged. "It'd be disappointing, but it's only a two-hour train ride. If you wanted to see me, I could do that on weekends."

It was the opposite of Freddy's answer. And I kind of hated him for giving it.

"What about you? What are you going to do in the fall?"

Dan made a wry face. "That's a contentious question right now. I'm working on convincing my parents that no, I'm not going to rabbinical school."

"Why not?"

He looked suddenly uncomfortable. "Promise you won't laugh?"

"Absolutely not."

He thought for a moment, pushing his plate away. Then he looked up, his blue eyes earnest and kind and . . . some other emotion I couldn't recognize. "I want to be a photojournalist."

"A what?"

"Someone who takes pictures for newspapers." He looked down again, and I couldn't tell if he was embarrassed at the admission or just unsure how I would react. "I know. There's not a lot of money in that line of work. I understand if it puts you off."

"I don't give a fig about money," I said. He looked back up at me, almost smiling, but not quite.

"That's because you grew up with it—you don't know what it's like to not have it."

"And what do you know about that either?"

We locked eyes. "Nothing, really. I have friends who do though. But, Marilyn—I'd photograph weddings and work at a corner shop and whatever else it took if we . . ." He realized his gaffe and trailed off. "If my family needed the money."

"That right there," I said, pointing at him. "That's the problem. 'I.' I don't want someone who solves problems for me. I want someone who lets me be an equal partner. And I know that may not exist, but if it doesn't, I'm fine being like Ada and not being tied down."

"Okay," he said. "Say you never get married. What are you going to do? Take over the matchmaking game?"

"It's not a game. She's got it down to a science. And no."

"Then what? You mentioned writing?"

I shut my mouth firmly.

"I wouldn't want you to give that up if it's what you love," he said softly. "Besides, I bet you're great at it. You'll make more than I will."

"And you'd be okay with that?"

He shrugged, but he was smiling. "Why not?"

A busboy came and took our plates and our waiter returned, asking if he could show us a dessert menu. "No, I don't think so," I said. "Just the check, please."

"Miss Heller has already paid the bill."

"Of course she has," I said, rolling my eyes. "We should have ordered extra lobsters to go. Had a picnic on the beach."

"Sounds awfully romantic. You sure you'd be up for that?"

He was teasing, but I pointed at him again. "Don't you start." I rose from the table, and Dan followed suit. "Let's go."

Dan threw some bills on the table as a tip, and I stalked out of the restaurant, him in pursuit. He looked at me standing by the car. "I didn't do well enough for a second date, did I?"

He had said all the right things. But there was a big difference between saying he liked me as I was and actually living it. He needed to understand that I didn't follow the same rules that he did. I eyed him carefully, then looked down at my watch. "It's early. You driving back tonight?"

"I don't have to. What did you have in mind?"

I grinned and started walking up toward Dune.

He followed, confused. "Where are we going?"

"Can you sing?" I asked.

"Sing? Not well."

"Shame," I said. "But probably a good thing you decided against being a rabbi, then."

The bay stretched beyond us at the end of the street, the sun just descending over it now. I looked at it briefly, thinking how this was the actual opposite of the sunrise with Freddy. Then we headed south toward 36th Street.

The sign for the Black Eagle glowed neon in front of us. Avalon didn't have much of a nightlife other than the small boardwalk. But I had heard about this place even if I hadn't been.

"A bar?"

"They have live music on weekends," I said. "Come on."

He looked unsure but opened the door for me, the smell of alcohol and cigarettes smacking us in the face.

"You twenty-one?" a bartender called to us as we walked in.

"Twenty-two actually," I lied. The restaurants in town had had no issue with me drinking wine, but the bar was stricter.

"You got ID to prove that?"

"At home—Dan, show him yours."

Dan pulled out his wallet. "Isn't the drinking age eighteen?"

"In New York," the bartender grumbled, inspecting Dan's driver's license. "Twenty-one here since Prohibition. And I get fined if you're not twenty-one."

"I'll vouch for her," Dan said.

"I don't need to drink if you don't believe me," I said. "You can give me a Shirley Temple, and I'll be perfectly content."

He shot me a grumpy look, then asked what Dan wanted. "I'll take a Coke."

We got our drinks, Dan sliding the man a dollar, and then I took his arm and pulled him toward the tiny stage where a band was playing a decent rendition of that new yellow polka-dot bikini song that was all over the radio.

The band finished, and I jumped out of my seat. "What are you doing?" Dan asked.

I flashed him a flirty look over my shoulder. The band was discussing what to play next when I sauntered up. "Hey, boys," I said. The lead singer glanced up and smiled at me. He looked familiar.

"Marilyn, right?"

I studied him. It was the lifeguard who often shared a chair with Freddy. "In the flesh. What's your name again?"

"Louis."

"Well, Louis, think I can get a favor?"

"Sure. What song do you want?"

I shook my head, smiled, and told him what I wanted. He conferred with the band, and they said they thought they could figure it out. Probably helped that the song was a couple years old. Louis offered me his hand, and I took it, climbing up on the stage. I took his place behind the mic as the band launched into "Stupid Cupid," by Connie Francis.

I had danced around my bedroom to that song too many times to count, so I knew all the words. And Louis did the claps behind me as I sang the lyrics, asking Cupid to leave me alone, swaying my hips and making sure I looked directly at Dan at that part. But he wasn't taking the hint. Instead, he was smiling, nodding along.

I rolled my eyes as the joint applauded, then took a quick bow and waved to the room. "Wanna do another?" Louis asked. "A duet maybe?"

"Nope." I pointed to Dan, leaning into the microphone. "But my friend over there wants to sing one."

The color drained from Dan's face. I hopped off the stage and went over to the bar-top table where he sat. "I told you, I can't sing."

I shrugged, sitting down and taking a sip of my Shirley Temple. A waiter arrived, bringing two old-fashioneds on a tray. "On the house," he said.

I picked mine up and took a long drink. "It's not about how good you are. It's about if you can keep up with me."

Dan looked at me for a long moment, then downed most of the drink in front of him, choking slightly on it. "If I do this, I get a second date."

"Sell me on it up there," I said, gesturing toward the stage.

He rose, looking at me one last time, then went to the band. Too quietly for me to hear, he said something to Louis, who then turned around to ask the band, who all nodded, one after another.

I leaned back in my chair, eyeing Dan suspiciously. He was going to chicken out.

But he didn't. He loosened his tie, then removed it and unbuttoned the top two buttons of his shirt. A woman at the bar wolf-whistled. Then the band launched into Elvis's "It's Now or Never," another song that was dominating the radio waves that summer.

To his credit, Dan was telling the truth when he said he couldn't sing. But he *could* do an Elvis impression, leaning the mic down and crooning off-key toward me as he sang the lyrics, asking me to be his tonight.

And despite myself, I found a smile on my face. He bumbled his way through the second verse, but he didn't quit. And he didn't take his eyes off me the whole time.

When he finished, the patrons rose and cheered. Louis clapped him on the back, and he jumped down, coming back toward me.

"How was that?"

I bit my bottom lip in mock concentration. "Well . . . vocal quality was a C, if I'm being generous. But you do get an A for the effort there."

"So a B average?"

"If I'm being generous."

"Do I get another date?"

I smiled again. "You get a continuation of this one. Let's go get ice cream."

He offered me his arm, and I took it.

CHAPTER FORTY-ONE

We got soft-serve cones at Avalon Freeze and then walked down to the boardwalk—a quiet one in Avalon, more for strolls than carnivals—where we sat on a bench, watching the moon reflecting in the rippling waves.

"I see why you don't want to go home," Dan said. "It's peaceful here. You can hear yourself think."

"Not like the Catskills or the Hamptons, where it's all about impressing everyone." Our families had spent several summers at the same Catskills resort when we were kids.

"No. Nothing like that."

I laughed softly. "Were you there the summer that someone put a bunch of fish in the fountain in the lobby?" He grinned broadly. "What?"

"Who do you think put the fish in there?"

I smacked him lightly with the back of my hand. "You did not!"

He took my hand, and for a moment we both looked at each other. And I realized I wouldn't be averse to him kissing me. We'd already done that much anyway. But he kissed my hand instead, then kept it in his. "I did. The rabbi was *not* pleased."

"Is he ever?"

"Not with me lately, no."

"Sorry about that."

Dan's eyes reflected the moonlight. "Nothing to be sorry about. Takes two to tango. Or destroy the ark at a synagogue."

I looked back out over the water. "Why didn't you just ask me out?"

"I did."

"No. I mean instead of proposing."

He was quiet for a moment. "If we hadn't gotten caught, I would have."

We both contemplated the alternate life that could have been. The me of two months ago would have gone on a date with him. Maybe more. But I wouldn't have come to Ada, then.

"Did they ever replace the stained glass?"

Dan's mouth twitched into a smile. "It's a piece of plywood with some embroidery that my mother made over it. The synagogue board can't decide if they should recommission the stained glass or if they should do something more solid."

"In case I ever go back to shul?"

"Your name wasn't specifically mentioned, but yes. I think they'd opt for reinforced steel if you were home this summer."

I laughed. "What a mess."

"And I've got the scar to prove it." He held up his left hand, which did have an angry red mark.

I took his hand, examining it in the dimness of the boardwalk light, and running my thumb over it. "At least you'll always remember me."

He reached for my cheek with his right hand, his left still in mine. "I couldn't forget you if I tried," he said, our faces suddenly much closer as he leaned toward me.

"Then don't try," I whispered just before our lips met.

This was neither our first kiss, where he seemed to be asking if it was okay, nor the next ones, where we so hungrily devoured each other that we didn't know what happened until the whole congregation was staring at us.

This was slower, as if we had all the time in the world, and the sensation of falling now was all inside of me.

He pulled back, caressing my cheek with his thumb. "I should get you home before it gets too late."

"Ada doesn't care. I'm surprised she didn't shove a prophylactic in my purse."

Dan threw his head back in laughter. "Did you really just say that?"

I shrugged. "I thought that was what you liked about me."

He wrapped an arm around me. "It absolutely is. But I'm not rushing things this time." He looked down at the beach. "How far of a walk would it be to get back from here?"

I did the math in my head. "Only about five blocks."

"How does a moonlight walk on the beach sound?"

I stood up, still holding his hand. "Very romantic—like something the rabbi and my father would heartily disapprove of. Let's do it."

Ada had left the porch lights on, and the light of the television was visible through the den window. "She must have waited up for us. She goes to bed by nine thirty every night so she can get up and swim at six."

"You really care about her, don't you?"

I nodded. "She's—she's like me. She's entirely who she is. And she lives exactly how she wants to." I thought for a moment. "I don't know that I want to be alone my whole life, but she's taught me that I don't have to be like everyone else."

"I hope I get to know her better," Dan said.

"Come for lunch before you go back to New York tomorrow. Ada would love to have you."

"If you want me to, that's all that matters."

"I'm sorry I slammed the door in your face."

He shook his head. "I'm not sorry for any of it."

"Not even proposing?"

"Not even that. We wound up where we were supposed to be."

He kissed me goodnight, walking me up the porch steps and waiting until I was inside before going back down them. We decided to go to the beach in the morning before lunch, and he would leave for the city after that.

I went inside, shutting the door behind me, and leaned on it, grinning from ear to ear until the noise of the television distracted me from my reverie. "Did you really wait up for me?" I asked, walking into the den.

Ada lay in her chair, her body completely slack, her mouth open. My heart stopped beating.

"No no no no no! Ada. ADA!" I ran to her, hands shaking.

She startled awake and swatted at me. "What's the matter with you?"

I sat suddenly on the floor, breathing heavily. "I thought—you weren't moving—I—you scared me!"

"I fell asleep because you stayed out so late. And besides, I thought I was too mean to die?"

"You absolutely are," I said, shaking my head. "But can you not *look* so dead when you sleep? Jeepers creepers!"

"What's the fun in that?" she asked, her eyes twinkling. "Now tell me all about your date."

CHAPTER FORTY-TWO

Dan arrived at nine, dressed in a T-shirt and pair of trunks he had bought at Hoy's—which I knew because the trunks still had a tag attached. I pulled it off for him.

"Why didn't you tell me you didn't have a suit?"

He shrugged. "I didn't want you to suggest something else."

"No," I said, shaking my head. "I don't want games or you trying to impress me like that. I want you to be who you are. And be honest."

"That's fair."

My lips twitched into a smile. "I'd have just told you to go get one at Hoy's anyway."

We stood there grinning at each other until Ada came to the door as well. "I thought you two were going to the beach, not standing on my porch all morning letting flies in the house."

"What's that expression again? You catch more flies with honey than with vinegar?" Ada looked at me warily. "Don't worry. You're pure vinegar. The flies won't bother you."

She swiped at me, and I jumped out of the way, laughing. "Get out of here," she said. "Be back in time to get cleaned up. We have a reservation at one."

"I'll have her back on time," Dan said.

"Who cares about her? You're the one I want to have lunch with."

"Real nice," I said, taking Dan's hand and tugging him down the steps. "We're going now."

We climbed the path over the dunes, hand in hand. The beach was empty except for a couple of families, so it was easy to find a private spot. We spread our towels, Dan's sporting a Hoy's sticker. "Honestly, did you think we wouldn't have beach towels at a beach house?"

He placed a hand over his heart. "From now on, I will consult you before making any and all beach purchases."

"I'm just saying, if you're going to be a penniless photojournalist, there are better things to spend your money on."

"Like taking you out on dates?"

"Well, there's that. I assume Ada won't foot the bill forever. Then again, she seems to like you better than she likes me." I pulled off my caftan, and Dan's eyes widened at my bikini. I cocked a finger at him. "You behave now," I said as I sat on my towel.

He removed his shirt as well, then sat on his towel. "You asked why I didn't tell you I hadn't brought a bathing suit—you just answered your own question. Look what I would have missed if you said we should go play miniature golf instead."

"I wouldn't have suggested miniature golf."

"No?"

"No. I'm terrible at it and I like to win."

"Then we'll have to play sometime. Level the playing field after you made me sing in public."

I laughed. "I'm definitely better at golf than you are at singing."

"You, on the other hand, can sing. Ever thought about doing that for real?"

"Nah," I said, shaking my head.

"Then what *do* you want to do? You never answered that last night. I know housewife isn't your dream job."

I picked at my towel, suddenly shy. "Ada got me a typewriter," I said quietly. "I'm working on a book."

"That's right," he said. "Can I ask what it's about?"

"It's . . ." I stared off at the ocean. "I don't know how to describe it exactly. It's not about me, but it's about a girl who feels kind of trapped in the New York social scene and her family's narrow views."

"So your situation, just not you?"

I glanced at him to see if he was being sardonic, but he was watching me with genuine interest, so I nodded.

"I have a feeling—as unique as you are—that you're not the only one who secretly feels that way. Considering I'm bucking family expectations too and all."

"That's true. Maybe I'll make her become a photojournalist."

He grinned. "Do you know anything about photography?" I shook my head. "I'll bring my camera next time I come down here. I can teach you the basics."

"Next time, huh?"

He leaned in and kissed my cheek. "Yes."

I couldn't help but smile.

~

Ada took us back to the Whitebrier for lunch. I ordered the same salad with crab, Dan saying it sounded good and that he would have the same. Ada raised an eyebrow. "I thought you were a rabbi's son?"

"Son, yes. But that doesn't make me a rabbi."

"Touché," Ada said. She looked at me and suppressed a smile.

"What?" I asked her.

"Don't say, 'What,' say, 'Pardon me,'" Ada said. I rolled my eyes. "And don't do that either. I don't imagine Dan here would stick around if your eyes stayed like that."

He leaned over to me. "I would," he whispered.

She pursed her lips in amusement. "And in answer to your question, I was just thinking that this might be the best match I didn't make."

I patted her hand. "You forced me to go out with him, so I think you can take credit."

"Thanks for the crumbs from your table," she said, peeling my hand off hers.

"Is it still a match if we don't get married?" Dan asked. "Marilyn made it quite clear that's not on the menu."

"I suppose living in sin counts," she said.

I choked on my water while Dan hid his smile behind his napkin. "Ada!"

"What?" she asked and took a sip of her own water.

"Don't say, 'What,' say, 'Pardon me,'" I parroted sarcastically.

Ada leaned in conspiratorially toward Dan. "Are you sure you want to get involved with this mess?"

"Ada!"

Dan leaned in toward her as well. "Yes, ma'am. I've never been more sure of anything in my life."

"Well then, Marilyn," Ada said. "I suppose I can send you back to New York now. I've done what your father asked—minus the marriage part. Though I suppose you'll change your mind on that eventually. Most girls do."

I could feel the blood draining from my face. She was sending me back? I liked Dan and all but—

"No," I said. "You can't do that."

"Oh, can't I?"

"Ada, please!"

She smiled wickedly. "Shush. You're not going anywhere until you finish those scrapbooks. That was just for calling me all vinegar earlier."

My shoulders sank in relief. "You're terrible, you know that?"

"In the best possible way."

"I'll drink to that," Dan said. "Now what's this about scrapbooks?"

"Dan wants to be a photojournalist," I told Ada. "She's got me going through all eight hundred years of her life in photographs."

"Don't be impertinent," Ada said. "Photography was only invented last century. And believe it or not, it predates me." She looked back at Dan. "Tell me more about photojournalism. Why is that worth disgracing your father by refusing to follow in his footsteps?"

Dan glanced at me, hiding a smile at the question. "To be fair, they don't know yet. I'm breaking the news slowly and hoping they'll eventually think it was their idea. But it's—well—I suppose it's a little like writing." I tilted my head at that answer, sure he was about to prove he didn't understand what I wanted to do. "I like being able to tell a story, just in images. There's so much nuance to a good photograph. It can capture so much emotion, all by snapping the exact right moment and framing it correctly. You get to decide what to focus on and what to blur." He gestured to the ocean sprawling to his right. "A picture of the horizon doesn't tell you anything. But look at the family on the beach."

Ada and I both turned to look at the mother, father, and two children. The father sat in a chair under the umbrella, a newspaper in front of his face, while the mother fed the children sandwiches. As we watched, the little girl dropped her meal in the sand and began to cry. The mother picked her up to comfort her but shot an annoyed glance at her husband, who had not budged.

"Right there—depending on the moment you capture, it tells a different story. You could show a lovely vacation. Or an unhappy marriage. Or something straight out of Norman Rockwell."

"Close your mouth, darling," Ada said to me, tapping me on the chin. I hadn't realized it was open, and I shut it with a snap. Dan was right. That was exactly what I did. Just with the proverbial thousand words instead of a single picture.

"Meanwhile," Ada continued, "I set that couple up six years ago now. So you'd best not tell the story of an unhappy marriage with that picture or that novel."

Dan and I both laughed, and he reached for my hand under the table, squeezing it gently.

~

When lunch was over, Ada drove home, but Dan and I walked back toward the Princeton. "I'm glad you came," I said.

He pulled me in and kissed me lightly. "I am too."

"Will you come visit again? We don't go back to Philadelphia until Labor Day."

"I would love to. But what happens after Labor Day?"

I bit my bottom lip. "I don't know," I confessed. "I guess I'm supposed to go back to college if my father agrees."

"Would it help or hurt if he knew we were . . . well, whatever we are?"

I thought for a moment. It would help, of course. The prestige of the rabbi's son would overshadow how we found each other. But then I would have to go back to New York and the rules and expectations that went with being there. And Daddy expected me to get married. But even if I fell madly in love with Dan, I didn't see a scenario where I didn't wind up reading a book at the kitchen stove with children screaming in the background.

"I don't know."

He put a hand on my cheek, turning my face to his. "Hey—I'm not going to ask you to do anything you don't want to do. If college—and New York—aren't where you want to wind up, that's fine by me."

"Can we just take it one step at a time? I don't know what I'm going to do in the fall. I don't know if Ada will let me stay. I don't know if I want to go back. And I don't know if I have a choice."

He pulled me toward him in a hug. "You have a choice, Marilyn. I meant what I said last night. I can pick up extra jobs and do whatever it takes. If you don't want to go back and Ada turns you out, you still have a choice." He leaned back so I would look at him. "And when you become a world-famous author, we'll switch and you can support me."

I laughed. "How about another date before we make that decision?"

"That sounds perfect. Next weekend?" I nodded, and he kissed me again. "Come on. I'll drive you home first."

I climbed into the front seat of his car. "Do you know, I never learned how to drive?"

"You didn't?"

"Why would I in the city?"

He considered this for a moment, the different worlds that we lived in just based on the bodies we were born into and the roles our families expected us to play in them. "Do you want to learn?"

"I think I do, actually."

Dan smiled. "Sounds like a date. Next weekend."

"Next weekend," I repeated.

CHAPTER
FORTY-THREE

Ada cleared her schedule the day before Lillian was due to arrive and threw herself into a tizzy making sure the house was perfect.

"I don't understand," I said to Frannie as I helped her put fresh linens on Lillian's bed for the second time that week. "We just changed the sheets. No one has slept on them. And why does she care so much? Doesn't Lillian work for her?"

"I just do what I'm told," Frannie said with a shrug. "They're very fond of each other, and Miss Ada likes to make sure everything is perfect for her guests."

"Did she go to this much trouble for me?"

Frannie suppressed a smile.

"What?"

"No. But you're family."

I thought about that for a moment. I was blood, yes. And I supposed I had heard of Ada in my childhood from time to time, but I didn't know her before being sent to Philadelphia. She felt like family now. But there was more to being family than shared ancestors. I looked at Frannie, who was making sure the bed had perfect hospital corners.

"Frannie, how long have you worked for Ada?"

She straightened up, putting a hand to her lower back, and thought for a moment. "Going on twenty-five years now. I was nineteen when she hired me."

Before I was even born. And now she had a house here for her family to vacation. "And you have kids?"

Frannie nodded. "They're grown now. But they come down for the weekends over the summer."

I tried to picture giving our maid, Grace, a house for the summer. We didn't have the kind of money that Ada did, and we still paid her for the summer when we spent it at the Catskills so she wouldn't take another job. But it wasn't that kind of a relationship either.

"Frannie!" Ada called from downstairs. "When you're finished, I need help with the flowers—you're better at the arrangements."

"Coming, Miss Ada!" She turned to me as I was about to sit on the bed. "Don't you sit on that bed that I just made now, or I'll have to make it again."

I looked at the pale blue quilt, wondering what kind of tyrant I was about to meet if the house had to be so perfect that a wrinkle in a blanket would require a whole bed being remade. The summer had just taken on a rose-colored hue with the reintroduction of Dan, and I was loath to let that go. I went to leave but turned a glass perfume bottle on the dresser a quarter inch first, just for the satisfaction of making something not perfect for this stranger who was coming to spoil my summer.

~

Ada left the following morning to pick Lillian up from the train station in Atlantic City. I offered to go with her, but Ada pointed a finger at me. "You stay here and make sure this house is spotless," she said.

I pouted a little. I didn't like Lillian. She was already intruding on my time with Ada. She didn't need a paid companion anymore. She had me. And especially with Dan's confidence that we would figure something out even if I didn't go back to New York, I was leaning more and more toward staying. Perhaps I would feel differently once we were back in Philadelphia, but absence had made the heart grow fonder there. It didn't have to be New York. It had its own charms.

I went up to my room and tried to do some writing, but I was too moody and the words weren't coming. I felt like I was being replaced. Which was ridiculous, because I had come in and supplanted Lillian, not the other way around.

I wandered into Lillian's room. The perfume bottle had been returned to its proper position. I moved it again with the listlessness of a cat that knocks everything to the ground.

Finally, I heard a car outside, ran down the steps, and peeked through the screened living room window to catch a glimpse of her.

But before I even saw Lillian, I realized that Ada was *smiling*. Actually smiling. I thought back to the day she picked me up at the train. I hadn't gotten a welcome like that. And I vowed to be on my very best behavior, to Ada at least, to make it clear that she didn't *need* an outsider when I was there.

Lillian's hair was wrapped in a scarf, large sunglasses hiding her face as she opened her car door and stepped out. She was slender, but tightly girdled into a yellow shirtwaist dress. She pulled the scarf from her mousy brown hair and stood for a moment, removing her sunglasses to look up at the house. Then she leaned in to say something to Ada, who smiled and nodded, gesturing for her to go inside.

I dashed to the front door to avoid being caught at the window, and threw it open just as they reached the porch.

"Ah, the prodigal daughter herself," Ada said. "Lillian, this is my niece, Marilyn. Marilyn, this is Lillian."

I stuck out my hand, but Lillian pulled me in for a hug. "I've heard so much about you from Ada that I feel like I know you already." She leaned back to look at me, brushing my hair from my face. "Why, she looks like you," she said to Ada. "Look at those cheekbones."

I looked at Ada, fifty-five years my senior, trying to see any resemblance. I supposed there was some from the pictures of her youth, but I looked more like my mother than her.

Lillian was younger than Ada, but her face was lined around her eyes and mouth, the reason being apparent when she smiled warmly. And as much as I still didn't want her intruding, I felt the slightest twinge of guilt at moving her perfume bottle.

"Why don't you go rest for a little while?" Ada suggested. "I have a table reserved for lunch, but we can always have something here if you're not up to going out just yet."

"I just need a little nap and a shower and I'll be right as rain," Lillian said. "Besides, I've been missing that crab salad all summer."

"I'm sorry about your mother," I said.

Both women looked to me, as if they had forgotten I was there. Lillian took my hand and squeezed it. "Thank you, dear."

"Go get situated," Ada said. "You two can get acquainted later. Lillian needs to rest."

"I'm fine," Lillian insisted but allowed Ada to prod her up the stairs.

"I'm going to change while you nap," Ada said. Then she turned to me. "Why don't you run on down to the market and get some more flowers for the living room?"

I glanced at the living room, where no fewer than four bouquets sat on available surfaces. "Shouldn't we leave some for . . . anyone else on the island?"

Ada fixed me with a look that told me I would go if I knew what was good for me. "Okay, then," I said, grabbing my handbag. "I guess I'll be back with flowers."

On my way into town, I passed Shirley, who was returning with a bag from Hoy's. She glared at me. "Good morning, Shirley," I said. "I hope you're well."

"Very well, thank you. We just had a wedding after all."

She was trying to sting me—I wasn't completely sure if it was for throwing off her brother or for not seeking out her friendship after everything happened. And she would never understand that she couldn't upset me—at least not about Freddy. "That's right. I hope they're very happy."

"They are," she said with venom.

"Good. I hope you will be too."

She opened her mouth, but nothing came out, and I continued walking.

When I returned, having taken my time and gotten a cup of coffee at the bakery, Ada was in the living room reading. Lillian was nowhere to be seen. I handed the flowers off to Frannie, who muttered about being out of vases before taking them from me. Then I joined Ada in the living room. She didn't look up from her book.

"Lillian seems nice," I said eventually.

"She is."

I took a deep breath. "I was thinking—what if I didn't go back to New York in the fall?"

Ada was still in her book. "And what would you do instead?"

Not the response I was hoping for. "I was thinking I'd stay on with you—if you'd have me, that is."

"An interesting idea. What about young Mr. Schwartz?"

I rolled my eyes. "We had one date."

"Two."

"You came along for lunch. That doesn't count."

"But you went to the beach before that, which does." She flipped the page.

"Okay, we've had two dates. And he said we'll figure it out if I don't go back."

She hid a small smirk. "I'm not sure your parents would approve that idea—although dating the rabbi's son would probably help."

"Well, they're not sending me back to school yet anyway—"

"Actually, I received a letter from your mother this morning. It seems your father has finally agreed that you can return to college."

That startled me. Mama was writing to Ada? Her letters to me arrived like clockwork each Thursday. But I had never seen one from her addressed to Ada. And why would she tell Ada about college before me?

"I don't know that I want to go back."

"You could take writing classes." She was still at least pretending to read her book.

I hadn't thought of that. But— "I could take those in Philadelphia too." I came and knelt in front of her, taking her book and putting it aside, leaving her no choice but to look at me. "And I mean—you wouldn't have to pay Lillian. I can be your companion. I've done a good job of it this summer, haven't I?"

Ada examined me. "Aside from Mr. Goldman, I assume you mean?"

"I've already apologized for that. Nothing like that will happen again."

"And you'd have me just cast Lillian out? She's lived with me for fifteen years. Where would she go?"

"I don't have to replace her," I said. "I just thought—"

"I'm not your mother, Marilyn. I suggest you speak with your parents before you make plans." She reached around me for her book.

"Ada, please—"

"We have nearly four more weeks until Labor Day," Ada said crisply. "A lot can happen in four weeks. I don't make plans that far in advance regardless."

I got up, shaking my head angrily, my strategy to be on my best behavior and make myself indispensable to her forgotten. "You know, I'm trying to help here. It's not just me being selfish."

Ada flipped another page. There was no way she was actually reading. "Not 'just,' no. Thank you so much for your act of selflessness in offering to put one woman out on the street to stay with another and avoid your family. We truly appreciate your sacrifice."

I glared at her. "Fine. You two can sit around like the witches that you are, and who cares what happens to me?"

"My, it sounds like I've missed plenty of excitement this summer," Lillian said from behind me, making me jump.

Ada calmly folded down the page of her novel and placed it on the coffee table. "That was fast," she said, rising. "Are you hungry?"

"Famished."

"Wonderful. Let's go to lunch." She looked at me. "Are you done with your tantrum? I'm not sure they allow misbehaving children."

I shook my head. "You go. I'd hate to intrude."

Lillian put a hand on my arm. "Please come. I'd like to get to know you better."

Ada stalked past her. "Leave her be. She can join us for dinner if she's over this little pique by then."

Lillian sighed, following Ada, with a sidelong glance back at me.

But after they left, I went to the window to spy.

"—that about?"

I saw Ada shake her head. "She's been getting all my attention all summer and is jealous, I think."

Lillian made a tsk-tsk sound. "Oh dear. I'll win her over yet."

"You shouldn't have to. You've had a hard enough time."

Ada started the car, and I couldn't hear them over the engine, but Lillian said something that made her laugh.

Once they were gone, I went to the living room phone and called my mother, not caring that it was long distance.

"Kleinman residence," Grace answered, sounding bored.

"It's Marilyn. Is Mama home?"

"Marilyn? Is everything all right?"

"Yes," I said in annoyance. "Put Mama on, please."

"But why are you calling?"

"Grace. Put Mama on the phone."

There were murmured voices and a shuffling sound before my mother spoke. "Marilyn? What's wrong?"

"Nothing is wrong."

"Then why are you calling?"

I sighed. "Ada said Daddy is sending me back to school?"

My mother exhaled, then spoke more quietly. "I believe so, yes. He hasn't sent the check yet."

"Mama, what would you think if I stayed here instead?"

"Why would you want to do that?"

I didn't know how to answer that question and make her understand. "I like it here," I said eventually.

"Marilyn, I don't understand. Is it a boy? I spent all summer trying to get your father to come around after what you did, and now you're saying you don't want that?"

The last ray of hope I had been holding on to began to sink into the pit of my stomach. "It's not a boy. I—I just haven't decided what I want to do yet."

"Well, decide quickly that you want to come home, because he's going to sign that check any day now if he hasn't already." I didn't reply and she softened. "I miss you."

I missed her too. And Daddy, despite the circumstances under which we parted. But the idea of returning to my childhood bedroom in the brownstone made me feel sick. So I told her I missed her as well and that I had to go before I ran the phone bill up too high.

"Enjoy this last month," she said. "You're making such wonderful memories."

I wanted to say, "Like you did?" but I couldn't. If she hadn't told me, it wasn't fair to let her know Ada had. And she would suspect, if Ada told me, that I'd had my own troubles. So I agreed noncommittally, said that I loved her, and hung up.

Then I went out to the porch and lay down on the wicker love seat, wishing Lillian didn't exist.

CHAPTER FORTY-FOUR

I wandered down to the beach while they were gone, but I couldn't focus on my book. Instead, I wound up sitting on my towel, watching the waves break on the shore. Daddy was going to send the payment for college. I would be closer to Dan. But what if I didn't *want* to be closer to Dan? Dating him here felt safe and exciting at the same time. Dating him in New York—was there any scenario where I didn't wind up living the exact life I wanted to avoid?

My shoulders sagged. Why did it all have to be so complicated? I didn't want both a fiancé and my parents to die in order to live my own life the way Ada had. But what other options did I really have?

Clouds blocked the sun, and I shivered as a cold wind came in from town. The handful of people still on the beach were packing up, and when I turned to look behind me, I saw why: dark clouds menaced with an approaching storm. I quickly gathered my things, but I wasn't quite fast enough and wound up sprinting along the dune path in pelting rain that stung like needles when it hit my skin. I couldn't see more than a few inches in front of my face, and I nearly fell as the gusts flung random debris into my path.

By the time I reached the house, I was soaking wet and shivering as the wind whipped my towel and hair furiously.

Lillian threw the front door open just as I reached for it. "Oh, you poor thing. Come in, let's get you warm and dry." She took my arm and pulled me inside, shutting it behind me. "Ada! I need towels!"

I looked at her curiously, wondering if Ada would yell for her not to yell room to room, but she came flying down the stairs with two bath towels, stopping short when she saw me. "Good gracious. You look like a drowned rat."

"I feel like one," I sniffed miserably.

Lillian took a towel from her and wrapped it around me, rubbing my shoulders with it the way my mother did when I was little and had just stepped out of the tub. "She's ice cold," Lillian said. "Let's run you a bath."

"I'm okay, really. It just came out of nowhere."

A loud crack of thunder sounded, startling me. "Nonsense," Lillian said. "Let's get you warmed up. It'll blow over quickly, and then we'll all go have dinner tonight."

Ada was looking out the windows that faced west toward the bay. "I think this one will last. The worst is still coming."

"I'm going to start the bath," Lillian said. "You come on up whenever you're ready." She climbed the stairs.

"Still want to replace her?" Ada asked.

I made a sour face, daring her to tell me it would cause wrinkles. "At least *someone* cares if I live or die."

"Darling, I care if you die. I would have to figure out how to get your body out so the house wouldn't smell like something out of a Faulkner story."

I shook my head, muttering as I went up the stairs. Lillian was sitting on the side of the tub, pouring a liberal helping of bubbles into the water. "I took these from Ada," she said, winking conspiratorially. "Let's let that be our little secret."

"She'll probably smell them on me and know. She always knows."

Lillian smiled warmly. "Well, I'll handle that if so. Come on. Suit off. A hot bath will do its job, and you'll feel good as new."

She turned around to give me privacy, but I didn't remove my towel. Was she really going to stay while I took a bath?

As if she could hear my thoughts, she said, "It's okay, I'm a nurse."

"But you're not *my* nurse," I said.

"That's more than fair. I'll be just down the hall. Holler if you need anything."

I looked at her skeptically. "Ada always tells me not to yell room to room."

Lillian shook her head. "Too many rules, that one. If you need anything, you just call." She rubbed my shoulder affectionately, then left the room, closing the door behind her.

I let the towel fall to the floor and stepped out of my bathing suit, dropping it as well, then climbed into the bath. It was uncomfortably hot against my cold skin at first, but after just a minute, I was revived. I sank under the bubbles, getting the blown sand out of my hair, then came back up, lying against the edge of the tub, immersed up to my neck, the jasmine and lilac scent of the bubbles soothing my nerves, even as another thundercrack rattled the house.

Once I stepped out and wrapped a fresh towel around myself and another into a turban over my hair, I felt like myself again. I grabbed my robe from the hook on the back of the door and slipped it over my shoulders, then went down the hall to my room to dress.

I peeked out my window just in time to see lightning hit the bay. It was only a little after four, but I doubted we were going to dinner that night. Ada had been right. The sky was as dark as night.

Instead of the dress I would have worn to go out, I pulled on a pair of clam diggers and a blouse, then padded downstairs, where Lillian and Ada were talking in the living room, Lillian curled up on the corner of the sofa, her feet tucked under her, Ada in the chair perpendicular to her.

"There she is," Lillian said. "Feeling better?"

"Much," I said. "Thank you." But I hesitated. "I don't want to interrupt."

Ada looked at me appraisingly, but Lillian gestured toward the spot on the sofa next to her. "You're not at all, but how sweet of you. Come, sit."

"She is a little," Ada said.

"Hush. I want to get to know her for myself."

I looked at Ada, imagining her breathing fire like a dragon at being told to hush, but she looked quite content.

Score one for Lillian, I thought as I sat.

"Now, Marilyn. How are you enjoying Avalon?"

"She likes the beach patrol a little too much," Ada said.

Lillian suppressed a laugh. "Yes, your aunt told me about that debacle."

"*Debacle* is certainly the word for it," I said cautiously. "I ran into his sister in town this morning. She said they're happily married now."

Ada pursed her lips. "And his mother will be all over town seven months from now claiming a nine-pound baby was born prematurely."

Lillian's lips twitched as she tried not to laugh again. "You're terrible," she said to Ada. "But absolutely right." She turned back to me. "I hear you've been writing a novel?"

"You probably heard what it's about too, since Ada sneaks into my room and reads it."

"It's not sneaking if it's my house," Ada said. "And it's quite good. Needs editing of course. But you have a natural voice for storytelling."

I stared at her. If it wasn't up to snuff, she would be the first one to say it. And without any niceties couching it to spare my feelings.

"Well, I'm not the type to read something without permission," Lillian said. "But when you're ready, I'd love to."

Thunder boomed again, and this time the power went out.

"Oh for the love of—" Ada said. "It'll be out all night."

"And we've weathered worse before," Lillian said. She rose, feeling her way to the mantel, where a candle and matches sat. She struck a match and lit the candle. "Let's get the rest of these. Is the lantern still in the hall closet?"

"I believe so, unless Frannie moved it."

"Where *is* Frannie?" I asked.

"We sent her home as soon as we saw the clouds rolling in," Lillian said, heading to the closet. She returned with a Coleman lantern, bathing the room in soft light. "We can manage dinner on our own tonight."

"Everything in the icebox is going to go bad."

"Then we'll use what we can and go shopping tomorrow. Where's your sense of adventure?"

Ada scowled at her.

"That'll cause wrinkles," I said.

Lillian let out a merry peal of laughter. "I like this one," she said to Ada. "She's got spunk, like you." She turned back to me. "How are you in the kitchen?"

"Terrible."

"Exactly like your dear aunt," Lillian said. "But we'll make do. Ada, let's open a bottle of wine and see what we can come up with."

~

The luminescent dial on my watch told me we were eating dinner early, when we sat down to a meal of a salad, salmon, and corn, but we were on our second bottle of wine and absolutely no one complained. Perhaps it was the wine or the feeling of roughing it in the dark, but everything was delicious. "If Frannie ever decides to leave, you'll be set," I told Ada.

"Frannie's not going anywhere."

"Why would she?" I agreed. "She gets a beach house. It's a sweet gig. Even if she has to put up with you." I put my hand on hers affectionately. She pulled it out from under mine and whacked my arm with it.

"If my company is so inadequate, I don't understand why you want to stay through the fall."

Lillian looked at me with great interest. "Really?"

I bit my bottom lip. I was tipsy, but everything had been turned topsy-turvy today. "Maybe. But that one doesn't want me."

"I didn't say that," Ada said. "I said it was up to your parents."

"And you know full well Mama will listen to you after—" I stopped myself. I didn't know how much Lillian knew of our family business, even if she had been clued in on my affair with Freddy.

"I'm sure Rose would take Ada's advice into consideration," Lillian said smoothly. She was looking at Ada, not me, but I got the impression she knew exactly what she was talking about.

"If I were so inclined, it's likely," Ada agreed. "But I don't have much tolerance for people who won't abide by the rules."

Lillian shook her head. "Oh, Ada, lighten up. If the girl doesn't want to go back to New York, what good will forcing her do?" She turned to me. "It'll all work out."

"She's been trouble," Ada argued.

"And you like trouble, so don't pretend that's a problem. It's like you've forgotten that forbidding a twenty-year-old to do something is a guarantee that she'll do it."

The two women stared at each other for a moment, communicating something I couldn't understand from their shared past. "I'll think about it," Ada conceded.

Lillian patted my leg under the table and winked at me. And just like that, I realized that far from being a threat, she was going to be my biggest ally in this house.

~

Thoroughly in our cups, we wound up poring over the albums I had made by candlelight. "This is marvelous," Lillian said. "Truly."

I glowed under the praise and the warmth of the wine. I had a blanket over me, lying sleepily on the sofa.

I had half dozed off when an exclamation from Lillian woke me. "There I am!"

I sat up. They were only in the second album. I hadn't gotten close to photographs from the last fifteen years yet. "Where?" I asked.

Lillian pointed to a picture of a group of women in nurse's uniforms in front of the Trevi Fountain. Ada was in the middle. I recognized her in her youth easily by now. Lillian's finger tapped one of the younger women, at the edge of the group. "Right there."

I turned to Ada warily. "You said you didn't remember who the other nurses in Italy were."

She grinned and shrugged.

"You've been friends that long?"

"We met in Europe," Lillian said. "I got married, and we lost touch for a while. Then Don died, and Ada wrote to me when she saw the obituary. We corresponded for a few years, and once my kids were out of the house, Ada asked if I wanted to come stay with her for a bit. Fifteen years later, here we are."

"You have kids?"

"And grandchildren now. They come to visit most summers, but they went to Chicago instead for the funeral this year."

I tried to picture children running around this house. There was no way. Ada must have rented them another house. Then again, this was Ada. She probably owned six rental properties in town.

But the war ended in 1919. Which meant they had been friends for over forty years. No wonder Ada reacted that way when I suggested she didn't need Lillian anymore.

I studied Lillian's young face in the flickering light. I would look more carefully now to see if she popped up again. But that was a job for the following days as I could hardly keep my eyes open. So I excused myself and stumbled up to bed, the blanket from the sofa still wrapped around me as Lillian and Ada continued drinking and flipping through the photo album.

CHAPTER FORTY-FIVE

I woke up convinced I was dying. Someone was drumming on my head, and my mouth felt gritty, like I had eaten sand. I had drunk too much before, but never wine. And I was pretty sure that a wine hangover was a level of Dante's *Inferno*.

By the time I made it downstairs in search of aspirin and water, it was almost nine.

"It's alive," Ada said from the living room.

I blinked at her. She didn't look like she'd had a drop the night before. That woman probably still woke up at six and went swimming. She clearly wasn't human.

Lillian looked a little worse for the wear but was more functional than I was. "Frannie has breakfast ready for you. Ada wanted to wake you, but I said to let you sleep."

"Bless you," I said. Lillian chuckled, and I staggered into the dining room. A place was set at the table with two aspirins next to the plate.

Frannie poured coffee in the waiting cup, and I topped it off with cream and sugar, using that to wash down the pills. Eggs and toast appeared in front of me. "The food didn't spoil?" I asked, not sure I would be able to keep anything down even if it was good.

"It did. I stopped at the store on my way in this morning."

"You really are the best," I said, gingerly nibbling on a piece of toast. Frannie ducked her head, and I heard the doorbell ring. "She has clients this morning?"

"Of course," Frannie said. "She doesn't take many days off."

"Are there really that many unmarried people?"

Frannie nodded. "They come from all over in the summer."

I shook my head, instantly regretting the motion. "I don't know how she does it."

"I don't either. But she's good at it." She looked at me pityingly. "Drink a lot of water. It'll help more than that coffee."

I didn't think that was true, but I drank as much as I could without risking bringing it back up. How a seventy-five-year-old woman out-drank me, I couldn't say. But here I was.

After breakfast, I snuck a peek in the living room, despite being forbidden to do so. Lillian was seated at Ada's side, taking notes. No chair in the corner for her. I shrugged. She could have that job. I preferred daydreaming and concocting stories about the photographs I was cataloging anyway.

~

By the end of the week, it felt like Lillian had always been with us. She was funny and kind and enjoyed getting Ada's goat as much as I did. Ada wasn't softer, exactly, with her there, but she was more likely to acquiesce to Lillian than to me. And Lillian was perfectly happy to take my side in disagreements.

I never would have made it out the window to meet Freddy with Lillian there though. She was a bedtime talker, coming in before she went to sleep, sitting on my bed, and asking a million questions about me and what I was writing.

Then again, I still thought Ada knew what I was up to the whole time.

Thursday night, I handed Lillian a stack of pages. "What's this?" she asked.

"Chapter one."

Lillian clutched it to her chest, then pulled me in for a hug. Neither of us needed to say anything. I was sure Ada had told her that I had suggested she send Lillian packing before I met her, and she clearly understood that sharing my work with her was a sign of acceptance.

The pages were at my place at the dining room table when I came down for breakfast the following morning. The two of them stopped talking as I entered the room. I hadn't had more than a glass of wine at dinner with them since the first night, though they didn't drink as heavily when there wasn't a blackout either. And I made sure to be on time. Ada frowned if I entered late, and, despite knowing I had an ally in Lillian, I still craved Ada's approval.

"When can I see chapter two?" Lillian asked by way of greeting.

I slid into my seat. "Does that mean you liked it?"

"My dear girl—this is what you were born to do."

I beamed at her.

"You're going to give her a big head," Ada said.

The corners of Lillian's mouth twitched up as she turned back to me. "Don't you believe a word your aunt says. She's the one who told me you were a natural storyteller after all."

Ada picked up her newspaper as I grinned down at my plate.

"What time does this young man of yours arrive?" Lillian asked.

"Tonight. But he's not my young man. We've only been on one date."

"Two," Ada said from behind her newspaper.

"Well, I'm excited to meet him. It's so romantic that he came down here to find you after that whole debacle."

"They're a good fit," Ada said, her face still hidden.

"Where is he staying?" Lillian asked.

Ada lowered the newspaper, and they both looked at me. "Uh . . . I assume at the Princeton again."

Lillian shook her head with a tsk-tsk sound. "Well, that won't do, will it? He'll stay here."

"Here?" I asked.

"Of course," Lillian said, a twinkle in her eye. "As long as you two can stay in your own rooms at night."

Ada let out an actual snort at that. I dropped my fork, staring at her open-mouthed.

"Close your mouth," Ada said. "You look like a fool." She looked at Lillian. "Are we sure that's wise? Marilyn isn't exactly the epitome of virtue."

I could feel my cheeks flushing.

Lillian smirked. "Were you? At that age?"

Ada was trying not to smile. "At that age? Yes. You, on the other hand . . ."

"Europe was interesting," Lillian said to me. She turned back to Ada. "And I married him after all."

"Yes, well, we didn't all have that option."

"Can I hear that story?" I asked.

"Absolutely not," Ada said.

I tried to picture her at thirty years old, having an affair with a soldier during a war. Then pieces of a puzzle fell into place. My eyes widened. "Ada—did you have an affair with Ernest Hemingway?"

Both women looked at me as if I had grown a second head. "With whom?"

Lillian laughed. "The bell tolls."

"He was an ambulance driver in the war—you were a nurse. That's basically the plot of *A Farewell to Arms*. You have a house in Key West—so did he. And you said you met the Fitzgeralds. You had an affair with Hemingway, didn't you?"

Ada shook her head. "You have some imagination, I'll give you that. No. It wasn't Hemingway."

"Come on—there's no way you didn't cross paths with him with all that in common."

She shrugged. "If I did during the war, I wouldn't know. He wasn't Hemingway then. He was just a kid driving an ambulance."

"Yeah . . . I'm not buying it."

Ada shook her head. "Suit yourself," she said. But she winked at Lillian, who wouldn't quite make eye contact with me.

I tried to remember if I had seen any Hemingway books when I had been in her room, but nothing stood out. I decided I was going to sneak in and look again the next time she left the house. His writing would definitely not be her style, so if they were there, it was evidence enough.

And even if it wasn't true, the story in my head was too good. I wouldn't use Hemingway himself, but the aunt's wartime affair was absolutely going to find its way into my book somehow.

CHAPTER FORTY-SIX

Lillian and Ada kept up a running commentary while I prepared for dinner with Dan.

"She's wearing the fuchsia dress," Lillian called down the hall after peeking into my room.

"Tell her the dark green is better," Ada yelled back.

"Don't yell room to room," I shouted.

Lillian laughed, and I heard Ada's footsteps. "I don't know why I tolerate that sass."

"Yes, you do," Lillian said. "She's just like you."

I ducked my head. It was a compliment I would take even if I'd pretend not to. "Only about a million years younger."

"Watch it," Ada said mildly, coming to sit on my bed. "And change into the dark green."

"I like the fuchsia."

Ada made a face.

"What's wrong with the fuchsia?" I asked.

"Nothing," she said, reaching into the pocket of her dress. "But it'd clash with this." She held out the Guerlain lipstick.

I stared at her for a moment before I reached for it, but she pulled it back. "The green," she insisted. "You can't wear red lips with a fuchsia dress."

Reaching up to undo the zipper, I stripped out of the pink, hung it carefully in the closet, and pulled out the dress she preferred. Once it was on, I went to the mirror. She was right, of course. It brought out the green in my eyes and was a much better choice. I turned around—they were both sitting on my bed now, Sally between them—and held out my hand. Ada placed the lipstick in my palm, and I looked in the mirror to apply it.

"Ada, how did you know I took it before?"

"I didn't."

"Then how—?"

"I was fishing. You took the bait."

I looked at her in the mirror. "You're the most aggravating—"

"Careful or I'll take it back."

I pursed my lips at my reflection. "Thank you for the lipstick—even if you originally stole mine."

Lillian held Sally up—Sally hadn't been more than a few inches from Lillian since she returned, and I had begun to wonder whose dog she actually was. "Ada just likes to be the alpha dog, doesn't she, sweet girl?" Sally licked Lillian's nose, and Ada made a face.

I expected Ada to have a snappy reply, but she said nothing. It dawned on me that Lillian may have been the real alpha of this house. Ada didn't fight her decision that Dan would stay here, and I doubted she would give me the lipstick without Lillian's prompting.

"How do I look?" I asked, twirling around.

Ada frowned. "Don't ask questions you already know the answer to."

But Lillian shook her head. "Don't listen to her. You look lovely."

All three of us looked up at the sound of a car outside the open window. "That'll be him," Ada said.

"I'll get it," I said, moving past her to the door.

"Don't be silly," Ada said. "He's going to be our guest after all. Come on, Lillian. I'll introduce you."

"Wonderful," Lillian said, heading into the hall. Sally jumped down and followed her.

I trailed after them, wondering if the lipstick was worth the price.

Ada reached the door just as Dan was raising his hand to knock, two bouquets of flowers in his other hand. "Welcome," she said, suddenly all sunshine and rainbows. "Come on in. I'd like you to meet my friend Lillian."

Dan shook her hand warmly, but looked down, biting the inside of his cheek. "I would have brought a third bouquet if I'd known."

"Don't be silly," Lillian said. "We can happily share."

Ada took both from Dan and handed them to me. "Go put these in water," she said, taking Dan's arm and leading him toward the living room.

He looked over his shoulder at me helplessly. "Hi. You look beautiful."

I smiled, then went to the kitchen, where I attempted to hand the flowers off to Frannie. "What on earth do you want me to do with those?" she asked, a hand on her hip. "We're out of vases."

"I don't know. Use a milk jug?"

"Were you raised in a barn?" She shook her head and stormed into the dining room, returning a moment later, her arms laden with three vases full of extravagant blooms. "Miss Ada better not mind me consolidating some of these."

"I doubt she will."

Frannie shook a finger at me. "It's on you if she does."

"I didn't bring the flowers!"

"No, but you brought the boy who brought the flowers."

I shook my head. "Love you too, Frannie."

She grumbled something that might have been "Too much trouble" or "Go blow a bubble." Either way, I wasn't her favorite person, and she attacked the flowers.

Dan was seated on the sofa, Lillian and Ada opposite him in chairs. "Shall we go?" I asked.

Dan started to rise, but Ada stopped him with a look. "Go?" she asked. "He just arrived. No. We have arrangements and rules to discuss."

I looked to him in alarm, but he didn't seem concerned. "Arrangements?"

"Yes. Dan will sleep in the spare room. And there'll be no funny business while he's here. I run a respectful house."

"Ma'am, I would never—"

Ada made a wry face. "Never say never—you might live to regret that." Dan blushed, and I stifled a laugh. He had a lot to get used to with Ada.

"Don't mind her," I said. "She had an affair with Hemingway."

Dan looked from me to her and back to me. "You're joking— aren't you?"

"Yes," Ada said at the same time I said, "No."

Lillian leaned forward and put a light hand on his knee. "Are you sure you wouldn't prefer the Princeton after all, dear?"

∿

By the time we left for dinner, Lillian had obtained most of Dan's life story. "Sorry about that," I said sheepishly as we walked down the stairs.

"Nothing to be sorry about." He took my hand and pulled me in, giving me a quick kiss. "Hi though."

I smiled. "Hi." But when we reached the car, he handed me the keys. "What do you want me to do with these?"

"Hop in. Your first lesson can be taking us to dinner."

"I can't drive us to dinner. I've literally never driven."

"No time like the present. Come on. I'll show you."

"But there are children in town. What if I hit a child?"

Dan chuckled. "Try not to do that."

"No. Shouldn't we go to a parking lot or an abandoned road for this?"

"Marilyn, you'll never find a more abandoned road than the streets here. Most people walk everywhere. You're the one who taught me that."

I looked at him uncertainly. "Have I finally found something you're afraid of? Other than marrying me?"

I set my jaw. "I'm not afraid of anything."

"Good. Climb in."

I got into the driver's side and slipped the key into the ignition. "Now what?"

Dan smiled. "It's an automatic transmission. If it was a manual, I'd have taken you to a parking lot. But this, anyone can do." He slid into the middle of the bench seat, his leg just touching mine with an electricity I didn't expect. Then he took my hand and placed it on the shifter next to the steering wheel. "This is reverse," he said, moving my hand with his. "Turn and look behind you so you don't hit anything, and VERY gently press the right pedal."

"What if I hit something?"

He shrugged. "That's what insurance is for."

"But you clearly love this car. Look at it."

"It's a car," he said. "I do love it. But you can replace a car."

I swallowed, the unspoken part of his sentence holding a lot of weight. "Okay. Here we go."

I turned to look behind me, stepped on the gas, and suddenly we were flying into the street. "Other pedal," he said calmly. I did as he said, and we jolted to a stop. "Gentle touch with your foot. Very gentle. Like you're worried there's glass on the pedal."

I moved my foot toward the gas again, but he stopped me with a hand on my knee. "Wait. Let's put it in gear first so we don't wind up on the beach."

"Could be fun."

"Let's stick to the road for now."

He put my hand on the shifter and showed me how to move it into gear. "Gently," he reminded me again as I stepped on the gas, this time moving forward slowly. "Look at that. You're driving."

I felt a smile spreading across my face. It changed into sheer terror when we turned onto Dune and other cars were coming toward us, but except for a momentary steadying hand on the wheel, Dan let me do the rest, even directing me very crookedly into a parking spot.

"Are you sure you haven't driven before?" he asked.

I shook my head. "I'll have to swipe Ada's keys to practice during the week."

"Or you can use mine next weekend."

I grinned at him. "What if I don't invite you back?"

He took my hand and kissed the palm. "You're not getting rid of me that easily."

CHAPTER
FORTY-SEVEN

The four of us ate breakfast together the next morning, Lillian asking Dan questions about everything she hadn't covered the day before. Ada didn't even have her newspaper at the table for once.

"What are you two doing today?" she finally asked.

"I figured we'd go to the beach," I said. "Then maybe Atlantic City tonight."

"How fun," Lillian said. "You'll take him to Hackney's of course."

I nodded, but Ada spoke. "I believe we'll join you on the beach today."

Lillian pursed her lips and put a hand on Ada's. "Let the two love-birds be. We can go another day."

"Nonsense," Ada said. "Besides, we don't stay as long as they do."

"You should definitely join us," Dan said. I shot him a look, and he nudged my leg with his under the table.

"How romantic," I muttered.

"Did you say something?" Ada asked pointedly.

I put my elbows on the table and leaned my chin in my hands. "It's just the most perfect dream date ever."

"Elbows off my table." She turned to Dan. "You really want all this sass? It's not too late. I could find a nice girl for you instead of my witch of a niece."

He hid a smile with his napkin. "She'll be so convenient at Halloween though. I won't even need to decorate for the kids."

Ada turned to Lillian. "I told you I liked this one."

We all went to our separate rooms to get ready, but Dan and I were the first ones back downstairs. "What's in the bag?" I asked.

He pulled it off his shoulder and unzipped it to show a camera, the letter *F* on the top, the word *Nikon* just below it.

"You weren't kidding, huh? That's a fancy camera."

"Just a single-lens reflex. But it shoots beautifully."

"Why are you bringing it to the beach? Aren't you worried it'll get sand in it?"

"Nah," he said. "I'll be careful. And I told you I was bringing it."

"What would you do with pictures of me though?"

He leaned in and kissed my cheek. "I just like photographing beautiful things."

"I'd tell you to get a room, but I don't want any broken windows," Ada said.

I jumped about a mile. "How does someone your age sneak up on people so well? Shouldn't your joints be creaking?"

She ignored me. "I hope you know how to put up a beach umbrella better than Marilyn. She almost killed people the last time she tried."

"I believe I can handle that."

"She exaggerates," I said. "Besides, the only one I'd want to kill is her."

"And it'll take much more than an umbrella to do that," she said. She turned to the stairs. "Lillian! Are you coming?"

"I am," Lillian called back.

"Why *are* you allowed to call room to room when I'm not?" I asked.

"Because it's my house."

"Then why is Lillian allowed?"

Ada looked at me shrewdly. "Because she's not as easily cowed as you are."

I shook my head. "We're going to go get the umbrella and chairs. Unless you'd prefer a broom to sit on."

"A chair will be lovely," Ada said. She touched Dan's arm as he turned to leave. "I meant it. You'd be a catch for a nice girl."

I dragged Dan out the door.

~

We set Ada and Lillian up with chairs and the umbrella, both of them so covered from any amount of sunshine possibly getting near them that I began to wonder if perhaps they were actually vampires. It would certainly explain how Ada snuck around so easily.

Dan and I spread towels a little way from them so we could actually talk.

"This really is a little slice of heaven, isn't it?" he asked.

"Avalon? Or the beach?"

"Both. We should come here until we're as old as they are." He gestured behind us.

"Are you planning our future again?"

He held up his hands in innocence. "Me? I didn't say we'd be married or bring our kids. For all I know, we're leaving our spouses to come here together."

"How scandalous, Mr. Schwartz."

He turned on his side to face me. "The rabbi would have a heart attack."

"I'm surprised he didn't when we crashed through that stained glass."

Dan laughed. "Me too, to be honest."

I leaned up on an elbow. "Do they know you're here this weekend?"

He hesitated. "They don't."

"And why is that?"

He sat up. "Because I figured they'd tell your parents."

I considered him for a moment as he looked out at the ocean. If he wanted me back in New York, the quickest way to get me there would have been to make sure my parents knew we were talking. Daddy would have yanked me back to New York so fast I would have whiplash.

I opened my mouth to ask why he hadn't, then, but he stood and offered me his hand. "Come on. Let's go in the water."

I took his hand and followed him into the surf, realizing I already knew the answer: he didn't want to force me into anything.

~

That night, as I got into bed, well past midnight after our trip to Atlantic City, I thought back to that moment on the beach. I had never met a man whose sole interest in me wasn't getting his own way. My father and my brother both wanted me to be the perfect reflection of the family, seen but not heard. It was a role I was destined to fail in. I didn't have my mother's stoicism or ability to let things roll off her back. And Rabbi Schwartz didn't care if I wanted to marry his son; he just wanted to save face. Even Freddy cared about what I could do for him—putting off college so he could finish his school and then assuming I would marry him to save him from his mistake.

Not one of them had ever actually asked me what I wanted or respected the fact that I had a brain in my head. Until Dan.

I rolled onto my stomach, hugging my pillow. I still didn't want to get married anytime soon, but I was happy Dan had come back into my life.

~

The following morning, we walked into town after breakfast, ducking into Hoy's and chasing each other up and down the aisle with silly trinkets. He pretended to cry out in pain when I got him with a crab claw pincer toy, then pulled me to him, both of us laughing.

He bought me a bracelet with a starfish on it and a pair of goofy sunglasses for himself. "What will the rabbi think of those?" I asked as we left the store.

"I couldn't care less," he said. "If you like them, that's what matters."

"What's going to happen when you tell him you're not going to rabbinical school?"

Dan bit the inside of his cheek. "I'd imagine they'll react much the way yours did to"—he gestured to the space between us—"everything. Except I don't have an Ada."

I didn't know Rabbi Schwartz well. He was an imposing figure in my youth, never tolerating childish shenanigans in temple. And Dan had always seemed so well behaved. But his admission that he had put the fish in the fountain at the Catskills . . . "So becoming a rabbi is your version of marrying a rabbi's son and being a dutiful wife and mother?"

He grinned. "Not sure how dutiful a mother I'd make."

I elbowed him playfully. "You know what I mean."

"I do. And yes. As the only son, that was—is—the expectation."

"Your mother too?"

He hesitated. "I think it's even more her dream. The only thing better than being a rabbi's wife is being a rabbi's mother."

I looked at him for a long moment, wondering how I hadn't seen the parallels of our circumstances. He didn't want to wind up leading services any more than I wanted to be reading at a stove. And neither of us had a way to make our families understand.

"Did you always want to be a photojournalist?"

"No. But I always loved taking pictures. I got a Brownie box camera when I was eight." He smiled. "Actually—maybe I did and just didn't know the word for it yet. My father took a group of boys from the synagogue to a Yankees game that year. And I didn't care at all about the score—I brought that camera, and I still have the pictures I got of

Joe DiMaggio and Yogi Berra. I caught DiMaggio just as he connected with the ball. It's one of my favorite pictures I've ever taken to this day."

I knew nothing about baseball and would have been more excited about a photograph of Mr. DiMaggio's ex-wife, but I could have listened to Dan describe the whole game in detail. "You'll have to show it to me sometime."

He smiled. "What about you? How long have you wanted to write?"

No one had ever asked me that. And I thought for a while before I answered. "I think—I think it's the same kind of thing. I used to make up stories. My bedroom was a tower that I was trapped in. But I didn't want a prince to come rescue me. I wanted to rescue myself. And somewhere along the line, those stories became the way to do just that."

"Two peas in a pod," Dan said, taking my hand.

I stiffened slightly at the use of Ada's expression to describe me and my mother. But he was right. I didn't know how either of us would manage the dream-shattering disappointments we were about to lob at our families, but there was a sense of comfort in knowing I wasn't the only one.

～

We stopped at the bakery for sticky buns and coffee on the way back to the house. Ada and Lillian were out when we returned, and the sky had turned gray and menacing, so we sat on the wicker sofa on the porch with our respective books. Dan was reading Ada's copy of *Hawaii*, and I had turned my attention to *Exodus*, by Leon Uris, at Ada's suggestion. By the time Ada and Lillian returned, just before the rain started to fall in huge drops that pelted the rocks and flowers, I was stretched out, my head pillowed on Dan's legs as he read above me, a hand wandering down from time to time to wind itself in a lock of my hair.

"Well, don't you two look cozy," Ada said.

"Let them be," Lillian warned.

"Who's not letting them be?"

251

Ada craned her neck to look up at the sky. "This'll blow through quickly. You should be fine to go home this afternoon. Though you're welcome to stay as long as you like."

"Does that go for me as well?" I asked.

She pointed a finger at me. "Don't get your hopes up." The rain began to fall in earnest as the two women went inside. "I sent Frannie home so she wouldn't get caught in all this—we'll have to muddle through lunch ourselves."

"We've done as much before," Lillian said.

The windows were open so we could still hear them as they continued into the house. "Yes, but we have company."

"He may be family soon enough by the looks of them out there."

"We can hear you," I called through the open window.

"Don't yell room to room," Ada replied.

I laughed, but Dan folded down the corner of his page and shut his book. "What's wrong?" I asked, looking up at him.

"Absolutely nothing. I just want to soak in the moment."

"Quite literally if the wind changes."

He shook his head. "Shush. You're ruining the mood."

I placed my book facedown on my chest. "Will you come back next weekend?"

His face spread in a smile. "I would love to."

Marking the page and closing the book, I sat up, nestling into the crook of his arm as we silently watched the rain fall together.

CHAPTER
FORTY-EIGHT

Dan went home for the week. He was clerking at a newspaper, trying to get a break in photojournalism, though his father still believed it was a lark and that he was going to rabbinical school in the fall. I had no idea what I would be doing in three weeks when Labor Day came around. I hadn't officially received word from my parents about whether I would be welcomed back into the fold, but with each passing day, I hoped more and more that they would allow me to stay where I was.

I broached the subject once more with Ada, who mumbled something about wayward girls, but I paid her no mind, especially when Lillian winked at me. Ada might have been the figurehead of our little family, but what Lillian wanted went.

And it *was* a family now. I felt more at home with them than I had in the first twenty years of my life. Yes, the pattern and routine would change again once we returned to the duplex in Oxford Circle. But there would always be next summer at the shore. And the summer after that. And I was certain I would settle into my own place in Philadelphia as well. Maybe I would even enroll in some writing classes, though I wasn't worried about earning a degree. Daddy had only sent me to college to find a husband after all. And as much as I enjoyed school, it was the freedom I loved. I had found that here, and much more of it.

August was a little faster paced for matchmaking at the shore than June and July had been, largely because more young men joined their families for their two weeks of vacation. A couple of handsome ones came through our door, frog-marched by determined mothers. A few weeks earlier, I might have found a reason to pop into the living room. But now I was content to mind my own business as I sorted through the photographs of Ada's life. I had a system and moved much quicker, watching as first her father, then her mother disappeared.

When I reached the bottom of the box from the late 1910s, my hand brushed a piece of fabric. That was a first, so I peered inside and pulled out something wrapped in a handkerchief, tied with a red ribbon.

I held the parcel in my hand for a moment. I wanted to open the ribbon. But something about it felt too personal. And the handkerchief was monogrammed with the initials *JWS*. It wasn't Ada's.

Instead, I set it aside, staring at it as if I could will it to tell me what was inside without violating Ada's trust. But the parcel said nothing, and I found myself waiting until Ada had finished with her clients for the day.

When the last mother and daughter had left, I knocked at the door to the living room. Ada was at the desk in the corner, Lillian across from her as they looked over notes from the day, Ada wearing the reading spectacles that she never let anyone other than Frannie and us see her in. They both looked up at my knock.

"Yes?" Ada asked.

I was suddenly shy. Whatever was in that parcel—I'm not sure how I knew it was personal, but I did. And I was even a little apprehensive about bringing it up in front of Lillian, though I was sure there were no secrets between them. But curiosity and I suppose a sense of duty propelled me toward them.

"I found . . . this," I said, holding the wrapped parcel out.

"What is it?" Lillian asked.

"I don't know. I thought—I don't know. I didn't feel comfortable opening it."

"Whyever not?" Ada asked.

"It felt . . ." I trailed off. "It just felt like I should ask you before I did."

Ada's lips twitched into a half smile. "How unlike you. Do you feel well? Lillian, see if she has a fever."

"I'm fine," I said, swatting Lillian's hand away from my forehead. "I just—is it love letters?"

"No," Ada said. "Those are in the Philadelphia house."

I briefly wondered how much a love letter from Ernest Hemingway would sell for. It would set me up for life, I assumed.

"No," she continued. "You may open that."

"Is that—?" Lillian began.

"Let her see," Ada said. "It'll answer her questions about my wartime activities."

"Hemingway?" I asked, pulling the ribbon. "These aren't his initials."

"No," Ada said. "They're not."

With the ribbon untied, I unfolded the handkerchief to find a stack of black-and-white photographs. My shoulders sank slightly in disappointment. But as I looked at the top one, I saw that the woman was Ada. She was in France, Notre Dame looming behind her, but she wasn't looking at the camera. Instead, she was looking at a man in uniform, her face positively glowing. I traced the line of her body. Her hand was clasped in his, but as I followed his arm up to his face, hidden slightly by his army hat, I stopped, looking back up at Ada in confusion.

She shook her head. "And you think *I'm* old-fashioned," she said.

The man's complexion left no doubt about his race.

I flipped it over. Ada's handwriting on the back read "John and I, Paris, November 1918."

"Who is John?"

"Does he look at all familiar?"

I turned the picture back over, holding it closer to my face, but no. I shook my head.

"He should. You're acquainted with his grandson after all."

I thought for a moment. "Thomas?" I squeaked. Ada nodded. "I don't understand." Ada chuckled as I tried to work it out. "You and Thomas's grandfather—" I flipped quickly through the rest of the stack of photographs. The third one down was them kissing under the Eiffel Tower. "I—" Nineteen eighteen. I quickly did the math. She would have been thirty-three. And if Thomas was in medical school—"Is—are you his grandmother?"

"Of course not," Ada said, taking the photographs from me and thumbing through them. "We couldn't have married. I thought at the time—especially if we stayed in Europe. But he was right, of course. It wasn't even legal in a lot of states. It was in Pennsylvania, but he had family down south. If we'd ever gone to see them . . ." She shook her head. "I loved that man to pieces. But he understood what I didn't. I couldn't. I hadn't lived it." She touched his face in the photograph in front of her.

"No," she said softly. "He came back home and married the girl who was waiting for him. Had four kids, including Thomas's father." She looked up. "I told you I'd been in love twice. John was the first great love of my life."

I sat there processing this as she spread the photographs in front of me. It explained her fierce devotion to Thomas. But it also didn't. How could she watch the children and grandchildren who could have been hers if the world was different and not feel bitter about what she never got to have?

I didn't ask that question out loud, but Ada could read me. "It took me a long time," she said. "I was willing to give up my family, my life, everything. And I know he loved me too—it was why he wouldn't do the same. Ours wasn't a story with a happy ending, no matter how you looked at it. If we came back here, odds were good we'd find a cross on our lawn, if not our house on fire, even in Philadelphia. I didn't really know how the world worked yet. I thought if we loved each other enough, we could find a place where our differences wouldn't matter." She shook her head again. "I was young and stupid and sheltered. John knew better. The world loves to destroy what it doesn't understand. Some things can be hidden to be protected. Some can't." Lillian reached over and took her hand. Had it been me, she would have swatted me away, but she let Lillian's remain, smiling at her tightly.

I tried to imagine an Ada so in love that she was willing to flout some of the most ingrained rules of our society. I didn't know any mixed couples even now. Though to be fair, I didn't know many people who weren't Jewish. We tended to huddle together on this side of the Atlantic, even more so since the hazy events in Europe during my early childhood. And marrying outside the faith was so strictly forbidden. Conversion for marriage was relatively new and still viewed as strange. Even I, rebel that my family thought I was, wasn't immune. It certainly hadn't been a pastor's son whom I crashed through a stained-glass window with.

And Ada, born more than half a century before me, was willing to be someone whom her family sat shiva for over a man who married someone else soon after.

It was too daunting to fathom.

"When we came back from the war—not long after those pictures were taken—I opened my eyes. I saw how people actually treated others. And I realized that John was smarter than I was." She shook a finger at me. "And you know I don't say that lightly." She thought for a moment. "No. We both wound up where we were supposed to be." She grinned at me. "We're a lot of scandalous women masquerading as house cats in our family. Me, your mother, your aunt Mildred, you—"

"What did Aunt Mildred do?"

Ada laughed. "That's a story for another day."

But one thing still didn't add up. "How did you go from a broken heart after the war to matchmaking?"

"She was good at it," Lillian said. "She fixed me up with Don."

Ada waved her free hand in the air. "That was nothing. He never took his eyes off you. He thought you weren't real. An angel who had saved his life. You were just the first face he saw when he woke up in the hospital."

Lillian shook her head. "She lies, you know," she said to me in a conspiratorial whisper. "He saw her first, but she told him I was the one who saved him."

"He was too nice for me. And I was otherwise occupied—"

"With John?" I asked.

They both looked at me. "No," Ada said slowly. "That was before I met John."

Hemingway, I thought triumphantly.

"To answer your question," Ada said, annoyed at the interruption. "I started with some soldiers and nurses in Europe. When we got home, I somehow had a reputation of being able to make perfect matches. I did it for free until the mothers came calling. Then I realized it was a way to support myself. My father was gone by then, and I had his money, but I wanted to earn my own. And now I have forty years of experience."

"And Thomas?"

"I wanted a fresh start after the war, with my parents gone, and John had spoken so lovingly of Philadelphia that I decided to go see it for myself. Before long, it was home. Eventually, we ran into each other, as was bound to happen in a city of nearly two million people—if you don't want to see someone happy with their wife, that as much as guarantees that you will.

"We kept in touch after that though. His wife is lovely. There's no bad blood there."

"Does she know about you?"

"She does. They had a good marriage."

"Had?"

Ada shook her head. "He died a few years ago. Heart attack. They ran in his family."

"I'm sorry," I said.

"It was a loss for his family, for sure."

But that didn't answer my question about Thomas. "Are you paying for Thomas's education?" I asked bluntly.

"What a leading question. He has a scholarship to medical school."

I looked at her from the corner of my eye. It was certainly possible that he had gotten a scholarship, but she hadn't said no. "Is it a scholarship funded by the Ada Heller Foundation for Matchmaking Sciences?"

Lillian burst into laughter. "Oh, Ada, I adore this one. She's the most like you of any of the family."

Ada shook her head. "No, you bigot. He earned that all on his own."

I stared at her again, marveling at this woman whom I had begged my parents not to send me to for the summer, thinking she would be a stodgy old bore. But she was wrong—she wasn't masquerading as a house cat. She was a leopard, camouflaged against her surroundings, but still living her life exactly as she saw fit.

And I hoped, when I looked back on my life a half century from now, I would be doing the same.

CHAPTER

FORTY-NINE

The mail brought two items of interest that week. The first was an envelope marked "Photos—do not bend" from Dan. I tore into it as soon as Ada offered it to me.

"Have at least a little self-control," she murmured.

"Why? He's not here to see it."

She shook her head but didn't leave, clearly wanting to see the contents of the envelope as well.

I emptied it onto the coffee table, a stack of black-and-white images tumbling out. The top one was me in the ocean, a wave just breaking at my back, my mouth open in an expression of surprise at the cold water and the joy of the moment. I smiled, wondering how he managed to snap it at the exact perfect moment. The next was me splashing toward the camera, which, as I recalled, caused a hasty retreat on his part. There were posed ones where I lay in the sand. I had been going for sexy and carefree, but the photos were more artistic than I expected. He had an amazing eye. There was a close-up of my face. I wasn't looking at the camera. Something else had captured my attention, and I was struck by how beautiful I looked— so much more so than when I looked in the mirror. Another of me sitting at the end of the jetty. I hadn't realized what he was going for when he posed me, but when I saw the picture, I instantly knew—it was the Little Mermaid sculpture in Denmark, spray coming up behind me again at the exact second needed to capture the essence of the moment.

"He's quite good," Ada said.

I had forgotten she was there. And was suddenly embarrassed. These felt so intimate, and not because I was in a bikini in most of them.

"He is," I said quietly.

The next shots were from Atlantic City. He had captured both the diving horses and my reaction of wonder to them. Me on the Ferris wheel, the lights of the city blurred beneath us. And one of the two of us, when he had handed his camera off to another couple with a camera, trading picture for picture. "A handsome couple," Ada observed.

I couldn't disagree.

I flipped to the next one, desperate for more, only to find that it was Ada and Lillian who had caught his attention. They sat under their umbrella, engrossed in conversation, their bodies angled toward each other under the yards of fabric and shade. The next was the same, but they were smiling at each other. And a third was a close-up of just their hands, Ada's on top of Lillian's.

"I think these three are for you," I said, offering them to her.

"I believe so," she said. "But why our hands? Mine look so old."

It was true. She could pass for younger everywhere else. But hands never lied. Mine still had the dimpled knuckles of someone who had never done a day's honest labor. But Ada's were spotted and worn, with pronounced knuckles and veins. It was a reminder that, as much as she claimed she wasn't going anywhere, nothing lasted forever. And it made me double down on my determination that I was staying with her when the fall came.

~

Unfortunately, the second piece of mail made that plan much more complicated.

My mother's weekly letter arrived a day late, on Friday instead of Thursday. I'd wondered aloud if everything was all right at home when the postman didn't have her letter, but Ada said she was sure it would arrive the following day. It did, and I opened it, sitting on the sofa in the den to read, hoping against hope that my father had decided against college.

> *Dearest,*
>
> *Wonderful news! Your father has sent in your tuition payment. It's taken most of the summer, but he recognizes that you made a mistake and that you will be your best, diligent, and obedient self when you return (so see that you are, please). There will be no more talk of the rabbi's son either— his parents say he's met someone. We're hoping he'll announce an engagement by the High Holy Days and then that scandal will be forgotten. The holidays are late this year, so I really think it will be blown over by Rosh Hashanah, and we can all start our new year with a clean slate as intended.*
>
> *We'll be wiring you money to return next week—you can take the train right from Atlantic City and bypass Philadelphia entirely. Ada will send any of your belongings you may have left in Oxford Circle when she returns after Labor Day. And that will give us time to go shopping for your school wardrobe and your books.*
>
> *I hope you've enjoyed your stay with Ada. I know she's wonderful, but I've missed you. And the condition to this all is that you'll be living with us during the year, not the dormitory. So that's a blessing in disguise, as I'll get more time with you.*
>
> *With love,*
> *Mama*

My chest was heaving by the time I finished reading. Next week! I couldn't leave next week! I had another two and a half weeks at the shore.

I couldn't go back to that prison of a house. And what would happen when it came out that I was the girl Dan was seeing but there would be no engagement? They would hound me day and night until I wanted nothing to do with him. And how long would it be before they wore me down, and I ended up stirring a pot of something inedible at the stove, nose in a book, my own writing festering in a drawer while I bore child after child?

No.

I wasn't going back.

Not even if they came here themselves and dragged me by my hair.

"Bad news, I take it?" Ada asked from the doorway.

I jumped. I hadn't realized she was there.

"Mama says I'm supposed to go home next week," I said flatly.

"I see."

"Ada, you—you'll let me stay, won't you?"

Ada came into the room and sat opposite me. "It's not that simple," she said. "If they agree to allow you to stay with me, you're welcome to. But I can't keep you here if they say no."

"Why not? I'm twenty. Can't I just stay?"

"You're going to need to talk to your father. There's only so much your mother can do."

I studied her. Her face was too bland. She knew something I didn't. "What did Mama say to you?"

Her lips flattened into a line. "It wasn't your mother."

"Daddy? You talked to Daddy?" She nodded, and I felt my stomach drop. The conversation hadn't gone well. That much was obvious.

"If I can convince him—"

"If you can, you can stay. But he was firm with me that I was not a permanent solution."

"But why? He doesn't want me there. I'm just trouble and a disgrace."

She took my hand. "Because that's what he sees me as. He knows why your mother came to me all those years ago. And the fact that I never married—well, he doesn't want my life for you."

I leaned away from her, aghast. "He *said* that?"

She closed her eyes for a few seconds. "He said I should understand that, in my line of work. I think he thought that was why you were coming for the summer. And the fact that I didn't make a match for you . . . He's not all too pleased with the way you've spent your summer."

"How much does he know?"

"Only what you've told your mother. And that you're as far from being engaged as you were when you left New York."

It made sense. If he had even an inkling about Freddy, he *would* have dragged me back by my hair.

But he had apparently sent me here to find an appropriate husband, a mission in which I had failed miserably and instead spent my summer sunning myself and working on a novel, which he would view as more wasteful than my afternoons on the beach. Reading was fine, but a woman's place was in the home as a wife and mother—even if she burned the roast.

I swore softly, assuming Ada would admonish me, but she surprised me, saying, "That's just the word for it."

"What do I do?" I asked her. She knew everything. She would know how to fix this.

But she shook her head. "You know your father better than I do. Appeal to him." She rose and went to leave but stopped at the doorway. "I want you to know that I did try."

There was a lump in my throat, preventing me from replying, so I nodded. Her head bobbed once in return, and then she left me in solitude to cry.

CHAPTER FIFTY

I was no closer to a solution when Dan arrived that evening. But with one look at my face, he took me into his arms. "What's happened? Is it Ada? Is she—?"

Ada came down the stairs. "Ada is just fine," she said. "Marilyn's parents have summoned her home, and she doesn't want to go."

He pulled back to look at me, holding my face in his hands. "That's all?"

I turned and ran up the stairs while he called after me. "Give her a little time," I could hear Ada say before I shut my bedroom door and threw myself onto the bed.

It took me an hour to come back downstairs. Dan was in the den with Ada and Lillian, each of them with a drink. Ada and Lillian both excused themselves, rising to leave when they saw me. I nodded to them as they walked out but said nothing.

"I'm sorry," Dan said, standing. "I didn't mean it like that—I assumed someone was dead from your face. I know you don't want to go back to New York."

I sighed. "It's okay."

"Ada filled me in some—but let's talk about it. Or not, if you don't want to."

I came and sat on the sofa, and he sank back down next to me. "I don't think I'm going to be much fun this weekend. Are you sure you don't want to just go home?"

He shook his head. "I'm not here for the beach and the boardwalk rides, Marilyn. I'm here for you." I smiled weakly. "Come on. Let's go for a walk. We'll get ice cream."

"But we haven't had dinner."

"Since when do you follow rules?"

He had a point.

~

"I'm not saying we'd have to get married—but if you were in New York, we'd see a lot more of each other."

"I think we'd see less of each other if they knew marriage wasn't the plan," I said over our cones. "And they would harass us nonstop until we caved." I didn't think he fully understood my aversion, but I appreciated him not pushing.

"What if we just didn't tell them we were seeing each other?"

I shook my head. "He doesn't trust me to live on campus. I'll have no freedom at all if I go back. I'm not leaving that house unless you come to the door and sit with my father first."

He reached out and touched my hair. "And I suppose this is too short for me to climb up to get to your window."

"Hah."

"Okay, here's the next idea—we run away together."

I looked at him warily. "And do what, exactly?"

"Whatever we want. We'll be bohemians. Live on a beach somewhere. Drink out of coconuts to survive."

"The world doesn't actually work like that."

"What if I work for a year and save up as much as I can, and then we leave?"

A year. A year in that house. I couldn't do it. Now that I had been free, I couldn't go back into a cage and sing and pretend I was happy.

He took my hand. "Then actually marry me. It won't be like your parents. I'll support you while you write. There are ways to not have kids—we won't until you want to—if you ever want to. And if I can't make enough money doing photography, well, I'll do whatever I need to."

I looked at him curiously. "Do you actually *want* to marry me?"

His eyes widened. "I don't know the right answer here."

"The truth is the right answer."

He took a moment before he responded. "The truth is, you're not like anyone I've ever known. I'm alive when I'm with you. And I want to be with you—in whatever way you'll have me. If that involves rings and a ketubah, yes. If it's coconuts and sleeping in a shack on the beach, that's great too. But I'm just trying to find a solution that helps you right now."

It was the right answer.

"Let me talk to my father," I said, aware that my heart was racing. "And we'll save all that as a very last resort."

"Okay," Dan said. "But the offer stands."

~

We spent much of the next day working out what I was going to say, flip-flopping between the idea of a letter, a telegram, and a phone call. Dan even role-played my father. But when he thundered that I was to come back that instant, I knew it had to be a letter. I was a writer, after all, and a phone call would likely end in a screaming match. I drafted it, then showed it to Dan, Ada, and Lillian, all of whom agreed it was the best I was likely to be able to do. I outlined my desire to write and my plan to enroll in writing classes, and implied that I was seeing someone Jewish and appropriate down here.

"He can't refuse that," Dan said.

Lillian agreed, but Ada looked less certain. "Add that my eyesight is failing," Ada said.

I looked at her in confusion. Her eyes were sharper than mine.

"Tell him you read to me and are helping me run the business. Tell him I'll rewrite my will if you stay."

I felt a chill, as if the temperature of my blood had dropped suddenly. It was the first time Ada had hinted at death being a real possibility for her.

"Ada—"

"Don't 'Ada' me. I'm not going anywhere. But we need to throw everything we've got at this and see what sticks."

I revised the letter.

It wouldn't go out until Monday's post, but Dan and I dropped it in the mailbox near the center of town on Sunday before he left.

"Call me when you hear," he said and kissed my forehead. "And I meant what I said. I'll do whatever you need."

"Least romantic proposal ever."

He pulled me back by the shoulders. "Marilyn Kleinman," he said. "The day you let me know you would be open to accepting that, believe me, I'll make the show you want of it. Until then, this will have to do." And he pulled me in to him, kissing me deeply until the world spun.

"Where did a rabbi's son learn to kiss like that?"

"Do you really want to know the answer to that question?"

"No," I laughed. "But do it again."

He obliged. And for a moment, I believed that the letter would do its job and things could continue exactly as they were.

CHAPTER
FIFTY-ONE

I jumped when the phone rang on Monday afternoon. Ada pursed her lips in annoyance. "You can't expect to hear from your father before Wednesday, you goose," she said.

I knew she was right, but I was too on edge to be much good to anyone. I tried to focus on the final scrapbook, but there were huge time jumps. Either Ada had years where she didn't take many pictures—which did make sense, once she was older and alone in Philadelphia—or I was just too scatterbrained to put the pieces together.

When I finally gave up in annoyance, I sat at my typewriter, but the words weren't flowing. Instead, I picked up my stack of pages, realizing it had grown far thicker in the last couple weeks, and sat downstairs with them and a pencil, hunting for typos and plot holes.

That provided the distraction I needed, and I quickly found myself immersed in the story I had told. It was closer to finished than I realized, but I didn't quite know how it ended. My idea of a happy ending wasn't the same as most people's after all. And I still wasn't sure if the aunt character lived or dramatically died at the end. It would propel the story along if she died, but it felt like too much of a jinx for my own irascible aunt.

No, she would live. There wasn't a way to write a happy ending if she didn't.

"What's got you so wrapped up?" Ada asked, coming to sit opposite me.

"Debating whether to kill your character off or not," I said tartly.

Ada shrugged good-naturedly. "You wouldn't be the first to try."

I wouldn't steal her backstory, but she had proven to be a much juicier character than any I could have created. "Who was your second great love?" I asked.

"Pardon me?"

"You told me you'd been in love twice. I know about John—who was the second?"

She shook her head. "No. That one belongs to me." She stood to leave. "And you won't find it in those boxes of photographs either."

I spent the next half hour debating ways to kill her character out of spite. I wouldn't do it, but there were days when it would be satisfying.

~

Wednesday came and went.

"It's a good sign," Lillian said, patting my hand affectionately. "Truly. It means he's writing a reply. If he were angry, you'd get a phone call or a telegram."

Ada said nothing.

Thursday morning, the two of them were in the living room with clients as I applied rubber cement to the back of photographs and then stuck them in the scrapbook. I would be done soon. I had reached the pictures from my mother's trip by Tuesday. Now I was firmly in my own lifetime, and the last box of pictures was nearing the end.

I hummed along to a song on the radio, turned down low so as not to disturb Ada and Lillian at work, and had just turned to a fresh page when a pounding sound startled me. I poked my head out of my bedroom, listening. Ada would be mad if it was Frannie.

But it was the front door. Heart in my throat, I ran down the stairs, skidding to a stop and narrowly avoiding crashing into Frannie, who was in the process of opening the door.

I righted myself and looked up into the angry face of my father, my mother standing pale behind him.

"Pack your bags," he said, eyebrows drawn together. "We're leaving today."

"Hello to you too, Daddy," I said drily.

Then Sally ran up and bit his pant leg, tearing at it angrily and growling as my stoic father tried to get away from the tiny little monster.

"Get this—thing—off me!" he said, trying to kick at her with the leg she wasn't holding.

"Come here, Sally," I said, scooping her up. She released his pant leg at my touch but growled at him in my arms as Ada entered the front hall.

She looked my father up and down, then observed Sally in my arms. "An excellent judge of character," she murmured to me as she passed. "Walter. Rose. I do so wish you'd called first. I have clients this morning."

"We'll be gone soon. I'm here to collect my daughter."

"And if she doesn't want to go?"

I had only seen Daddy's face go purple once before and that was at the synagogue. He started to sputter something, but Lillian walked out of the living room, took in the scene, and said, "Oh dear. I'll send the Levines home and call to cancel the rest of today's appointments. You all go talk in the den. I'll have Frannie bring some coffee and finger sandwiches." She took Sally from my arms and returned to the living room.

"After you," Ada said, gesturing to my parents.

My father stomped into the room, but my mother stopped to embrace Ada, who patted her back in return. Ada and I exchanged a look, but she shook her head and held a finger to her lips, indicating that I should let her talk first. I nodded and followed her into the room.

Mama and Daddy had sat together on the sofa. Ada took one of the chairs opposite, and I took the other.

"Don't you bother sitting," Daddy said. "You go pack your things."

"With all due respect, Walter, she is a guest in my home. I'd like her to sit and for us all to have a discussion."

"She's my daughter."

"And you're married to my niece, if we're really going to analyze the generational hierarchy."

If I could have crawled into her skin and become her, I would have. She was fierce and ferocious and feminine all at the same time.

Daddy nodded his assent for me to sit and I did.

"Now," Ada continued. "Let's discuss young Marilyn's future, shall we?"

"There's nothing to discuss. She's coming home."

Ada looked at him. "You'd rob an old woman of her companion in her twilight years? Marilyn has been indispensable this summer."

"You have a companion," Daddy said. "That one who's making the phone calls now. What kind of house are you running if you need two?"

"A business," Ada said. "Marilyn takes notes on meetings as well as evaluates prospective clients." It had been weeks since she let me near the business. "I honestly don't think I could keep doing this job without her."

"Then retire," my father said. "You certainly have the resources."

"I'm afraid I'm not ready to do that."

"Then hire someone else. She's coming home. You already filled her head with this writing nonsense. No respectable man wants a woman with a career."

I was seething. Both at the implication that all I was good for was marrying someone and also at the insult to Dan, who had been clear that if I wanted to write, that was what he wanted me to do.

"Just because *you* don't want that doesn't mean no one does," I spat. "It's not 1933 anymore. Times have changed."

"They haven't changed as much as you think they have," he said ominously. "And *people* don't change. You want to wind up like her? Alone? Begging for a niece to come stay with you so someone can find you when you die?"

"I beg your pardon—" Ada started, but I put a hand on her arm, silencing her.

"I'd rather be like her than like you! Trying to sell your daughter off to the highest bidder. I'm not some prize cow! I'm writing a book. And it's a good one. And I'm *not* going back to your stodgy old life just to rot away like Mama does!"

My mother stiffened, and the purple hue crept back up my father's neck.

"Your mother is perfectly content—"

"Even you know that's not true. I don't believe for one moment that you actually bought THREE ovens just because Mama told you it wasn't her fault dinner burned. She's got her nose in a book the whole time she's cooking because it's the only escape she has."

"That's enough," my mother said as my father turned to stare at her. "Rose?"

She glared at me, then turned to my father. "Yes, I read while I cook sometimes. Cooking is dull once the food is in the oven and with the children grown, it's a way to stay occupied. And sometimes I lose track of time. But that doesn't mean I'm unhappy." She looked back at me. "You're making a lot of assumptions."

"Fine. Even if you're perfectly happy, it wouldn't make *me* happy. Can't you understand that?"

"No," my father said. "Unless you're trying to tell me you're some kind of deviant."

My mouth dropped open. "Some kind of—*what?*"

"Now, see here—" Ada said.

"No," Daddy said. "*You* see here. She's my daughter. And she's not spending another night here."

"I'm an adult," I said. "I'm not fifteen. You don't have any legal right to make me do anything."

"You won't see another penny from me if you stay here," he warned. "No clothes or makeup or frills."

"I'm willing to bankroll her writing career," Ada said. I looked at her in surprise. We hadn't discussed the financial aspect of me staying. And truth be told, it hadn't occurred to me that I was working for my room and board with her.

A triumphant look entered his eyes, and my heart sank. I knew that look. He had just won, and he knew it. I just didn't know how yet.

"I hope you're prepared to be both her mother and father, then. Because if she stays, we will sit shiva for both of you."

It was the ultimate threat from a Jewish parent. A step beyond disowning. Parents could always reinstate a disowned child. Once someone sat shiva for you, you were dead to them for the rest of their life.

I looked to Ada, confident she would defuse this somehow. If anyone could, it was her. Her expression hadn't changed, but the color drained from her cheeks. She wasn't looking at me though—her eyes were fixed on my mother.

I followed her gaze to Mama, who looked so small and lost, like a wounded child, next to him. And looking back at Ada, I understood what she saw—the girl who had come to her in despair twenty-eight years earlier. I hadn't been broken when I arrived—far from it. I was arrogant and far too sure of my ability to get around the chaperone my parents had selected to mend my wicked ways. But as I watched, Ada set her jaw and lifted her chin, and for a moment, I allowed myself to hope. No one had ever gotten the best of Ada Heller. She would call my father's bluff and fix this.

Then she turned to me. "I'll send Frannie up to help you pack," she said. "I'm sorry it came to this."

The world tilted upside down. "Ada—no!"

She put a firm hand on my arm. "Go on. I'll be up soon as well."

"I'm not leaving you!"

"Go on," she repeated. "I'll be there directly."

I rose and ran out of the room, the tears falling before I even reached the bottom step.

CHAPTER
FIFTY-TWO

I didn't pack. Instead, I threw myself onto my bed. They could sit shiva for me. I wasn't going back to that house, no matter what Ada said.

I don't know how long I wept into my pillow for what I was about to lose, but eventually the door opened, and I felt the bed shift as Ada sat on it, the familiar smell of her perfume wafting over me as she stroked my hair.

"Imagine kicking up all this fuss," she said. "You didn't even want to come here."

I picked my head up. "That was before."

"I know. But you're no plucked flower that will wilt and die in the city. You, my girl, are a phoenix. And it may feel like the end of the world, but you will rise from the ashes into something even stronger."

"Only if I burn the whole house down," I said darkly.

"Then do that—metaphorically, preferably. I don't fancy visiting you in Sing Sing. Though it would be entertaining to slip you a file in a cake."

I smiled sadly, despite myself. I could see her doing just that. "Can't I just stay? I don't care if they disown me."

"I care," she said lightly. "Your mother cares. And you will too, someday." She turned her head, staring off at something I couldn't see. "My parents—well, it was the opposite, really. Papa was the supportive one. But Mother was in charge." She took my hand in hers. "I wouldn't do a thing differently. But I wish I'd had more time with them. And if you stayed with me, you would regret it. You don't want to be the person who lives with that kind of regret."

I shook my head. "If I go back, the only way out is marriage. And I don't *want* that."

"You would be happy with Dan."

"Is that Ada the matchmaker or Ada my aunt?"

She flinched. "Touché. But it doesn't mean it's wrong."

I sighed. "I might want to marry him *someday*. But I want it to be my choice."

Ada nodded. "It's the curse of our family, I'm afraid."

"What is?"

"That desire for freedom. A gilded cage is still a cage. Most people don't see the bars that hold them. You and I do."

"And Mama?"

"Your mother—" Ada hesitated, then shook her head slightly. "She climbed into the cage of her own accord. She saw the outside world and decided against it."

I had never seen it that way. But maybe she didn't burn meals because she was unhappy. Maybe she burned them because she was too content to remember to check.

But that didn't matter now. Because I still didn't have a way out other than Ada allowing me to stay. "Please," I begged. "Don't make me go back there. I don't want to leave you."

For a moment, she said nothing, and I allowed myself to hope. Then she shook her head. "You have to go home," she said, patting my hand. "But don't you worry. I've got tricks up my sleeve yet. You really think I'm going to let Walter Kleinman get the better of me?" She rose, going to my wardrobe. "Just pack what you need for now. I'll send the rest along later. I doubt all your things will fit in your father's car."

"Ada—"

"No more tears," she said. "Don't you know that's the most important thing? You never let them see you cry." She pulled out a couple of dresses and laid them across the bed. "No. You go down there with your head held high and you be an obedient daughter—as much as you know how to be, that is." She paused, contemplating the typewriter. "And take that, of course. You'll have plenty of time to finish your novel there. And an easier time getting it into the right hands in the city."

"I don't know how to finish it. This is the worst possible ending."

She crossed to me and cupped my chin in her hand, forcing me to look at her. "This isn't the end of anything except our summer. You hear me? You're going to be a writer, and you don't let your father or anyone else make you think you can't do that."

I swallowed thickly, then nodded. "Will I see you again?"

"You will see me again. And in the meantime, we'll write." I wiped my nose with the back of my hand. "A handkerchief, darling. That"— she pointed at my hand—"is disgusting."

I let out a hiccupping laugh through my tears. "I'm going to miss you."

"And I you, trouble though you are."

"You like trouble."

"That I do. You remind me of me." She paused for a moment. "And you *do* know the ending of your book." I looked at her questioningly. "She drives off into the sunset to live exactly how she wants."

~

When I went downstairs, carrying only my valise, a hatbox, and my typewriter, my parents stood. "Where did you get that?" my father asked, pointing to the typewriter in its travel case.

"From me," Ada said coolly. "And it's poor manners to refuse a gift."

He started to sputter, but my mother put a hand on his arm, murmuring something that quieted him. "Into the car," he said finally. "We have a long drive ahead of us."

Lillian was next to Ada, Sally in her arms, Frannie behind them. I set the bags down and went first to Frannie, embracing her. She squeezed me back, tears in her eyes. We nodded at each other before I moved on to Lillian. "I'm so sorry I wasn't kinder when you first arrived," I said.

"I never even noticed," she lied. "Dear, sweet girl. Please write to us."

"I will," I promised, hugging her tightly. She pressed a warm kiss to my cheek before releasing me. I took a minute to pet Sally, who nuzzled into my hand. I felt my breath hitch, but remembered Ada's admonition and took a deep breath to steady myself.

Then only Ada remained. "Thank you," I said. "For everything."

"Don't you make a fuss," she warned. "This isn't goodbye."

I didn't believe her. If the last time she had been to New York was my brother's bar mitzvah twelve years earlier, I didn't see her making the journey now. And there was no chance my parents would let me visit her in Philadelphia again. But it was a choice—believe her and be able to leave, or not and stay rooted to the spot, tearing my family apart. So I chose to believe her, if only because it was what she wanted.

She pulled me in for a brief but tight hug, and I wondered if she was telling me not to make a fuss so that she didn't cry in front of my parents either.

"I'll see you again soon," I whispered.

"You'd better."

My father cleared his throat and Ada released me. I looked back at her one last time over my shoulder before descending the porch steps.

My parents loved me because I was their child. But there was a lot they would change in me if they could. Ada was under no such obligation to love me. And, no matter how many critiques she had of my behavior and manners, she wouldn't change a thing. Leaving her felt like I was leaving a piece of myself behind. But I was stronger for having known her. And even if I never did see her again, that part of her would always be with me.

Squaring my shoulders, I blew her a kiss, then followed my parents down the steps and settled into the backseat of my father's black sedan for the long ride home.

CHAPTER
FIFTY-THREE

My childhood bedroom seemed smaller. Which was ridiculous because it was bigger than my room at either of Ada's houses. But the walls were closer. The windows smaller. And everything in it a reminder of what I didn't want.

It was better than the rest of the house though. In my room, I could sit at the desk where I'd done my homework in high school, my typewriter in front of me—my old one discarded to the back of my closet. It would never produce a novel. It was a relic of the girl I used to be. And, for those hours while I wrote, the room receded. My character wasn't me, but she lived in the now-familiar spaces of the world I had just left. And Ada was right—I did know how it ended.

I appeared for meals only because my father told my mother, which I heard through the vent in the floor, that if I didn't join them, she wasn't to bring me food. And as romantic as the idea was of wasting away in my tower to punish the dragon downstairs who kept me hostage, this wasn't what broke me. Because it wouldn't have broken Ada.

I wrote to her Thursday night and Friday morning. But Friday afternoon, a telegram arrived from Lillian, telling me to write to them at the Philadelphia house. They had ended their summer early, for the first time ever.

That revelation left me pacing my room and chewing my cuticles to shreds. There was a week and a half left before Labor Day. Going back to Philadelphia meant losing nearly two weeks of matchmaking. What were they thinking?

But Ada said she still had tricks up her sleeve. That my father wouldn't get the best of her. My hopes rose for the first time since returning home—if she went back to Philadelphia, she had to be planning something.

If they were back, it meant she wouldn't see my first two letters. I sat down at the typewriter, pulled a fresh sheet of paper through the roller, and began to write to her, combining what I had said into one new missive.

My mother came to the door, wanting to talk about my summer. Thursday night, I had turned her away. But now that I knew gears were in motion in Oxford Circle, I let her come in.

She sat on the bed. I was still at my desk, the letter finished, chapter 30 of my book in front of me.

"Is that the book you said you were writing?" I nodded. "Ada said it's wonderful so far."

At that, I turned to face her. "How often do you write to her?"

She looked surprised. "Why, every week."

"Why didn't you ever visit her?" The guilty look on her face told me the answer. "I found the picture of you and her on the boardwalk in Atlantic City. She would have liked it if you went to see her, other than to retrieve me."

"I know," she said quietly. "I regret that."

"You don't have to do what he tells you."

My mother shook her head. "It wasn't your father." I made a disbelieving face. "I doubt he would have been thrilled, knowing what he knows, but he never would have stopped me. I didn't want to go."

I thought of her face in that picture. "Why?"

She sighed. "There are so many things you can't possibly understand."

"Try me." She didn't reply. "I know why your parents sent you to her."

Mama looked up in alarm. "Ada shouldn't—"

"You're right. She shouldn't have. *You* should have."

For a long moment, she said nothing. "May you have your own daughter someday and have to account for every mistake you made."

"No," I said. "It's not a mistake if you learn from it. But that doesn't explain why you never went back."

She was quiet again, studying her hands in her lap. "After . . . after. I made the decision to put that behind me. To live my life as if it hadn't happened. I missed Ada, but I couldn't go back there. It would be too painful."

"So you sent me instead."

She reached for my hand, and I moved it away. "It wasn't a punishment—or at least, I didn't mean it as one. Ada—Ada was the best thing that ever happened to me. I regret what led me to her, but she gave me my life back. She's the reason I married your father and the reason you're here. If she hadn't taken me in that summer . . ." She trailed off, unable to finish the thought. She shook her head sadly. "I hoped she would have the same effect on you. But I guess a lot can change in twenty-eight years."

I stared at her. "Mama, she *did* do that for me. But I want a different life than you do. That doesn't make it wrong."

She didn't understand. And she never really would. She looked at the world through her own lens and didn't know how to see it through mine. And I supposed I couldn't see her life through hers either. Ada had said she was happy in her choice. I didn't understand how, and she would never understand how I could be happy with a different one. Which made me sad, knowing even if she accepted me for who I was, there would always be a judgmental rift born of a lack of comprehension.

But then she surprised me. "I'd love to read what you've written. If and when you're ready."

"I'd like that," I said, despite a flutter of nerves in my stomach. She would be a tough audience, reading as much as she did. And the notes she left in margins of books that I read after her were frequently critical but always accurate. "It's still rough though."

She smiled, though it was tinged with sadness. "We're not as different as you think. I dreamed of being an editor once." She shook her head. "It wasn't a world for women then."

"You still could be."

"No. But I do want to read your book."

I handed her the stack of papers next to me. "I have some corrections in pencil. But I'm finishing the draft before I go back and make the changes."

"Do you want me to make any notes if I find errors? Or just read?"

I felt tears springing to my eyes at the respectfulness of the question. Especially because she said *if* instead of *when*. "Whichever you want."

She stood and leaned down, kissing my forehead, and then plucked a pencil from my desk before going to the door.

"You're leaving?"

She turned, the stack of papers clutched to her chest. "I have a book to read."

CHAPTER FIFTY-FOUR

I refused to go to synagogue with my parents on Saturday. My father was visibly relieved, my mother, concerned.

"Wouldn't it be better—?" she began.

"She said she doesn't want to go," Daddy said gruffly.

Amazing that you care what I want NOW bubbled up in my throat, but I forced myself to swallow the tart response. Egging him on would only result in my being dragged there against my will. I wanted to see Dan. But not with the whole congregation staring at every look that passed between us. My mother's comment about not visiting Ada rang in my ears, and I could see her point.

"Stay out of trouble," my father warned.

"Honestly, Daddy—" A sharp look from my mother stopped me.

Bide your time, a voice that sounded like Ada's whispered in my head. I sighed. "I'll be good."

"No writing," he said. "It's Shabbat."

I bit the inside of my cheek to keep from exploding at his hypocrisy. Besides, writing wasn't *work*; it was my escape. And there were plenty of Saturdays when he caught up on paperwork in his office. He also had no problem with my mother cooking or using electricity. But I exhaled through my nose. "I'll read a little and maybe take a walk."

"No walk. You'll stay home. We'll tell people you didn't feel well."

"Right."

My mother kissed my cheek, then whispered in my ear, "I'm up to chapter twenty. I stayed up late reading. It's wonderful, dearest."

Thus buoyed, I waved goodbye, watched them leave, then retreated to my room to resume work. The book was nearly finished.

But I had only typed two lines when I heard a sound from downstairs. It came again, and I poked my head out of my bedroom door, listening. Someone was knocking at the front door.

Normally, Grace would take care of it, but Daddy felt it was wrong to pay someone on Shabbat, so she didn't work Saturdays. Sighing, I went downstairs. I didn't feel like dealing with anyone ill-bred enough to come selling something on Shabbat to a house with a mezuzah, but I wouldn't be able to focus until the pounding stopped. Even with the radio on.

I flung open the door. "We're not inter—oh!"

Dan stood on the step, a light rain plastering his hair to his head.

I looked around to make sure no stray neighbors were looking before pulling him inside, where he kissed me against the door.

"What are you doing here?" I asked breathlessly as he released me.

"My mother said you were home. I told the rabbi I had a headache and then came here. I was watching for your parents to leave."

"You can't stay. If they catch you here—"

"I won't," he said. "But I had to see you. I didn't want to call."

I wrapped my arms around his waist, burying my face in his damp shoulder, inhaling his scent, already so familiar. Being with him felt like home.

"Are you okay?" he asked. "What happened?"

"I am now." I gave him the short version of what had transpired, leading him into the living room to sit.

But he didn't look happy that I was in the same city as him. "What about us?"

My shoulders sank. That was the problem, wasn't it? My parents didn't trust me to go anywhere. They had sent me to Ada thinking it would be even more of a prison than home. And if we told them we were seeing each other, they would trust me less unless it was clear an engagement was imminent. Our behavior at the shul was evidence enough we couldn't be alone together. And they could never understand that everything had changed between then and now.

"I don't know."

"Marilyn, we have to tell them. There's no other way."

I shook my head. "Without an engagement, they wouldn't allow it. Your parents wouldn't either. The whole congregation would think we were just sleeping together. We'd never live it down."

"Then we get 'engaged.'" He made air quotes around the word. "We don't get married until you're ready, but we give them enough of what they want to be able to see each other."

"It won't work. They'll start planning the wedding immediately."

Dan thought for a moment. "We—I—tell them I want you to finish school first. That buys us two years."

"The whole reason my father is sending me back to school is to meet a husband. He wouldn't fall for that."

He looked down at his lap, studying his hands for a long moment. When he lifted his head, something steely had resolved in his face. "Then I'll go to rabbinical school, like my parents want. Your parents can't argue against waiting until I can make money to support us."

"No."

"Marilyn—"

"I'm not letting you give up your dream just so I can keep mine."

"You're more important than photography. I can still take pictures."

"No. I don't want to be a rabbi's wife any more than you want to be a rabbi."

He reached over and took my hand in his. "I don't have to finish. It just gives us time."

I took my hand back. "What if I'm never ready to get married?"

The look in his eyes broke what was left of my heart.

But he pressed on anyway. "Then we break up when you decide. And I'll take the blame with both families."

"No." He opened his mouth to argue, but I took his hand, silencing him. "If it comes to that, I'll take the blame."

His eyes widened. "Do you mean—?"

I nodded, defeated. I couldn't see a scenario in which he changed so much that he asked me to forfeit my writing. And the idea of a long engagement, while difficult to manage with our families, allowed us the freedom to figure out what our lives would look like if we did follow through.

But the corners of Dan's mouth turned down. "No. Not if you look like that saying yes."

I moved over until I was sitting on his lap. "Daniel Schwartz, there is no one else on this earth whom I would consider marrying. Now propose to me properly so we can actually see each other and decide what we want to do."

He pulled my face in and kissed me. "It's hard to do it properly when you're sitting on my knee."

I laughed for the first time since my parents arrived in Avalon. "I suppose we should make a show of it, for my parents. And yours."

"I don't care about them. I care about you." He nudged me and I stood, while he slid off the sofa and knelt in front of me. "Marilyn Kleinman, will you pretend to consent to marry me to appease our parents?"

My eyes narrowed. "Not even engaged yet and the romance is gone."

He rose, wrapping me in his arms. "Believe me, we're just getting started." His face moved closer to mine.

"Yes," I said. "I can't promise more than that, but yes."

CHAPTER
FIFTY-FIVE

I slept fitfully that night. I wasn't sure I was up for years of pretending. But the engagement, however real or unreal it was, would allow us to see each other. And after losing Ada, the idea of also losing Dan was too much to bear.

Dan was to come the following afternoon. We debated whether he should ask my father first but agreed that he had already secured his approval once and a surprise was better for our purposes. I asked if he was going to tell his parents before he came, but he said no. They would insist on coming with him if he did.

Breakfast was a quiet affair, my father buried in his newspaper, my mother trying to make conversation and receiving one-word answers from both of us until I retreated upstairs to write. I had been admonished the previous afternoon for the sound of typing coming from my room and wound up writing late into the night after my parents went to bed, tiptoeing past their room with my typewriter to the kitchen downstairs, where they wouldn't hear me. There were maybe two or three chapters left to go, but my characters weren't quite behaving and didn't seem to want to leave the world of their novel behind.

Just before lunch, my mother knocked on my door. "I hate to interrupt, but I want more," she said.

"You finished already?"

"I did. What's next?"

I nodded to the stack of new chapters next to me. She returned the others and took the new pages. "I'll leave you to it," she said.

I turned toward her. "Mama?" She looked back. "Is it any good?"

"This is what you were meant to do," she said, crossing to caress my hair. "I'm so proud of you."

I couldn't quite reply around the lump in my throat. And as much as I wanted to be back with Ada, I understood that she had been right. I would care if I walked away from my family with no avenue back.

~

I couldn't focus after lunch. Instead, I sat watching the clock on my nightstand tick closer and closer to Dan's arrival.

Finally, exactly at the stroke of two, there was a knock at the door. *Showtime,* I thought, leaving the sanctuary of my room. I came down the stairs, just as Grace asked Dan to come inside. He winked at me, and I offered a tight smile in return.

My father came out of his study, then looked from Dan to me, and I could see the wheels turning in his head at our combined absence from synagogue the previous day. "What's this about?" he asked as my mother came in from the kitchen.

"Don't be rude, Daddy. Invite him in for heaven's sake."

He started to sputter, but Mama put a hand on his arm. "Won't you come in, Daniel?" She gestured toward the living room. The two of us sat on the sofa, my parents in the chairs opposite us.

"Dr. Kleinman," Dan began. "I'm here today to ask for your blessing."

He looked at Dan warily from the corner of his eye. "I gave it to you in June, but Marilyn refused you."

Dan nodded. "I asked her again yesterday, and she said yes."

My parents' mouths dropped open in unison and for a split second, they sat there like gaping fish. I could practically hear Ada saying they'd catch flies like that. Then they were on their feet, hugging each other, the two of us, Daddy clapping Dan on the back and calling him son.

"The season is all wrong," Mama said. "It'll be a long engagement, I'm afraid, until the spring—early spring, of course, so it won't start too late at night . . ." She trailed off, an idea hitting her. "Or I suppose a fall wedding would work. October maybe, before it's too cold."

"No," I said as Dan shook his head.

"I've decided to go to rabbinical school after all. So we would have to put the wedding off a few years. I can't marry her until I can support her."

"Of course you can," my father said. "You'll live here until you finish."

We hadn't seen that one coming.

Dan started to come up with an answer but was interrupted by the ringing of the phone. "Grace will answer it," my mother said.

"October it is, then," my father said.

I shook my head. "Spring. You can't have your only daughter not have a spring wedding."

My mother nodded. "She's right."

My father threw up his hands. "Women," he said conspiratorially to Dan. "We'd best leave those details to them."

Grace came into the room. "Champagne," my father said. "We're celebrating."

"Right away," she said. "But there's a phone call for Marilyn."

"For me?"

"She's occupied," Daddy said. "Take a message."

"I said that, but she said it's urgent."

Ada. "Excuse me," I said, rising. "I'll be right back."

I hurried out of the room to the phone in the kitchen. "Ada?" I asked as soon as I picked up the receiver.

"It's Lillian," the voice said thickly. "Oh, Marilyn. I'm so sorry. Ada—Ada died. This morning."

CHAPTER FIFTY-SIX

I sank to the kitchen floor, the phone dropping with a clatter next to me. My mother came running in, but I couldn't speak to her. Not yet. Instead, I reached for the receiver, bringing it back to my ear and asking Lillian what had happened.

"It was sudden. She didn't suffer. She asked me to go pick up bagels—Frannie was off—and I did. When I got back, I found her. They said it was her heart."

She was alone. She was alone because I wasn't there. While yes, I would have been the one sent for bagels, Lillian would have been there. She would have called an ambulance. And maybe she wouldn't be gone now. But I wasn't there.

"What happened?" my mother asked, kneeling beside me, but I waved for her to shush. Lillian was still talking.

"—funeral. She wants to be cremated, but she left instructions about a service." There was a pause. "She left instructions about everything."

"I'll take the train down tonight," I said weakly. "Ask Thomas if he's willing to pick me up, but if not, I'll take a cab from the station."

"I'm sure Thomas won't mind," Lillian said. "Ada would throw a fit at you taking a cab alone at night." She sounded bereft.

"Oh, Lillian. I shouldn't have left. I should have been there—I—"

"She told you to go," she sniffed. "No one won against her. Except time, I suppose."

"I told her she was too mean to die."

"She knew that was a joke," Lillian said. "She loved you. You know that, don't you?"

I nodded even though she couldn't see it. "I'm going to pack. I'll call from the station when I know what time I'll arrive."

My mother was ashen by the time I hung up. "Ada?" she asked faintly. I nodded and she closed her eyes. My breathing was ragged, but no tears had fallen yet.

"I have to go. Lillian needs help planning the—the funeral."

I stood and my mother followed. "I'm coming with you."

"No. I'll call once we set the funeral. You'll come for that with Daddy."

"I—"

I cut her off. "I need to do this. Myself."

She looked at me for a long moment before nodding, then pulled me close in a tight hug. "I'm sorry," she whispered.

I couldn't reply.

Dan wanted to drive me, but I said no. I would take the train. The three of them would come down in a couple of days.

"Call me, please," Dan said. I told him I would and kissed his cheek.

My father didn't argue about me going, but I didn't say a word to him, even when he insisted on driving me to the station and seeing me on the train. "I'm sorry," he said as they called for me to board.

I finally looked at him. "Are you?"

He seemed taken aback. "Of course."

"You're the one who said she only wanted me there for someone to find her when she died. She was alone when it happened. Do you know that?"

He flinched, turning pale. "Marilyn—"

I shook my head. "I don't want to fight. But I should have been there. And I wasn't because of you."

I turned, picked up my valise and typewriter, and stepped onto the train.

As it rumbled down the tracks toward Philadelphia, I tried to rest. But every time I closed my eyes, I heard Lillian saying, "Ada—Ada died," over and over again until I thought I was going to scream.

Finally, the train pulled to a stop at the 30th Street Station. And as I stepped out onto the platform, I thought about how different the circumstances were from the last time I stood here. I dreaded going to Ada's house both times, but for such different reasons. It was going to feel so wrong without her.

I walked out into the night air, still hot in this little city that had grown on me so much, and looked around for Thomas. But I spotted Lillian instead, Sally in her arms.

Setting down my suitcase, I embraced her, Sally straining between us to kiss my chin. "How are you holding up?" I asked her.

"I've been better," she said. "She'd hate that I drove her car here."

I almost laughed at that, but a choking noise came out instead. It was true. She would have been livid. But that was how I knew it was true. If anything would bring her back from the dead to argue, it was that car.

"She's really gone, isn't she?" I asked.

Lillian nodded, dabbing at her eyes with a handkerchief. I was dangerously close to needing my own.

"How are we going to stay in that house?"

She shook her head. "I don't know. But I'm glad you're here."

~

It wasn't until I was back in my bedroom, the clothes that I had left in Avalon boxed in the corner, that the tears began to flow. And once they started, I didn't think they would ever stop.

I don't know when I fell asleep, but my dreams were a mix of Ada being alive and realizing she was dead all over again. So when I woke, it took me a minute to remember what was real and what wasn't. And once I did, I didn't want to get out of bed. It would be so much easier to stay under the white coverlet, selected by Ada, and let the grief consume me until I joined her.

But I heard Sally whine, and it reminded me that Lillian needed me. So I rose, went to the bathroom to wash my tearstained face, and then dressed to go downstairs.

The next two days blurred together. We met with the rabbi, who tried to dissuade us from following Ada's request for cremation, as it went against Jewish custom, but Lillian stood firm. I remembered something Dan's father had said at my grandmother's funeral, about the tradition of mourners shoveling dirt onto the casket themselves. "It's a mitzvah to honor her wishes over our own," I told him, not knowing if that was actually one of the six hundred and thirteen official mitzvahs or not. But that language spoke to him, and he agreed to perform the ceremony as Ada had wished. Before he left, we had set the date and time.

He knew her well enough to give his own eulogy, but he asked if either of us wanted to speak as well. Lillian shook her head. "I don't think I could get through it," she said.

"I'll do it."

The rabbi turned to look at me in surprise.

"She was—*is* my family." Lillian patted my leg, and the rabbi agreed, rising to leave.

Then there were decisions about shiva and notifying the community and my family. Lillian dealt with the crematorium, and I made the other phone calls—an arrangement that worked for me. I couldn't talk about her remains like that.

Dan and my parents drove down Tuesday night and came to the house to see what they could help with, but I asked them to stay at a hotel instead. I didn't want my father in Ada's house, and Dan couldn't stay with us without more chaperonage. No one argued with me—a first with my parents. We ate a solemn dinner that a silent and drawn Frannie had cooked, and then they prepared to leave for the night.

"How are you?" Dan asked as my parents went down the front steps, my mother clutching my father's arm. "Really?"

"Numb," I said. "I just need to get through tomorrow."

"What can I do?"

I smiled tightly at him. "You've already done it. Just be here."

He pulled me in for a hug, and for a moment I melted against him, letting him hold me. But I couldn't fall apart. I had to finish my eulogy and figure out how I was going to make it through reading it in the morning.

Once they were gone, I went back to my room and sat at the vanity, looking down at the typewriter that Ada had given me. But the words didn't come.

"Oh, Ada," I sighed out loud. "How am I supposed to do this without you?"

I thought of my first glimpse of her. How she took my lipstick. Our night in Atlantic City. The way she called me stupid after Freddy, but made it clear all along that she would take care of me, no matter what happened. Her forcing me and Dan together, seeing what I couldn't. *You do know the ending,* she repeated in my head. And I began to write, pausing only to wipe away tears.

CHAPTER
FIFTY-SEVEN

I woke to the sound of the alarm clock Ada had put by my bedside months earlier, my eyes opening on the day I dreaded. Yet the house still contained her presence. It felt impossible to believe that when I went downstairs, she wouldn't be at the breakfast table, her newspaper in front of her face, a tart remark on her lips about the hours I kept.

But when I made my way down after dressing, the table was empty, save for a place set for me.

I didn't want breakfast, but I forced myself to nibble on some toast, knowing I needed fortification to make it through the funeral.

The synagogue was only a few blocks away, and Lillian drove us there in Ada's car. Had we been going to a gravesite as well, we would have hired a limousine, but it seemed wasteful when we were just returning to the house for shiva. Shiva itself seemed wasteful. Who would come other than us, my parents, and Dan? Harold wasn't even coming down with his wife for the funeral. But Lillian said shiva was always in Ada's plan. She could have told me she wanted her urn carried in on elephants while a brass band played "When the Saints Go Marching In," and I would have complied. Anything to assuage the guilt of not having been there for her.

"Are you ready?" Lillian asked me as she parked the car in front of the synagogue.

"No," I said honestly. "But I'm as ready as I will be."

She patted my arm. "You don't have to speak."

"Yes. I do."

Lillian nodded. "I know she said she wanted this, but she would have hated the fuss."

It was true. Splashy as she was, she preferred to be the one pulling the strings. Which she was to the last, with the exacting funeral plans. "That's why she chose cremation—she didn't trust anyone else to pick her clothes or do her makeup."

Lillian smiled sadly. "You know, I think you're right. Heaven forbid she spend eternity in a dress from a sales rack."

I almost laughed. "Or in the wrong shoes."

"She'd haunt every last one of us."

I imagined Ada as a ghost, yanking the blanket off my bed if I slept too late and howling if I yelled from room to room. I would welcome the haunting if it meant I could see her again.

"I'll try to do her proud today."

"You already have," Lillian said. She opened her car door. "Come on. Let's give the old girl what she asked for."

"You're definitely getting haunted for that one."

Lillian smiled less sadly. "I hope I do." She turned to look at me as we got out of the car. "She's not really gone, you know."

I nodded. She would be with me for the rest of my life, even if she wasn't haunting me. I knew that much.

~

We were the first to arrive, and we were brought to a room for family in the back with the rabbi. My parents and Dan arrived shortly after, as did Dan's parents—an unwelcome surprise. My mother's sister, Mildred, entered with her family as well. I asked them all to excuse me as I went over my eulogy in a corner. I didn't want their sympathy. My father tried to say he was sorry again, but Dan successfully navigated him away, with a nod to me.

Eventually the rabbi told us it was time and led us into the sanctuary, where I stopped in my tracks.

A sea of heads turned to look at us. It was standing room only, people lining the back and side walls, pressed tightly together, with only the front two rows, reserved for family, open.

"Who—who are these people?" I asked Lillian in a whisper.

But the rabbi turned and answered. "Ada brought thousands of people together in her lifetime. This is just a fraction of them."

I glanced over my shoulder at Dan. She hadn't been paid for us, but we numbered among those. Mama and Daddy too, in a less direct way.

As we moved through the crowd though, two people caught my eye—largely because they stood out from the rest of the assembled throng, but also because one of them was just about the only person I recognized other than my family. Thomas stood, in a suit, next to an elderly woman, whom I assumed was John's wife.

We reached them, a few people from the back, and I wrapped my arms around Thomas in a hug, drawing both whispers and a couple of gasps, all of which I ignored.

"You okay?" I asked him.

He nodded. "This is my grandmother. Grandmama, this is Miss Ada's niece, Marilyn."

"I'm so sorry for your loss," she said, shaking my hand.

I clutched hers with my left as well. "Thank you for being here." The rabbi cleared his throat at the holdup, and she extricated her hand, using it to pat me on the arm.

I didn't know her. But somehow that kindness gave me the push I needed to make my way to the front, where Ada's urn rested on a cloth-covered table.

The rabbi spoke first, leading the congregation in two readings before giving his own eulogy.

"We gather here today to remember Ada Heller. So many of us were blessed to know her, though this may be the first time she set foot in this building for anything other than a wedding."

People stirred uncomfortably, unsure of whether they were supposed to laugh or not. The rabbi shook his head as his joke fell flat.

"Ada dedicated her life to the service of others. Both as a nurse, serving in the first World War, and later as a matchmaker, bringing together the Jewish community of Philadelphia in so many happy marriages, which is one of the greatest mitzvot a person can provide.

"There are those who say that a person who creates three successful matches automatically ascends to the highest level in the afterlife. I don't know if Ada believed in all that. But I do know why this is such a holy calling. It is the first thing that the Lord did after creating man—creating a match for him. We are each only half a soul, and when Ada made a match, she created whole families, both the partners and the children who were born of those marriages."

He paused, taking a deep breath. "I, myself, am one of those children, born of an Ada Heller match. As are my own children. How many here can say the same?"

There was the sound of fabric swishing all throughout the room and I turned, watching how many dozens of hands went up.

"None of us knows for sure if there is an afterlife until we leave this world. But what I do know is that we live on through the memories we leave. And that is Ada's legacy. She will live on through all of us in this room. As long as we remember her and tell our children and our children's children of the woman who created our families, Ada will never truly die."

He led the congregation in the Mourner's Kaddish, then introduced me. I winced as he called me her great-niece, then rose and went to the bimah with my typed eulogy clasped tight in my hand.

"The first thing to know about Ada," I began. But then I made the mistake of looking out into the sea of people, and my voice broke. I couldn't do it. I wasn't going to be able to make it through this.

I took a deep breath, trying to compose myself, and focused on a spot at the back of the sanctuary. But a woman moved in front of the door, and I startled.

She wore a turquoise Hermès scarf around her hair, a pair of cat eye sunglasses covering her eyes, her lips a shade of red I recognized at a glance. She lowered the glasses and winked at me.

She wasn't really there. I knew that. And by the time I looked down at my notes and then back up at the door, she was gone. But her presence in that moment, real or imagined, gave me the strength to go on.

"The first thing to know about Ada," I repeated, my voice strong now, "is that she would have dressed you down, regardless of who you were, Rabbi, for calling me her 'great' niece. Implying Ada was a day past thirty would earn you her scorn." People stirred. "Go ahead and laugh," I told them. "Ada despised anything maudlin and would have walked right up to the front if she were here and told you all to go home if you were going to be mopey. So we're going to make this a celebration of her instead of a goodbye. Deal?"

"Deal," a few people repeated. I glanced down at the front row and saw Dan next to my mother. He nodded at me, flashing me a discreet thumbs-up. I looked back at the door one more time, hoping to see her there, but my imagination could only produce her once.

"Ada was the most cantankerous person I've ever met in my life." I turned to her urn. "You hear that? It's true." A few chuckles. "But she was also my best friend. Something I never expected to say about a seventy-fi—I mean, thirty-year-old." More chuckles.

"I think even down here in Philadelphia, it's common knowledge how I came to spend the summer with her. And I honestly thought it was a fate worse than death when I arrived. On the car ride back from the station, me holding on for dear life in the backseat—if you've ever jumped onto a curb to avoid falling victim to Ada's driving, you know what I mean—Ada confiscated my lipstick. Apparently it made me look 'like a tart.' Which, quite honestly, was exactly the look I was going for.

Not three minutes later, she was putting it on at a traffic light. She told me she could pull it off."

I looked out again. People were smiling. "She could though. There was nothing she couldn't make look effortless, from my lipstick to a fur stole in Atlantic City in ninety-degree heat. If Ada wore it, it was fashion. Plain and simple.

"She was a hypocrite to the last. A stickler for rules she never followed herself. The epitome of *do as I say, not as I do*. But the secret behind that was she delighted in being called out on it. Few dared. I was one of them. And by all rights, she should have sent me packing. But Ada valued wit and a wicked streak, both of which my family wish I had inherited far less of from her." I looked down at my father. "Sorry, Daddy." Genuine laughs this time.

"Ada's business was love. I know that when you hear the word *matchmaker*, you think marriage, not love—or at least I did. But despite never marrying herself, Ada understood love better than anyone I've ever known." I looked into the crowd at Thomas's grandmother, who was nodding. "And that's why her matches worked. She looked for what made people happy and helped them find more of that in another person. She encouraged me to write, and strong-armed me into giving the boy who got me banished down here a chance." I held the back of my hand to the side of my mouth in the pose of a mock whisper. "You're welcome, Daddy." The crowd roared, and though he tried to hide it, I saw a smile creeping across my father's face. "And you know what? She was right. About everything."

I looked at the door one more time, closing my eyes briefly and seeing her there in my mind. "She was vain and mischievous and selfless and kind all in one. And if I live to be a hundred years old, I doubt I'll meet anyone like her. But my challenge to you today echoes what the rabbi said. Remember her. Tell your best Ada stories to your children and grandchildren. And more than that, live your life the way that *you* want to. Not the way society or anyone else tells you to. Because you only get this one chance. That was something that Ada understood better than anyone. She did exactly what she wanted. She should have been miserable. A meddling spinster with a bad attitude. But she wasn't. She was happy and free and lived and loved exactly how she was meant to. And I don't think there's much more that anyone can wish for.

"So instead of being sad tonight, drink a glass of champagne and raise it to Ada's life and legacy. Because she would want you to celebrate instead of mourn." I paused. "Okay, she would want you to mourn a *little*. She *was* vain after all." I paused for laughs. "But then she would want you to pick yourself up and be happy. And that is what all of us"—I looked down at Lillian, then my mother and aunt, who were dabbing their tears, and Dan, who was smiling at me with shining eyes, and sought out Thomas, who was doing the same, his grandmother's hand clasped in his—"who loved her most are going to try to do for the rest of our lives as well, despite the hole she leaves behind."

~

Lillian and I hosted the shiva, which was an exhausting revolving door of community members. But as we accepted condolences for what felt like the nine hundredth time, I began to understand that this was for them as much as for us. I didn't want them in Ada's house. I wanted a quiet space to remember her. But there was comfort in the stories they shared with me.

A couple of hours in, the crowd began to buzz. I glanced up at the door to see Thomas standing uncertainly, a hat in his hands.

I excused myself from the conversation with one of Ada's neighbors and went to greet him with a hug. He pulled me off him gently but firmly. "You don't need more gossip," he said. "I just wanted to pay my respects . . ."

"I'm glad you came. I have something for you. I was going to call you this week if you didn't," I said.

"For me?"

"Come on," I said, taking his arm and leading him toward Ada's study. I felt eyes on us, so I left the door open and offered him a seat on the sofa while I went to retrieve the parcel, still wrapped in a handkerchief and tied with a ribbon, from the desk.

"I don't know how much your grandmother told you," I said, suddenly realizing this might be an unwelcome surprise. "But I think—I think Ada would have wanted you to have these."

He looked at me curiously and untied the ribbon, then opened the handkerchief. The picture on top was the one of Ada smiling up at John. Thomas examined it carefully for a moment, then moved on to the next picture, stopping and looking up at me in surprise when he got to the one of them kissing.

"You didn't know, then?"

He shook his head. "I knew they met in Europe, before he married my grandmother. He said in a different life, he would have loved her."

"According to her, he did. She said—she said the world loves to destroy things it doesn't understand. That he knew that, but she had to learn it for herself."

Thomas nodded. "She was a wise lady, that one."

"How did you start doing odd jobs for her? She never explained that, but I know she adored you." *Like the grandson she never had,* I thought.

A wry smile spread across his face, and I realized Ada was right. He did look like his grandfather. "It was two cars and eleven years ago. A 1946 Cadillac. It was making a noise, and she was convinced her mechanic was robbing her on account of her being a woman. So she called my grandfather and said she absolutely hated to bother him for something like this, but would he take a look. He brought me with him. I was twelve and didn't understand why Granddaddy was helping this rich white lady. On the trolley ride over there, he explained. He said it didn't matter if you were Black, white, green, or purple. If someone was a good person and needed your help, you helped them if you could."

He looked at me, and his grin was absolutely wicked. "Ask me what was wrong with the car."

I couldn't resist. "What was wrong with the car?"

He could barely respond for laughing. "She had a family of birds nesting under the hood."

"Birds?"

"One of them flew at her when Granddaddy opened the hood. First, last, and only time you ever saw Miss Ada scream, I swear."

The image was too delicious, and I laughed too. "I'd pay good money to have seen that."

"She tried to give me a dollar for helping get them out of there, which she said was really to not let anyone know she'd screamed, but my grandfather handed it right back to her. He told her there was absolutely no need and that we were happy to help." His smile turned wistful. "When Granddaddy was finishing up the car, she slipped me the dollar again and told me to come back and visit her sometime."

"And you went?"

"Absolutely not. My grandfather caught me trying to spend that dollar on candy and marched me right back up to her house to give it back again. I don't remember their whole conversation, but there was a lot of hand-waving and finger-pointing, and it ended with him saying I was going to earn that dollar." He looked back down at the photographs in his hands. "She didn't need me and tried to say I could just go home and tell my grandfather that I hung some pictures or some other non-sense. But he and I didn't keep secrets—except this one, I suppose—so I told her I'd best actually hang some pictures, then. She looked at me like I was crazy but said, 'Come on, then. Let's find something honest for you to do.'" He looked back up at me. "I liked her. I know that's such a strange thing to say but—"

"I get it."

He nodded. "I suppose you do. I started coming by on Sunday afternoons after church, just to see if she needed help with anything. It was just her and Miss Lillian in this big house, and I—I wanted to be someone my grandfather would be proud of."

I felt tears pricking at my eyes. "I know I never met him, but I know he's proud of you. And Ada is too."

Wiping at his eye with the back of his right hand, Thomas nodded. "I hope so."

I put my hand on top of his left, which still held the photographs. "I know so."

For a long moment, neither of us spoke. "Thank you for these," Thomas said eventually, gesturing to the pictures.

"Of course." I hesitated. "She said your grandfather was one of the two loves of her life. She wouldn't tell me who the other was. I guess I'll never know now." Thomas shifted slightly. "Wait. Do you know?"

"Not for certain, no. But I think love looks different to different folks." He tilted his head at me. "If it didn't"—he held up a picture—"I think I'd look different today." He stood. "You should probably get back to your guests. Thank you again."

I wanted to hug him. In a different life, we would have been cousins. But my earlier hug had made him uncomfortable, and we were in a room alone together with my father and new fiancé down the hall. "Can I shake your hand?" I asked eventually.

"Yes, Miss Kleinman. I'd like that."

I held out my hand. "Please just call me Marilyn."

He smiled over our clasped palms. "I hope we meet again soon, Marilyn."

I watched him leave, then took a deep breath and steeled myself to return to the assembled guests.

CHAPTER
FIFTY-EIGHT

On Friday, Ada's lawyer came to the house at nine. Lillian wanted to deal with the will before people descended on us for the third day of shiva. We decided not to do the full week of mourning and would cut it off with Shabbat that evening. We were exhausted and, as Ada would have said, it was simply too much fuss.

Mr. Cohen arrived, and we showed him into the living room.

"I'll leave you two to it," I said as they sat.

"Marilyn," Lillian said. "You don't understand. Mr. Cohen is here for you."

"For me?"

The lawyer nodded. "Ada changed her will quite recently, leaving you as her primary beneficiary."

I shook my head. "I'm sorry, it's been a difficult few days. I'm afraid I didn't hear you right."

Lillian reached up and took my hand. "You heard him correctly. Sit, please."

I sank onto the sofa as Mr. Cohen pulled a sheaf of papers thicker than my manuscript from his briefcase and set them on the coffee table in front of us. "It appears you're quite a wealthy young woman," he said as he began outlining properties, stocks, and other assets.

My head was spinning.

"I'm sorry, just a moment please. Lillian, this isn't right. You deserve it. Not me."

She shook her head. "She already gave me what I was getting. And we both discussed this before she made the change." She squeezed my hand, which I hadn't even realized she was still holding. "You're free."

I blinked rapidly, trying to process the implications of what they were saying. The Avalon houses. The Philadelphia properties. A building in New York City—a whole building. The car. The jewelry. This house.

"I can't," I said. "I don't know what to do with this. It's too much. Lillian, please, split it with me at least."

But Lillian shook her head. "This is what Ada wanted. And me as well. Be happy."

"There are a few conditions," Mr. Cohen said. "There's money in a trust for Thomas for after he finishes medical school."

"Of course."

"There's an account set up for"—he glanced down at his notes—"a Frances O'Donnell as well."

"Good." Of course Ada took care of Thomas and Frannie.

"And Ada wanted Lillian to have Sally."

"She never liked me anyway," I said.

Sally licked my hand from Lillian's lap as if she understood and disagreed. But then it dawned on me—

"Lillian—you're staying here, aren't you?"

She shook her head. "No. I'm not."

"You have to. Please. It's your home."

"No. Home was where Ada was. And this no longer is."

"But—" I remembered Ada asking where Lillian was supposed to go when I suggested dismissing her. "No. You have to stay."

"No," she said lightly. "I'm going back to Chicago."

"Please don't go."

She smiled sadly at me. "I have to. And you have your own life to begin. With the resources to do whatever you like."

I thought for a moment. "I want the Avalon house that Frannie uses to go to her," I said to Mr. Cohen, who nodded. "One of the row houses too. I—I don't know what I'm going to do yet, but—Ada always said real estate was the smartest investment. And she left me so much more than I could ever need." Lillian squeezed my hand again, and it was as if I could feel Ada's presence nodding approvingly at me.

"One to Lillian." She started to protest, but I shushed her. "I don't care what Ada gave you. This is what I'm giving you. And the money necessary for its upkeep." She didn't argue. "And one to Thomas—but can you tell him Ada left it to him, not me? I'm afraid he'd refuse if he knew it was from me."

"I can stretch the truth a little there. I believe Ada would approve."

"Good." I may have been her blood, but Lillian, Frannie, and Thomas were her family before I even knew she existed. And that mattered so much more than any wealth I could ever accrue.

"There's one more provision."

"Which is?"

"She wants you to scatter her ashes." He looked down at one of the papers in front of him. "This was extremely specific. You're to go to the end of the jetty at the north end of Avalon—I assume you know where that is—alone. She was quite clear on the *alone* part. And scatter her ashes into the water there, on the ocean side, not the inlet side." He looked up again. "I'm not sure I understand the difference, but she made me include it."

"It's where she swam to every morning," I said. "I know where it is."

"Excellent," he said. "There's more to discuss, but Lillian said she wanted me gone by ten." He handed me a business card. "We'll need to sit down at some point when you're ready to discuss investments and to sign the paperwork for the transfer of properties, but I'll initiate those with the city this afternoon."

"Thank you, Mr. Cohen."

He shook my hand. "I look forward to a long partnership, Miss Kleinman."

Lillian showed him to the door, while I stayed on the sofa, trying to wrap my head around the extent of my newfound wealth and what it meant for my future.

I was still there when she returned. "People will be here soon," she said.

"I wish you would stay."

She came and sat next to me. "I'll always just be a phone call or a letter away. But you need to go live your own life now. And so do I. It's what Ada wanted for both of us."

"I don't know how to begin."

"Yes, you do," she said, echoing Ada and bringing a tightness to my chest. The doorbell rang, resonating through the too-empty house. "That'll be your parents most likely. Speaking of where to begin." She rose, but I took her hand.

"You'll always have a home here, if you want it."

Lillian leaned down and kissed my forehead. "I'm glad you came into our lives."

I wrapped my arms around her waist. "I am too."

She held me close for a moment until the doorbell rang again. "Best get this over with," she said. I released her but stayed on the sofa. The amount of money and properties that the lawyer had outlined was quite simply staggering. I could buy and sell my parents many times over. I could buy a villa in the south of France.

But without Ada, it was a hollow victory.

"I'd give it all back for ten more minutes," I whispered. She would never hold a copy of my finished novel in her hands. The book that wouldn't exist without her not-so-gentle nudging. If I caved and married Dan, she wouldn't be there. I owned the Avalon house now—could I go back there in the summers without her? Or would the memories be too heavy, the entire Jersey shore tainted by the hole she left behind?

Part of me wanted to give it all away. But she wanted me to have this. The ability to do what I wanted.

When did she change her will? I wondered. I would have to ask Lillian. Was it before I left? Or after? She made the offer to my father, but knowing Ada, that didn't mean it wasn't already done.

The house was beginning to fill with people, and I heard my mother call my name. I finally stood, feeling far older than my twenty years. *You need to go live your own life now,* I heard Lillian say again in my head.

I found my mother in the kitchen, looking for me. "I need to talk to you and Daddy," I said. "I'll go get him. You wait for me in Ada's study, please."

Dan was standing between his parents as his father spoke with Ada's rabbi. I caught his eye, and he excused himself. "Come with me," I said.

"Are you okay?"

I looked at him, our freedom stretching out beyond us. "Never better. Come on."

Daddy was in the den, looking through the items on the shelves, which were mine now. "Daddy," I said. "I need to talk to you and Mama. In Ada's study, please."

"What's this about?" he asked, noticing my hand in Dan's. "Should the Schwartzes join us?"

"No."

He looked puzzled but followed us to the small office, going to sit next to Mama on the sofa against the wall. I gestured for Dan to sit in one of the chairs across the desk, which I perched on the edge of. Mama's eyes widened. "We need to move the wedding up to the fall, don't we?"

"Pardon me?"

"That's what this is about, isn't it? You're . . . ?" She trailed off, but I understood her implication.

"No! Mama!" Daddy looked from her to me in horror. "There isn't going to be a wedding. At least not anytime soon."

Dan's face fell, and I held up the fingers of my left hand in a tiny *wait* gesture to him. "Ada's lawyer came to see us today. It turns out, she redid her will sometime this summer. And she left me pretty much everything."

"Wonderful," Daddy said. "That means you can get married while Dan is in rabbinical school. No need to delay the wedding at all now, regardless of . . . other circumstances."

"Would you all stop insinuating that I'm pregnant?" Everyone winced. "There's not going to be any rabbinical school, and there's not going to be a wedding. At least not unless Dan and I both decide we're ready for one."

My father's eyes narrowed. "Explain yourself."

"Dan doesn't want to be a rabbi. He wants to be a photojournalist—"

Daddy scoffed. "There's no money in that."

"That's my point, Daddy. We don't need the money now. We can do what we want."

"Now see here, young lady—" His finger was pointed at me, but I cut him off.

"No, you see here. I have houses. Money. Stocks. Even a car—"

"You can't drive!"

"Dan taught me. And I'll get a license. But the car isn't even a drop in the bucket. And you can't hold money or school over my head as a way to get me to go home now."

"I meant what I said." He stood up. "If you stay here—"

My mouth was open to speak. I saw his face on that train platform. While he might have meant it in Avalon, the threat was empty now, and I had no problem arguing until he came around. But my mother beat me to it, putting a hand on his arm. "Walter, enough. With Ada gone, the only blood family I have left are Mildred, Harold, and Marilyn. We're not disowning anyone."

He began sputtering, but she wasn't done. "You can't bully her into being who you want her to be. She's different. The world is different. And she's an incredibly talented writer—something she was probably too scared to even try because you hounded her so. I want her home even more than you do, but she's grown. And I want her to be happy. She's never going to be happy doing what you want." She turned to me. "Will you at least stay engaged in name to keep gossip down?"

I nodded. That was fair.

"Then we give you our blessing."

"I—" my father began, but my mother didn't let him continue. She moved around until she was directly in front of him.

"We give them our blessing, Walter. And if you can't do that much, then I'm moving to Philadelphia too."

His mouth dropped open. Mine wanted to follow suit, but I kept it firmly shut. I had never seen Mama stand up to him like this. She always waited until he cooled down before launching her quiet campaigns. It was the first time I saw a hint of Ada in her, and I wondered if it was being in this house that did it.

Eventually his shoulders sagged, and he nodded, mumbling something that sounded like a blessing.

I turned to Dan, whose eyes were wide. "What do you say? Want to stay engaged and take pictures?" He looked at me for a long moment, then suddenly I was in his arms and he swung me in the air. "I take it that's a yes?"

"As long as you'll still let me buy the ring."

I smiled, shaking my head. "Ada has one I want to use. It was her mother's."

"I think she would like that."

I agreed.

~

Slowly people started to leave as afternoon turned into evening. We'd had a full house until ten the previous two nights, but custom dictated that shiva end at sundown on Shabbat and the visitors knew enough to leave before that, even if no one in our house would be observing.

Dan's parents had left around noon to return to the city in time to lead Shabbat services at our synagogue, but Dan remained with my parents. My mother and Dan helped me, Lillian, and Frannie clean up while my father read Ada's untouched *Philadelphia Inquirer* in the den.

My mother and I wound up alone in the dining room. "Mama," I said. She looked up at me. "Thank you."

She leaned over and squeezed my shoulder, then busied herself again, piling leftovers onto a plate. "What will you do now?" she asked lightly.

"I don't know," I said. "But I'm leaning toward staying here for a while."

"And you'll finish your book, of course." I nodded, though part of me didn't want to. I had started it with Ada. And finishing it would be closing that chapter of my life even more. "I'll pass it on to Paul when you do." Paul Stein was Daddy's editor friend who sent her books early.

"You will?"

"Of course." She looked surprised by my question. "If he doesn't want it—and I think he will—I'm sure he'll have recommendations of who else we can take it to."

"We?"

Her mouth twitched up into its first real smile since the phone had rung in the brownstone. "I'll even waive the customary percentage that literary agents get. Though you *can* afford it now."

A sound escaped my throat, and it took me a moment to realize it was a laugh. "Oh, Mama."

But the corners of her mouth turned down again. "I should have stood up to your father earlier. It shouldn't have taken Ada dying for you to be able to live the life you wanted."

I wondered if there had been any way to get here without Ada dying. After all, it had taken Ada's fiancé dying for her parents to agree to let her stay single and go to nursing school. Perhaps my father had been bluffing all along. But with the clarity of time, I now recognized the remorse on his face when I told him it was his fault Ada had died alone.

I thought back to how angry I had been when they made me go home. And at my father at the train station.

That was gone now, replaced with an aching exhaustion. I just didn't have it in me to be angry anymore, even at Daddy. He was a product of his time. And not everyone could be like Ada and reject the norms that they were raised in. Not everyone wanted to. I saw that now.

I also saw my mother more clearly. She had surprised me in Avalon with her admission that she read because cooking was boring, not because her life was. Maybe she really was just a terrible cook. Which would mean I came by my lack of culinary skills quite honestly. A giggle rose up in my throat at that disloyal thought, but I swallowed it down.

Instead I wrapped my arms around her and hugged her. "Sometimes things work out how they're meant to," I said. "Ada understood that."

"She did."

"And this is what she wanted—me to be able to be free without losing my family." My mother opened her mouth to speak, but I cut her off. "You did exactly the right thing. There's no need for apologies."

She smiled again, sadly. "When did you get so wise?"

I grinned, shaking my head. "Sometime between that stained glass window and becoming possibly the wealthiest woman in Philadelphia. It's been quite a summer."

"That it has." She looked toward the kitchen. "I'm glad you and Dan found each other. He's good for you."

Two months earlier, that comment would have sent me running. But the idea of the stove no longer scared me. Besides, I was an even worse chef than my mother. There was no way I was doing the cooking in any scenario. "I am too."

She reached up and tucked a piece of hair behind my ear. "It's hard letting your baby go off into the world. But I know you're ready for it."

"Thank you, Mama."

She nodded briskly. "And don't you take too long finishing that book. I expect to see you on the bestseller lists soon." She picked up the plate she had been working on and carried it into the kitchen.

I sank into one of the dining room chairs, elbow on the table, my chin resting on my hand, contemplating how completely the world had turned upside down in the last few days. Ada always did like to shake things up. *Don't ever think that I don't know what I'm doing,* she said in my head, just like my first night in Philadelphia, when she threw the rock that landed me in a bush.

"Thank you," I whispered to the empty room.

And for a brief moment, I swore I smelled her perfume, as if she had walked behind me with a nod.

CHAPTER
FIFTY-NINE

Lillian left on Sunday. Our goodbye was tearful, but she promised I would see her again soon. She held Sally tightly. "You come find us, okay?"

I said I would. I had never been to Chicago, but it seemed like a good place to go on an adventure. And I had time for adventures now. I scratched behind Sally's ears and kissed the top of her head. "Goodbye, you little terror. What kind of dog is she anyway?"

"A schnauzer," Lillian said.

"If you'd told me I would miss that dog . . ."

"She'll be happy to see you," Lillian promised. "She's a wonderful judge of character."

I nodded. "That she is."

Thomas took her to the train station in Ada's car, promising to return it after he dropped her off. "I'm not worried," I told him.

We embraced one more time, and then Lillian was gone. Frannie offered to stay over if I wanted the company until Dan returned the following day to go to Avalon with me. But I told her to go home to her family.

She cleared her throat. "I just wanted to say thank you—"

"No. Thank you, Frannie. Ada loved you dearly. And I appreciate everything you did for me this summer."

"But you didn't—"

I smiled at her. "What would Ada say right now?"

She grinned wanly. "To take the gift, say thank you, and shut up about it."

I chuckled. "That is exactly what she would say."

"I can come back in the morning—"

"I can handle toast and coffee. Take the week off. And once I figure out what I'm doing, I'll let you know."

She hugged me tightly. "Ada loved you. Even if she didn't say it."

I squeezed her back. "I do know that. Now go on home and enjoy your family."

And then I was alone in the house that would always be Ada's to me.

I spent the evening looking back through the albums I had made for her. And because it was Sunday, I put on Ed Sullivan, poured myself a hearty glass of wine from her generous stock, and had a running commentary with her empty chair about that night's "really big shew."

In the morning, I opened the door to her bedroom. I half thought she would be sitting on the bed, ready to admonish me. But the room was empty. I looked around. It was mine now. I could take the biggest bedroom if I chose.

I shook my head. Maybe someday. But not now. Instead, I went to her vanity, took the jewelry box, and brought it to the bed, where I sat with it. I knew what I was looking for.

It was in the third drawer. The sapphire engagement ring that had been her mother's. The one she let me wear to Atlantic City. That would be my engagement ring from Dan. I knew I should wait for him, but I slipped it on my left ring finger. It fit perfectly, as if it belonged there.

There was still time before Dan was due to arrive, so I looked through the rest of the jewelry before moving on to the closet.

Her closet was a sight to behold. Dresses for every occasion. Hats. Shoes. More jewelry. Furs. I discovered there was an entire other row behind the one in the back. I felt behind the second row, wondering if there would be a third, but my hand brushed a door frame.

Curious, I pushed the clothes aside, revealing the narrow door. *Narnia,* I thought. I reached for the knob, half convinced I was about to meet Aslan and the White Witch and that instead of Ada, I was the one who had died. The other half of me was sure it would be locked, its contents remaining a mystery.

But the knob turned easily. I peered through the darkness, then stepped through into another, empty closet. I opened the door and stepped out into Lillian's room.

That was anticlimactic, I thought, returning the way I came into Ada's closet.

I was trying on a black Givenchy dress that was a dead ringer for the one Audrey Hepburn wore in *Sabrina*—though it wouldn't quite zip over the bust—when I looked at the clock and realized more than an hour had passed. Dan would be there soon, and we were driving straight to Avalon to carry out Ada's final wishes.

After stepping out of the dress, I hung it back in the closet and replaced all the jewelry except for the ring.

But I stubbed my toe on something sticking out from under the bed. Cursing, I bent to see what it was and came away with a photo album. It wasn't one I had put together. I sat back on the bed with it and quickly saw it was an album of Ada and Lillian. They were in Avalon, and in front of a theater, and many, many more, smiling brilliantly and looking so happy in each other's company.

I should send this to Lillian, I thought. Why was it under the bed though?

I shrugged. I would deal with it later. When we got back from Avalon.

The shore house was closed up, but we were planning to spend the night there, then drive back here to decide what came next. I liked the idea of staying in Philadelphia for at least a little while, and Dan was going to talk to some local newspapers to see if they were hiring. I told him he didn't need to work if he didn't want to, but he insisted. If it was some masculine thing about money, I was going to be annoyed, but he asked if I was still going to write now that I had money.

Ada had made a better match than she realized in us.

The doorbell rang, and I went downstairs to let Dan in.

CHAPTER SIXTY

Once we got out of Philadelphia, Dan pulled over. "What are you doing?" I asked him. There wasn't a place to eat or use a restroom in sight.

"Switch with me," he said. "You're driving."

"I can't drive all the way to Avalon!"

"Why not? There's no traffic going that direction this time of year. It's the perfect practice."

I looked at him for a moment, then he got out and came around to the passenger side while I slid over into the driver's seat. "This is a more powerful car than mine," he warned. "So go easy on the gas pedal. If you crash it, I think Ada is going to haunt you."

I smiled. "She'd come back to murder me."

"Let's stay alive, then."

I put the car into drive, Dan sitting close enough to grab the wheel if I needed him to, and we continued along the Black Horse Pike until we reached the Garden State Parkway, where we went south toward Avalon.

By the time we were on Avalon Boulevard, I felt comfortable driving. The marshes loomed on both sides of the road as we crested the hill and the town came into view.

"I miss her," I said as we entered town.

"I know. I do too. And I didn't know her nearly as well as you did."

I reached over and touched the urn on the seat between us. "Do you think she can hear us?"

"I never really believed in an afterlife," Dan said. "But I think she can. If anyone could, it's her."

"She'd love how Mama stood up to Daddy."

"She would."

I pulled to a stop in front of the house. "Let's go in for a minute. I need to use the restroom, and I want to call Lillian in Chicago. Just let her know we're here."

Dan agreed, and we climbed the steps. I used a key on the ring to unlock the door, something I had never done. It stuck a little, but I jiggled it, and the door opened.

The furniture was covered in sheets to protect it from dust. But we were only staying the night. It wasn't worth opening everything up just to redo it.

Sleeping arrangements would be more interesting, I realized as I washed my hands in the powder room. Dan would respect whatever I chose, but we could do what we wanted now. I looked at my reflection in the mirror. I didn't honestly know if I was up to it yet. I wanted our first time to be special, and tonight was likely to be sad. Not how I wanted to start our lives.

I sighed and went to the phone in the kitchen, pulling the number Lillian had left me from my pocketbook.

I dialed the operator and told her where to connect me. The phone rang four times before an unfamiliar voice answered. Which wasn't unexpected. Lillian had told me she was going to stay with her sister for a couple of weeks before getting herself a place.

"Hi, this is Marilyn Kleinman. I'm calling for Lillian?"

"Lillian?" the voice asked. "Why would Lillian be here?"

"I'm sorry, the operator must have given me the wrong number. I'm looking for Lillian Miller."

"Lillian is my sister, but she's not here."

"I—she told me she'd be staying with you."

"If so, that's news to me. Isn't she in Philadelphia?"

"No."

"Hmm. Well, I suppose you can give me your phone number, and if I hear from her, I'll tell her to call you."

I complied, giving both the Avalon number and the Philadelphia number.

"What's wrong?" Dan asked.

I sat in a chair at the kitchen table. "Lillian isn't staying with her sister."

"Does she have more than one sister?" he asked. I shook my head. "Huh. That's strange. Maybe her train was delayed?"

"Maybe. But her sister didn't know she was coming." My shoulders dropped. "She said she would always be just a phone call or a letter away. I don't understand."

"It's a misunderstanding," Dan said, putting a hand on my shoulder. "She'll be in touch soon to let you know where she is."

I looked up at him and nodded. "I'm sure you're right."

"What now?"

I sighed. "I guess it's time to say goodbye."

We walked to the jetty at 8th Street, and I climbed up onto it, then Dan handed me the urn. He climbed up as well, but I put a hand on his chest. "I need to do this alone," I said.

He nodded and kissed my cheek before climbing down. "I'll be right here if you need me."

I picked my way along the rocks carefully, holding the urn under my arm, until I reached the end.

"I guess this is it," I said to the urn. "I'm so, so sorry I wasn't there, Ada. I am. But thank you. For everything."

I unscrewed the lid and peered inside.

But instead of ashes, there were papers.

I blinked heavily. The crematorium had messed up. Of all the mistakes to make. I shook my head angrily and fished out the papers.

Then I dropped the urn.

They weren't papers. One was a photograph of Ada and Lillian, holding hands in front of a house I had never seen, lined with palm trees. They were facing each other, looking into each other's eyes, and if I didn't know better, I'd have thought they were a couple. There was an address on the back.

The second was a postcard from Key West. The tiny hairs on my neck stood on end as I turned it over.

There, in Ada's unmistakable scrawl, was a note.

> *My darling Marilyn,*
> *Live the life you want. Love whom you want. And don't*
> *forget to write.*
> *XOX,*
> *Ada*

For a moment, the world spun. *Love whom you want.* The picture. The secret door to Lillian's room. The album. The refusal to tell me who her second great love was. Saying I wouldn't find it with the other photographs. *The world loves to destroy what it doesn't understand.* Lillian's hand on hers when she said that.

My mouth fell open.

But—

Don't forget to write. My book. She meant my book.

Except—

The Key West house wasn't among the assets Mr. Cohen had outlined.

She already gave me what I was getting, Lillian had said.

I've got tricks up my sleeve yet, Ada had told me as I was leaving Avalon.

She's not really gone, Lillian had said as we walked into the synagogue.

The woman at the back of the funeral.

Don't forget to write.

The address on the back of the picture.

Don't forget to write.

My eyes widened, realizing that like so many things Ada said and did, there was a double meaning there.

~

Dan was waiting for me at the base of the jetty, just like he said he would be. "Where to now?" he asked.

I smiled broadly. "Have you ever been to Key West?"

He shook his head. "I haven't."

"Up for the drive?"

"I'll follow you anywhere," he said.

"Good. Let's go. Tonight."

"What's in Key West?"

"Everything," I said.

Ada was right. I did know how this ended all along.

ACKNOWLEDGMENTS

This book was born on the beach in Avalon, New Jersey, just a couple of days after *She's Up to No Good* came out. Marilyn's character came to me as my husband pulled our umbrella out of its sheath, and by the time he had put it up (something that I, like Marilyn, couldn't have done easily), I had a general plot. I wrote half of the outline on my phone under that umbrella and the rest after the kids went to bed that night. And then the story just poured out of me.

Thank you to my editor, Alicia Clancy, and the entire team at Lake Union for taking a chance on this story before I had even written it. And thank you for gently rejecting the two ideas before this one—they weren't right, and when it's the right story, it just flows. And, boy, did this one flow!

Thank you to my agent extraordinaire, Rachel Beck. Even though I didn't join you in a third pregnancy, we're bonded for life, and I love both that and you.

Thank you to Liza Dawson and the whole team at Liza Dawson and Associates for taking over seamlessly when Rachel was out. I was nervous, but you were amazing!

Thank you to my husband, Nick, for picking up the slack so I could write this on such a tight deadline. Thank you for letting me bounce ideas off you with zero context and letting me talk my story out so it would work, and the million other ways you support me.

Thank you to my children, Jacob and Max. I know it's a lot right now (not that you can read this yet) when Mommy has to work two jobs, but please know that I'm doing this for you, my loves. (And Sandy and Gracie.)

Thank you to my mother, Carole Goodman. I've never let anyone see unfinished work before. But because I was on such a tight deadline, I sent her this, a chapter a night, and she read it as I wrote—frequently sending me angry messages, telling me to write faster because she wanted more. Thank you, Mom. For everything.

Thank you to my father, Jordan Goodman, for knowing practically everything and knowing exactly who to ask the few times when you didn't. Mom may say I'm Google, but I think that makes you the encyclopedia—the original know-it-all, and I appreciate you so much.

Thank you to my grandmother, Charlotte Chansky, for the lifetime of stories, support, and love.

This book would absolutely not exist without my aunt and uncle, Dolly and Marvin Band. They were 90 percent of my research, and there is no way I could have finished it on time without their help. From the cars, to how to get to Atlantic City before the AC Expressway, to what you wore on the boardwalk (with adorable pictures to prove it!), to how people did their hair back then, the two of you knew everything and answered every single question I had immediately. Thank you, thank you, thank you for being so generous with your time, your memories, your support, and your love.

Thank you to my cousins Ken and Arlene Sirmarco for finding the perfect location for Ada's house and sharing your memories of growing up in Philadelphia in the 1960s. You saved me hours of research, and I'm so, so sorry Ken isn't here to see the finished product.

Thank you to my brother, Adam, sister-in-law, Nicole, and nephews Cam and Luke. Love you to the moon and back.

Jennifer Doehner Lucina. Are there even still words? I couldn't do any of this without you. Thank you for catching every typo, and thank you for twenty-eight years of friendship (which is CLEARLY bad math because we're both younger than that, and I refuse to hear otherwise). Love you so much!

Thank you to my uncle Michael Chansky and aunt Stephanie Abbuhl, for letting us use your Avalon house so generously. (And to my cousins Andrew, Peter, and Ben, for not being in town the week I came up with this book!) I hope the references to familiar places make you smile.

Thank you to my cousin Allison Band, for being such a huge champion of my writing. Here's hoping we get to see some of these on a screen soon!

Thank you to my "Band" cousins, Andy Levine, Ian and Kim Band, Mindy and Alan Nagler, Maddy Levine, Jolie Band, Trevor Band, and Matthew Nagler.

Thank you to Mark Kamins, for handling all the financial aspects of my life so I don't have to actually understand how taxes work.

Thank you to Kevin Keegan, for making me the writer that I am today—even though you're also why I'm too em-dash happy. And yes, we'll find you a role in the movie.

Thank you to Sarah McKinley, for dropping everything to be a beta reader for this and for our group chat, which kept me sane while writing this during the start of the school year. Love you!

Thank you to Rachel Friedman, for being my partner in crime on this journey through motherhood, life, and all the things in between.

Thank you to Sarah Elbeshbishi, for being my go-to person. Beta reader, dog sitter, babysitter, personal assistant, and friend.

Thank you to Sonya Shpilyuk, for keeping me sane at my other job.

Thank you to Paulette Kennedy, for believing I could do this even when I didn't think I could. Your faith in me made this book a reality.

Thank you to my crew of author friends, Jennifer Bardsley, Elissa Dickey, Mansi Shah, Annie Cathryn, Lacie Waldon, Maddie Dawson, and Rochelle Weinstein.

Thank you to Katie Stutzman, Jan Guttman, Reka Montfort, Kerrin Torres, Laura Davis Vaughan, Haben and Mike Asghedom,

Joye Young Saxon, Christen Dimmick, Amy Shellabarger, Christine Wilson, Jessica Markham, Allison Kimball, Shelley Miller, Jenna Levine Liu, Jeremy Horton, Sophia Becker, and Kim Thibault, for being my people.

Thank you to Carol Goddard, for supporting me in both careers. I can't tell you how much I will miss you!

Thank you to my Bookstagram fam, for being my street team. I owe you all so much.

Thank you to the Confino family.

Thank you to my youngest supporters, Charlotte, Genevieve, and Nathaniel Lucina; Aurora, Elena, and Zara Asghedom; Maya and Rosa Shpilyuk-Franklin; and Belle and Sam Wilson. I'm not a celebrity, but I love that you think I am!

Thank you to my students, past and present.

And finally, thank you to my readers, for making my dream a reality.

ABOUT THE AUTHOR

Photo © 2022 Tim Coburn Photography

Sara Goodman Confino is the bestselling author of *She's Up to No Good* and *For the Love of Friends*. She teaches high school English and journalism in Montgomery County, Maryland, where she lives with her husband, two sons, and two miniature schnauzers, Sandy and Gracie. When Sara's not writing or working out, she can be found on the beach or at a Bruce Springsteen show, sometimes even dancing onstage. For more information, visit www.saraconfino.com.